CW00498500

The Other Boy
Andrea Hicks

Nightingale Lane Publishing

www.andreahicks-writer.com for a free excerpt of the next book in the
Jagged Edge Psychological Thriller Series
THE DESTRUCTION OF BEES

CHAPTERS

Newton Denham, Hampshire. 15th December 1999 - 1   *** 1

Christmas 2018 - 2   *** 3

Christmas 2018 - 3   **11

December 1999 - 4   **23

Christmas 2018 - 5   **26

Christmas 2018 - 6   **39

December 1999 - 7   **50

Newton's Mill - 8   **53

New Year 2019 - 9   **59

The Contempo Gallery - 10   **68

March 2019 - 11   **71

March 2019 - 12   **85

Slaughter's Wood - 13   *100

April 2019 - 14   *102

April 2019 - 15   *106

April 2019 - 16   *114

Slaughter's Wood - 17   *122

The City - 18   *124

May 2019 - 19   *132

June 2019 - 20   *138

June 2019 - 21   *146

June 2019 - 22   *153

June 2019 - 23   *160

June 2019 - 24   *166

Late June 2019 - 25   *169

Late June 2019 - 26   *177

July 2019 - 27   *191

July 2019 - 28   *196

July 2019 - 29   *198

July 2019 - 30   *207

July 2019 - 31   *212

July 2019 - 32   *220

July 2019 - 33   *229

Late July 2019 - 34   *233

Late July 2019 - 35   *238

St. Nicholas's Church - 36

Newton Denham, Hampshire
15th December 1999

1

Don't go outside, they'd said, and she'd assured them they wouldn't. Anyway, it was dark and she was afraid of the dark. Aaron wasn't. He told her he wasn't afraid of anything and she believed him. Aaron didn't know how to be afraid.

The front door was open, just a little, enough for her to see the bonnet of their old grey car parked outside. Her breath caught up in her throat.

'Aaron,' she called. He didn't answer. Her school pencil case was in her hand, torn pink plastic decorated with felt tip pen and unicorn stickers. Annette, a girl in her class had decorated hers with a big red heart with an arrow through it, her initials at the arrow end, and at the pointy end two different initials, RT, for Ryan Turner. Everyone loved Ryan Turner. And everyone loved Annette who was pretty, tall, and slim. Lacey had found a picture of a gazelle in a book she'd borrowed from the library and it had reminded her of Annette with its slender legs and long-lashed doe eyes. Annette had long brown hair that flicked up at the ends and hazel eyes, not dirty-fair hair and green eyes like Lacey's. She hated it when people mentioned her eyes. Some of the kids at school called her "The Green-Eyed Monster". It was because she loved Ryan and everyone knew about it, and they wouldn't let it drop even though she tried very hard not to look at him in class or when he was in the playground, following Annette around like a little puppy.

Ryan loved Annette and it made Lacey want to cry. Sometimes she did cry. There were other times when Lacey felt a burning in her chest and when she watched them, wanted to hit Annette really hard; would have liked to knock her over in the playground and laugh at her as she fell onto the gravel. Hopefully it would make her pristine games kit all dirty and covered in muck and not so bright-white it made your eyes hurt to look at her. And the creases her mum had ironed into the sleeves would get roughed up. Her hands and knees would get grazed and she'd have tiny bits of stone stuck in the cuts in her hands, and they would sting so much her eyes would water. And maybe everyone would laugh at her like they laughed at Lacey when she got pushed over. She would have enjoyed it, everyone laughing at Annette instead of her. Maybe she could make it happen. It wouldn't be so hard to give her a quick shove in the ribs during break time.

It didn't matter what everyone thought, anyway. She was only a bit jealous, not enough for them to call her a green-eyed monster. Or worse things sometimes. Rude words that meant something else, like her dad used sometimes when he was talking about the neighbours because they'd ignored him in the street or he'd got thrown out of the pub or they'd said he was a waster. She hated it when the kids at school called her names. It made her angry. So very angry.

Newton's Mill, Newton Denham, Christmas 2018

2

Sarah pulled aside a curtain in the living room and peered out of the window, watching the abundant snowflakes as they fell from a coal black sky. The darkness was almost impenetrable and she thought about their flat in London. Light pollution was something she and Dan were used to. It had never disturbed her because if ever Dan worked away it made her feel like she wasn't completely alone, like a comfort blanket of activity. The pinpoints of light in the darkness and the glow from the windows of the high-rises, and even the traffic noise which was always there, day and night, were part of their life. She loved picking out a car from the trail of vehicles, watching its taillights as it got further and further away, wondering about the people inside and where they were going. The mill was totally different. The only light outside was from the Victorian streetlamp in the front garden, but it was on the other side of the house. The nearest house to the mill was down a winding lane surrounded by an orchard of fruit trees separating the two properties, with only tiny dots of light like pinpricks puncturing the blackness. The rest of the house was completely obscured. She pulled the curtain back across the window and sighed. Dan had phoned an hour before to tell her he couldn't get home because the train service to St. Denys Station had been brought to a halt thanks to the knee-deep blanket of snow on the tracks and the high winds blowing it into impenetrable drifts.

'You'll be alright, won't you?' he said. 'I'm sorry to leave you alone on our second proper night in the mill but there's nothing I can do. I should be back about lunchtime tomorrow. Jed's offered to drive me if there's still no service. I'm sorry, Sarah.'

She'd felt her stomach tighten but had taken a deep breath. 'I'm a big girl now,' she laughed. 'I wondered if you'd be able to get home. It's bad, isn't it? I don't remember seeing it like this. Don't worry. I'll be okay. I've still got plenty of unpacking to do and we need to get everything organised for Christmas Day so there's more than enough here to keep me occupied.'

She'd meant to make him think she didn't care that she was alone and she was pretty sure she'd achieved it, but a surge of anxiety went through her. Being left at the mill by herself on their second night wasn't something she'd anticipated. The house was too quiet, and for a moment she wondered at the wisdom of buying somewhere with so many rooms. The apartment had been compact, small some might say, but it had always made her feel as though she and Dan were cocooned, cradled in a safe place. The mill was an unknown quantity, rangy, sprawling, with unfamiliar noises and places yet to be explored. It was only five thirty in the afternoon but it already felt like the middle of the night, and outside was a density of darkness she had never known before.

Wandering into the study she stood by the window, looking out onto the beam falling from the streetlamp onto the lawn, illuminating individual flakes of snow sinking onto the landscape, shivering at the intense wave of déjà vu like an aura encircling her. She shook her head telling herself not to be so silly. Why would snowflakes around a streetlamp make her stomach lurch? She'd seen it in London lots of times and thought how lovely it was, ethereal and maybe a little Dickensian; London her spiritual home, the place she knew more than anywhere else.

Loved more?

A dense thump from above her on the first floor startled her and she frowned, glancing up at the ceiling. She swallowed and waited with bated breath in case it happened again as a frisson of something she couldn't quite place went through her. She breathed out slowly then tutted, shaking her head.

'For God's sake, woman, stop scaring yourself.' Her thoughts went to the unpacked boxes in the bedroom awaiting her attention and she grimaced. I'm just being lazy, she thought, finding any excuse not to do the job everyone hates. She glanced up at the ceiling again. She didn't want to go up the antique wooden staircase and onto the gallery with the leaded light windows looking out onto the night-time shadows, but how else was she to get the job done?

As she opened cases and dumped the clothes onto the floor before sorting them into piles, the evening news on their bedroom TV simply confirmed the heavy snowfall, with scenes of a snow covered United Kingdom grinding to a halt, the motorways strewn with abandoned cars and interviews with travellers wrapped in blankets and regaling their tales of danger and daring-do in the snowbound countryside. Sarah smiled to herself. The slightest flurry always caused chaos in the UK. She thought of one of her clients at the art gallery who came from Maine and thought the British were wusses because they couldn't handle a bit of snow as the broadcaster explained the heavy snowfall had been unexpected and had caused travel chaos across the country.

'Ain't that the truth,' she grumbled. An hour later, after completing only half of her task, she realised she hadn't eaten since breakfast, so went down to the kitchen to look for something interesting. A baked potato with cheese seemed to be the only thing on the menu. 'Really exotic,' she said to herself at the first bland forkful. 'Merry Christmas, I don't think,' she said aloud, and threw the remaining half in the bin. As she rinsed her plate under the tap, the lights over the island and underneath the cupboards flickered on and off then went out just as the iron knocker rapped against the front door. She clutched her stomach and inhaled a sharp breath. 'What the hell is going on tonight?' she said aloud. She waited for a moment, her heat thudding in her chest, not wanting to open the front door while the house was in darkness, then the lights flickered back on again. She closed her eyes and blew out a breath of utter relief as the door was knocked again, louder this time and with more impatience.

Through the glass in the door, Sarah could see the shape of a woman behind it, her outline shifting in the coloured glass of the stained glass panel as she bobbed and fidgeted from side to side, clearly irritated at being kept waiting. Sarah opened the door and smiled uncertainly, curious as to why, and how, someone would choose to visit during such bad weather.

The woman was about mid-twenties but her expression was world-weary and etched with annoyance. Clearly attractive her natural prettiness was concealed by a too heavy foundation caked on her skin. Her lips shone with sticky gloss and Sarah's eyes were drawn to her overdeveloped pout that was clearly not as nature intended. Her once white padded coat had a broken zip which she held together with her arm at the waist to stop the two sides of the jacket flapping in the wind. Sarah smiled, thinking she must be a local, perhaps calling to see how they were settling in. Strange she'd chosen the worst night of the year to do it.

'Hello,' Sarah said in her most welcoming voice, aware she was a newbie in the area. Making friendships didn't come easily to her and she knew she needed to make the effort. 'Can I help?' Her friendly smile slipped from her face when the woman didn't return it and spoke to her curtly in a monotone, broad Eastern European accent, minus the niceties.

'Where is Dan? I must talk to him.'

'He's not here I'm afraid.' Sarah opened the door a little wider. The contrast of the freezing air from outside against the comforting warmth of the hall felt like a cold blast, and the vibes she got from her visitor were just as icy, but she was curious about the woman who had turned up uninvited claiming to know Dan. 'Who wants him?'

'I want him. Yelena. He knows me.'

'Well, he's never mentioned you, sorry.'

'It's not important whether or not he has mentioned me,' she said with a wave of her hand. 'I'm going home and I need to leave Tobias with him. I can't take him with me...it's not possible. He has no passport.'

Sarah stared at her. 'I think you must have the wrong house. We only moved in a couple of days ago. Are you sure you have the right Dan?'

Yelena's expression darkened. Her tone changed from curt to openly hostile and she raised her voice. 'Don't be stupid. Of course I have the right house. He told me he was moving away from London. He had to tell me where he was going. He's the father of my child and I would have made life hell for him if he had gone without telling me where he was going. I know where he works. I know his friends.'

Sarah's eyes widened and she chuckled slightly. Someone had got their wires crossed. 'The father of your child? What child?'

Yelena reached behind her and dragged a little boy to stand in front of her. He was dressed in a red and blue tartan dressing gown, red jogging bottoms, and grubby trainers. 'This child. He is Dan's son and it's time he stepped up and did his bit for the boy.' Sarah laughed and shook her head, and taking a backward step into the hall went to close the door, but Yelena was too fast for her. She pushed her body against the door and shoved hard, sliding a scuffed boot onto the inner doorstep. Yelena's stare didn't leave Sarah's face and her lip curled as she spoke. 'You think you are better than me. Your kind always think they're better, but really, you're no different from me. All women whore in one way or another so you can stop looking down your nose. You've chosen the easy way by not having his child so your life is comfortable, but I know who the father of my child is and after all this time it's his turn to look after him. He has done nothing until now, but now he must.' Sarah couldn't speak, her voice stuck in her throat with shock. Yelena's expression darkened. 'For fuck's sake, say something. It's too cold to be standing here waiting for you to do something. Leave the child in the snow on your doorstep if you want. If you can't be bothered with him it is of no concern to me. And I'll tell you, he is difficult. Hardly says a word. I don't know what's wrong with him. Anyway, no matter. I am leaving. I cannot take him. Tobias cannot come with me. He has no passport. I must leave the country and go to my home. He is Dan's child. He is his responsibility.' She turned to leave.

Sarah stepped out onto the porch steps and grabbed Yelena's arm. 'Just a minute! Whore! Who the hell are you calling a whore? If you are this little boy's mother you need to take him home. Right now. What kind of a woman are you? Get your arse back here.'

Yelena yanked her arm out of Sarah's grip. 'This Dan's home? This is Tobias's home. Dan is his father so his home is Tobias's home and it is about time. You can get as loud as you like but it makes no difference. Look. There's no one to hear you.' She patronisingly waved both hands in the air. 'Women like you...you want, want, want. You think you will have your own way, don't you?' She shook her head and stuck out her chin. 'Not this time.'

'Wait!' Sarah cried. 'You can't just leave the boy here. Dan's not here. He doesn't know me. You have the wrong house, the wrong Dan.'

Yelena's eyes narrowed and she drew her face close to Sarah's, their noses almost touching. 'Is he Dan Kenyon?' Sarah's stomach lurched when she heard Dan's name and she pushed Yelena away. Yelena shoved the boy, whose hair sparkled with snow, further towards her. 'This...is his son.'

Yelena retraced her steps down the path leaving her exiting footprints in the thick snow, past the streetlamp and towards the gates. The yellow light from the lamp made her hair look brassy and highlighted her unkempt appearance. Sarah ran after her, shivering in the freezing air, her feet sodden, her face and hair wet with snow melting as it touched her, falling from an inky sky. She yelled at Yelena, her lone voice sounding odd even to her. 'Do not leave. Do not go. You cannot leave the boy here. What the hell are you thinking? Get back here now.'

Yelena opened the gate making gestures with her fingers and thumbs. 'Yadda, yadda, yadda, keep talking, no one cares.' She got into an old green Citroen parked in the lane and started the engine which emitted a low growl and clouds of smoke from the exhaust. She left without a backward glance. Sarah watched the taillights of the retreating car as they disappeared down the lane, then turned dismally towards the house and went back to the steps, her arms wrapped around her. The boy stood on the top step, clutching a patchwork elephant to his chest, staring up at her and looking frozen to the bone. She gently turned him around and pushed him into the hall, shutting the front door against the freezing air and Yelena's retreating footprints, the heat from the fire hitting them with a wall of warmth.

It was quiet, the only sound the crackle of flames as they licked around the wood in the grate. Flakes of snow that had fallen on the boy's head had melted and flattened his dark hair against his scalp. He and Sarah considered each other carefully, she looking for Dan in his features; the chestnut brown hair, the sparkling tawny eyes fringed with dark lashes and the creamy complexion. They were all there. Tobias was Dan's mini-me, and it shook her to her centre. Her thoughts ricocheted from one thing to another beginning with the hope that maybe Yelena had made a mistake. She said Dan Kenyon. How many Dan Kenyons are there?

'How old are you?' she asked Tobias quietly. His eyes swept to the left and he stuck a finger into his mouth as he thought about what she'd asked him. After a few moments he held up four fingers and his thumb. She closed her eyes and lowered her chin to her chest. She and Dan had been together for over six years.

They'd agreed not to have children. They'd met through an internet dating site and both had said they hadn't expected to meet anyone who would become important.

'Just looking for a roll in the sack, were you?' she'd laughingly asked him on their first meeting. She'd been pleasantly surprised at the restaurant. He was already waiting, and he actually resembled his photo.

He'd laughed and raised his eyebrows. 'I was curious,' he said.

'Curious? Curious about what?'

'Internet dating. My colleagues had all tried it with varying degrees of success.

I thought I'd see for myself.'

'And?'

'And…it's pretty good so far.'

They had been inseparable after that, together only six months before deciding to get a flat. Their conversations about their future went long into the night, both agreeing their respective careers were far too important to them both to want the responsibility of a family.

'You're sure about this, Sarah?' he'd asked her. 'You might change your mind as time goes on. I don't want to be the one to deprive you of having children if it's something you want for the future. It would be wrong of me to expect it.'

She'd slipped her arms around his neck and kissed him. 'I'm one hundred percent sure,' she said. 'I love my job at the gallery, Dan. it's the work I've dreamed about since I was a teenager. I worked long and hard on my fine arts degree and it would break my heart to give it up. Having a family is not really something I've thought about. We both want the same thing.'

As she stood with Tobias in the hall that conversation seemed eons away. Nausea rolled into her throat as realisation struck her with a hammer blow. Dan had slept with another woman during their relationship and the result was standing like a sculpture watching her, barely blinking. His stare unnerved her and she turned away. It's a mistake, just a huge mistake. It couldn't be right, could it? Dan's smiling face loomed into her mind's eye and her thoughts went into overdrive. This has to be wrong. Dan loves me. There's no way he would hurt me like this. To have covered this up for so long would mean I don't really know him. And I know him, don't I? The essence of Dan? I know him. I know all of him.

'Would you like some warm milk...and...and...a biscuit?'

Tobias nodded and pointed behind her. 'And boy.'

She frowned and turned to look behind her. 'What?' She stared into the space, then felt silly at being taken in.

'Boy,' he said.

She shook her head as Yelena's words about Tobias came back to her. He followed her into the kitchen where she heated a mug of milk in the microwave and placed it with two biscuits on the table. Watching him for a second as he sipped the milk, the fabric elephant still held tightly under his arm, she grabbed her phone off the counter and went into the living room, perching on one of the sofas as dark notions of Dan and what he'd done scuttled around her mind like cockroaches. She pressed his photo on the display and stared at it, then put the phone to her ear. It rang out and went to Voicemail.

'This is the Voicemail of Daniel Kenyon. I'm sorry I can't take your call at the moment. Please leave your name and number and I'll return it as soon as I can. Many thanks.' His voice was cheerful, trustworthy, one she knew so well. The automated voice instructed her how to leave a message and Sarah half-listened to the robotic voice, emotionless in a bubble of hurt, numb. In the fifteen minutes since Yelena made her getaway Sarah had been too shaken up to cry. Her shock at Yelena's appearance at the mill had made her so disorientated she couldn't think straight, but now silent tears ran down her cheeks. As she sat staring unseeing at the television blinking light and shade into the room she couldn't work out whether what she was feeling was pain, devastation and utter disappointment in Dan, or blinding anger so intense, so powerful if he walked through the door at that moment she would punch him.

Her phone had gone silent, a black void of nothing waiting for her to fill it with a message. She swallowed, not knowing how to start, waiting for inspiration to hit her, mulling it all over, wishing she'd written something down before making the call, wondering how or why Dan had betrayed her. She clutched at straws—perhaps Yelena was lying and he had no knowledge of Tobias. Or...the straws slipped out of her grasp...he had hidden the existence of his son and had lied and lied. A lie by omission is still a lie. And the more she thought about it, it seemed increasingly as though he had lied. Dan had assured her if she'd wanted a family he was the wrong man for her, yet he had a son, conceived not long after they'd got together and hidden away like a guilty secret, a deception so damning he couldn't bring himself to tell her, hadn't trusted the strength of their relationship to see it through. Hadn't trusted her.

Disappointment crushed her and her face crumpled. The happiness and contentment she'd felt in their new home had been short lived. The future didn't look the same anymore, the rosy existence she had imagined and the one they'd planned together crumbled to dust, and in her heart there was a fracture that ripped her to her core. She bent her head and closed her eyes, resting her mobile against her forehead. 'Oh, Dan,' she whispered.

The small mound under the eiderdown shifted slightly but didn't make a sound. Tobias, still in the dressing gown he'd refused to take off was fast asleep, the ever-present patchwork elephant still in his arms, but now upside down. She swallowed the lump in her throat as tears pricked under her eyelids. Somewhere in her innermost core she felt a deep sorrow, a sense of pity for the little boy. Tobias was in the way, an inconvenience because he didn't fit in with his mother's plans. Sarah wondered why it was so vital for Yelena to return home, and why she couldn't take Tobias with her. She could have organised a passport. He was her son. Wasn't he meant to come first? A thought struck her. Did Dan want him? Had either of them ever wanted him?

She stood by the bedroom window looking out onto the garden at the front of the house, at the lane running by the property and the field beyond, drawing comfort from the lamp throwing out light onto the garden. Even though its glow was muted she could at least see some of the outside. The trees were black smudges against an indigo sky. The snowfall had been relentless but it was calm now, with cascades of white powder tumbling from trees and bushes as the breeze caught them and tipped the weighty cargo from their branches. The back of the house was in total darkness and she made a note to remind Dan they needed some lights out there.

Dan. Would they really be discussing garden lights when he came back from London? The thought of his name felt like a thunderbolt, jarring her body and dragging her into reality. She sank to the floor and sobbed. There was no way out of it. Dan had betrayed her.

Waking with a start, her eyes flicked open to find Tobias standing in front of her. She'd left him in the bedroom in the middle of the night and curled up on a chair in the breakfast room, drifting off to sleep, groggy with exhaustion.

'Tobias! How long have you been standing there?' Glancing at her phone she ran her fingers through her dishevelled hair and got up, letting the blanket fall to the floor. Making her way across to the kitchen she licked the dryness from her lips and reached for the kettle. Tobias stayed by the chair watching her every move and she closed her eyes, drawing in a breath of tiredness. When she opened them Tobias was still staring at her.

'Are you hungry?' she asked him. He nodded and she tried to remember what it was kids had for breakfast. 'I s'pose you like cereal, but we only have muesli. I'm not sure you'd want it.' He said nothing. 'Right.' Sarah opened the fridge. 'How about…a boiled egg, and soldiers. Everyone likes those.' Tobias left the chair and walked over to the table where he had sat the previous evening. He didn't reply, but climbed onto the chair and waited. 'I guess that's yes.'

She boiled an egg and cut a slice of buttered bread into soldiers, placing them in front of him. 'Enjoy.' He picked up his spoon which hovered over the egg, but changed his mind and put it back on the table. Sarah frowned. 'Don't you want it?' Tobias gazed at her, then at the egg. The penny dropped. 'Oh.' She took the butter knife from the counter and sliced off the top of the egg. 'Can you feed yourself?' He took the spoon and dug it into the egg, allowing the bright yellow yolk to dribble down the sides. He picked up one of the soldiers and wiped the yolk from the plate, eating as though he hadn't been fed for a week. Sarah shook her head. 'This is so wrong,' she said under her breath.

While Tobias was eating Sarah showered and dressed, then sat at her dressing table and applied some makeup, knowing that she was filling up time before Dan returned and the inevitable confrontation. She held a lipstick in front of her mouth. Lowering her hand she stared at her reflection. Her hair was long, way past her shoulders, and dark with a fringe sweeping across her left eye and just past her cheekbone. She had worn it like this since she was seventeen, the same style, the same colour. Up until then she had worn her hair short in a gamine style. Pixie hair someone had called it once. It was a name she'd liked and had revelled in being called a pixie which was so far removed from the names she had been called before. And she'd been blonde with blue streaks, an element of rebellion in her teenage years that had pleased her because it meant it was her decision, a way to take a little control over who she was, who she wanted to be. But that was before the fight with Deanne Trainor, a big bully of a girl who had goaded Sarah day after day, week after week, until Sarah had snapped and lashed out at her. The ensuing fight went down in the school's history as the worst it had ever seen. And it had been bloody; the floor of the courtyard ran with blood, mostly Sarah's. This was because Deanne had hidden a penknife in her boot and had produced it when she felt she was in danger of losing. She had sliced it with force down the left side of Sarah's face leaving her with a long scar that had faded from a red and inflamed wound to a wide silver thread. It could still be clearly seen, running from the outside corner of her eye to just under her earlobe close to her jaw, pulling the skin taut towards her hairline. Every day she applied the same concealing makeup. Every day she cursed the memory of Deanne Trainor and the school which had been so remiss it had allowed her to inflict a mark on Sarah that would stay with her for the rest of her life.

The memory stilled her hand and she inhaled a breath to the bottom of her lungs before continuing to dab concealer on the scar. Without warning an image of Dan and Yelena having sex flashed through her mind and she cried out, dropping the cosmetic sponge as she grabbed the top of the dressing table. This image was the one she had tried to push away, the one keeping her awake for most of the night until she'd fallen into a sleep she couldn't prevent. Her dreams had been laced with scenes of recriminations and tears; Dan's face, his mouth pulled into a wide grin, the one she'd come to love, smiling at her as she asked him about Yelena, her voice wobbling as he evaded her questions. She wanted to hurt him for what he'd done, yet at the same time…needed to love him…needed him to love her.

As she continued to apply the concealer to the side of her face she sensed a movement behind her. She turned expecting to see Tobias but there was no one there. She turned back to the mirror but it was not just her reflection she saw. It was as if the glass had been overlaid with another, a smeared greasy image in grey, as though her face had been reproduced in shadow just centimetres out of kilter. She rubbed at it with her sleeve, frowning because she couldn't wipe it from the glass. 'Why won't it rub off?' she said under her breath, buffing it furiously. Then it disappeared as swiftly as it had appeared and she sat back staring at her reflection, now clear, now sharp. She heard laughter; a child's voice, throaty, distinct. She got up and went to the window, peering down into the garden and the lane glowing with white, but it was empty of people. There was no one in the lane and no footprints apart from those leading from the front door to the gate; hers, Yelena's and a line of small prints, obviously Tobias's. Going out onto the landing she peered over the bannister. 'Tobias? Was that you?' she called gently. He didn't answer and she went back into the bedroom, and finished her make up quickly, not wanting to leave him alone for too long. As she descended the stairs tears welled again and she brushed them away angrily, wondering what kind of life they would have now that everything had changed.

At nine-thirty her mobile rang. It was Dan. This was the moment of no return. There was no thinking about how she would approach Tobias's arrival with him, no rejecting one way and constructing another just because it made her feel more comfortable with what she had to say. It would never be comfortable. This was it.

'Hello.'

'Hi, babe. How goes it?'

'Well, I'm still here if that's what you mean. Just.'

'Right.' She could hear the frown in his voice. 'You okay, Sarah?'

'No, not really.'

'Has something happened? The tree didn't fall over, did it?' He laughed. 'I thought it was a bit precarious before I left yesterday. Might have to get Owen from the garden centre in before tomorrow. Don't want it to fall on my mum, do we?'

Sarah steadied her breathing. She didn't want her voice to wobble, or sound strained. She was as angry as hell but she needed to control it, to let him know she'd made a rational decision. Losing it meant losing points. 'It's nothing to do with the tree, Dan. If only it was so simple.' She took a breath. 'Yelena happened.'

Dan's utter shock filled the space between them. His disbelief, and perhaps fear because his secret had been spilt without his knowledge and permission didn't need to be put into words. The silence was a cacophony of guilt. It was there, between them, solid and immoveable. 'Yelena?' He swallowed and she heard it click as it got stuck. 'What...how?' He took a deep breath, the nervous tightness of his throat evident as he tried to speak. 'What happened, Sarah?' His voice sounded alien, with a strange pitch, one that made her stomach roll.

'I think that's my line.' She laughed but it was without humour.

More silence and another swallow. 'I don't know what to say.'

'I'll bet, but you knew what to do didn't you, the result of which is sitting in the breakfast room.'

'Yelena's at the mill?'

'No, Dan.' She gave pause to add weight to her words. 'Tobias. Your son.' Another pause. 'Funny really. Did you not say, if I remember correctly, you didn't want children? I didn't imagine it did I, or is it just me you don't want them with?' She waited for him to say something, but the silence from his end made her think he'd disappeared into the ether, imagined him with his phone to his ear, the expression of horror on his face because his secret was out, his eyes searching around for a plausible explanation but realising there wasn't one. 'So, are you coming home for Christmas or do I have to entertain your son by myself? Oh, yeah, and your family are meant to be visiting tomorrow, aren't they? Don't worry, everything's under control. There'll be plenty of food and drink chosen and paid for by me, oh, and presents I made the effort to buy...for your family. How many have *you* bought? Did you get Yelena anything? She is the mother of your child, after all. And what about Tobias? Is he getting anything? They weren't on your list so I'm afraid I haven't bought presents for them.'

'I'm coming home.' Dan's voice was flat and dark, and Sarah felt her heart breaking.

'Does your family know about Tobias?'

'No.'

'So, he's just your dirty little secret, is he?'

'Enough, Sarah. We need to talk. I'll explain.'

She laughed, ironic and brittle, her voice seething with anger. 'I'll say when it's enough, you bastard, and I haven't even started yet. This one's going to run and run isn't it? How's Dan Kenyon going to extricate himself from this little problem? You shagged someone else. You've got a child. Bet you didn't give me a second thought while you were getting your rocks off.' She pressed the end button and stared at her mobile as Dan's image faded from the screen. She closed her eyes and tried to stop her heart from splintering into a million pieces.

A noise from the living room reminded her she'd left Tobias on his own. She was sure it was a child's voice she'd heard but surely it wasn't Tobias. He'd hardly spoken since Yelena had left him at the mill. When she went into the living room she found him curled up on the sofa watching CBeebies. Sarah raised her eyebrows. He'd found the remote and switched on the television, so he clearly knew what to do. She sank to her haunches in front of him.

'Are you okay, Tobias?' He turned his head to look at her, then raised his hand to his chest in a fist and bent it towards her from the wrist.

'Does your sign mean, yes?' He made the same sign. 'Did Mummy bring some clothes for you? I didn't see any. Maybe she forgot to take them out of the car.' He held his hand up again, palm facing her and waved it to the side. He got off the sofa and went into the hall, then waited until she joined him, pointing to the front door. Taking Tobias's hands she led him across to the staircase, and sitting on the second step gently put her hands on his arms and stood him in front of her.

'Can you talk to me, Tobias? Can you say what you're trying to tell me?' He stared at her, his gaze steady and unflinching as if he was thinking. Sarah knew he understood. 'Are you frightened?' she asked him gently. For the first time Tobias's gaze wavered, and he lowered his eyes. He inspected the floor as though he had lost something, then became frantic, turning around while he searched the floor. 'What is it? What are you looking for?' Tobias anxiously touched his nose with the flat of his fingers, sweeping his hand down in front of his face. Sarah frowned, frustrated because she couldn't interpret his sign language. He made the sign over and over again, and gradually it dawned on her. The sign was like an elephant's trunk. 'Is it your elephant?' she asked. 'Have you lost your elephant, Tobias?' He made the sign for, 'Yes.' She was sure she'd seen it under the table so took his hand and led him into the kitchen. Together, they bent down to look. Tobias crawled under the table and retrieved it, clutching it to him like it was the most important thing in the world, rubbing his cheek against the fraying fabric with his eyes closed. Sarah's heart lurched when she saw how it made him feel finding the elephant. She remembered Tobias had pointed to the front door when she'd mentioned his clothes. 'Are your clothes outside?' He hesitated then made the sign for yes.

In the porch, under the slatted seat, was a scruffy sports hold all. Sarah dragged it through the front door into the hall, and when she unzipped it an overpowering smell of nicotine and cigarette smoke hit her full in the face. 'Ugh, oh my God.' Tobias stood silently in the kitchen doorway, his intense gaze never wavering. 'I think this lot needs to go in the wash, don't you?' He turned silently and went back into the kitchen without making a sound. She picked up the bag then noticed a small white envelope on the floor of the porch. She glanced at it briefly then picked it up and pushed it into the back pocket of her jeans to open later.

As Tobias's clothes were loaded into the washing machine she heard a whimper from the breakfast room. Peering over the island she could see him cowering under the table. 'Tobias?' She went around the island and got down on her knees, putting a hand out to the distressed little boy, but he cowered away from her fingers and began to scream. Sarah quickly pulled her hand back and sat on the floor, leaning against the table leg and looking towards the hall, not speaking, allowing him the space to decide when he wanted to come out. When he didn't move she stood without comment and went back behind the island, pushing the filthy clothes from the hold all into the washing machine with her foot while holding her breath. 'What is the woman thinking?' she said under her breath as she pushed the washing machine door shut with her knee until it clicked. At the sound of the click there was a shuffling from under the table. Tobias stood on the other side of the island.

'Are you okay now?' she asked him. He stared at her, a crease between his dark eyebrows. 'What was it that frightened you? Can you tell me?' Again, no response. She sighed and bit her lip. 'It was something I did,' she said to herself. She glanced at the washing machine. 'Is it the washing machine? Don't you like it?' Tobias frantically shook his head.

'It's the washing machine?' He stood stock still. She walked around the island and held her hand out to him. 'We'll go into the living room and watch The Night Garden, shall we? Do you like The Night Garden? Daddy's nephew loves it,' she said, sighing when she realised he probably didn't know what a nephew was. He stared at her for a moment longer, reached up and took her hand.

In the living room he appeared at ease on the sofa, cocooned in a fur throw she'd tucked around him. She felt his ankles between his pyjamas and his slippers. They were stone cold.

'Sit here for a moment. I'll get you something warm to drink while we wait for Daddy to come home. Do you like this?' she asked him as Iggle Piggle and Upsy Daisy danced across the screen. He glanced up at her and nodded. Her stomach wobbled at the sadness in his eyes and she wondered what kind of life he'd had with his mother.

'You don't like the washing machine, do you?' she said gently.

He looked at her from the outer corner of his eye. 'Hurts,' he said, and rubbed his upper arm with a small pale hand.

'What hurts, Tobias? Does the washing machine hurt?' He frantically shook his head and his breathing changed, his breath coming fast and shallow. 'Okay, okay,' she said. 'It's fine. I won't ask about it anymore. Would you like some hot chocolate?' He raised his hand and bent his fist towards her then turned away, his attention drawn back to the television.

She leant against the windowsill in the kitchen and watched snow fall onto the already pristine white lawn. The flakes were soft and fluffy; from the East where they make soft fluffy flakes apparently. She laughed to herself, thinking the world focussed on inconsequential things instead of important things, the things that really mattered.

'Who cares,' she said under her breath. She slipped her mobile out of her pocket. Two thirty p.m. She inhaled a deep breath, and before she could release it, she heard the sound of a key inserted in the front door lock. Her heart jumped and she closed her eyes for a moment releasing the breath by degrees. This was it, the moment when she would confront Dan about Tobias and his affair with

Yelena. Shit! She wasn't ready. She was pathetically unready. Why hadn't she played it out, talked to the mirror and roleplayed, anything other than feel so unprepared.

The front door slammed and the sound of Dan's footsteps on the parquet floor echoed in the hall. She waited for him to join her in the kitchen but the footsteps stopped, so she went to the kitchen door and stood by the frame. Dan was leaning against the wall, watching Tobias in the living room. She tried to read the expression on his face but couldn't. It was blank, his jaw a rigid line, his eyes telling her nothing. She thought she'd see something there, something close to regret, or even guilt. When he realised she was there he turned and looked at her. They stared at each other for a few moments then Sarah lowered her eyes and went back into the breakfast room, sinking into one of the chairs by the fire. He followed her in and dumped his briefcase on the floor. He stood by it for a moment, clearly waiting for her to take the lead.

'Are you going to say something?'

'Oh, I've got lots to say, but I'm not sure you want to hear it.' Her voice got higher in anger and she wrapped her arms around her body, her fists balled so tight her fingernails dug into her palms. 'You had sex with another woman, and if that wasn't enough you've lied to me for over five years about the son you had with her. What would you do if you were me?'

'I...don't know.'

'You. Don't. Know. Bullshit, Dan. Complete bullshit. You know exactly what would happen. I'd be out of here with my kid in tow. Wouldn't I?' She stopped for breath, her body shaking with pent up rage. 'Why didn't you tell me?'

'I couldn't. I thought you'd leave me if you knew.' He swallowed the nausea in his throat. 'I made a mistake, Sarah, a huge mistake. I thought about telling you but the longer it went on the harder it got.' He rubbed his eyes with his fingers as though attempting to rub her away from his vision so he wouldn't have to face the music. 'I don't suppose sorry is going to be enough, is it?'

'Sorry is what you say when you've forgotten someone's birthday or left your clothes all over the bedroom floor. It's not enough for when you've fucked someone else and produced a child you decided not to tell me about, particularly as you were adamant you didn't want kids.' She glared at him. 'Now I know why.'

He walked reluctantly to the other chair and sat facing her. 'It wasn't the way you're making it sound.'

'Oh, right,' she cried. 'That's okay then, as long as it wasn't how it sounds. So, you didn't fuck Yelena, and Tobias was the result of an immaculate conception. If that's the case why the hell is he here?'

Dan reached for her hand, but she pulled it away. 'Don't touch me! Don't ever touch me again. I fucking hate you. I mean, do I actually know you? You've cheated on me and had a child while we were together and you've been living a lie for the last five and a half years. And you've made me live a lie too. And now she's dumped her kid on us. Why, Dan? Because it's Christmas and she wants to go out partying?'

'It's not his fault.'

'Oh, I know. I know exactly whose fault it is, and it's not his and it's not Yelena's. It's yours.'

She went into the kitchen and filled the kettle, slamming it down on the hob with a bang. She was on automatic; filling the kettle when she was angry was more to give her something to do other than sitting and waiting for the war of words to begin, but this went deeper than just anger. She felt crushed, sick to her stomach, sidelined. Dan had something with Yelena, a woman he'd had an affair with he didn't have with her. Something meaningful and permanent.

A little boy.

As she listened to the kettle bubbling, she felt her eyes fill with tears, and for a split second a black, seething hatred went through her. She hated Dan for ruining everything. As they stared at each other there was a tinkling crash from the hall. She went to the kitchen door. A glass Tiffany angel; a gift to each other on their first Christmas together had fallen from the Christmas tree and was on the floor, the wings lying apart from the body. She stared at it for a moment, wondering how it could have fallen as tears ran down her cheeks before picking up the pieces, returning to the breakfast room and throwing them at him. One of the wings struck him on the cheek and fell to the floor, shattering into tiny shards, sending sparkling glass fragments skittering across the wood. 'There it is. A metaphor for our relationship, smashed to pieces thanks to you. What did you do, take her to an empty house and fuck her on the bed? Was it this house? Our bed?'

'I wish you'd stop talking like someone who isn't you. You never talk that way.'

'No, I don't.' She narrowed her eyes. 'But I bet she does. I didn't think you liked rough. Because she is, isn't she? Dog rough.' He looked embarrassed. 'Do you want to know something?' Dan stared at her. 'That woman…that…that mother, if she has the nerve to call herself a mother drove away from here without even a backward glance at that little boy in there. She couldn't have cared any less if she'd tried. It was as cold and heartless as if she'd taken an unwanted puppy back to a pet shop, just dumped him on the step and disappeared into her new life.' She paused, seething, and turned off the gas as the kettle began to whistle. 'So he has two parents who don't give a damn about him.'

'I never said I didn't care about him.'

'No, Dan. It's me you don't care about! Actions speak louder than words. Has no one taught you that?' she yelled. She went into the living room to sit with Tobias. He dragged his eyes away from the television and gazed at her for a few seconds as if acknowledging her presence but didn't lose the haunted look shading his face. He turned away again and hugged the patchwork elephant to his chest. Sarah suddenly realised he didn't have any toys apart from the elephant. The following day was Christmas Day and they didn't have anything for him. Her face crumpled and she pulled her knees up to her chin, burying her face into them as she cried, not wanting Tobias to see, wondering if it would make any impression on him even if he did.

A noise at the door startled her and she raised her head. Dan stared at her, his face the colour of stone. 'If Yelena and I hadn't had a child you wouldn't have known.'

The irony wasn't lost on her. He'd said Yelena and I, like they were a couple. It sounded so... permanent, more respectable and solid than she knew it was. Shaking her head with astonishment, she said, 'So we would have lived a lie. For how long? For always? Well, I know for definite you would have. I've been doing some sums. It must have been when you were on the business trip to Prague a few months after we met. Did you have to pay her? How much was it? I hope she was worth it.'

'Don't be ridiculous.'

'Oh, what? Are you so fabulous and in demand you've never had to pay anyone?' Something dawned on her. 'Have you got a secret life, y'know like those guys with two or three wives who don't know about each other? Is that what's happening here?'

'You're being ridiculous. When the hell would I have the time to have a secret life, for God's sake? And no, I've never paid anyone. I would never do it and you know it, and I know you're trying to hurt me, Sarah. I get it.'

Puffing out a little laugh she grinned, but without mirth. 'We've begun our new life in this wonderful house with a big fat lie you've hidden, and *I'm* trying to hurt *you*? Really? Well, I wonder why that is?' Her eyes went to Tobias, then dragged them back to Dan, shaking her head. 'I feel so sorry for him. He must wonder who the hell he is, and more importantly who we are. We're nothing to him. We're strangers. He's been dumped on strangers.'

Dan wandered over to the window and stared out, his hands stuck resolutely in the pockets of his jeans, his shoulders slumped. 'Do you have to say things like that in front of him? He has ears.'

'Yes, he does. He also has issues. Did you know? I mean, do you actually know anything about your son?'

He half turned his head. 'Of course, I know. I'm his father.'

'Yeah, his father. But who's his Dad?' she asked him, her eyes wide. 'Not you, that's for sure. You're too selfish. Have you ever read him a bedtime story? Have you tucked him up at night and told him you love him? Were you there for his first day at nursery? Did you go to his Nativity? I'm guessing by the look on your face the answer is no.'

'How could I do those things? Yelena's a nomad. She goes where the work is.'

'And it never occurred to you it might be better for Tobias to be with you, where he could have had a solid upbringing and some stability in his life. Did you never ever think of him all the time you were working on your precious career? He's your son, Dan. Your little boy. How could you just…dismiss him like he didn't exist?'

He rounded on her, his face blazing. 'You didn't want kids, did you? I did it for you.'

She threw up her hands. 'Oh, here we go. Same old, same old. You'll always find someone else to blame. How do you always manage to do it?'

'I didn't want you to feel you were obliged to take Tobias on. And let's face it you've never been the mothering type. And while we're talking about careers, isn't it what you've got? Your career is as important to you as mine is to me. How could you have taken care of him?'

She got up from the sofa and faced him with a smirk, pushing her face up close to his, realising Dan was doing what Dan always did. Every time they had a disagreement he would shift the blame somehow. 'Well there's the rub, Dan. I wouldn't have.' His eyes hardened again, the blazing fire she'd seen in them only a second earlier quickly extinguished and replaced with ice. 'This has happened because of you,' she said pushing a finger into his chest, her teeth clenched in rage, her voice getting louder. 'Because you couldn't keep it in your trousers and you lied about the result. You should have been honest about it from the start. Okay, it might have split us up but at least it would have been rooted in truth. You've taken my choice away from me and Tobias's choice away from him. When are you going to take responsibility for what you've done and behave like an adult?' She went into the hall and took her parka off the peg, then remembered the envelope in her back pocket and shoved it in the bag she'd hung over the finial at the bottom of the stairs. 'The food delivery will be here in an hour. I'll let you deal with it. I'm going into town to get Tobias a present for tomorrow. I'm guessing you haven't thought about it.' Dan sighed and lowered his gaze. 'No...I thought not.'

15th December 1999

4

Lacey sat on the stairs and stared at the open front door. A cold draft trailed up the hall making her shiver, and she wrapped her arms around herself, deep in thought. She left her pencil case on the step and walked down the hall towards the door, putting a rough-skinned hand with bitten-down fingernails on the handle, opening the door a little wider.

'Aaron,' she called softly. A bud of fear sprouted in her chest and grew downwards into her stomach. They said they wouldn't be long. They said she was in charge and if anything went wrong she'd be in trouble. They said they'd belt her to within an inch of her life if she didn't do as they said. Her dad always said it, that they'd belt her to within an inch of her life. Lacey didn't know what it meant but it didn't sound good. If it was like when he clouted her around the head for being cheeky she was sure it would be something to be avoided.

Outside, the street was silent. She gritted her teeth and waited for a few moments, listening, wondering if Aaron would suddenly run through the door like a hurricane, shoving her out of the way and laughing his head off. He was always like it. Her Nan had said there was something wrong with him because he never listened and was out of control; a child should be seen and not heard and be still at least some of the time. Aaron was never still, and never quiet.

Silver smoke trails snaking out of the chimneys reached her nostrils, and breathing it in gave her a semblance of comfort because it meant she wasn't totally alone. Most of the houses in the street still had open fires, which was just as well her Nan said. More often than not the money meant for the electricity meter would go down the pub and stay there. It's what her Nan said anyway when she moaned about her dad, which was most of the time. She didn't think her Nana liked her Dad.

Lacey eyed the houses across the street. Some had brightly coloured fairy lights in the windows, pinpricks of garish glow illuminating the front gardens sloping down to the road. Christmas Day was only ten sleeps away and her mouth pulled into a grin of excitement. The streetlamps were inefficient; throwing out shafts of dim yellow light like an apology puddling on the ground at the foot of every metal pole, each thick with layers of lumpy grey paint which the council had enticingly called "a community refurbishment". In those sallow beams myriad pinpricks of sleet were highlighted as they danced in the air. Her eyes widened, hoping those tiny grainy pearls would turn into fluffy flakes of snow, the anticipation of hurtling down the snow-clad slope on their sledge making her shiver again.

Her foot reluctantly crossed the threshold and she stood on the concrete path running from the front door to the road, hopping from one foot to the other on a patch of scrappy grass serving as a front garden.

'Aaron.' Her voice was louder this time, thinking he'd probably gone to see his best friend whose house was at the corner of the street. Her gaze was drawn back into the hall, its comfort and safety drawing her in, and she wondered if her parents would want her to leave the house to follow him. Her thumb went into her mouth, the gnawed at a nail already chewed down to the quick. A silent curse left her lips, using the word her mum had cried that morning when she'd stubbed her toe on their old vacuum cleaner, the flex of which was still sprawled across the kitchen floor. Retracing her steps she shut the door and went into the lounge, then through to the kitchen, praying he was in the house.

Upstairs, the floor in Aaron's bedroom was covered in the usual childhood detritus, toy cars, farmyard animals, broken train tracks and discarded drawings, but no Aaron. A sketch of their elderly neighbour was on his desk, so faithfully drawn the likeness was like a photograph. And there were others, all people she knew; Mum, Dad, Nana, Aaron's teacher, Mrs. Crane, and Lacey. The drawing made her look pretty and a sensation of pleasure went through her, then disbelief that their Aaron had drawn them, the little brother who caused her so much grief, whose snotty face was always filthy and whose language was worse than anything she heard from her parents. He smelt horrible too, and her nose wrinkled at the thought of him. The drawings slipped from her fingers and floated to the floor, making a whispering sound as they fell like chiffon, one against the other.

Chewing on her thumb again she slowly descended the stairs to the hall as realisation hit her. Aaron was not in the house. Going to her room and contemplating what to write on her pencil case had seemed so important. As untidy and uncared for as it was, her room was her private space where thoughts of Ryan Turner comforted her, but now she was in trouble even though she hadn't done anything wrong. Aaron had gone without giving a thought to what would happen to her. He was a pain in the arse just like her mum said, and Lacey knew he was doing whatever he was doing to scare her and get her a beating.

She ran into the kitchen, and taking the spare key off the hook, grabbed her coat from the hall floor where it had been dropped after school. The house felt wrong, like a bubble of silence, an empty space without Aaron's presence. Lacey opened the front door again, almost relieved to be out of the house, and stepped out onto the path. A light wind had got up which tugged and teased a pale green tarpaulin stretched across the front of a house on the other side of the road. The sound of the sheet flapping against the charred building irritated her, and the thrashing snap and pull of the tarpaulin prevented her from thinking straight. The house had caught fire eighteen months earlier and was yet to be repaired by the local council. Her mum and the neighbours had moaned about it, saying the snotty, up-themselves councillors wouldn't want such an eyesore in their street, and if it had been it would have been fixed up months ago. The green tarpaulin had become a familiar sight to them on their side of the road. It felt like it had been there forever.

As Lacey slammed the front door and looked down the street a tremor of fear went through her. She was breaking a promise by leaving the house, but she had to find Aaron and get him back into the house before her Mum and Dad came back from the pub. He probably hadn't gone far, maybe just to his mate's, and they didn't need to know they'd left the house. She had to find him soon because it was nearly Christmas, and if she was belted to within an inch of her life it would be all Aaron's fault and she'd never forgive him.

Thanks for coming out to the mill. I didn't know if you'd make it.'

'You'll have to get used to the weather conditions here sometimes, particularly where you are. Not much protection from icy drafts. It is worse this year though. People think it's a good thing for us taxis, more punters, but we have the same trouble getting about as everyone else does.'

Sara reached into her bag for her purse. 'What's the damage?'

'Give us a fiver. That'll cover it.' Smiling at the taxi driver she handed him the note. 'What will you do about getting back?'

'Oh, I hadn't thought.'

'Our office is in George Street. When you're ready to go home, pop in there. Someone will take you. It might be me.'

'Thank you….?'

'Dave. Dave Crowther.'

'Thanks, Dave. Sarah Anders.' They shook hands across the front seats. 'I might see you later then.'

She got out of the taxi and looked up at the sky. It was still the grim grey it had been all day, full of threatened snow. She slammed the car door and looked up and down the high street wondering where the toy shop would be. Everywhere has one, even a village as small as Newton Denham. Maybe I should just ask someone, she thought. It would be quicker than walking up and down the street looking for one. A passer-by directed her to The Toy Box halfway down the high street, towards the church. Sarah had anticipated it would be buzzing with shoppers but it was surprisingly empty. The bell over the door tinkled as she went in, and the matronly woman standing behind the counter smiled at her.

'Merry Christmas.'

'Merry Christmas. I thought you'd be really busy today.'

'Oh, no, dear. Everyone's already bought the kids' presents. The Christmas trade is over for us. We were quite busy this morning but we'll be closing soon. Are you looking for anything in particular?'

'Er…I'm not sure.' Sarah bit her lip.

'Suppose he or she has got everything?' the woman said. 'They all have these days.'

'Something like that.'

The woman nodded. 'Yes, it's so difficult to know what to get to interest kids today. Most of them seem to spend their lives staring at one screen or another, but some of the old-fashioned toys are still popular. Prince or Princess?' Sarah frowned, and the woman laughed. 'Girl or boy.'

'Sarah laughed with her. 'Oh, right...boy.'

'Left hand aisle. There's loads of ideas down there.'

The shelves were stacked high with games and books. Further along the shelves were huge gaps. 'The gaps are where this years' most popular toys were,' the woman called from behind the huge gondola. 'Snooker tables are in again this year. And robots. They always do well,' she said, quieter, as she tidied the counter, as if to confirm it to herself. Sarah didn't answer, confused by the array of games and boxes on the shelves.

'I've got absolutely no idea what little boys like,' she said under her breath. 'Only big boys.'

'I'm Mary.' Sarah jumped as the woman appeared by her side. 'Can I be of any help?'

Sarah wondered if she should tell her exactly what had happened but thought better of it. Newton Denham was a village. She assumed everyone knew everyone, and probably all their business. She hadn't even computed the shock of Tobias arriving on her doorstep yet so would probably regret it afterwards, even though it would have been good to get it off her chest. 'It's for...an unexpected guest. We weren't anticipating her bringing her little boy with her so we didn't buy him anything. I...we don't have any children so I'm not really very up to date on toys and what's popular.'

Mary narrowed her eyes. 'You're the new couple from Newton's Mill, aren't you?'

'Yes, we took ownership a couple of weeks ago but we've just moved in.'

'You're brave.'

Sarah frowned. 'Oh. Why?'

Mary began moving boxes around on the shelves. 'Well, we're in the middle of winter aren't we? Not the best time to move. It's always so much easier in the summer.'

'Yes, I suppose it is. The move was okay, though. No problems.'

'How old is he?' Sarah glanced at her blankly. 'The little boy? The unexpected guest?'

'Oh, five.'

Mary reached up to a middle shelf and found a box of Lego for small hands. 'These are perfect for five-year olds. They've always been very popular. Still were this year. Or here's a Take Apart toy racing car. They've been flying off the shelves.'

'Okay, they'll be fine. Do you have anything bigger?"
'Bigger.'
'Yes, y'know, like a main present.'
'Um, I've got a trampoline in the back. It was ordered by a mum and dad and cancelled. The little boy's aunt had already bought him one. Does it sound like something he would like?'
'Perfect. I'll take all of these, and some colouring books and wax crayons please, for some after Christmas lunch peace.'
Mary raised her eyebrows and grinned. 'You'll be lucky.' She went out to the back of the shop and brought back a box with an image of a blue and green trampoline on the front. 'He'll love this. He can use it inside and in the garden.'
'Thank you…for your help.'
'It's no trouble. Would you like me to phone TipTop Cars? You'll never get down the street with all this, and it's really coming down now. I really had no idea it was going to be so bad.'
Sarah peered out of the shop window. The light was fading and huge white flakes drifted past the glass and settled softly on the pavement. It was beautiful; the old-fashioned cobbled street looked so lovely lit up with fairy lights and decked in snow, the quintessential English village at Christmas, but sadness overtook her and part of her just wanted to shut it out.
'Thanks. That would be great.'
Turning to look out of the window again a lone man walked by the shop, hunched up against the snow, hands pushed deep into the pockets of his jacket. He glanced into the toy shop window and when he saw Sarah did a double-take, a frown creasing his forehead. Embarrassed, she averted her eyes and waited for Mary to finish her phone call. When she looked back through the window he'd gone past and was sauntering towards a coffee shop, greeting another man waiting outside. Before going inside he glanced back at The Toy Box for a long moment, then disappeared. She shrugged and picked up some of the carrier bags as Dave drew up in his taxi. She was glad it was him. He seemed nice and it would be a wise move to get to know the locals. Being stuck out in the sticks wasn't conducive to getting cosy with the neighbours. The effort would be worth it, even with things the way they were.
Dave came into The Toy Box rubbing his hands together and breathing out vapour like a dragon. 'It's bloody cold out there. Just seen your Lukey, Mary. Gone across the road with his mates. Alright for some.' Mary rolled her eyes and grinned at Sarah. 'C'mon let's get this stuff in the car and get you home. My missis is doin' a big stew and dumplins' tonight and I can't wait.'

Mary laughed. 'You don't change much, Dave Crowther. All you ever think about is your stomach. You were the same at school if I remember right.'

'Well, someone's got to think about it. It might as well be me.' He took the bigger box and Sarah picked up the small ones. 'You ready?'

'As I'll ever be. Bye, Mary. And thanks for your help. You've been a lifesaver.'

'And you have a lovely Christmas. I hope the little boy, whoever he is, appreciates his lovely presents.'

'What little boy?' Dave asked.

'He's staying at the mill with...?' Mary glanced at Sarah quizzically. 'Sarah. Sarah Anders.'

'With Sarah.'

'Oh, right.' His eyes went to Mary, and he nodded. 'Well, you have a good 'un, Mary. See you in the New Year, I expect.'

'And you, Dave. And you, Sarah.'

The street was virtually empty, the shopkeepers were locking up for the last time before Christmas and Sarah glanced up and down the street as Dave piled the bags into the car.

'Dave, would you mind taking these things to the mill for me? Dan's there. He'll pay the fare.'

Dave was surprised. 'Er, yeah, if that's what you want. You not going home?'

'Not yet. What time do you finish?'

'I'm on 'till ten, but if I'm not around one of the other drivers will take you.' His eyebrows drew together in a frown. 'I wouldn't leave it too late if I were you. Christmas Eve is always busy and we don't know what the weather's going to do.'

'I won't. Thanks, Dave.'

'No problem.'

She watched as Dave drove up the narrow street then walked the same way. The shops in the centre of Newton Denham were closed and there was a ghostly feel to the place even though every building was strewn with chains of fairy lights and every window had a Christmas display. The village shopkeepers had gone to town and Sarah was impressed. They rivalled some of the ornate displays she'd seen in London. In the centre, on the green, was a huge decorated Christmas tree. There was to be a Christmas Carol concert around the tree that evening, and Sarah had hoped she and Dan would go, but it wouldn't happen now. A wave of utter sadness crushed her. Her shoulders began to shake and she prayed no one would come along the path. She wondered if she'd made the right decision not to go back to the mill, but the thought of returning there felt wrong. She didn't want to be there, couldn't face a little boy who had been abandoned by his parents without breaking down, not just by his mother who had so brutally left him with a stranger, but Dan too.

By the time she reached The Crown Hotel in the centre of the village she'd stopped crying. Rummaging around in her bag she found an old tissue and wiped her face before going inside. She glanced up at the fascia of the old building, its stonework and mullioned windows, and the wisteria crawling across the front, no longer in flower but in its winter garb, hanging with icicles and sparkling with snow. She bit her lip, took a breath, and stepped across the threshold.

An open fire danced and crackled in the grate, the only sound in the deserted reception area. Behind the desk was a young woman about Sarah's age. She looked up and smiled when Sarah approached the desk.

'Hello. How can I help?

Sarah swallowed hard, hoping the receptionist wouldn't ask her any awkward questions. 'Do you have a single room available?'

The receptionist checked the computer. 'You're in luck. We have a single room on the top floor. How long would you like it for?'

'Just for tonight. For now.'

The receptionist nodded as Sarah handed over her credit card. 'Is your luggage in your car? I can get one of the porters to get it for you if you like. It'll save you going out in the cold again.'

'Er, no, no luggage.'

The receptionist's eyes met Sarah's but her smile didn't waver. 'That's fine. Here's you key card. Dinner is from seven onwards, or you can get snacks at the bar. I hope you enjoy your stay.'

'Is there room service?'

'Yes. We have twenty four hour room service.'

Sarah sighed with relief. 'Thank you.'

'No problem.' Sarah began to walk to the lift. 'If there's anything you need just let me know.'

Sarah turned and the young woman nodded, her eyes soft, her smile, sympathetic. 'Thanks. I will.'

Sarah stared out of the window onto the street below. The snow had stopped and a fog had settled on the village, swirling around the roof tops like an ethereal ribbon in the muted lamplight. Below her window, on the green, people gathered in readiness for the carol concert. She watched as bobble-hatted families arrived together with excited children breathing hot vapour into the cold air, and mums and dads snuggled close to each other to stave off the breath of a winter's eve. Tears rolled down Sarah's face as a school band struck up the first cords of, Oh Come All Ye Faithfull, and the gathering began to sing her favourite carol. She closed the curtains and pulled the cover off the bed, laying on the duvet underneath. She wanted to close her eyes, to shut out the noise of her thoughts invading her peace and forcing her to face up to the thing she couldn't confront. The tears came easily and she sobbed, her body wracked with sorrow as she cried. Dan had a child, a child with someone else. He had lied the whole time they had been together. The duplicity he had hidden so easily made her stomach churn and she ran to the bathroom and threw up, then splashed her face with cold water and laid back on the bed, exhausted, praying sleep would come so she could obliterate the images in her mind.

Her phone buzzed and she picked it up. Laying the phone on the pillow she watched Dan's image disappear as the phone rang out. It buzzed again, and again his smiling image lit up the darkened room and gradually faded. A beep followed indicating a text. She accessed her message box.

"Where are you? Please Sarah, come home. I need to talk to you."
Ignoring it she exhaled, and switched the phone to silent.

Christmas Day. The hotel room looked different in daylight. Last night it had felt like a cocoon, a sanctuary, somewhere for her to think, to cry, to rage, and to work out what to do next. Now it was like any other hotel room, impersonal, a little jaded; not a place where any comfort could be had. She got out of bed as someone tapped on the door.

'Room service, Ms. Anders.' The young waiter brought in a breakfast tray and left it on the luggage rack. 'Do you need anything else?'

'No, it looks…great. Thanks'

'Reception wondered if you were staying tonight.'

Sarah took a deep breath. 'No, no, I…I won't need the room, thank you. What time do I need to leave?'

'We ask guests to vacate their rooms by ten thirty.'

She glanced at her phone. Seven thirty. She had three hours to make up her mind.

After eating a hurried breakfast which she realised was her first meal since yesterday morning, Sarah showered and dressed. There had been eight missed calls from Dan and more messages, and she made a promise to herself to answer next time he called. She didn't have long to wait.

'Yes?'

'Sarah! Thank God, I've been so worried.' He paused and Sarah didn't say anything. 'Where are you?' he asked quietly.

'I stayed in a hotel.'

'A hotel?'

'Where else would I be? I'm not exactly spoilt for places to go.'

'I wish you'd come home.'

'Yeah, well, there's the thing. It doesn't feel like my home anymore.'

'No...well, I understand. I...will you come back? Please, Sarah.'

'Do you have any idea what you've done, what you've done to me and how it's made me feel?'

'I've hurt you.'

'No Dan, you've crucified me. I feel sick every time I think of you and her together.'

'I know...'

'And do you know Tobias's mother isn't the only one who looks bad in all of this? You left him with her, someone not fit to be his mother, and now she's left him with you, a stranger. You're both the same, utterly selfish. I don't know who's worse. And I don't know where it leaves me...or...or what the hell I'm going to do.'

'I'm not proud of what I've done. I'm so sorry I lied to you. Please come home, Sarah. It's Christmas Day. Could we just get through Christmas, and afterwards...well, you can decide.'

The taxi made its way out of the centre of the village and onto the dual carriageway.

'Didn't think I'd see you today,' she said. 'What time do you finish?'

'Oh, I'll be home in time for lunch, don't you worry about that. Keeps me out of the way of all the flapping about whether we've got enough food and how could we have forgotten to get sprouts. Does my head in.' He looked out of the side window. 'These roads aren't too bad,' said Dave, making small talk. 'It's the roads where you are that cause the most problems.'

'I guess we didn't think of it when we bought the mill. It was incredibly cold on the day we decided to move here but there wasn't any snow. It might have been a different decision had there been.'

Dave eyed her in the rear-view mirror. 'You from around here?'

Her eyes met his. 'No,' she said, shaking her head. 'We've come down from London. Both Dan and I work in the City but we got fed up with the rat race. It's one thing working in it. Living in it as well became too much.'

'S'pose you had one of them posh apartments?' Her phone beeped with a text. *"Are you on your way?"*

'Well, actually, we did.'

'Thought so. I could tell.'

'Oh, dear. That obvious is it?'

Dave shifted in his seat and continued to glance in and out of the rear-view mirror. 'It was obvious you didn't know these parts.'

Her fingers hovered over the keys, ready to type an answer, but she changed her mind. 'Why?'

'There's a lot of history here.'

Sarah closed her eyes momentarily and pressed her lips together, pushing her phone into her bag. 'There's a lot of history everywhere.'

He nodded and pulled a face. 'True.'

They pulled up outside the mill and Sarah looked into the distance. Tiny pale yellow lights from the house down the lane pierced the half-light across the landscape as snow began to fall again, but they seemed so far away they looked like distant stars.

'Right,' he said, rubbing his hands together. 'Have a good one. You on your own today?'

Sarah reached into her purse and pulled out a ten-pound note. 'If only,' she said under her breath. 'No, we've got family coming. If they actually get here.'

'Oh, good. Safety in numbers, that's what I always say. Good to have the family around you. I'm expecting some chaos as well.' He grinned. 'They're all coming to us. Saves 'em money, see, eating me and the missus out of house and home.' He reached out from the open window and took the note from her, delving into his pocket for change.

'No, Dave, it's fine. Merry Christmas.'

'Oh, right, well, thanks Sarah.' He saluted her and nodded to Dan who had appeared at the front door, pushing the note into his pocket. 'Merry Christmas.'

As Sarah put her purse back into her bag she saw the envelope she'd picked up from the front porch. Making her way up the steps to the hall she slipped her finger under the flap and pulled the envelope open, thinking she was seeing things when she pulled out a little figure made of bent twigs. She held it up in front of her, then realised it had a sharpened twig pushed through its stomach. Grimacing, she pushed it back into the envelope. 'Maybe it's a local Christmas custom,' she muttered.

'Sorry?' Dan called as he turned into the hall. 'I missed what you said.'

Sarah shoved the envelope back into her bag. 'Nothing. Just talking to myself.'

'Where's Tobias?'

'He's in the living room watching television.' He reached for her but she stepped back. 'I'm glad you've come home. I was so worried. I didn't know where you could have gone.'

She indicated the boxes Dan had stacked in the hall, ignoring him. 'You'd better have a look at those. Mary from The Toy Box included some wrapping paper as well. Maybe you could take them upstairs and wrap them.'

Dan reached for her hand. 'We need to talk, Sarah.'

'Talk?' She raised her eyebrows. 'I can barely look at you, never mind talking. Anyway, what's to talk about? It is what it is. To be honest I need some space. Now isn't a good time to thrash out this mess. There's still loads to do. Your family is coming in a few hours don't forget, and the last thing I want is their opinions on the subject, although I can't imagine what they'll make of it. What are you going to tell them?'

'I don't know.'

She pulled her hand away from the fingers he'd entwined around hers. 'You could try the truth. It's done now. It can't be undone. Tobias is your son. If you lie to them now you'll be denying him. He and I are two people you've forgotten when it suited you. Are there any more?' He rolled his eyes. 'You can't hide Tobias away any longer. Tell them the truth, and shame the devil.'

He glanced at her and his eyes narrowed. 'What?'

'You should tell them how it is. They'll accept it better coming from you. Your mother won't care anyway. You know you're her little darling who can't put a foot wrong.'

'Sarah.'

'No, Dan. That *is* the truth. She certainly won't see my side of it. You slept with someone else when we were together and had a child you hid away for five years. As far as she'll be concerned it'll be put up or shut up. I know what she thinks of me.'

'And what does she think of you?' he said with a sigh.

'That I'm not good enough for you. But let's be honest, Kate Middleton wouldn't have been good enough for you.' Slipping off her parka, she hung it on the peg. Dan ran a hand through his hair but said nothing. 'You're her little prince, and you always will be. I don't know how the hell I'm going to get through today, and you might not like me saying this, but I'm dreading it.'

Dan took Tobias's presents to wrap upstairs. Sarah ironed his clothes, wishing she'd bought him something decent to wear when she'd been in the village. The clothes from the hold all were rough, probably second hand, the jumpers and shirts frayed at the wrists. In the hold all had been a check shirt, and a pair of jeans with holes in the knees she was sure she could make look funky by fraying the holes even further. As she worked on them she heard Dan's phone ring from where he'd left it on the arm of the sofa. She picked it up and looked at the screen. It was Yelena, her photograph more attractive than the real thing. Sarah bit her lip.

'Dan's phone.'

'I need to speak to Dan. Put him on.'

Sarah felt her hackles rise. 'When you speak to me properly, Yelena, I'll get Dan.'

'Just put him on.'

'You've got five seconds to change your attitude. If you don't I'm going to cut you off and delete you. It's your choice.'

Yelena inhaled a breath. 'Put Dan on. Please.'

Sarah ignored the sarcasm with which Yelena had laced the last word. 'Not perfect, but much better. Remember it for next time. I won't take any crap from you.' She paused. 'Dan!' she called loudly with the phone next to her mouth, hoping it would deafen Yelena. 'There's a call for you.'

Dan bounded down the stairs, and glancing at the screen took the phone from Sarah. He rolled his eyes, pausing before speaking. 'Yelena.' His eyes went to Sarah as he listened. She knew Yelena was complaining about her. 'I called you because I want to know what the hell you think you're doing.' He waited. 'Yes, I know he's my son, but you said you wanted him with you.'

Sarah tapped Tobias gently on the shoulder. 'Let's go into the kitchen, Tobias,' she whispered. 'We can have some milk and biscuits.' He scrambled off the sofa and took her hand, his eyes focussed on her face. 'Do you understand me, Tobias? You know what I'm saying, don't you?' He continued to stare at her, then nodded.

'You're doing what?' Dan shouted at the phone. 'So, when are you coming back? What about Tobias?'

In the kitchen Sarah could hear Dan's raised voice and she shook her head. 'What a mess,' she said under her breath. Tobias slid on to a chair and watched her as she moved around the kitchen, heating milk and putting biscuits on a plate as she listened to a one-sided conversation Dan was having with Yelena, which ended with, 'Go to hell.' Afterwards he joined them in the kitchen and sat at the table.

'That went well,' Sarah said, pulling a face. 'I suppose we've got a lot more of it to look forward to. She's so bloody rude.'

'She's going to Europe…Russia.'

'I could have told you that. Why is she ringing you now? Bit late in the day all things considered, isn't it?'

'She doesn't know when she's coming back.'

'Meaning…?'

'Meaning Tobias is ours for the foreseeable.'

'Ours?'

He rolled his eyes. 'Mine,' he said in a small voice.

Sarah's heart dropped at the look on his face. 'Have you considered Tobias might have some issues, maybe autism?' she said.

Dan studied the floor, then his eyes met hers. 'Autistic Spectrum Disorder. It was clear there were issues with him right from the start. Yelena kept saying he was a pain and wouldn't listen to her, and when anything happened he didn't like he would throw himself on the floor and scream. He even bit her once.' He looked away from Sarah. He seemed reluctant to talk, as if negotiating with himself how much he should tell her. 'He knocked his own baby teeth out banging his head against the wall when he lost control. We took him to a specialist to be assessed but Yelena said it was all rubbish, he was just a brat who wanted his own way and what he needed was a good slap. I didn't pursue it any further because she couldn't be relied upon to take him to appointments.' Sarah nervously shuffled her feet. She didn't really want to hear what "they" had done. She'd wanted to ask about the gap in his teeth but hadn't in case it was because of something Yelena had done. The less she heard her name or had to repeat it the better as far as she was concerned. In any case it wasn't her business.

'Couldn't you have taken him?'

'I offered to, but when the first appointment was due she made sure she wasn't around, working she said, so when I went to pick him up there was no sign of them. I hung about outside the building where she was living but she didn't materialise so I gave up. I decided if Yelena didn't want it to happen, it wouldn't happen.' An uncomfortable silence fell between them. 'Anyway, I need to finish wrapping Tobias's presents. When it's done I'll help you with lunch. Maybe we can discuss everything.'

'You keep saying we need to talk but it won't change anything, Dan. What's there to discuss. You're Tobias's father. What're you going to do, dump him again? It doesn't matter how I feel does it?'

'I've already abandoned him in your eyes, I know you think I have, but it's you I'm thinking about now. We need to talk about you and how you feel.'

She didn't say anything, or look at him, or acknowledge what he'd said, but went upstairs to run a bath. Her favourite oils fragranced the room and she relaxed, sinking into it, the steam from the hot water fogging up the mirror and shower screens. Sarah closed her eyes and tried not to think. Thinking meant she had to decide. And to decide meant acceptance. If she didn't accept what Dan had done it meant leaving everything she'd come to know and everything she'd anticipated for her future...their future. And accepting meant living forever with the knowledge that Dan had slept with Yelena and made a child while she and Dan were together. And it was this sticking in her throat like barbed wire.

She wrapped herself in a towel and went into the bedroom. Dan had made up a bed for Tobias in the dressing room, a kind of snug leading off the main bedroom, and as she peered in her heart pitched with sadness. She sat at the dressing table and ran her fingers across her cheek. The steam from the bath had melted the concealer she used to disguise her scar, and now its presence was exposed through the camouflage. No amount of concealer could hide it completely, so she wore her hair with a side parting and allowed it to cover the area of her face most affected. It didn't always work. When it was windy or she forgot and tucked her hair behind her ear, the scar could clearly be seen. She sighed and wondered if she'd ever be able to trust another plastic surgeon. The one who had assured her the scar would be virtually invisible after the operation had bodged it.

Dan's reflection faced her in the mirror as he came into the bedroom. He stood at the door and waited, looking awkward.

'About today,' he said quietly.

Her eyes found him in the mirror, watching his reflection as he tried to keep his voice emotionless, businesslike, even though it was clear to her he didn't want to talk about his family's visit which would be impossible to get through without something going wrong, even without Tobias's presence. She squeezed some moisturiser into the palm of her hand and dotted it onto her face. 'What about it?'

'There's still time to cancel. I rang them. They haven't left yet.'

Turning on the chair she gave an ironic smile. 'What, and have your mother blame me for ruining her Christmas. I don't think so.

Unless you're going to leave here, which in usual circumstances would be the right thing to do. You could stay in the company flat and have them all there.' She blended the moisturiser into her skin with her fingers, efficient, methodical, as though her feelings were made of stone. 'Good luck with that.'

'You want me to leave?' His expression drew in on itself, his face squeezed into a quizzical frown. 'It's Christmas Day. I want to be with my family. With you. And Tobias…here at the mill. If you don't want them to come I could say one of us is ill…or something.'

'No, Dan. You mean you'll say *I'm* ill. There's no way you'll let her blame you. And while we're on the subject.' Her eyes hardened. 'I know what you're doing. Don't make this my problem. This is your problem, of your making, and if you want to cancel, do it, but do it because *you* want to. I know you don't want to face them with Tobias because it means you'll have to tell them you're less than perfect. Well, it's tough, because you're not perfect, just like the rest of us. Maybe they'll realise you're human after all. And while we're on the subject, this is all about you. You tell them…tell them how, when and why. I knew nothing of any of this until a few hours ago so please don't expect me to make a comment on what should or shouldn't happen. Right now I'm busy working out how I'll get through today, so discussing anything about our future is off the menu unless it's a decision for you to give me some space. I'm struggling to get my head around it, so please, don't push it.'

'It's a huge tree, Dan. Did you really need one quite so big? Whose idea was it?'

Dan's mother, Coral stood in the hall, one hand on her hip, her lip curled in disdain as she surveyed the huge sparkling Christmas tree. Sarah stood by the kitchen door on the periphery of the group. Coral always had a sharp remark ready to deliver like the stab of a knife and Sarah dreaded being in her company.

Dan stood by the front door, his arms full of coats. 'We both fell in love with it, Mum, and it looks great in here doesn't it?'

Coral sighed. 'I guess so, although I don't know why you had to move so far from London. It's so cold…and barren.' She glanced at Sarah when she said it, and Sarah knew she was having a pop at her because they hadn't started a family. You've got a shock coming to you, Sarah thought. There's no way you can blame me. If I wasn't the person I am I'd relish your discomfort, but there's someone here far more important than you. Sarah glanced at the floor not wanting to make eye contact.

'Has everyone got a drink?' asked Dan, holding up a bottle of champagne.

'Uncle Dan, we haven't,' said Matthew, Dan's eldest nephew.

Dan looked at Melody, his sister. 'Hey, Mel, get the boy a drink, will you?'

Melody, who was Coral in training, her long white-blonde hair volumised with myriad extensions looked pointedly at Sarah, but Sarah stood her ground. 'Oh, for goodness sake,' she said, slamming her champagne flute down on the hall table. 'Why do men always assume it's the woman who has to do all the fetching and carrying? What about James? I suppose he's not capable.'

When everyone had a drink in their hands Dan toasted the new house. He glanced at Sarah as she sipped her champagne. His eyes were troubled, and he tried to smile at her, but it got lost as Coral led the stampede past him into the living room to get the best seats. Sarah went into the kitchen under the pretext of checking the turkey. This was the moment. They had a couple of hours before lunch, enough time for the shock to sink in and for Coral to get what she thought of the situation off her chest.

Dan followed Sarah into the kitchen, his fingers absent-mindedly rubbing the slender stem of his glass. 'I think we should bring Tobias down now. He's been on his own long enough.'

'Far too long, Dan. How's he going to cope with all this? They're not the quietest people in the world. You know there might be tears. Recriminations. Are you ready for it?'

'I've got to be, haven't I?'

She shrugged. 'I'll get him.'

As she turned to leave he put his hand on her arm. 'Sarah,' he whispered. 'I want to make this right with you, but I can't do it while they're here. The timing couldn't be much worse, could it?' He looked into her eyes. 'Please help me, Sarah.' She raised her chin and stared at him for a moment, saying nothing, then went upstairs to get Tobias. He was sitting on the floor with the present Sarah had given him without Dan knowing, unable to comprehend why he shouldn't have something to open on Christmas morning like every other child. Dan had been so caught up with worrying about what his family would say about Tobias he hadn't even noticed it had disappeared from under the tree.

'Hi, Tobias.' He glanced up at her, his eyes holding hers with a steady gaze. 'Daddy wants you to come downstairs now. You can bring your new car. Do you like it?' He made the sign for yes. 'You've got other presents downstairs…and there are some people who want to meet you. They're Daddy's family and he's going to introduce you to them. I don't want you to be frightened because they're very nice.' He looked away. 'Come on. Let's get this over with,' she whispered, and held out her hand to him. He got up and stuck the car under his arm, holding his other hand out to Sarah, but suddenly remembered his elephant and ran back into the room, scooping it off the floor and hugging it to him. He suddenly stood motionless, as if he was held in the room by an invisible cord.

'Boy. Boy to come.'

Sarah shook her head, frowning. 'Tobias, who do you mean? Can you tell me?' He stared at her, then began to giggle, throwing his head back and laughing, then hopped from one foot to the other, pointing behind her. She turned, thinking perhaps Dan was being jokey to amuse Tobias, but the galleried landing was empty. 'What are you doing? What are laughing at?'

'Boy…silly.' Tobias was grinning from ear to ear, and was the happiest Sarah had seen him look since he'd arrived at the mill.'

'Is he your friend?' she asked him, thinking the other boy was someone he'd made up because he was lonely. She knew children did it all the time.

40

He nodded, still grinning. 'Other boy. Tobias friend.'

When they went into the living room, Dan reached for Tobias's hand but he didn't move. 'Come on, mate.' Dan's faint voice gave away his apprehension. 'I want you to meet everyone.' Sarah watched as Dan encouraged Tobias into the room which suddenly went quiet. Coral looked up, her mouth set into a straight line. One by one each pair of eyes turned towards Dan and Tobias. 'Who's this?' Coral said, frowning. She peered behind Dan to Sarah. 'Is he something to do with you?'

Sarah shook her head. 'No, and I think this is a moment for the family. I'll check on lunch.'

She went into the kitchen glad to be away from them, but as Dan began speaking her curiosity got the better of her and she returned to stand by the staircase, listening as Dan began to explain, starting with a breath she heard wobble in his chest. 'This is Tobias. He's my son.' Sarah's throat went dry as she waited for the fallout. The room was a hushed vacuum as though everyone had been petrified in a moment devoid of the impetus to move forward.

Melody spoke, breaking the spell. 'How can he be your son?' she said, a frown in her voice. 'You don't have a son.'

'Well, yes, I do, Melody. And here he is.'

'You didn't tell us you and Sarah had a kid. Why wouldn't you tell us? We're family.'

'He's not Sarah's,' said Dan. 'He's mine...and someone else's.'

Coral looked down at her glass, her chin jutting out in anger. She threw a look across to her husband who shrugged, looking like a rabbit in the headlights of her laser gaze. Sarah drew in a silent breath as she waited for Coral to ramp up her tirade.

'So, you had a child, and you didn't think to tell me, your own mother.'

'I didn't tell anyone. Sarah didn't know until the day before yesterday.'

Coral's eyes narrowed. 'And what's she making of this? I'd have thought you and she would have had your own kids by now. I'll be in a bloody old people's home by the time you two get going.'

'Mum, this is nothing to do with Sarah. The reason we don't have kids is because when we got together we agreed not to have a family. It was our choice, and nothing to do with anyone else. But...I made a silly mistake and some not altogether clever decisions.'

Coral smirked. 'Tobias? What kind of name is that?'

'It's a Russian name,' said Dan. 'His mother's Russian.'

Melody released a patronising laugh. 'Fuck me,' she said. 'You been doing your bit for world peace, Dan?' She waited for everyone to laugh but no one did, and she flounced out of her chair to refill her glass. 'Well, Mum. Looks like you've got yet another grandson.'

'Yes, I suppose I'll get used to it.' Her eyes went to Dan and Tobias again. 'I'm not very happy, Dan. You should have told me. Out of everyone you should have told your mother, but you've told me now and to be honest I'm glad you've fathered a child. I'd hoped you would even if it's not been the most conventional way of starting a family. Everyone needs a family. Even you.' She thrust her arm towards Tobias. 'Come here.' Tobias didn't move and Coral looked annoyed. 'Come on,' she said, her face pulled into an expression of annoyance. 'What's the matter with you? I'm your grandmother, probably the only one you've got.' She stared at Dan. 'What's the matter with him?'

'He has autism.' Sarah's eyes widened, surprised he'd found the courage to tell his family about Tobias's challenges. Perhaps now he was willing to confront the truth and do something about it.

'Autism? How can he have autism? Where did he get it from? You don't have it.'

Dan sat in the chair opposite Coral and pulled Tobias onto his lap. 'We don't know why he has it.'

Coral was exasperated. 'Oh, great. So, what does it mean? Is he…what, slow, disabled, what? And what about his real mum? Isn't she doing anything about it?' Sarah felt a flame of heat in her stomach. It slowly rose into her chest and flowed like an electric current into her throat, the burning acidic sensation threatening to suffocate her. It was intense anger at this stupid, difficult woman, and more than anything she wanted to slap her. 'What's to be done about it?'

'Nothing, Mum. Nothing can be done.'

'Can't he have treatment? It's not like you can't afford it. This place must have cost a fortune.' She paused and lowered her voice. 'I suppose *she* doesn't want to spend the money on him.'

'We haven't had time to discuss it and I don't think you should be saying those things in front of him. He's not deaf. He can hear what you're saying.'

Coral sniffed. 'That's as maybe.' She turned her attentions to her husband. 'Lewis. You agree with me, don't you? The boy should have treatment to sort out his problems.' Lewis shrugged and took a long swig from his brandy glass.

'I've just told you, Mum. Nothing can be done, but I will do everything I can to help him, hopefully with Sarah's help.'

Sarah heard Coral laugh. 'I think you're living in cloud-cuckoo land. Why should she lift a finger to help you? The boy's not hers.' Coral glared at Lewis. 'I wouldn't.'

After lunch they went into the sitting room for coffee. The boys were running around the house causing mayhem, and Sarah's nerves were on edge. As she stacked the dishwasher she heard Dan come into the kitchen.

'When are they going?' she whispered. 'I don't think I can stand much more of it.'

'It's Christmas Day, Sarah. They're my family. Cut them some slack.'

'I know they're your family, Dan, it's just a shame they don't know how to behave.' He rolled his eyes and went into the dining room to clear some of the used crockery. A scream from upstairs startled him and he ran back into the hall. 'What the hell...?'

Sarah was already there, looking up the stairs to the landing. 'Is everything alright?' she called. 'What is it? What's happened?'

Melody and James' youngest son, Leo came down the stairs holding his arm. 'That boy hit me,' he said.

'What boy?' Dan asked him.

'The new boy. The one with the funny name.'

Dan's eyes went to Sarah's. 'Tobias?'

'Yeah, him. He hit me. Really hard.'

'No, he wouldn't hit you.'

'He did, Uncle Dan. He hit me with Matthew's lightsabre. I hate him. He's a horrible boy. He should go back to his own house. We were here first.'

Melody stood by the door, drink in hand, her eyes misty with alcohol. 'What's up, baby,' she said to Leo, stroking his face. 'Have you hurt your arm?'

'Mum, the new boy hit me. Tobias. He hit me with Matthew's lightsabre and he's really hurt my arm. I think it's broken and it's all his fault.'

Melody frowned at Dan. 'Where is he? Where's Tobias? He needs to be told he can't get away with hitting people when he wants to.'

'Hang on a minute, Melody. Let's get the story straight before everyone starts throwing accusations around.'

'What's to get straight? He hit my son and it's unacceptable. We're guests here and I don't expect my child to be bullied, or for you to ignore it just because he's yours, or because you say he's got issues. He should know how to behave in company.' Her eyes drifted back to Leo. 'Leo, where's the boy? Where's Tobias?'

'He's up there,' he said, pointing upstairs with his apparently broken arm.

'Well, tell him to come down. I want a word with him.' She swayed and grabbed hold of the doorframe.

Coral appeared in the hall and Sarah inhaled. Here come the fireworks.

'What's going on out here?'

Melody assumed a pained expression. 'Dan's boy, that Tobias. He hit Leo with Matthew's lightsabre.'

Coral looked at Dan and Sarah, her lips twitching, ready for a fight. 'So get him down here and tell him it's not nice to hit people. He needs to be punished.'

'I'll deal with it,' said Dan, who grabbed hold of the wooden finial, hopped past Leo and ran up the stairs. Leo followed, clearly hoping to witness Tobias being reprimanded.

Sarah went back into the kitchen wishing they would go. Her thoughts went to Tobias. She was sure he wouldn't hit anyone. He was too gentle, too timid, surely, to do something like that. And if he did hit Leo it was probably in self-defence. She smiled to herself. Leo and Matthew needed taking down a peg. She just hadn't imagined it would be Tobias who would do it.

She glanced at the clock. It was just past four and she wondered if Dan's family expected to be fed again before they went home, praying they wouldn't. Surely no one would want to eat again after the huge lunch they'd served. There was a movement at the door. Coral was leaning against the doorframe, glass in hand.

'So, what are you making of all this, Sarah. It must have been quite a shock to find out Dan had a child.'

Keep it light, Sarah advised herself as she looked across to Coral. 'Yeah, it was, but it is what it is. It's a shame Yelena's so difficult.'

Coral frowned. 'Yelena? The boy's mother, I take it.' Sarah nodded. 'You've met her?'

'She turned up here and literally dumped the poor kid on the doorstep. She phoned Dan and said she was going home to Russia for a while. Why she didn't take Tobias with her is anyone's guess. Any mother would have. But not Yelena it would seem.'

'And where do you stand on this?'

Sarah's eyes widened. 'What do you mean?'

Coral stepped further into the kitchen and Sarah pictured a cold-eyed rattlesnake preparing to strike. 'He cheated on you, didn't he? Dan said the boy is five. If he's five he slept with his mother when you two were together. You've been with him, what, six and a half years?' Sarah nodded again. 'Are you going to stay with my son?'

'Dan and I haven't had a chance to talk about it, Coral, but as soon as a decision is made about the state of our relationship and what will happen to Tobias, Dan will tell you I expect.'

Coral took a swig of her drink. 'I should hope so. I'm Dan's mother and we're his family. And while we're on the subject, no chance of your family joining us today I suppose?'

Sarah's breath caught up in her throat. 'I don't think so.'

'Mm.' Coral turned away, a triumphant smirk across her face. 'Well, don't forget. I have a right to know what's going on in my son's life.'

'That may be the case, Coral, if it's what Dan really wants, but you don't have a right to know what's going on in mine.' Coral paused for a moment and Sarah saw her stiffen and inhale. As she went into the hall, Sarah heard a gleeful laugh behind her. She turned, frowning, then shook her head. Her stomach rolled and she felt herself go hot as she closed her eyes and rested her chin on her chest. 'What the hell's happening?' she said under her breath.

Coral turned at the doorway. 'What did you say?'

Sarah lifted her chin and shook her head. 'Nothing, Coral. Nothing.'

She watched as Melody and Coral whispered to each other, and Sarah was in no doubt she was the subject of their spite. Then she heard Dan's voice. He was in the hall with Tobias by his side.

'I've asked Tobias about hitting Leo but I'm not getting anything from him.'

Melody sneered. 'Course you're not. He's hardly going to admit it is he, but he's as guilty as hell.'

'Give it a rest, Melody. He's only a child. You're not helping matters.' He got down on his haunches in front of Tobias. 'You didn't hit him, did you mate?' Tobias glanced into the kitchen at Sarah who appeared at the door. He looked back at Dan and shook his head.

'There. What did I tell you? He didn't hit Leo.'

'The other boy,' Tobias said in a small voice.

'What?' Dan gently held Tobias's arms and pulled him closer. 'What did you say, mate?'

'The other boy. The other boy, up there,' he whispered. He pointed at Leo. 'That boy, he…,' and put his hands round his own throat and squeezed. 'The other boy say, no. He say, no, no, no. Leave Tobias. Leave Tobias alone. *He* hit with the stick. Not Tobias. Other boy made him…not to do this,' he said, animated now, his hands still around his own throat.

Sarah listened quietly, tears threatening to flood down her cheeks. That voice, pleading to be believed, and Dan's family so determined not to listen. Melody stormed out of the hall into the sitting room.

'He's lying. What a liar. My Leo would never do anything like that. Of course he hit my son. Well done, Dan. S'pose he gets it from his "Russian" mother. James, James, shift yourself, we're going.'

James woke with a start. He'd been snoozing since lunch and the contents of his wine glass balanced on his not inconsiderable stomach had spilled down the front of his shirt as he dozed. 'Wha...what? What's up, Melody? I thought you were going to ask Dan if we could stay the night.'

'I've changed my mind. If we leave now we'll get back before Doctor Who starts. The boys want to see it...even if it is a woman.' She tutted. 'Bloody ridiculous if you ask me. Doctor Who's always been a man.'

'But I've been drinking. I've had...a lot.'

'So get some coffee and sober up,' she shouted. 'Come on, James, move it. Why does it always take you so long to cotton on to anything? Honestly!' She threw him an acerbic look and began to stuff their things into a bag.

'Are you leaving so soon?' Sarah asked Melody as she joined everyone in the living room. She said a silent prayer and almost crossed her fingers.

'What does it look like?' Melody replied, rudely. 'I won't have my son being bullied by Dan's brat. I don't care what the hell's wrong with him, he's got enough about him to say it was someone else who hit my Leo. It was obviously him. We don't even know him.'

'Would it have made a difference if you had?' asked Sarah, her expression unreadable.

Melody slowly raised her head, narrowed her eyes and stared at her with daggers. 'What I meant was, I don't...like...bullies.'

Sarah left Melody to it, went into the dining room and stood by the window. The scene outside was enchanting; snow lay beautifully unblemished on the lawn, undulating in waves like the Italian meringue cookies from Zanzibar's Patisserie she and Eve, her work colleague treated themselves to every Friday, and the trees shimmered like a fantasy in the increasing twilight. She thought about her parents and how much she would have loved them to see her new home. Coral had known exactly how to hit below the belt; the barbed comment about her family had stung her and her eyes suddenly filled with tears again, unbidden and unwanted. She closed her eyes and went into herself.

A soft hand stroked her face lightly and she forgot herself and leant into it, thinking it was Dan. She came to and flinched, expecting to see him, but there was no one. She breathed in, her face a portrait of sorrow. It had felt so real, the hand that had touched her skin. She had wanted it to continue, it had brought her comfort, but she thought she must have imagined it.

The sky was clearer now, and stars twinkled in the darkness turning the garden into a fantasyland. Her spirits brightened and she brushed the tears away. The weather had improved—the snowfall had stopped, and the blanket around the mill had begun to soften—and she thanked everything that was Holy for the rise in temperature. She heard the voice of the weatherman from the television in the other room say the snow on the roads was thawing and the motorways were almost clear. It meant there was really no need for anyone to stay over, and she was glad of it.

'Sarah, everyone's going now,' Dan called. Fixing a rictus smile on her face Sarah went into the hall where he stood with Tobias, and watched Dan's family as they shrugged on their coats. James was still complaining he'd had too much to drink to drive home. Coral told him to stop moaning and just to be careful and not fall asleep at the wheel. Melody was still sulking because of Leo. Lewis was silent as usual and the boys were fighting. It was pretty much the same as when they'd arrived, except in reverse. Sarah was glad it was in reverse.

Later, when everyone had gone Sarah went into the living room and settled back against the sofa. She felt Dan's hand slip into hers and opened her eyes to see a box lying in her lap, beautifully wrapped in luxury tissue and tied with a silver bow. She stared at it for a moment until her gaze slid over to Dan.

'I thought we weren't doing presents this year.'

He shrugged. 'I couldn't resist it.' She continued to stare at him. 'It's not a bribe, Sarah. I bought it weeks ago.'

She unwrapped the present. It was a diamond tennis bracelet, something she'd always wanted. As she held it up in front of her it sparkled in the candlelight. 'It's…beautiful. Thank you.'

'I've emailed Jed and told him I'm taking some time off,' he said. 'I need to sort things out and get to know Tobias.'

'Right. And what about afterwards?'

'How d'you mean, afterwards?'

'Well, you'll have to go back to work at some point. What will happen to Tobias?'

'I'm not sure yet. Maybe a nursery, or preschool. He's bit old for a nursery, isn't he?'

'He's five. He should go to school. A proper school.'

'Will they take him? He doesn't speak.'

'He does. He spoke earlier. You heard him.'

'A few words. Is it enough for a mainstream school to take him?'

'I'm not sure. It depends on the school. I looked it up. It seems most schools have a unit for children who are on the autistic spectrum. Or he could go to a special school. I think it hangs on whether he can get a statement, depending on what his needs are.'

'A statement?'

'An educational statement.'

'You've been busy.' She shrugged and looked down to her lap where the bracelet sparkled alluringly, pulling her into Dan's plans, obfuscating reality with its sensuality, like a siren calling to her. 'And how do I get one of those?'

'GP first, I think.'

'Okay,' he said. 'I'll take him in the new year.'

'He doesn't like the washing machine for some reason. He says it hurts.'

Dan looked dumbfounded. 'He actually said that to you.'

'Yep.'

'What does he mean, it hurts.'

'I've no idea. Perhaps you should ask him. Yelena left the hold all here, y'know the one I put out in the garden by the bins. It had clothes in it for Tobias, and they absolutely stank, so I opened the washing machine door to put them in and he had a kind of meltdown. He was very scared, so I'm guessing there's a reason for it.'

'Oh, my God.' Dan ran his hand across the stubble on his chin. Sarah loved this unconscious action and her heartbeat quickened. She looked away, wishing she could turn the clock back to when they first saw the mill. It was such an amazing day and she couldn't have loved Dan any more if she'd tried. As if reading her mind, he asked her, 'Can you forgive me, Sarah?' She scrunched up her face then stared at the ceiling and he chuckled. 'I'm not sure if your face is telling me you will, or whether you'd rather I didn't ask you.'

'I haven't had time to really look at how I feel,' she said.

'You don't suddenly stop loving someone. It's not something you can switch on or off.' She glanced away. 'I'm not sure how much I like you though. And also because there's a child involved. And he's here, with us. His perspective of the world at the moment is our responsibility, something I'm aware of even though he's not my son.

I'm guessing he may have already seen some violence, verbal, maybe even physical. I can't do it to him. I think he's been through enough.'

'I thought I'd take him out tomorrow and buy him some new stuff.' He reached across the divide between them and slipped his fingers around her hand. 'Would you like to come with us? We could have some lunch somewhere. A Boxing Day treat to make up for today. It might be nice.'

The warmth of his hand comforted her and she wanted to forget the revulsion she'd felt for him yesterday, but it was impossible. She pulled her hand away and pushed the bracelet back into its velvet box, the tissue now torn and crumpled. 'Like happy families?'

'Not if it's not what you want, but your help would be appreciated.' He slowly pulled his hand away from her, looking uncomfortable. 'I'm new to all this.'

'Please don't look for sympathy, Dan. I'm afraid I'm all out.'

He sighed and rubbed his chin. 'Mum said you told her she has no right to know about your life.'

'That's right.'

'I guess it includes talking about your family.'

'Oh here we go.' She looked hard at him. 'Why are you bringing it up now?'

'I'm your partner and I don't know anything about them.'

'You're my partner when it suits you, and...there's nothing to know. Were you thinking about that when you were shagging her?'

'Come on, Sarah.'

'How can I tell *you* about them when *I* don't know about them.'

'What d'you mean?'

'I don't know them. I haven't seen them since I was...what, about ten.'

'Why?'

'You'll need to ask them. They dumped me in a children's home and I never saw them again.'

He tried to hold her hand again and again she pulled away. 'Don't.'

'I'm so sorry, Sarah.'

'Well, don't be. You don't miss what you haven't had.'

She was scared. The darkness made her feel vulnerable because only grownups went out in the dark and it was the latest she had ever been out on her own. The drawn curtains in the other houses meant the kids who lived in the street were already in bed. It's where she and Aaron would have been if he hadn't left the house. She'd planned to make hot chocolate on the stove for them and see them both to bed early so her parents would think she was sensible and that they could rely on her. The thought of their anger made her shiver again, not with cold but with a surge of anxiety stroking her neck and cheeks, knowing the rage her father would fly into, fuelled by beer, would be taken out on her.

She wondered if Aaron might have been sitting cross-legged by the school railings. He was often to be found up there, playing with his favourite Lego figure, hoping someone walking by would slip him a pound so he could go across to the shop on the crossroads and buy sweets. Their parents didn't discourage him from behaviour most adults would think was unsafe, in fact the opposite. Their dad said he was a chip off the old block, and one day he'd be a millionaire and he'd better not forget his old dad, as he ruffled Aaron's hair and pretend-punched him in the stomach. Aaron basked in this rare show of approval while Lacey stood and watched, wondering what it was she had to do to get the same kind of attention.

Peering down the street towards Slaughter's Wood bordering the lower half of the estate, her throat went dry. She called him once more, praying he'd appear out of the darkness, his hands in his pockets, his nose running with snot. There was no sign of him. She began to walk, slowly, looking around her as she went in case Aaron crept up on her and jumped her. As she got to the end of the row of houses, she noticed the front door of Aaron's friend's house was slightly open. She ran up the steps holding onto the rusty handrail, wincing at the coldness of the metal. Someone was in the hall, hanging a coat on a peg.

'Mr. Duffield?' He turned and walked towards the door. He was out of breath, his nose nipped red with cold which he wiped with an upwards sweep of the back of his hand.

'Lacey? What are you doing out this time of night?'

Her eyes widened. 'What time of night?'

Ray Duffield glanced at a clock on the wall. 'It's quarter to nine.'

Lacey shuddered. 'Have you seen Aaron? He's gone walkabout again.'

'No, love.' He shook his head. 'My two are in bed. Been there ages.' He frowned 'Do your mum and dad know he's out?'

'They've gone for a drink at the Grapevine. I'm meant to be looking after Aaron. He unlocked the front door and left the house without telling me. He's not supposed to go out but he never listens. I'll be in trouble now and it'll be all his fault.'

'I doubt he got far, Lacey. Have a look down the street but don't go into the woods. It's no place for kids at this time of night. Poachers, see. And they've got guns.'

Staring up at him with wide eyes her heart began to beat faster. 'Guns?' she echoed in a whisper.

The steps outside the Duffield house were already glassy with frost, so she took each one with care, her bottom lip under her teeth. As her foot reached the pavement she paused, her eyes squinting into the darkness and her fear went up a gear. There was no choice but to search the woods for Aaron. It was the last place for her to look.

At the end of the street the grassy bank sloped down to the river. It was dank and smelt cloyingly of mildew and Lacey wanted to be anywhere but there.

'Aaron,' she shouted. 'Aaron, if you're in there you need to come out now. Mum and Dad will be home soon. You'll be in big trouble if you don't come home.' Her voice wobbled with panic. 'And so will I,' she mumbled.

It was always like this with Aaron. Never an easy moment. Her frustration with her brother got the better of her. 'Aaron, for fuck sake, come out now, you little git,' she screamed. Her fists squeezed into tight balls, clenched in anger, pushing the blood out of the palms of her hands. There was nothing for it but to go into the place she didn't want to go. It was either that or go home and face the music when her mum and dad found out Aaron was missing.

'I'll kill the little bastard when I get hold of him,' she said under her breath.

Lacey looked back up the street. The sleet had stopped: all that was left was a fine mist clinging to the rooftops and blurring the yellow glow from the streetlamps. She ran down the slope to the stream and picked her way across, using the stepping stones she and her friends used to get to the other side. The trees swayed in the breeze as the trunks made contact, creating a clunking sound.

She bit her lip. She'd never been in Slaughter's Wood after dark and to her it felt other-worldly. She thought of the book on her shelf in her bedroom, and the wicked queen in Snow White and the Seven Dwarfs and drew in a shaking breath.

Underneath the trees a mantle of leaves, crisp and shrivelled by cold crunched under each step until she reached the dark interior where the undergrowth was soggy with decay and smelt pungently of mildew. The freezing damp penetrated her trainers, turning her toes to what felt like tiny icicles, and further in, where the winter sun's rays weren't strong enough to infiltrate the trees' canopy, the bitter cold trailed up the sleeves of her coat, cleaving through her skinny arms and into her bones.

As her eyes got used to the gloom she recognised shapes she was familiar with; the tree where they had tied a length of blue nylon rope so they could swing backwards and forwards pretending to be monkeys, screeching, and laughing uncontrollably, brushing against the dense covering of leaves as they flew through the air, the log where they sat and put the world to rights, eating crisps and smoking the cigarettes Aaron had stolen from the newsagents, and the huge pile of leaves they'd made together only that afternoon. Her breathing slowed and she realised she was in the place where they always played. It's just the dark, she reassured herself. It's the same place, it just looks different.

Lacey called her brother again, praying he would answer this time.

'Aaron. Aaron, stop playing around. We need to get home. Please, Aaron. Let's go home. It's so cold.' The bitter odour of wet earth filled her nostrils and she could hear something rustling the leaves as it moved around the undergrowth, a bird or a squirrel. There was no other sound apart from the wind and the trees. She tried again. 'You'll be in so much trouble when Mum and Dad get home,' she cried. 'It won't just be me who gets the strap. You will too.' Nothing. 'Aaron!' she yelled.

She'd expected him to jump out on her, frightening her half to death like he often did. He always thought it was hilarious and would run around her, fist-pumping and saying, 'Yeah, yeah, I got you good that time.' At that moment, as alone and scared as she was, Aaron's crazy behaviour would have been welcome.

Newton's Mill
New Year 2019
8

'What's happening?'

'I've got to go in.'

She shook her head with frustration. 'You said you wanted to do the best for Tobias and you would put him first. If you want this to be sorted, we need...' She bit her lip. 'We need to talk properly, without recriminations. I'll do my best not to get angry. I can continue being mad at you and feeling bitter, but it won't change anything and it's making me feel lousy. We've been dancing around it for days. Phone Jed. Let's sort this out.'

Dan scratched his head. 'Okay. Okay, I'll phone him.'

'I'll go and see if Tobias is awake. Perhaps we could try and get him to say something.'

Sarah made Tobias breakfast and they let him play with his toys for a while, aware they would have to tread carefully with him. The meltdowns he'd had over the past few days had been horrendous and she wanted to try and avoid it at all costs. She and Dan had hardly spoken and she wondered if he'd picked up the atmosphere between them, but apart from the volcanic meltdowns he had seemed strangely content. He seemed relaxed with his own company, almost self-contained.

They made him comfortable in the sitting room and switched on the TV.

'He likes Mr. Tumble,' she said. 'I'm pretty sure he learns some of his signing from there.'

Dan smiled warmly at her. 'He has an imaginary friend too. It's funny really. I can remember doing something like that when I was a kid. Melody was such a pain I invented my own playmate just to get away from her.'

'What makes you think he has an imaginary friend?'

'He was kind of murmuring sounds under his breath when I was watching him yesterday, like he was communicating with his mate, looking up and smiling. Nice really. My friend was real to me. I guess his is real to him.'

'He's different to you though, right?'

'Well, course he is. But, he's still a kid. Didn't you have an imaginary friend? I thought everyone did.'

She stared at her hands, not wanting her eyes to betray her. She missed Dan, needed him, wanted to be close again but not quite able to bridge the yawning chasm dividing them. Forgiveness was all very well but the thought of his betrayal kept opening its jaws and biting her. 'I don't remember it to be honest. It's nice you understand him, but...he won't be the same as you were. You'll have to accept Tobias's life will be different from the one you had when you were a boy. He has...different challenges, different needs for which solutions need to be found.'

Dan puffed out a breath, then nodded. 'I know.'

They sat on the sofa in the living room, a picture of family togetherness. Tobias was sitting on the footstool in front of them, his attention fully on Mr. Tumble.

'Tobias?' Sarah said his name softly. He didn't respond. 'Tobias?' He turned and stared at them. 'Do you remember Leo?' Tobias got off the footstool and found the tattered elephant laying by the television, holding it close to his chest. 'Do you remember the boy who was here the other day? Leo? You were playing with him and Matthew upstairs. Do you remember him?' Tobias held the elephant in front of his face, staring intently into its button eyes, doing his best to ignore Sarah. 'Tobias?' His gaze went to them again. He nodded.

Sarah glanced at Dan then back at Tobias. 'You remember him?' He nodded again. 'So...do you remember when Leo said you hit him?' Tobias made the Makaton sign for yes. 'You said you didn't hit him. Was that the truth? You're not in any trouble. Daddy and I just need to know. Did you hit him?' He held his right hand in front of him and swept it the right.

'I think he means no,' said Dan. 'Do you know who did, mate?'

He averted his eyes to the side. 'Other boy,' he whispered.

'The other boy? Do you mean Matthew? Is Matthew the other boy? Did Matthew hit him with his lightsabre?' Sarah asked him. Tobias shook his head and Sarah's stomach tightened. 'Who was it, sweetheart?'

He opened his mouth and began to scream, walking backwards, away from them, holding the elephant by the trunk and flinging it around in the air, striking it against the footstool and the television, shrieking as though he was scared to death. 'Other boy! Other boy! Other boy!' He threw himself on the floor and began kicking out. 'Boy! Boy! Boy!' Sarah slid off the sofa and tried to catch his flailing arms and legs. She managed to catch an arm, but one of Tobias's feet caught her in the chest, winding her, and she doubled up. Dan grabbed him and pinned his legs down as Sarah held his arms to his side.

'It's okay, Tobes,' said Dan. 'It's okay. Calm down, Tobias. It's over.' Tobias wriggled away from them and ran out the room. They heard his footsteps as he clattered up the stairs, his breath coming in short gasps as though he was being pursued. Dan put his head in his hands. 'Oh, God.'

'That went well,' breathed Sarah.

'What does he mean, other boy?'

She shook her head. 'I've no idea. I don't think an imaginary friend can hit anyone with a lightsabre. Maybe he's saying it because he doesn't want to get into trouble. I just can't imagine him hitting anyone though. He's too...gentle, too contented. The meltdowns only happen when he's being cornered. I can't imagine how he feels.'

'I'm so sorry, Sarah.'

She turned away from him, wishing he'd stop saying sorry. 'You said, and it's not helping.'

'I know. I know I've said it before, and it sounds hollow even to me, but I don't know how to put it right.'

She walked to the window, pressing her fingertips against the cold glass, staring out onto the thawing snow, wishing the problem could be dissolved as easily. 'It's not something you can put right, is it?' She turned to face him. 'You can't mend this or stitch up the rip in our relationship and make it new again. Our lives have changed. The life we thought we were going to have...well, it isn't possible. Everything has altered. Everything is different. And the reminder of what happened between you and Yelena is upstairs.

'It's not his fault,' she whispered. 'And as much as I thought I would never have what it takes to get close to a child...I feel for him, because I know he's confused. He doesn't know us, and yet we're talking to him as if we should be important to him. Why should he think we're important, Dan? Why should he think you're important?'

'I know.'

'And when Yelena told me what had happened and pushed Tobias towards me telling me he was your son, you became a stranger to me too. It was like everything I thought I knew about you was wrong. You became a different person, one I couldn't trust. Do you understand?'

As he nodded his lip trembled and tears ran down his cheeks. 'You're describing someone I wouldn't like,' he whispered. 'Someone I'd avoid.' He looked up at her, his eyes glassy with tears. 'And I don't know what to do about it because if you leave me,

Sarah I'll have lost everything. I love you, and this,' he glanced away, 'secret, I've been carrying around with me...to be honest, I'm relieved it's out. I used to lay awake at night wondering what you would do, if, when, you found out about Yelena and Tobias. It would make me sick to my stomach going over and over it, wondering if I should just tell you. I've made a terrible mistake and I feel like the biggest shit ever to walk the earth.'

'You should have told me, Dan. Hearing it from her made it so much worse.'

Quiet contemplation descended over them. Neither knew what to say to the other. Sarah wiped her face on her sleeve and Dan noticed how pale she was. A crash from above their heads startled them, and they ran out of the living room and up the stairs, Dan two at a time. A photo of Sarah and Dan holding glasses of champagne at a wedding had fallen off their bedroom wall, the glass broken into three pieces, the silver frame buckled.

'I couldn't have fixed it up properly,' said Dan, looking at the now irredeemable frame in his hands. 'Shame. Mum and Dad bought this frame for us when we moved into the flat.' He carefully pulled the photograph out of the frame. The image was intact apart from a deep slash across his face. 'The photo's had it too. I wonder how it fell off the wall.' He pulled at the nail. 'Nail's still intact.' He shrugged. 'Oh, well, we've got others.' He looked up at Sarah but she wasn't listening, she was staring at the mirror on the dressing table. 'Sarah?'

'What's that?' She was pointing to the mirror, now scrawled on with her red lipstick, the scattered remains like discarded breadcrumbs on the dressing table top. 'Someone's written on my mirror.'

Dan's mouth settled into a straight line and his jaw hardened. 'Boy. It says, boy.'

'Jesus, Dan. What the hell's going on? There's something not right here.'

Dan shook his head. 'I'll go and ask him, little sod.'

Her eyes widened. 'I don't mean that, and ask him what?'

'Well,' he puffed out a breath. 'Ask him why he's written all over your mirror. He needs to find other ways to get his point across.'

'Are you kidding me? When did he learn to write, Dan? He can barely string a sentence together. Did you teach him?'

'You know I didn't.'

'So, you think his mother showed him how to write, someone who can't even be bothered to clothe him properly.'

Dan rubbed his chin and gave a derisory laugh. 'Well, he knows how to write one word, doesn't he?'

'Does he?' Sarah crossed her arms in front of her. 'And why would he know that word rather than any other?'

Dan lost his patience and raised his voice. 'I don't know, Sarah, but I'll find out. Go downstairs and I'll deal with it. Looks like it was Tobias who hit Leo, doesn't it? He lied, didn't he? How fucking embarrassing. And now he's trying to blame some imaginary boy he's invented. I'm not having it. I'll get the truth out of him, and then we can forget all this "boy" crap.'

She watched him as he left the bedroom, then sat on the end of the bed. She couldn't accept that Tobias would hit another child. They'd been in each other's company only a few days, but Tobias hadn't shown any viciousness towards anything, and certainly not towards her or Dan, at least not intentionally. He was a sweet boy. She'd worked out his meltdowns were more in frustration with himself, and when he kicked out he wasn't aiming it at anyone, he was just frightened.

Later, when Sarah was cuddled up with a throw on the sofa, Dan came into the living room. He looked tired, his eyes ringed with dark smudges.

'Well?' she asked softly. 'What did he say?'

'Not much he could say. How could he deny it? He's the only other person here, and while we're on the subject, he's the only one who keeps talking about this boy he's fabricated.' He sat on the sofa, his elbows resting on his knees. 'Let's get one thing straight, if he does something he shouldn't he gets punished, just like any other kid. And what he did was wrong. He can't go around drawing on mirrors with your lipsticks to get his own back. It's not on.'

'No, I know...but.'

'What? You think because he's on the spectrum he shouldn't be punished when he does something wrong?'

'I wasn't saying that. You're assuming he did it, and, honestly, Dan, I don't know how he did. He doesn't have that skill does he?'

'For fucks sake, what are you saying? If he didn't do it, who did? Come on, Sarah, get real. We don't know what he can do, not yet anyway. Of course he did it, unless you think there is another boy here doing all this stuff.' He pulled a face. 'I mean, whoo hoo hoo,' he said, patronisingly waggling his hands by the side of his head. 'Have we got a poltergeist?' He blew out a breath of derision and shook his head. 'I'm getting a beer.'

She watched him walk away, disappointment tightening her chest. You're not the same, she thought. She stared into the space he'd left as he'd gone into the kitchen. You're not the same.

He stroked her hair as they lay beside one another. She closed her eyes, ready for sleep, exhausted by everything, wanting the comfort blanket of the night when nothing could be done about anything, when the world around them closed down, and just for a few hours she could forget.

'Do you love me, Sarah?' he whispered. 'Enough to forgive me?'

Her eyes flicked open and she gazed at him, then lowered her lashes, the intensity of his scrutiny too much for her. She turned onto her back and closed her eyes again. 'I wish I knew.'

New Year 2019
9

There was hardly any light, just pinpoints of slim rays illuminating the wet pavement in the velvety darkness. The chilling air seeped underneath her scarf, moistening her skin like clammy fingers stroking her neck. She raised her shoulder to her cheek, shrinking away from someone or something examining her without her permission, turning the roots of her hair into a tingling mass. Trickles of perspiration rolled down her back. She swallowed, bending her body slightly as she peered into the darkness. At the top of the hill was a dark distorted blotch of a building where chimney stacks imposed heavy black shapes onto the distant skyline. An iron gate opened and shut again as the wind blew against it, the constant clanging ringing in her ears like a funeral bell. Shaking her head with frustration she exhaled through pursed lips, compelled to move away from where she stood and follow the path down the hill. Behind her the pavement stretched down towards a cavern of darkness where no light revealed its ending. Her instinct told her she must go there, but the fear she felt was overwhelming.

A dark figure outlined by one of the yellow rays from the street lamps walked up the hill towards her. Narrowing her eyes she struggled to focus. He was unrecognisable, a man with skin the colour of parchment, the features smeared across his face as if they had been rubbed out with an eraser. He walked towards her, his shoulders leaning in to the increasing wind rushing towards him. She was terrified, shocked by the panic coursing through her body. Instinctively she understood this person would do her harm and she opened her mouth to scream. No sound left her. Pushing with her chest she tried with all her breath to cry out for help, but her throat closed against her voice. Her jaw relaxed allowing her lips to meet as he got closer and closer.

She turned away from him in slow motion, lifting her foot to run. I want to go home. I must get home. Her thoughts were in turmoil but her legs were like lumps of lead, heavy, impossible to lift. Her mouth opened to scream as his hand reached out to touch her….

'Sarah! Sarah, for God's sake. What is it? Jesus!' The sensation of being pulled upwards woke her. Opening her eyes she met Dan's worried stare. He searched her face, shaking his head at her. 'Sarah, you…I think you were dreaming.' He frowned at her, waiting for her to say something. 'I'll do it,' he said as she fumbled towards her nightstand for the carafe, her throat like sandpaper. 'Let me pour it for you.'

She drank deeply from the glass, panting as she wiped her mouth on the back of her hand. 'Thanks.'

'Are you okay?'

'Yeah, I'm alright,' she whispered, hoping he wouldn't ask her about the dream.

'What was it? A dream...a nightmare?' She raised her chin as he pushed her hair away from her face. 'You want to talk about it?'

'No, it was nothing.'

He raised his eyebrows. 'It didn't sound like nothing.'

She settled down against the pillows and pulled the duvet up to her chin, closing her eyes, and feeling Dan do the same she waited, trying not to breathe, and after a few minutes he was snoring lightly again. The relief allowed her to exhale, craving the time to think without being questioned about the dream even though deep down it was something she didn't want to think about. It was happening more and more, and each time was worse as its grip tightened on her. She turned gently on to her side, dreading the dawning of the following day because Dan would question her about the nightmare. She understood why. It was what she would have done, full of worry, a need to protect.

It wasn't the first time she had woken crying. Before, when they were in the apartment, he had mentioned doctors, a psychiatrist, 'It's something hidden in your mind, troubling you', he'd said. 'We need to find out what.' This was something she didn't want. It'll give it more strength, she thought, and it's the last thing I need.

She imagined herself walking away from it all, leaving Dan and Tobias, packing her bags and closing the door on the mill for the last time. A taxi would take her to the station, maybe Dave would be driving and he'd ask her if she was seeing friends, shopping perhaps, because she was going to London. It's what people always thought when someone went to London; a day of shopping, a happy day, a day of laughter and fun. She'd get on the train and maybe stay at Eve's until she could find somewhere of her own. She imagined all of this as hot tears rolled across the bridge of her nose onto her pillow, soaking the pillowcase under her cheek. She wanted to sniff but daren't in case she woke Dan again, so she got out of bed, quietly slipped on her dressing gown and crept out of the bedroom.

In the hall she paused at the bottom step and looked up to the top of the Christmas tree. They should have taken it down but neither she nor Dan had their heart in it, such a reversal of how they'd felt when it had been delivered from the nursery. In the darkness it looked drab. The branches had begun to droop and there were no lights illuminating it to make it ethereal and beautiful. The decorations seemed gaudy and cheap. If she'd had the strength she would have torn it down and thrown it into the garden, an allegory for the relationship she thought she had with Dan, but it stood erect, solidly mocking her hopes of a happy ending. The night she and Dan decorated it was such a beautiful moment, their first Christmas tree at the mill. It had meant so much to them. They'd made love that night; he had given her love and she had returned it, enjoying him, revering his body while he took her into pleasure she had only fantasised about, but the picture she had painted of them was fake, their relationship was based on deceit and she didn't know how to get past it, or whether she ever could.

Settling into one of the chairs by the fire, the fading embers flickering orange flashes of Morse code into the room, her eyelids began to droop. She was tired, exhausted by stress and the constant interruption of her sleep. She drifted, the pull of sleep encouraging her into its velvety depths until she was aware of the sensation of not being alone. Her instinct told her it was Tobias; she could feel him standing a few feet away from her, staring at her like he always did. She sighed, sleepily. 'Tobias, I'm okay. Go back to bed, little man, you'll catch cold. Do you want me to come with you?' When he didn't reply her eyes flicked open. Tobias wasn't there. She looked around the darkened room. The fire had died down leaving smouldering embers and the room in darkness. 'Tobias?' she said quietly into the blackness, sure there was someone there. 'Tobias, you can come out now. You must go back to bed or you'll be too tired for school in the morning. You can't be late on your first day.' She sat forward in the chair waiting for him to come out of the shadows.

A movement at her peripheral vision startled her and she turned towards it. As she tried to focus, a hazy shadow drifted by her, a soundless whisper touching her face like a cobweb in a light breeze or a gentle sweep of a feather. Her heart thumped like a drum in her chest as she flinched and put her hand up to brush it away. It was a reflex action, the anticipation of something or someone about to touch her. The shiver flashing through her gave her goose bumps and the roots of her hair tingled and stood on end. A gossamer breath of a sigh hovered above her head, then fell like tiny droplets of fine cool mist onto her skin. Her blood pulsed in her ears and she didn't dare breathe. This is what it feels like to be really scared, she thought. I know there's no one here, there can't be. Dan's in bed, and if it was Tobias he wouldn't play games like this with me. He doesn't know how to.

She began to leave the chair, then faltered in fear, then leapt forward towards the light switch, flicking it on as fast as she could, flooding the room with light and glancing around the room, hoping perhaps it was Tobias she had felt touch her, who had caused the air in the room to shift and her skin to chill making the fine hairs on her arms prickle. Releasing her breath she inhaled again. She shook her head at her own foolishness. 'What's wrong with me,' she muttered. 'Idiot.' Switching the light off, she pulled her dressing gown around her and tied it at the waist, then turned on the strip lights over the counter to give her confidence.

Nightfall had always comforted her. The darkness in their apartment in London and the glow of the lights from the other apartment blocks around them had reassured her, but in the mill everything felt different. The security she had experienced in her former home, the proximity of coffee shops, boutiques, nail and hair salons, the formality of the flower beds, and trees regularly clipped into angular shapes by young gardeners who greeted her by name as she walked by; all of this had made her feel safe, wrapped her in a cocoon, the protection of familiarity she took for granted, ensuring her feelings of wellbeing and confidence.

Her short time at the mill had swiftly stripped those feelings away. Instead of being part of something as she had in The City, the mill felt more like a satellite; the closest neighbour to them was way down a lane and hidden behind a copse of tall trees and an orchard, so there was no comfort to be had there. She could hardly believe in such a short time her conviction in herself could melt away to nothing. And all because she lived in a different place? Surely it was ridiculous. She was the same person, still had confidence in her abilities as the manager of an art gallery, continued to love what she did. Yet here…here she was thrown into confusion, like a fish out of water, a square peg in a round hole. She loved the mill, had fallen for it when she'd first seen it. So what was it? What was the thing making her feel so out of sorts, so…empty, as if she were bereaved? She swallowed hard, tears misting her eyes, her sense of isolation making her anxious. She didn't want to feel like this. It wasn't how she wanted to be.

It was the dream. It must be the dream.

Sarah sipped her coffee and watched Tobias as he played with his porridge, lifting the spoon and allowing the beige soggy gloop to fall back into the bowl. The patchwork elephant sat on the table, and each time the porridge hit the bowl a shower of lumpy specks splattered the tatty fabric.

'Don't you want it, Tobias? Would you like something else?' He shook his head. 'Aren't you hungry?' Again, he shook his head.

She pushed herself away from the counter and went across to the island, sitting on her haunches beside him. 'What's wrong, sweetheart? Are you looking forward to school?' He turned his head to look at her and she smiled. 'You'll meet all your new friends today. Won't it be nice, to meet your new classmates?' He didn't answer. Sarah sighed and closed her eyes. Somewhere, somehow, she couldn't connect with him. Dan joined them in the kitchen, pulling a sweater over his head.

'Bloody hell, it's cold today.'

'Yeah,' she nodded and raised her eyebrow. 'And not just the weather.'

He frowned. 'What's up?'

Sarah blew out a breath and ran a hand through her hair. 'Oh…maybe I'm expecting too much.'

'Sarah?'

'Just, having a morning.'

He grabbed her hand and pulled her across to a stool at the island. 'Sit. Have you eaten?'

'No.'

'Why not? You're not eating are you?'

'I don't have an appetite.'

'Yeah, well you need to eat. I'm going to cook you something.'

'Dan, honestly, I don't want…'

'I don't care. You need to eat something. And I'll take Tobias to school. You and I are going out for the day. We must sort everything out before I go back to work.'

He got bacon, eggs, tomatoes, sausages and hash browns out of the fridge and loaded them, apart from the eggs, into a frying pan he'd drizzled with olive oil. Sarah watched him as he attempted to fry everything and couldn't help smiling.

'Maybe you could have grilled some of it. It looks like you're cooking a stew.'

'Oh, right.' He looked down at the overflowing pan. 'It'll be alright, won't it?'

She went across to the oven, retrieving the bacon and sausages from the pan, laying them under the grill. The hash browns stayed where they were and she got another pan for the eggs. 'Don't give up your day job.' She glanced at Tobias sitting patiently at the table. 'Maybe he'd like some of this. Why don't you ask him?'

Dan pulled out a chair next to Tobias. 'Fancy a fry up mate?' he asked him, retrieving the sticky bowel from the table. 'Instead of this extremely cold and yucky porridge?'

Tobias slid off his chair, grabbing the elephant as he went. He went into the hall and they heard him pad upstairs to his room. Dan and Sarah watched him go and Dan shook his head. 'I don't think he wants it.' He rolled his eyes. 'And I don't think he likes me, either.'

Sarah checked the bacon and sausages under the grill. 'Give him time.'

'I don't think it's time he needs. And we still haven't got to the bottom of the lipstick thing.'

'You done some research online, haven't you? Did it not give any advice about what to do?'

'Yeah, but the spectrum is so wide. I need to find out where he is on the spectrum before we can do anything else. I was thinking about speech therapy, but he does speak. I think he only speaks when he wants to.'

The bacon spat and sizzled under the grill, and she nodded as she dished up the breakfast, sliding the fried eggs onto a plate. 'I think so too, when he trusts the person he's speaking to.' She glanced at Dan, but he didn't acknowledge what she'd said.

'And the other boy thing. What's that about? I can't say I'm thrilled about it. Apparently some kids with autism fixate on things. Maybe Tobias is doing it, fixating on this imaginary friend.'

'Mm, maybe.' She took the loaded plates over to the island and sat opposite Dan who forked sausage and egg into his mouth and chewed while thinking. 'I mean, there can't be another boy can there? Jesus, why am I asking the question? There isn't anyone else here. Even contemplating it is bloody ridiculous.'

Sarah lowered her eyes. 'No, but we need to get to the bottom of it,' she said quietly. She felt his eyes on her and she looked up. Here it comes, she thought.

'Are you okay now?'

Her heart sank like a stone. 'Yeah? Why?'

He frowned. 'You were very upset last night. I'm guessing you had a nightmare. Was it the same one you had before?'

'Before?'

'You've had it before, right? The nightmare? When we were in the apartment. You've had bad dreams because sometimes you cry out...in the night. And this was before all this recent stuff. With me and, well, y'know? So, I know it's not the only thing bothering you.'

'I...I don't know.' She bent her head towards her plate and momentarily closed her eyes. 'It's nothing, I'm sure. Just one of those things.'

'But something's bothering you, isn't it? Isn't that what they say? Your dreams are related to what has happened or happening in your life?' He finished his breakfast and positioned the knife and fork carefully on the plate. 'What happened recently...' Her expression was as impassive as she could make it as she glanced up at him. 'You know it won't happen again, Sarah. Ever. I know I've hurt you and behaved like a proper prat, and I don't think I'll ever forgive myself.' He waited for her to speak but she said nothing. 'But, I think these nightmares have been bothering you for longer, not just recently.' Sarah didn't say anything and his eyes softened. 'Do you think it's because of what happened with your parents? I mean, it makes sense, doesn't it? It must have been very traumatic for you, bearing in mind how young you were.' She played with the food on her plate, and again said nothing. 'I...I just want to help, Sarah. If you're struggling...' He looked away. 'I know I haven't helped much lately.'

'I'm not sure what you want me to do. Lots of people have nightmares. Does it have to mean anything? Maybe I ate too much cheese at bedtime, or perhaps it was one of the box sets we watched. We like psychological thrillers and crime. Maybe I should watch more comedy or chick flicks.'

'So, you're saying it's nothing.'

'I'm saying it's nothing.'

Dan shrugged and took his plate to the dishwasher, but Sarah knew it wasn't the last she'd heard of it. He was one for getting things fixed. Now he had custody of Tobias, legal or not he would get the issue sorted. It was one of the things about him she'd fallen in love with. He was a doer not a talker. If he believed in something he believed in it passionately and would be a great advocate for whatever it was. She knew he would ask her about it again and next time she needed to be prepared with an answer. The problem was not knowing what the dream meant, but like Dan, she knew it meant something, something her unconscious couldn't, or wouldn't let go.

'We're off.' Dan came into the kitchen with Tobias. The little boy was dressed in his grey and red school uniform, a Minions lunchbox in one hand, the elephant in the other. She got his coat from the peg in the hall and helped him into it.

'You have a good day,' she said to him. 'Do I get a kiss goodbye?' He stared at her for a moment then leant forward and placed a gentle kiss on her lips. She looked at him in astonishment. 'Oh, Tobias, thank you. What a lovely kiss.'

Dan raised his eyebrows. 'You're honoured.'

'I so am.'

'Come on, mate.' Dan reached for Tobias's hand, but he flinched away. Dan looked crestfallen. 'Tobias, come on. Don't be like that.'

Tobias shook his head animatedly from side to side. 'No,' he said. 'Not…not.' He flung his arms around Sarah's neck, nearly knocking her onto her back. 'Saha. Saha. Me and Saha…and boy.'

Sarah gently placed her hands on to Tobias's arms and leant forward. 'Dad'll take you to school, Tobias. It's your first day and he'd like to take you. It's a special moment for both of you.' She gave him one of her brightest smiles, trying to lessen the tension surrounding the moment, glancing up at Dan with regret, his face a mixture of sadness and irritation. 'You've got everything, haven't you? Your lunch…and elephant. Elephant will look after you. You'll be fine.'

Tobias pulled away from her and launched his lunchbox across the kitchen. 'Not, not,' he screamed. 'Saha. Want Saha. The boy says. The boy told me. He told me only Saha.' He began to scream, shrill and ear-penetrating.

Dan screwed up his face at the noise and began to unravel his scarf from around his neck. 'He wants you, Sarah,' he said morosely, flinging his coat onto the island. 'Obviously he hates me.'

'No, Dan, he's just…' She shook her head with frustration. 'He's just having a bad morning. I think you must expect these things to happen. He's nervous about school. It's a big thing, starting a new school. He'll probably hate me tomorrow.'

'If I'm not going to take him to school and he doesn't want to spend time with me there doesn't seem to be much point my being here. I might as well be at work.'

'Of course there's a point to you being here. You're his Dad. How are you going to get to know him if you run away every time it gets difficult?'

'So, you think I'm running away?'

'We haven't got time for this. I'll run him to school. I'm guessing your offer of a day out to discuss things has gone by the wayside.' He shrugged and turned away. Sarah went into the hall, taking her coat of the peg. 'This is what's wrong with us. It always has been. You don't listen. Ever. Do you want to know what I think?' His eyes were ice when he looked at her and he raised his chin, ready for the onslaught. 'I think you need to grow up.'

'Thanks for your opinion.'

'It's not an opinion, it's a fact. You're not Prince Daniel here, regardless of how you're treated at your parents. You're a father now, and to be honest it's time you behaved like one. Stop sulking for Christ's sake, and bite the bullet. This was never going to be easy.' She pulled on her gloves and a woollen hat over her hair. 'And while we're on the subject, as much as I hate to say it because it's not his fault, he's not my child, he's yours and Yelena's, although she's no kind of mother anyone would want. I don't know what you're expecting me to do but I have a job too, one I would like to keep. I've already been off longer than I said I would be and I'm going to need to show my face at some point. I've done everything I can to help, Dan, even though some would say I'm bonkers for even accepting the situation we're in.' Pulling on her gloves, she sighed. 'I'm not Tobias's Mum. I want to keep my job. Yelena could come back and take him with her at any time. What will I have left? A relationship down the toilet and a job I love under threat. None of this is sorted yet. You know it isn't.'

He nodded, and she saw him swallow down his disappointment. Her heart dropped for him, but he needed to know how it was.

The Contempo Gallery
Bond Street, London
January 2019
10

'So what now?' asked Eve as they stood in the gallery's kitchen sipping the first coffee of the day. 'This hasn't worked out quite the way you thought, has it? Will you stay with Dan? He cheated on you, Sarah. And with…' she flicked her hand. 'Someone like her.'

Sarah smiled wryly. 'I don't think it matters who it was he slept with. He did it and lied by omission for the last five years. I'm asking myself if I can trust him. I want to. He was distraught at what he'd done.'

Eve blew out a laugh. 'Distraught at being found out, you mean.'

Sarah couldn't help laughing at her friend's disapproval. 'You're so cynical.'

'Damned right I am. What I want to know is why you haven't ripped both his arms off and smacked him over the head with the soggy ends? I'm not getting it, Sarah. He needs something to happen to make him realise his behaviour is bloody disgusting. I like Dan, but honestly? What's he's done is way beyond acceptable. If madam hadn't come to your door you would still be in the dark about the kid. She took matters into her own hands, didn't she? And let's face it she didn't give a damn about Tobias, or how you would feel.' She shook her head. 'Makes you wonder what kind of woman she is. I couldn't leave my kids with a stranger. Every morning I feel bad when I drop them off at nursery even though I know they're well looked after. It's the price we working mothers have to pay, guilt at not contributing, guilt at not working, guilt at working, and guilt about being a rubbish mother. Honestly, we can't win. It's something she doesn't worry about by the sound of it.'

Sarah tipped the dregs of her coffee into the sink and rinsed the cup under the tap. She wiped her hands on a tea towel and leant against the counter, folding her arms. 'It's Tobias I feel sorry for. Poor little boy. He must wonder who the hell he can rely on.'

'Not his mother.' Eve glanced quickly at Sarah. 'Or Dan?'

Sarah sighed. She knew Eve was right. 'He's trying.'

'Mm,' Eve said as she left the small kitchen. 'And not before time. Regardless of how much Dan would like to forget his one-night stand with Tobias's mother he can't just shove a child under the carpet because his existence is an inconvenience. He's treated both the boy and you appallingly. You must be questioning what you do next.'

'I've thought of nothing else, Eve, but it's not easy. I love Dan. We've been together a long time. Yes, what he's done is bloody awful, but...' She puffed out a sigh and looked up at the ceiling as if searching for the answer. 'Oh, I don't know.'

Eve linked her arm through Sarah's. 'Sorry, Sarah. It's none of my business. No one can say what they would do if they were in the same situation. Just make sure you know what you'd be taking on, particularly with the autism thing.'

Sarah glanced at her. 'Do you know about it?'

'I know a family who have two children who are on the autistic spectrum. Don't get me wrong their parents adore them, but it's changed their lives. Family life isn't what they thought it would be. There's so much for them to consider with regards to education, or before they do anything or go anywhere. And the future isn't very certain.'

'Is it for anyone though? None of us knows what the future holds.'

Eve smiled and squeezed her friend's arm. 'True.' They were quiet as they went into the gallery, each to their respective desks. Both began to look through their diary to plan their appointments for the day. Eve was still smiling, and as her eyes found Sarah's she laughed. 'You've fallen in love with him, haven't you?'

Sarah grinned. 'Who?'

'You know who. Tobias. You've found your mothers' instinct.'

Sarah shook her head. 'I didn't find it. It found me.' She rested her chin on her hands. 'Dan and I agreed not to have children. I was happy with the decision. I'd never craved having a family. I guess I didn't want the responsibility. Dan assured me he felt the same. And, honestly, I think he was telling the truth at the time.' She looked down and shuffled her papers together for her first appointment. 'But I didn't know he already had Tobias. On the face of it, it looks really selfish of him, but I didn't object, so I don't think I can turn around now and say I've changed my mind and now I want my own kids.'

Eve raised an ironic eyebrow. 'You're very generous.'

'I don't think it's about generosity, Eve. I'm dealing with what's in front of us. Yelena has deserted Tobias. The person who was the mother figure in his life is no longer around. Dan has hardly been father of the year. It seems he didn't have much to do with Tobias's upbringing before Yelena decided to leave him with us. Neither of his parents would get a medal for the way they've treated him. I'm not sure I want to do the same thing, to show him I'm as irresponsible as they've been by baling on him.'

Eve looked at her from under her eyelashes, her mouth pulled into a grin. 'Maybe you wanted kids after all. Who knew? But he's not really your responsibility is he? Being a working mother is not an easy option, Sarah. And you've hardly been eased into it gradually. Dan has almost taken the decision for you. Once you commit, that's it, you're in for the long haul. I hope you've given it lots of thought.'

Sarah stood and smoothed her mid-length black pencil skirt over her slim thighs. 'What is it they say about raising a child? It takes a village… The happiness and security of a child is everyone's responsibility. What's happening to him isn't his fault, it's his parent's fault and it's not right he should suffer because of them.'

Sarah watched with wonder as the evening drew in a little later each day. This one seemingly small thing elated her and made her feel stronger. The dark winter nights and the short days were more apparent in the countryside and she welcomed the extra daylight. Living amongst the busyness of London she had hardly noticed as one season changed into another, rather the days blended like ombre, the changes acknowledged simply by a change of wardrobe; a jacket for a coat, a skirt and pumps instead of trousers and boots. She smiled to herself and thought how shallow it all seemed.

She had left work early as her last appointment had cancelled. This had left her glad rather than concerned at the missed opportunity to sell a piece of art. The day before she had sold a painting by an up and coming artist to one of their regular clients for £150,000, so felt the few unexpected hours to herself had been duly earned. Marcus Townsend, her boss and owner of the gallery had surprised her and Eve with a bottle of champagne to mark her success.

'Welcome back, Sarah,' he said. 'You've been sorely missed.'

She laughed and pulled a, "You must be kidding" face. 'I was here, Marcus, in body if not always in mind, I admit that, and I'm grateful to you for understanding.' She grinned her thanks. 'Aaand, I know for a fact Eve made a stonking sale a week ago. You couldn't have missed me that much. She's stellar at what she does.'

'You and Eve are a great team. I know your circumstances have changed, Sarah, but, well, to be honest I've been worried. Committed art lovers who have the qualifications you have are hard to find. You know about art, you've studied it to the nth degree which is why Gerard Coleman comes back to you time and time again. He knows he has never made a bad purchase from us yet. He has just called me. He's thrilled with his new Renton. Carl Renton is going places. He's young and talented and of the moment. The painting you sold him today will probably double in value over the next couple of years or so. He can't lose.' She smiled, pleased at his flattering comments. Sarah was confident in her own abilities, but even she had to acknowledge it was nice when they were recognised by someone else, particularly the man who paid her salary. Marcus sipped his champagne and held his glass up to her. 'And while we're on the subject, neither can you. You've just earnt yourself a shedload of commission.' It was strange how she always forgot. She was so interested in her subject, so bound up in the art world she had forgotten it was how she put food on the table.

Eve glanced across at her and chuckled. 'How can you not think about commission? It's all I think about. Wait until Tobias is nine or ten and wants the latest trainers, or bike, or games console. He'll expect you to think about it, believe me.'

Sarah had smiled and nodded, but couldn't envisage Tobias at the age of ten, or whether she would be in his life then. The future was the last thing on her mind. All she could think about was dealing with the now.

She had grown close to him, realising it was probably because even at his tender age he subconsciously recognised his need for a mother. She tried not to assume she was particularly special to him or that he couldn't get along without her. Would it have mattered who I'd been, she thought with a twinge of sadness? Chuckling, her thoughts went to Coral and Melody. You'd have to be pretty unlucky to end up with a stepmother like either of them and an image of Coral with her sinewy feet trying to squeeze her knobbly toes into a glass slipper had made her grin to herself, but her face had fallen again when Dan's image appeared in her mind's eye. Apparently it was a 'perk' of the job to be introduced to women when they were on business trips, one of the reasons why Sarah wasn't sure she believed Dan's vehement assurance it had never happened before or since. It was only now, when the dust had settled and the bruises had outwardly healed, she could think about it rationally. Dan had done everything he could to reassure her he loved her and only her. And she had already concluded it wasn't this concerning her the most. She was sure he loved her, in fact, she had never doubted it. But she also knew if he was working within a culture where casual sex was on the menu it would be difficult for some men, and some women, to turn it down. Was Dan one of those men?

She went back into the house and leant against the counter, hating thinking about him like this. She loved him more than she had ever loved anyone. He was her world, her soulmate. They discussed everything, even down to the colour of the towels they would have in the bathroom. Silly, silly things, important only to them. He was the only person she could be utterly ridiculous with and know he wouldn't judge her, just laugh with her and be totally ridiculous too. They'd done everything together, had revelled in each other's company, stayed up talking until dawn broke through the curtains, danced in their living room to their favourite music until they could dance no more. He was her best friend, wasn't he? Yet he'd changed, she couldn't deny it. She'd tried to push it away, looked for the man he was before they'd bought the mill, but she'd struggled to find him.

She put her head in her hands, her light mood evaporating into a dark cloud hovering above her head. When she hadn't been looking, when she had taken her eye off the ball, someone, something, somewhere had decided the script of her life was to be rewritten. Had she ever written it for herself? Had any of her decisions been made because she actually knew what she was doing?

She sank to her haunches and laid on the floor, pressing her forehead against the flagstones and breathing in the earthy smell. She closed her eyes and wished she could be the person at home she was at the gallery; confident, sure of her own abilities, a people person with a ready smile and a knowledge of her subject which would floor most people. Faced with Dan's persuasiveness and the forceful influence of his family those positive assertions seemed to dissolve, and she would feel herself reverting to the girl she once was, the one Deanne Trainor had scarred for life.

She sat up, frowning, a sound on the edge of her consciousness. It was singing she was sure of it. She recognised it…from…somewhere, a song they would creep around to when they were kids, holding each other's hands, not worrying about the lyrics, not caring if they got the words wrong. It was the joyfulness of it, the closeness she'd felt with her school friends as they'd screamed out the words and laughed and laughed at the line about getting old and losing hair. They'd all point at Mr Greening, the maths teacher, laughing at his comb-over flapping in the breeze as he made his way across the playground, worn out by the kids and their antics, an exhausted man who couldn't wait for his impending retirement when he could forget about the damned school and its troubled, disrespectful pupils.

I can see you.
When you're old.
Losing hair
And going bald.
I can see you
From behind.
You can see me
In your mind.

The song had always had a creepy feel about it and she remembered they would use shrill scary voices to sing it to each other. Sarah got to her feet and strained to hear the song. In the living room the television was cold, the screen black, but the sound of a reedy voice coming from upstairs was still discernible.

'Tobias,' she called, going out to the hall and standing at the bottom of the stairs. 'Tobias.' She waited for a moment, listening. The singing had stopped, and she leant her head over to one side and wondered if she'd imagined it. 'I'm going mad,' she muttered to herself. 'I'm hearing things. I must be losing it,' but still curious ran up the stairs to find Tobias sitting on the floor of his bedroom surrounded by sheets of A4 he'd taken from the study, and a line of colouring pencils in size order at his side.

'What are you drawing, Tobias?' She picked up one of the sheets of paper. It was a drawing of Dan, the likeness undeniable, except in Tobias's drawing Dan didn't have a mouth. 'Is this picture of Daddy finished?' she asked him. 'I think you've forgotten something,' she said, kneeling beside him and gently brushing his hair back from his forehead. 'Why don't you finish it for when Daddy comes home? He would be so pleased. Look,' she said, pointing to the area where the mouth should have been. 'You can draw a mouth here. Daddy doesn't look right without a mouth.'

Tobias snatched the drawing out of her hands. 'No,' he cried, looking agitated, and stamped his feet on the other drawings scattered around him. One was clearly of her and she was astonished at the quality of the drawing. It had a maturity and flair she could only have dreamed of at Tobias's age. 'This is lovely, Tobias,' she said, picking it up to save it from Tobias's feet. 'Can I keep it?' He lifted his gaze, steadily observed her and nodded. 'Thank you. Thank you very much.' She waited for him to begin drawing again, then remembered the song she'd heard. She hummed it slowly. '*Hm, hm, hm, hm...hm, hm, hm,*' and sat on the bed, wondering if he would sing it with her, hoping he would, wanting him to recognise the tune and join in. It would confirm her imagination wasn't playing tricks on her, assure her the little voice she'd heard was real. It must have been his. Tobias turned his head to look at her. His expression gave nothing away and a shiver went down her back. He observed her coldly for a few moments then picked up a pencil and stabbed the picture of Dan, making holes through the paper and into the rug beneath.

'Tobias, no,' Sarah cried, trying to pull the pencil from his hand. 'What are you doing?' He stared at her resolutely, fighting her, trying to pull his arm away, his fingers wrapped tightly around the pencil.

As his arm went limp he allowed her to clasp his fingers. She pulled him towards her and put her arms around him. 'What was that about?' she asked him, pushing him gently away from her and looking into his face. 'Why would you hurt a picture of Daddy?' His eyes were so dark their depth seemed endless. She waited, determined not to speak first.

'Man is bad,' he whispered.

Sarah felt a trickle of perspiration run down the side of her neck and her heart dropped. 'What do you mean? Which man is bad?' He raised his chin and stared up at the ceiling. He was hedging. He didn't want to answer her. Gently putting her hand to his cheek she turned his face towards her. 'Tobias,' she whispered. 'Which man is bad, sweetheart?'

'The boy telled. The boy telled man is bad.' He looked down, his expression distraught. 'Boy sad.'

'Which boy? Which boy said the man is bad?'

'Not Tobias. The other boy telled the man is bad.'

'Where's the other boy? Where is he now?'

'Gone 'way.'

'Gone where?' He didn't reply so she tried again. 'Why is the boy sad?'

Tobias screwed his face up and winced. 'Got a hurt.'

Pulling him towards her she rested her chin on the top of his soft, brown curls. 'You know Daddy's not bad, don't you? Daddy isn't bad, Tobias. He's not bad just because he's a man. Daddy loves you. I don't know who this other boy is and I don't know why he's saying what he's saying, but please believe me, Daddy would never hurt you. And neither would I. Do you understand?' He nodded. 'Are you sure, Tobias, because it's important? If Daddy knew you thought he was bad he would be very upset.'

'Daddy not bad.'

Sarah shook her head. 'No, he isn't.'

'Not to Tobias.'

'No, not to Tobias.'

'Bad to Saha.'

'What?'

'Bad to Saha. Very bad. Daddy maked Saha have cry on her face.'

Sarah's stomach rolled and she wondered how she could explain it all away. A five- year old doesn't need this. He must have heard us arguing about Yelena. It occurred to her a problem with speaking did not necessarily indicate a problem with hearing. He knew what had happened between them and lying to him would be the worst thing she could do.

'Sometimes grownups make mistakes. Daddy made a mistake. Do you understand?'

'Made Saha's sound hurt.'

Tears welled in her eyes and she blinked them away, understanding immediately what he meant. He'd heard her voice when she was distraught, crying, berating Dan for sleeping with another woman. Part of her was embarrassed and she wondered how much Tobias actually understood. 'Yes, but Daddy is very sorry. He's sorry he upset me and we're sorry it upset you, but it's over now. Sarah and Daddy love each other and we love you.'

'And Mama too.'

It came without warning, the question she had dreaded. She had thought about it, how she would answer if Tobias ever thought to ask it. He had never spoken as much as today, and certainly never of Yelena. 'Daddy will always be Mummy's friend because she gave you to him which was a wonderful gift.' This seemed to satisfy him. He abruptly turned away and picked up his crayons and a sheet of paper. 'Do you want to go downstairs? Tea's nearly ready.' He stepped by her onto the landing without saying a word.

When she got downstairs he was sitting at the kitchen table, drawing. 'We've got your favourite tonight,' she said spooning mounds of glistening macaroni cheese into two bowls. You like macaroni, don't you?' He nodded without looking at her, and she wondered if she dared mention the drawing he'd done of Dan. 'What about Daddy's picture?' she said, placing the bowl in front of him. 'Maybe you could do another one to replace the one you did upstairs.' He didn't answer, simply pushed the paper and crayons to one side and tucked into the macaroni. Sarah took her bowl over to the table and sat beside him. The drawing Tobias had quickly sketched was a precisely observed picture of an elephant. Sarah was astonished at his accuracy. There were so many areas where Tobias needed help but in this he was exceptional.

'Where Mama?'

'Mummy had to go away for a while to see her family.' I need to change the subject, she thought. 'How about a walk after tea? We could go down to the river. Maybe we'll see some rabbits like the ones in Peter Rabbit, or a frog. And we could jump in all the puddles down the lane. Just for half an hour. We need some fresh air. It'll do us good.' Tobias scooped a huge spoonful of macaroni cheese into his mouth, threw the spoon in to his bowl and went into the hall to get his Wellington boots.

Outside, the sky was overcast, a gunmetal grey threatening another deluge on top of the already sodden garden.

'Hmm,' Sarah said, looking up and grimacing. 'This might not have been the best idea I've ever had. Never mind. We're made of sturdy stuff, aren't we, Tobias? We won't let it put us off.' She swung his hand to and fro, then stopped when he didn't seem to be enjoying it. 'Anyway, it'll mean more puddles for us to jump in.' He nodded and a small surge of happiness went through her. Gradually, Tobias was beginning to respond to her, and the almost imperceptible little nod meant everything. He was listening and understanding and making progress in small steps.

They walked down the spongy grass slope. Sarah held tightly onto Tobias's hand, the sound of running water and the strength of the current evident before they'd even got close to the edge. The river was swollen with the recent rainfall, flowing fast, coursing past the banks and taking lumps of earth and branches with it as it hurled by. Water surged under the bridge, meeting a current formed by the undulating riverbed. It eddied in the centre forming a greenish detritus filled whirlpool of mud and leaves. The sound of the rushing water sent a frisson of fear through Sarah, the resulting shiver making her skin crawl.

'I didn't realise it would be like this,' she said. 'I'm not sure I want to be here when it's like this.'

'Frog?' Tobias glanced up at her.

'I'm not sure a frog would last long in there, sweetheart. I think he'd need a big boat to get through all the swirling water.'

'Poor frog,' he answered.

'Yes. Poor frog.' As she spoke the heavens opened, releasing huge drops onto their heads. She pulled up Tobias's hood and then her own. 'Let's walk towards the lane. We might see some rabbits trying to get out of the rain, and we can jump in the puddles.'

They headed towards the lane and went through the gate behind the summerhouse which gave them access from the mill garden. The rain was falling steadily now, and Sarah wondered if she should take Tobias back inside, but he'd let go of her hand and was jumping in the puddles. He was going from one to the other, leaping in with both feet. She heard him laugh with glee when dirty water splashed over his wellies, soaking his jeans, and she didn't have the heart to stop him. It was the first time she'd seen him let himself go, to be a child with no thought other than to enjoy himself. She jumped in the puddle next to his, squealing loudly. He stopped and stared at her as if considering whether this was normal behaviour for an adult. She did it again and he gave a little grin, satisfied it was okay.

They jumped from puddle to puddle until the ground evened out near the property at the end of the lane. The light was failing and Sarah held her hand out for Tobias, deciding it was time for them to go. As they turned to walk back, she saw someone at the curve of the lane as it branched off to the property.

'Wonder who that was?' she said, as much to herself as to Tobias. There was no sound now. Darkness had fallen and she cursed herself for leaving it so late to get back. As they got to the puddles Tobias wanted to play again, but she pulled him away, increasing her pace as much as his short legs would allow. It felt like they weren't alone, as though someone was following them and she wondered who it was she'd seen on the lane. A rustling in the long grass beside them made her flinch and she frowned. 'I'm getting spooked over nothing,' she said under her breath. 'Woman up, Sarah.'

The silence now the rain had stopped had become almost oppressive and she kept looking over her shoulder. She heard a splash behind them as though someone had stepped into one of the puddles. There's someone there, she thought. I know there is. Why are they doing this? Why don't they show themselves? She picked Tobias up and tried to run with him but his weight slowed her down, so put him down again, urging him to walk faster. She got her keys out of her pocket, thinking if they were attacked she could use them as a weapon, jangling them so whoever it was behind them would hear them. Sarah broke into a run, pulling Tobias as fast as she could down the lane without dragging him off his feet. Her hood had slipped off her head and a fresh shower of rain was driving into them, turning her hair into rats' tails, dripping water down her face and into the neck of her padded coat.

The end of the lane came into sight, and relief flooded through her in a comforting wave. As she ran for the place where she knew they'd be safe she looked over her shoulder again. A man stood in the middle of the lane, the darkness shrouding him like a cloak. As they got to the end of the lane and went through the gate behind the summerhouse he disappeared from sight. Tobias ran towards the mill and Sarah was glad she'd left the lights on; the glow spilling from the windows made her feel safe. They were home.

As she got to the path leading to the front door she looked across the garden, down the slope to the bridge. A fiery orange tip from a cigarette burned in the darkness. It paled for a moment, glowing bright again as it was drawn on.

Someone was there. Someone had followed them. Someone was watching them.

Dan breezed in through the door, but as certain as she was they had been followed in the lane and someone had watched them from the bridge, reasoning had kicked in and she decided to keep it to herself. Dan was already on alert because of the nightmare, and it made her question her perspective on something which could have been completely innocent, a neighbour walking a dog perhaps, or someone going into the woods to shelter from the rain. And it would be something else for him to question her about. It concerned her that she doubted he would believe her. She should have been able to tell him, but her misgivings held her back.

'You look happy,' she said. 'I haven't seen you look so positive for ages.'

'The takeover is in the bag. Jed and I have done a sterling job and we'll definitely be rewarded for it. How would you like to go away for a bit? Somewhere sunny?'

'It sounds great. When were you thinking?'

'Next week?'

'Right? What about my job…and Tobias's school?'

Dan helped himself to macaroni cheese, spooning a huge helping onto a plate, and joined them at the table, kissing the top of Tobias's head. 'It won't be a problem, will it? I'm only talking a week.'

'I can't take another week off so soon after the last break I had, and schools don't allow you to take the kids out of lessons for random holidays. We'll get fined.'

He shovelled a forkful of food into his mouth. 'So we'll pay the fine. It can't be much, can it? We need a break. And Marcus loves you. You're the best person he has at the gallery. He's hardly going to sack you.'

'And do I get a choice in this? Sounds like you've already decided for me.'

He detected the annoyance in her voice and raised his eyebrows. 'Anyone would think I'd told you I was sending you to the salt mines. I just wanted to take us away for a week. We need it don't we?'

'I know, and it's a lovely idea, but I'm not taking more time off, and…I don't think you should take Tobias out of school. He's making progress now and it needs to be consistent. If you want to go away it'll have to be in the school holidays.'

'Which is when everyone else goes, and we'll be overrun with other people's kids. And it's more expensive.' He loaded his fork with more macaroni cheese and looked at her glumly.

'Yes, Dan, and these are the changes you must make if Tobias stays with you. Apart from anything else he's doing really well at the moment. His speech is really improving.'

Dan looked down at his food and sighed. 'Is it? I hadn't noticed. He barely comes near me. It seems you're the only one he wants. And you said "you", not "us". You need to tell me what you want, Sarah. You haven't been near me for weeks. Am I on a reprieve or am I going to be thrown out? I know I've caused havoc but you need to make a decision one way or the other.'

She glanced across to Tobias, wondering how much she should tell Dan. 'There's something we need to talk about, but not now.'

'Has something happened?' He laid his fork down. 'What now?'

'I don't think you're going to like it.'

'This is ridiculous, Sarah. You don't believe any of this stuff, surely.' Dan paced the room, a deep furrow between his eyebrows. He felt was doing his best to protect Tobias while at the same time trying to placate Sarah, but he couldn't understand why she was so determined to believe in Tobias's assertions they weren't alone in the mill.

'I don't know what to believe, but it pretty much answers why he doesn't go near you anymore. He's scared of you because you're a man and he's been told men are bad.'

Dan pushed his fingers through his hair, his eyes clouded with disbelief. 'And who told him because I can hardly believe a five-year old would say it without someone telling him. It's such a generalisation. Why would anyone say it? Was it someone in his class?'

'Look...I'm just telling it like Tobias is telling it. He says it's the other boy. He's talked about the other boy since he came here. And there's that business with the lightsabre at Christmas.'

Dan sunk down onto the sofa opposite her and rested his elbows on his knees, rubbing his face with frustration. 'There were just the three of them up there. He must have been talking about Matthew. I know for a fact he wouldn't think twice about clouting Leo if he thought he could get away with it.'

Sarah shook her head. 'I don't think he was.'

He leant back and observed her. 'You believe him, don't you? You actually believe there's something here, something we can't see and Tobias can. Come on, Sarah, we've always agreed this stuff is bullshit.'

'Like I said, I don't know what to believe. Listen to what Tobias is saying. Even if *we* struggle to believe in what he's saying he clearly does believe it, and at the moment isn't it what matters? He says there's another boy in this house so maybe we should behave as though there is. We need to humour him and perhaps we'll get at the truth.' Dan went quiet and she could only guess what he was thinking. 'He asked where Yelena was.'

'Did he? I wondered when it would happen. What did you tell him?'

'I said she was visiting her family. I was waiting for him to ask me when she was coming back but I changed the subject.'

'And what would you have said?'

'Pass.' Dan rested his head on the back of the chair and blew out a breath of frustration. Sarah raised her eyebrows, thinking, wondering how their life could have changed so much. 'Sorry to burst your bubble.'

'This autism thing with Tobias. I didn't realise how difficult it would be. Things haven't turned out the way I thought they would.'

She looked out of the window into the dark. 'Do they ever?'

'So, what now? Don't we have to make him realise there is no other boy? Show him he's the only one here. How are we going to encourage him to feel the same as other kids when he's talking like this?'

Sarah got up and went over to the fireplace. The logs were burning down and she felt the atmosphere in the room was cold enough without the fire going out. 'He doesn't feel the same as other kids though, does he? Because he's not the same.' She pulled a couple of logs from the log basket and pushed them into the embers.

'I just want him to stop talking about this invention of his. It's not normal,' he looked over to her, almost apologetically, 'for want of a better word. It seems like he listens to this…this thing more than he listens to us. And now he's been told by whatever "it" is I'm a bad person and he doesn't want anything to do with me. How am I supposed to accept it? I'm his Dad, and I want to be a good dad to him. I…know I've let him down, but I want him to know I'm here for him. I want him to understand if he needs anything he comes to me. I feel as though I'm competing with this thing.'

Sarah knew what she was about to say wouldn't go down well. 'How about you try to understand that if he's making up the other boy there could be a very good reason for it.'

Dan left the chair and stood in front of the fire, warming his hands over the flames. 'If? Of course he's making it up, Sarah. For Christ's sake, there's no such thing as ghosts. It is a ghost he's talking about, isn't it?' She nodded. 'They don't exist. It's a figment of his imagination and I'm going to get it sorted, once and for all.'

'How?'

'Harley Street. There's a child development clinic there. One of my colleagues told me about it. I'm going to take him there. Get some clarity on all this.'

'Well, it's a start.'

'Maybe they'll get to the bottom of this ghost thing.'

'Or maybe they won't.'

'They will, because it's got to stop. If he thinks I'm a bad person how am I going to have a relationship with him?'

'Actually, it wasn't you.'

'What do you mean, it wasn't me?'

'He didn't say *you* were bad. He said the boy told him "man was bad". He didn't say you. He didn't say Daddy was a bad person.'

Dan visibly relaxed. 'Right. You're sure?'

'I'm positive.'

'Did you ask him who?'

'He wasn't able to answer me.'

'Jesus. Where's this going to end?'

'We have to find out what's going on. I know how you feel about this stuff, but I'm not convinced it's nothing.'

'So, what you're saying is, you think it's real. You don't think he's making it up.'

She sighed, wishing he would be more flexible but knowing how stubborn he could be. 'I'm saying we should keep an open mind,' she said in a quiet voice. 'No one knows for sure, do they, not even you, oh, great philosopher.'

He chuckled and she was glad she'd made him laugh. It was the first time they'd laughed together in months.

'Okay. If it's what you think we should do.' He sat on the arm of the chair and reached for her hand, inspected her fingers intertwined with his, rubbing the backs of her hands, turning one over and lifting her palm to his lips to kiss it. 'This is the first real problem to test our relationship, Sarah. In London it was just us. We only had ourselves to think about. We hadn't lived, had we? God knows, we were pampered, cosseted from life. This is real so it's important, crucial we get it right no matter what it means. It'll either make us or break us. I hope it makes us stronger, makes us more resilient as a couple. You've been holding out on me and I don't blame you, but I need to know if I'm to be sent to the guillotine. You must know what you want by now.' Dan waited but Sarah said nothing. He was frightened to push it in case she said what he didn't want her to say. 'Do you like it here?'

She glanced at him. 'I like the house…but…'

'But?'

'I like the mill, Dan, don't get me wrong, but we've had nothing but problems since we got here. You can't expect me to say I'm happy after everything that's happened. I keep getting the feeling this place is cursed, that we'll never be happy again until we leave it behind. I'm worried it might have bad memories.'

He pursed his lips and blew out a sigh. 'You're kidding, right.' He scratched his head and pulled a funny face. She smiled because he always looked so boyish when he was baffled by something, usually at some remark she'd made he found funny. He often said it was this quirkiness that had attracted him to her, her propensity for stating the obvious then coming out with something totally profound and left field. He said she was the quirkiest, most intelligent woman he'd ever met. She hadn't taken offence at what she felt was an astutely accurate description. She'd rather liked it. It made her feel different. Unique. 'Ah, Sarah, here we go. You think a house can remember things. You think people become so ingrained in the four walls they inhabit they leave their memories behind?' He threw back his head and laughed.

Sarah shook her head, not in the least surprised by his reaction. 'What? What's wrong with getting emotionally attached to where you live? I loved the apartment, didn't you? It's part of who we are. We have our own memories there.'

'It was okay, yes, but when we moved out I forgot all about it and concentrated on living here. I don't feel like I've left a part of myself there for the new owners to deal with, just like I don't think for one second this house has hung onto the souls of people who have lived here before. Once I'm gone, I'm gone. I take my belongings and dump them somewhere else. It's called moving on.' He smiled at her, his eyes softening when she rolled her eyes. 'Maybe it's because I'm a bloke, but...there aren't any memories at Newton's Mill, Sarah.'

'And you know for certain because...?'

'...Because there's no such thing as apparitions, spooks, spectres, lost souls, whatever you want to call them. No Ghostbusters needed here. They do not exist. And houses don't have memories because if they did they'd all be in bloody therapy. You know I don't believe in all that stuff—clairvoyance, spirits, or whatever. It's all bullshit promoted by charlatans to make money out of gullible people. We've always said we don't understand how reasonable, seemingly intelligent people could be taken in by them. Now we're talking about it ourselves. It's just crazy. I can hardly believe we're considering it.'

'I know what we've said before, but we should consider it. We must listen to Tobias. It doesn't matter how we feel or what we think. We should listen to him.'

Mary unlocked the shutters across the windows of The Toy Box and pushed them upwards with a grunt. They made a loud rattling sound as they hit the top of the window and locked into place with a clang. She put a hand on the small of her back and rubbed the soft mass of flesh above the base of her spine. Her lumber region was playing her up again. The pain was excruciating and her bunions were giving her gyp as well. She shook her head and mumbled to herself. She should have retired years ago, but the possibility of a relaxing retirement seemed such a long way away it wasn't worth thinking about anymore.

The main street in the village was already bustling with out-of-towners who came from the middle of March onwards to visit the cobbled streets, to marvel at the old-fashioned buildings and revel in the quaintness of the place, so the prospect of making some money from their hopefully indulged kids kept her going; a comforting thought helped along by a nice sticky rum baba at elevenses. It would break her Slimming World diet but it was only a little treat. Life wasn't worth living without the little treats.

She stepped into the shop and took the cover off the new computerised till they'd had installed in the shop. It did everything but make tea, and she rubbed her hand across it thinking she would have rather spent the money on a decent holiday. The last time she and her husband, had gone away was three years before; a last minute all-in package deal to Benidorm. He'd got sunburn and had spent two of their six days lying in bed, his inflamed, raging skin covered in a thick layer of calamine lotion. He'd made such a fuss, expected her to wait on him hand and foot like she did at home. She laughed to herself and shook her head, wondering why she'd stayed with him all these years. He was a walking disaster. She'd told him so too. No matter what he took on he never seemed to have the nous to make a success of it. And he'd done a few things since they'd been married, trying just about everything; driving instructor, painter and decorator, caretaker, window cleaner, waiter. He'd even signed up for a private investigator course once and had imagined himself as Philip Marlow or Sherlock Holmes. For Christmas he'd asked for a spy camera, one he could pin to the lapel of his coat, and a recording pen for illicit conversations. She knew it was just the latest in a long line of faddy things he believed he could do, but when she mentioned to him he'd probably have to carry out surveillance for hours on end in the cold, wee small hours and perhaps not get the information he needed to get paid, it seemed to put him off. Anything that required any real effort put him off. She knew he was intrinsically lazy, and at his age, early-sixties, it was way too late for him to make a real go of anything.

She glanced around the shop and the bright colours of the toys on the shelves, the new games, the popularity of which were led by the media, the Barbie dolls and pots of slime, the computer games and pretend makeup, and thought no matter how much she complained about all the work she'd put in over the years The Toy Box had kept them out of debt and had put food on the table and a roof over their heads. They'd also raised two children, sending one to university, although precious little good it had done him. Their son had inherited her husband's lazy gene, and it was as much as she could do to get him out of bed some mornings. How he'd managed to get his degree she didn't know. And he hadn't made the most of it. He was content to do the jobs other people didn't want to do. He called them "COWs", Can't-Or-Won't, do-it-yourself-ers. He said they were the people who kept him in beer money. It seemed to be all he wanted out of life. There was no girl on the scene either, so no chance of him settling down any time soon. She went into the gloomy backroom and put the kettle on to boil. There was about ten minutes before she unlocked the door, so she decided to make the most of them and have a cup of tea before opening up.

Taking her tea into the shop she saw Max the street cleaner on his little cleaning buggy, swilling the cobbles with water and scrubbing them with two swirling brushes fixed to the bottom. They looked like the brushes sweeps used to clean out the chimneys, and Mary smiled at the sense of nostalgia warming her. No matter how hard the years before had been they were lucky to have the shop where it was; situated on a lovely old cobbled street with a beautiful church at one end and the high street at the other. Anyone wanting to visit the church would have to pass The Toy Box, and if they had children who wanted everything, and they had parents who gave them everything they wanted, so much the better. She sipped her tea and pondered the morning, wondering who she'd have in, hoping they would be big spenders with deep pockets. A tax bill had arrived the previous week she'd yet to tell Ray about, and if it could be paid without telling him so much the better. He was a so-and-so for moaning about the Inland Revenue as he called them. He'd contributed so little to the country's coffers over the years he hadn't realised they were now HMRC, but he didn't like her paying them either, regardless of what they were called.

Tutting at her thoughts she drained her cup and frowned when she saw Sarah standing on the pavement on the other side of the narrow street. She took off her specs, spat on each lens and polished them on her ankle-length floral skirt. Putting them back on her nose she narrowed her eyes and hardened her jaw. There's something about the new girl, she thought. Not sure what it is but I'm never wrong. She wasn't unpleasant, in fact the opposite, but something wasn't quite right. The story she'd told at Christmas about a little boy and his mum staying at the mill hadn't rung true at the time, and since then Mary had learned that Sarah and the bloke she was with, what's his name, Dan did she say, had enrolled a little lad up at St. Giles, the primary school on the estate. Funny business. Mary wondered who the boy was and decided to ask Sarah the next time she came in the shop. Mary had her finger on every pulse in the village and even if Sarah didn't tell her she'd find out eventually. Someone would spill the beans.

Watching her from the safety of the shop, Mary hid behind boxes of Lego and stacks of books. Sarah carried one of the pale blue and gold bags from *Bluebelle and Rouleau*, the posh lingerie shop on the corner opposite The Toy Box. 'You have to have money to shop there,' Mary said to herself. 'Of course, you're loaded, aren't you? You bought the mill and it must have cost you a pretty penny. Who are you, I wonder? And who's the boy?' she muttered. 'Not yours, I know. You would have said he was your boy, wouldn't you? There would have been no reason not to say he was yours, but you didn't. You said he was a friend's boy. So why is he living with you?'

She didn't have long to wait. Sarah looked over to The Toy Box and crossed the road. Mary darted behind the counter and made herself look busy. She looked up as Sarah got to the door, and waved and smiled and went to the front door to unbolt it.

'Hi, Sarah,' she said, going behind the counter. She made her voice lighter and friendlier than she felt. 'I haven't seen you since Christmas. How are you and the family?'

'We're fine. Just thought I'd come and say hello.'

Mary wondered how she could get the conversation around to the boy. Funny, she thought, how things worked out. Here's my chance to get the lowdown on the townies. 'How did the presents go down?'

Sarah frowned.' Presents?'

'The ones you bought for the little boy? At Christmas. Did he like them?'

'Oh, yes. Sorry. Um, yes, he loved them.'

'Settled in has he, at the school?'

Sarah stiffened and Mary was certain she'd hit a nerve. 'Yeah, he seems to like it.'

'Yeah, not a bad little school. Not always had the best reputation, but…well, when you live local you can't let it put you off. We should all support our community as much as we can. Got time for a cuppa?' Sarah nodded, and Mary congratulated herself for handling her curiosity so well. I'll get it out of you, she thought as she switched the kettle on. There's something there. I knew there was something there. I always know.

Mary took the cups and saucers into the shop and sat behind the counter after dragging a stool in for Sarah from the back room.

'Might as well make ourselves comfortable,' she said, and then we'll begin, said her inner voice. 'Do you think you'll stay here, Sarah, in Newton Denham?' She asked the question as lightly as she could, so it seemed as though she was just engaging in small talk.

'I think so, although it's been a bit of a culture shock for us?'

Mary frowned. 'Oh, in what way?'

'We came from the city…virtually lived on top of it. And we only had an apartment, so coming here and living in a mill was a massive change for us.'

'What made you decide to do it, to move away from everything you knew?'

Sarah shrugged and sipped her tea, thinking how quaint it was to use a cup and saucer. She only used them at Christmas for after dinner coffee. 'We wanted a change. Don't get me wrong, I loved living where we did. It was in the middle of everything and there was always so much going on. The busyness and never-ending stream of, well, just life really, became part of the problem. There was never any peace, always noise, and lights, and people, which is why I think I've struggled a bit since coming here. The quiet and isolation of Newton's Mill has taken some getting used to, but I think I'm okay now, and Newton Denham is so pretty. It's like going back in time.'

'It's why we get so many visitors. I think Newton Denham has become what they call a destination place which is good for The Toy Box. I need as many visitors as we can get.'

'Newton's Mill certainly isn't part of it. We rarely see anyone. Occasionally people walk by with their dogs, or maybe a group of ramblers or runners go by. I'm not sure people know it's there.'

Mary stared at her. 'Oh, they know it's there.'

Sarah placed her cup carefully on the saucer and raised her eyes slowly, meeting Mary's stare. 'Actually, Mary, it's the mill I wanted to talk to you about.'

'Newton's? I'm not very familiar with it I'm afraid. It's stood empty a few times I think. What do you want to know?'

'Apparently it had been empty quite a while before we came here. Ever since we moved in people have referred to the history of the place. Not just Newton Denham, but Newton's Mill in particular. Have you any idea what they're talking about?'

Mary looked down at her cup and sniffed, pushing her heavy-framed glasses further up her nose. 'Well, there was some talk a while back. I don't know if that's what you mean.'

'Go on.'

'You can't take this as gospel, Sarah. You know how people are. They like to gossip. We've got a lot of gossips in this town and to be honest if I don't tell you one of them will, and they're not as friendly as me.' Sarah said nothing. 'All I know is…in the past people have talked about a child's body being found there, in the grounds.'

Sarah's hand flew to her mouth. 'What?'

Mary waved a hand at her. 'Now don't look like that. It was just hearsay. Like I said, people gossip.'

'Do you know who it was?'

'No, not really. I heard a little girl was involved, but to be honest I don't really want to know and neither should you. It was a long time ago, and if we lived in a city like you did it would have been forgotten years ago. But Newton Denham is a tight little community, and when things happen or someone says something out of the ordinary those things are never forgotten because not much happens here. It becomes part of the history of the place, and mud sticks as they say. And believe me, it doesn't even have to be true.'

'What an awful story. Poor little thing. When was it?'

Mary put her cup and saucer on the counter and tapped her fingers against her chin. 'Now, let me see.' Her eyes slid to the right and she sighed as she tried to remember. 'It has to be at least twenty years ago, perhaps a bit more.' She watched as Sarah relaxed slightly.

'Oh. Not recently?'

'No, no, years ago. It might even be more, certainly not less. No one mentions it. It's not the kind of thing you talk about over tea and cake, is it? And if you want my advice you'll forget about it. Don't go around asking questions, will you, now I've told you, or I'll wish I hadn't said anything? No one talks about it, and it's not the best way to make friends in your new community, is it, asking about the death of a child?'

Sarah shook her head and stared into her cup. 'No, I guess not.'

'Now, don't go worrying about something that doesn't concern you. It was a long time ago and there's no way it can affect you. Put it to the back of your mind. Like I said, it's only what I heard and it could be gossip. You know how these things take hold. It could all be bunkum.'

'No, I know. It's just a bit of a shock. You don't look into the history of a place, do you, when you fall in love with somewhere? It's the last thing you think about. Actually, I didn't think about it at all. I would never have assumed anything so horrible could have happened there.'

'Just as well I'd say, otherwise we wouldn't do anything. What about London? You lived there and it didn't bother you, did it? I bet you never gave it a second thought. Read up on it. I love historical books and much of what's written is set in the capital. Some of our monarchs were treacherous, killing and maiming all over the place, including women and children. They didn't care who they got rid of if someone got in their way. Look up The War of the Roses. Now there's a bloody history of our country if ever there was one. They got up to all sorts in centuries past. Everywhere has a history.'

'That's what Dan says.'

'Well, Dan's right.'

Sarah left The Toy Box deep in thought. What Mary had told her had made her feel uncomfortable and she had a heavy feeling in the pit of her stomach. She wondered about the child who had been found in the grounds of Newton's Mill and wished she'd asked Mary more about it, but Mary had given the impression it wasn't something she wanted to expand on. She thought about going to the library and looking it up, but before she'd left home Tobias had complained of not feeling well and Sarah had left him with Dan and a bottle of Calpol. Her mobile buzzed and she took it from her bag.

'How is he?'

Dan sounded strained. 'He's been sick.'

'Oh, no.' Sarah wanted to laugh because of the revulsion in Dan's voice, but was concerned about Tobias. 'I'm coming home now. You can manage for a bit, can't you?'

'I think it goes with the job doesn't it? I'm not sure it's on my CV though.'

She put her phone back in her bag and made her way to the taxi rank. She looked for Dave, but he wasn't there. A young guy of about thirty came out of TipTop Cars and lifted his chin to her.

'Need a cab?'

'Yes, to Newton's Mill, please.'

'Oh, right,' the guy said, getting into the driver's seat. Sarah opened the door to the dilapidated Vauxhall Tourer and got in the back. She wrinkled her nose at the smell of the interior; greasy fast food and cigarettes, and another smell she couldn't quite place. There was a McDonalds bag and wax crayons on the floor—a lurid green one had been trodden into the grey carpet—and muddy footprints on the backs of the front seats where little feet had wiped the soles of their shoes. She shut the door and rolled the window down, taking in large gulps of fresh air. 'So, you're the new owner?'

'Sorry?'

'Of the mill.'

'Yes, with my partner.' The driver stuck the key into the ignition, but the engine took four tries before it came to life. 'Fucking useless car...oh, sorry. Shouldn't have sworn in front of a punter.'

She raised her eyebrows. 'Don't worry about it.'

'My wife says I swear too much. Every second word, she says.' Sarah nodded into the rear view mirror hoping he wasn't going to start a conversation with her, suddenly losing the desire to get to know the locals. For the first couple of minutes she got her wish as she Googled what Mary had told her about the body at Newton's Mill but found nothing, hoping it was obvious to the driver she wasn't up for talking. Once they were on the dual carriageway he struck up a conversation.

'What's it like, living at the mill?'

She looked up. 'Yeah, nice. Different.'

'Different to what?'

'Different from where we were before.'

'And where was that?'

She glanced down at her phone. There was a text from Dan. "He's been sick again. Christ, it's horrible."

'London. We lived in London.' She texted back. "On way."

'And now you've come here.'

'Yeah.'

'Funny really.'

Her brow puckered and she wondered if he was about to tell her something else she didn't want to hear. 'Why?'

'Most people can't wait to get away from Newton Denham,' he said, taking his eyes off the road and peering over his shoulder at her.

'Really? You're still here.'

'Yeah, I know, but if things had turned out different I wouldn't be.' Sarah argued with herself about whether she should ask him what it was he wanted to turn out differently but he didn't wait for her to ask. 'Got her pregnant, didn't I? Fucking stupid.' He glanced an apology at her in the mirror. 'Couldn't leave her on her own after getting her up the duff, could I? Leave her to the gossips.'

She looked down at her phone wishing Dan would ring her, thinking she really didn't want to know any of this. 'Well, what could they have said?'

'Anything they want. They might have said I'm a no good bum, a waster, and shit like that. I stepped up to the plate, I did, but those old biddies don't care whose life they ruin. No one's good enough for 'em. And they've ruined a good few around here let me tell you. One bloke I know was close to suicide because someone had put it around Newton Denham he was gay. He was a married man, like. Got kids too. If they don't know it they make it up. They don't care what they say about you. You wanna watch out for 'em. They might start gossiping about you.'

'Right. And was he gay?'

'Er, well, yeah, he was, but, it's not the point is it? It was nothing to do with them whatever he was.'

'Do the residents of Newton Denham not approve of gay people?'

'I dunno. I just think it was the next bit of juicy gossip. They probably started on someone else afterwards when they'd got bored with it. I don't mind 'em meself. Gays I mean. I've always said, as long as they leave me alone I'm okay with it. I believe in live and let live, but some of 'em 'ere don't think the same way as I do. They near crucified him.'

Sarah glanced out of the window and watched the countryside speed by, wishing the journey would go quicker. She prayed for the mill chimney to come into view across the fields because she'd know it was nearly over. 'I'll make sure I'm careful.'

'You do that.'

They pulled into the lane and she paid the fare as he leaned out of the driver's window.

'You wouldn't catch my missus living in a place like this.'

'No?'

'No way. Too spread out and too isolated. You don't know who the hell's about or what's happened here. Gotta be haunted hasn't it?

Ghosts? Isn't it why the others left?' Sarah stared at him. 'Yeah, sure that was the story,' he said, rubbing his chin, getting into his subject. 'We hear about everything in the village. There ain't any secrets in Newton Denham. Things happening they couldn't explain, see. Scared them half to death. And their kids went all funny too. One of them was in my Kylie's class. She said the girl was nice at first but then went all moody and thin and kept talking about strange things happening in the house and her mum losing it.' Sarah glanced at the mill and swallowed hard, then looked back at him. She couldn't think of anything to say which he took as an invitation to keep talking. 'And anyone can get in there. Like an open door that is.' He nodded towards the slope leading down to the river. 'Looks nice, but, nah. Asking for trouble. Pretty though.'

'Thanks.' She pulled a wry smile and rolled her eyes. 'Thanks anyway.'

'No worries. You take care now.'

'I'll definitely try to.'

Inside she found Dan sitting on the edge of the sofa next to Tobias who was lying under his duvet, his elephant beside him. Next to the sofa was a bowl.

'At least it's Saturday and he doesn't have to take time off school. Did he have Calpol?'

'Yeah, but he brought it back up again.'

'Tut, oh Tobias.' She slipped off her coat and indicated for Dan to move out of the way, sitting by the little boy. His face was pale but he looked glad to see her. 'How are you feeling now? Do you still feel sick?' Tobias shook his head. 'Do you want anything, a drink maybe?'

'Perhaps he should have some milk. He hasn't eaten all day.'

'No, not milk. It'll curdle in his stomach. It doesn't matter if he hasn't eaten for a few hours, it won't hurt him. He should have plain water until he can stomach something else. Maybe some toast.'

Dan grinned. 'How d'you know all that stuff?'

'What stuff?'

'About the milk, and toast, and curdling, which sounds gross.'

Shrugging she rubbed her hand across Tobias's forehead. 'I don't know. Common sense, I suppose. He's not hot anymore anyway. It's the high temperature that makes people sick. He'll probably start to feel better now his temperature is going down.' She tucked the duvet around the little boy. 'Are you hungry, sweetheart?' He nodded, and she glanced up at Dan. 'See. Nurse Sarah knows what she's doing. I'll make some toast.'

After dinner Sarah loaded the dishwasher and Dan took Tobias up to bed. After a while he came into the kitchen holding the patchwork elephant by its trunk.

'This needs a wash,' he said. 'It's acquired a new coat and a strange smell.'

She frowned and stepped back. 'Is it sick?' Dan nodded and pulled a face. 'Oh, God. Eewgh, hand it over. I'll put it in the washing machine with some anti-bacterial stuff. Does Tobias know you've got it?'

'Fast asleep. We'll have to get it washed and dried before he wakes up or he'll have a meltdown.'

'Okay. Priority mission.' She opened the washing machine door and flung the elephant inside. As it hit the drum two of the patches parted and a gap appeared as some of the stitching shredded. 'Oh, no, what have I done?' She reached into the washing machine and gingerly pulled the elephant out between thumb and finger. She held it up and peered into the hole, screwing up her eyes. 'I think there's something inside.'

Dan stood next to her squinting into the hole. 'What is it?'

'I don't know, and to be honest I don't want to touch it. It absolutely stinks.'

He opened the door of the cupboard under the sink and peered inside. 'Got any rubber gloves?'

'Oh, yeah. A pink pair. At the back. Still in the packet.' He ripped open the packet and handed them to her, taking the elephant from her fingers. 'I don't want to rip it too much,' she said, taking the sodden elephant from him. 'We need to get it back to him in working order so to speak.' She slipped a finger into the gap and hooked it around whatever it was inside, pulling it towards her. Something shiny fell out and plopped onto the floor. Dan picked it up.

'It's a sachet.' He closed his eyes sighing. 'What do you think this is?' He held it up in front of her, waving it in front of her nose.

Her mouth dropped open. 'It's not drugs, is it?' she whispered.

'Well, I don't think it's icing sugar. Any more in there?'

She pushed two fingers and a thumb in this time, not worrying about the stitching, and pulled out two more sachets. 'Oh, my God, Dan. What is it?'

'Cocaine by the looks of it.'

She snapped her head round and glared at him. 'How do you know it's cocaine?'

He pulled a face and shrugged. 'People do this stuff all the time.'

'Not us.' He didn't say anything and she continued to stare at him. 'You've tried it?' He nodded. 'When?' He shrugged again, and she shook her head. 'It was on the trips wasn't it? When you went abroad with Jed and the others for work. She closed her eyes and blew out a breath of frustration. 'Jesus, Dan. What's coming next?'

'I don't know why you're getting so upset. Everyone does it. It's nothing. It's like…having a drink.'

She threw the elephant into the washing machine. 'I don't even know if what you're saying is true, but what the hell is it doing stuffed into Tobias's elephant?'

'How should I know?'

'Well, I do. I bet it's Yelena's doing. She probably used Tobias's elephant to take it wherever she went. The police don't search kids' soft toys, do they? I suppose she was selling it. She must have forgotten about it in her rush to get away. Makes you wonder why she was in such a hurry. What a thing to do. What a bitch.'

Dan went to the island and slid onto one of the chrome and leather stools. He rested his elbows on the counter and put his head in his hands rubbing his eyes with the heels of his hands. 'She's something else.'

'Yes, she is. But I'm wondering what exactly.'

Dan raised his shoulders in a shrug. He looked drained and Sarah watched him through narrowed eyes, wondering if he deserved sympathy for the guilt she imagined was racing through him, or whether he needed a kick up the arse for being so irresponsible. 'I don't know, Sarah. I don't know what she is, but I do know she's let Tobias wander around with cocaine packed in his favourite toy.' He shook his head. 'How could she use her own son, an innocent child who has no choice?'

'Because she doesn't care about anyone but herself. She's not a good person is she, the mother of your child?' She felt bad for saying it, but her anger with him for what he'd done to them had still not diminished and things seemed to be getting worse. 'Are you going to contact her and tell her we've found her stash?'

'Would there be any point?'

'Yes, there would be a bloody point. She needs to know we're on to her.'

'I'll text her.'

Sarah whirled round to him, her face dark with anger. 'No you will not text her. Nothing in writing. If the authorities found out about this you could have a problem on your hands. She'll lie and lie to save her own skin. How do we know she won't say the cocaine is yours?' Something occurred to her. 'Did you take it when you were with her?' He rolled his eyes and breathed in deeply. 'You did, didn't you?' She shook her head in disbelief. 'And since?' He remained silent. She grimaced, screwing up her face with frustration, wondering if she knew him at all. 'Why? Why do you take it?'

'It's just…a social thing. People do it, all the time, even at work.'

'You?'

He shook his head and looked at her, his eyes shaded by contrition. He reminded her of a naughty schoolboy who had been caught smoking behind the bike sheds. 'No. Not at work. I'm not addicted, Sarah. It's just a bit of fun.'

'Fun? You think it's fun? Oh, yeah, this is hilarious. And what about Tobias? Is it fun for him? I could weep for him. God knows what he's been through, pushed around from pillar to post, used as a drug donkey…'

'Mule.'

'What?' She frowned.

'It's drugs mule, not donkey.'

She threw a pod into the washing machine and slammed the door shut with her knee, clicking the button to switch it on. 'I don't care what it's called,' she said walking towards the hall. 'It's bloody disgusting and you need to do something about it.' At the door she turned back. 'Something else for you to think about.' He glanced up at her, his eyes clouded with tiredness. 'Mary said a child was murdered here, she thinks a little girl. Her body was found in the garden.'

'You're kidding.' She shook her head. 'Nope. Still want to stay here? I'm beginning to think buying this place is the biggest mistake we've ever made.'

Sarah went upstairs and popped her head around Tobias's door. He'd kicked off his duvet—its cover decorated with Thomas the Tank engine—and it had slid onto the floor in a heap. His face was pale but relaxed, and his dark brown curls were stuck to his forehead. A sudden surge of a need to protect him went through her making her stomach roll. It startled her and she released an involuntary gasp. Tobias stirred, flinging his arm up over his head. His eyes opened and he stared unseeing into the darkness until his eyelids fluttered and closed again, his eyelashes dark shadows against his pale cheeks. Sarah slowly released the breath she was holding. If Tobias woke before his elephant had been washed and the stitching repaired he would never settle. As ragged and old as it was the patchwork elephant had been the only constant in his life, and now they'd discovered even this innocent looking toy had been tainted by his mother's neglect. Sarah had deliberately not washed it even though it was in desperate need of it, because she thought washing it would have changed its colour and smell and it would have upset Tobias because he was used to his elephant being the way it was, a comfort in spite of the odour and dirt. Now she wished she'd taken it away and washed it and they would have discovered what Yelena had hidden inside it way before now. Sarah suddenly went hot when she realised Tobias had taken the elephant to school with him. She closed her eyes when she thought of what might have happened if the stitching had split and the sachets of cocaine had fallen out in front of the teachers and other children.

'This is a nightmare,' she said under her breath as she turned away and went into the bathroom. She ran a bath, absent-mindedly swishing bath oil through the water as she sat on the edge. She watched the scented lilac bubbles fill the bath and rise up to the edge. The house felt cold and the chill had seeped into her bones. Her knees and elbows hurt and she shivered, wondering if the heating had gone off. A hot bath was her favourite way of getting warm again and she couldn't wait to slide in. Clouds of steam filled the bathroom, and as she got into the bath she heard the bathroom door open. She took a breath and shook her head, expecting Dan to slide into the bath with her, offering to soap her back, placating her, trying to persuade her taking cocaine was just a recreational thing and nothing to get hung up about, and she was the one out of step. 'I need some time, Dan,' she said without turning to face him. 'Give me some space. We'll talk later.' He didn't reply and she turned around. 'Dan?' The steam cleared a little. She was completely alone.

The bathroom door was slightly open, so she got out of the bath tutting and closed it, pushing against it with her knee to make sure it was shut. Frowning, she climbed back into the bath and slipped her shoulders under the scented water. She closed her eyes and let her head fall back, allowing the hot water to soothe her tense muscles and warm her aching joints. The heat calmed her nerves and she smiled to herself. Pure luxury. After a few minutes she opened her eyes and sat up, reaching for a sponge and soap from the glass shelf. A feeling of not being alone suddenly made her skin chill. A shiver went through her and she pulled her right shoulder up to her ear. It was as though someone was watching her and she turned her head to look over her shoulder.

In the darkness of the landing and through the decorative glass of the bathroom door there was a face, the motionless grey outline softened to opaqueness by the etching on the glass and the steam from the bath. The eyes were dark shadowy pools with indistinct edges in a flat grey expanse. There was a dark indentation just above the chin, pulled into what looked like a wide grin. 'Honestly,' she said under her breath. 'Like I need this now.' She squeezed the sponge, lathering up the soap. 'You're so not funny, Dan, and I'm not in the mood!' she called out, looking across to the door. 'Dan, it's not funny. Grow up.' She waited for him to burst in through the door, to make like a gorilla as he'd done in the past, arms waving in the air, a funny walk to make her laugh when they'd fallen out, but the door remained closed. She huffed with annoyance and her frustration got the better of her.

'Can I not even have a bath in peace?'

Sarah washed at her leisure, determined to take her time. After half an hour had passed she stepped out of the bath, and wrapping a towel around her glanced towards the door. The face had disappeared. She went out onto the landing which was in darkness. Tobias's door was as she'd left it, slightly open, so she peeked in. He was fast asleep, turned on to his side, his breathing soft and regular. Backing away from his room she looked over the banisters on the galleried landing, then walked to the top of the stairs. The television was turned down low, the voice of someone commentating the football match Dan was watching filtering up to her. She padded down the stairs leaving wet footprints on the wooden treads and went into the living room. Dan was stretched out on the sofa. He looked up when she sat on the chair opposite, and attempted a smile. When she didn't return it he raised his eyebrows and pulled a face, turning his gaze back to the television.

'Was it you just now?'

'Was what me just now?' He answered without looking at her.

'Looking through the glass panel in the bathroom door and pulling faces?'

He shifted position and smiled. 'Why would I do that?'

'Sometimes you mess about, y'know, when we've had a disagreement.'

He glanced at her. 'I get the feeling you're not in the mood for messing about, Sarah. Not with me, anyway.' He looked back at the television, glancing at her again when she didn't say anything. 'It wasn't me,' he said, shaking his head. 'I've been watching the footie for the last half hour. Maybe it was Tobias looking for you.'

'He's fast asleep, hasn't woken since you put him to bed.'

He shrugged and laughed. 'So, who was it?'

She bit her lip and thought hard about what she should say next. This was something she didn't want to share with Dan. More secrets. More things hidden. There was something there…on the landing. She'd seen it with her own eyes.

Something…

Someone…

'It was probably nothing.'

Dan smiled and nodded. 'Yep, probably nothing.'

Slaughter's Wood
15th December 1999
13

She made a plan to walk as far as the river, and if there was no sign of him she'd give up and go home. If her mum and dad lost it with her so be it. It wasn't really her fault Aaron had gone walkabout. They knew what he was like. Maybe they should have tied him up before they left for the pub so he couldn't go anywhere, like they'd threatened before.

The tumultuous sound of the river met her before she could see it. It was running fast, and Lacey hated the gurgling, rushing sound it made as the muddy, detritus laden water swept over rocks and into little gullies carved out by the strength of the surge. From where she stood on the bank, the top secret den they'd built with fallen branches last summer was visible on the opposite bank. It was big enough to take all of them; Lacey, Aaron and four of their friends. But not Annette. Annette had Ryan. She couldn't have everything.

The den was in the middle of a copse in front of The Big House. They called it, "The Big House," because it was bigger than any of the other houses on or near the estate, and you could only get to it by going through the wood and crossing the Rickety Rackety Bridge over the river. It was their secret. During the summer you would know where it was only if you were part of their inner circle, and in the winter people didn't venture so far because it was so boggy underfoot. Lacey, Aaron, and their friends had sworn an oath by spitting on the palms of their hands and pressing them together, swearing they wouldn't tell anyone it was there, or talk about it with anyone who was not part of their group. It was their place.

This is where Aaron will be, she thought, chastising herself for not thinking of it earlier, but she'd have to cross the Rickety Rackety Bridge over the surging river that sounded like a monster that had left its cave. The bridge had gaps where broken wooden slats had fallen into the river and some of the handrail had rotted away. Lacey wished with all her heart she didn't have to go across, but she had to find Aaron. Beginning a count to five like they always did when they were daring each other to cross, she ran swiftly over the bridge, holding her breath and not releasing it until safely on the other side. Her heart began to beat faster as she made her way into the copse then across to the den where she knocked three times on one of the branches, saying the password, 'McDonalds'. She bent down, peering through the gaps in the branches and smiled broadly. Aaron was inside, his bright blue fleece giving him away.

'Aaron,' she said in a singsong voice. 'I know you're in there. I…can…see…you...' She said the password again, louder this time. 'McDonalds.' He didn't answer. He was meant to say the return password, "Happy Meal". 'Aaron!'

Sinking to her haunches she crawled on her hands and knees through the front entrance, mud and soggy leaves sticking to her bare legs. Aaron was leaning against the branches at the back of the den, looking straight at her, his legs out in front of him. His hair and face were plastered with mud, as if he was in camouflage.

'I knew you'd be in here. Why didn't you say Happy Meal? You know you're meant to. If you don't do what you're meant to do, we'll have to kick you out of the club. Everyone has to say the return password.'

Aaron's stare didn't waver. His blue eyes were glassy and unblinking as blood bubbled out of his ear and ran down his neck, soaking his fleece and dropping onto pale, cold hands, resting in his lap.

'Aaron,' Lacey said in a whisper, her voice wobbling as she reached out to touch him. 'I think you've cut yourself.'

April 2019
14

The huge wooden staircase was like no staircase she'd ever seen before, beautifully carved and depicting trees of the forest, grapevines and birds in flight, the wings burnished with gilding. The polished oak handrail was wide enough for someone to sit on and slide down to the depths. The walls were deep red, and when she looked above her head her eyes widened with wonder at the highly ornamented ceiling swathed with gilded filigree like an oriental temple. She lowered her eyes and observed what was in front of her, feeling compelled to follow the staircase down to its end. Her instinct screamed at her to turn back. She stopped for a moment, determined to swallow her fear, pushing it to the very centre of her, grasping with the utmost clarity the force telling her she must continue. Shivering, her coat was no barrier to the increasing cold and she pulled it tighter around her and took another step down. The further down the staircase she moved the colder the air around her became, until her hand became stuck to the handrail where clumps of ice had fused her skin to the wood. She tried to pull her hand away, grabbed her arm with her other hand to give her more traction, but still the ice wouldn't release her.

A scream from below her startled her. It resonated through the air and bounced off every wall. He was hurting, and as his protector she was the only one who could stop the pain. With one last pull she wrenched her hand from out of the ice. Blood poured from her palm, staining the ice and falling like a cascade onto the step where she stood holding her wrist with her other hand and staring at the blood. Another scream followed the first and she began to run down the steps, slipping and sliding, round and round and round the spiral staircase until she reached the bottom where she slithered and tumbled, reaching out for the handrail to prevent herself from falling. Her hands were ice, her fingers like pointed icicles and she couldn't hold on. Her heart quivered in her chest. She knew what the outcome would be as the fight went out of her, and she sank into the black hole screaming his name, 'Tobias!'

She woke with a jolt. Dan was still sleeping, his snoring like gentle waves running back and forth across tiny stones on a beach. She rolled her eyes with relief, thankful she hadn't said Tobias's name out loud. Reaching for her mobile from her bedside table she held it under the duvet so as not to wake Dan and clicked it on. The battery had run out. Slipping it back on the table she turned onto her side, turning her pillow over and pulling the duvet across her shoulder, her eyes on Dan as the question she had wanted to ask him wouldn't allow her to sleep. What would you do if I'd had a child and kept it a secret from you for five years? There would have been little forgiveness. For you, things would be very different, she thought as she watched his chest rise and fall in unbroken rhythm. Your sleep hasn't been shattered. Terrifying nightmares haven't plagued you. It's all so different for you, you carry on your life as you did before. Nothing has really changed for you, your family, your job, your home, the tempo of your life carries on. There's been no condemnation of you, just acceptance, acceptance of your weaknesses in a kind of, "Oh, well, boys will be boys" way, and you've lost nothing.

She closed her eyes. In her heart she knew there was more to him than what had happened. It didn't define their relationship and their need for each other was irrefutable. He loved her she was certain. And she loved him. Still. Still and always.

Except...

Her eyes flicked open. She could just see the outline of Dan's face in the darkness, the curve of his chin and the way his hair curled at the nape of his neck. She wanted to wake him, to touch him, to run her hands over his body, to make love, have wild sex, to feel him inside her, on top of her with his mouth on hers, the weight of his body making her feel secure...and needed. The heavy, almost pitch-black darkness of their bedroom didn't stop her imagining his tanned skin against the pristine white Egyptian cotton bedding, the hipster designer stubble just close enough to a beard to be cool, and dark well-defined eyebrows framing soulful eyes fringed with thick lashes any woman would die for. She continued to observe him, then turned onto her other side pushing down the heat rising inside her body and closed her eyes. His image was framed behind her eyelids; good looking, charismatic, well educated...and a cheat.

'You're not in today, are you,' Dan asked her as he sipped his coffee. She shook her head. 'Why?'

'Marcus has closed the gallery for a couple of days. It's his father's funeral this afternoon.'

'Oh, right. You not going? I'd have thought he would have wanted you there.'

'It's family only. They know hundreds of people because of the gallery. Marcus and his sister were worried it would turn into a sort of crazy parade. He said they just wanted it quiet. It's what his father wanted apparently.'

'Do you have plans for today?' he said lightly.

She glanced up at him wondering if she should agree if he suggested they went out for the day. Agreeing would seem like she consented to everything, and she so didn't, but another part of her wanted things to get back to the way they were. Like they used to be. Before. She tucked her hair behind her ear, waiting for him to suggest something. 'No, no plans.'

'So, it's okay with you if I go into work? I'm sorry, Sarah, I really need to go in today. Jed and the bosses are making noises about the time I've taken off. I've been working almost part-time for weeks and they won't put up with it for much longer.'

'What about Tobias?'

Dan went into the hall and took his jacket off the stand, wrapping a scarf around his neck. Sarah noticed his briefcase was already on standby on the bottom step of the staircase, ready and waiting for his return to the city. 'Could you sort him out today? You know he loves you to take him to school. I'll make some enquiries about childcare for before and after school. I could take him in the morning before work, and maybe you could pick him up in the evenings? You finish before me, don't you? We could share it. For now. Until... What do you think?'

She put Tobias's bowl of cereal in front of him and rubbed her hand across his head as he sat at the island. He looked up at her, his way of saying thank you. 'I think I don't have a choice. A fait accompli, you might say.'

'I'm doing the best I can, Sarah.' He lowered his eyelids for a few moments to give him pause before looking back at her. 'I've taken time off to be with him, even though he'd rather be with you.' He put his case down and leant against the doorframe. 'Is this going to work?'

'It depends.'

'On what?'

'On whether there are going to be any more surprises, y'know, a one-night stand and a child one day, snorting cocaine the next. Is there anything else I should know about?'

He pursed his lips and lowered his eyes. When he looked up at her she was still staring at him, her gaze steady and accusatory. 'I don't blame you for being angry,' he said quietly.

'Well good, because I am. I'm as angry as hell, and I don't think you've got anything to blame *me* for, do you?'

He picked up his briefcase. 'You know we can't carry on like this?' She shrugged and looked away. 'I'll see you tonight.'

April 2019
15

Sarah stood in the sloping garden, watching the river as it swirled and eddied under the bridge leaving pockets of frothing water by the banks. She wrapped her hands around her coffee cup and breathed in, smelling the pungent wet earth. April had brought with it the promise of new growth. Snowdrops planted around the trees danced in the increasing wind. Crocuses, hyacinths, primroses and violets pushed through the grass and she felt a surge of optimism, and remembered a quote from Charles Lamb, her university lecturer had once asked them to illustrate in one of their art classes. *"Here cometh April again, and as far as I can see the world hath more fools in it than ever."* Maybe it will be okay, she thought, if I can get my head around it all. Forgiveness is meant to be a wonderful thing. A redeeming thing. I just wish I could find it, and the courage to put it all behind me.

Her thoughts went to Eve who had told her in no uncertain terms she hadn't punished Dan enough. She sighed heavily. Maybe she hadn't, but any punishment she meted out wouldn't change anything. She believed him when he said he loved her, but the sense of betrayal and mistrust made her stomach churn and it was a barrier she couldn't get across. Would she ever trust Dan again, enough for her to stay and build a future with him and Tobias? A few drops of rain fell on her hand and she looked skywards. The apocryphal April showers had become a reality with sudden bursts of heavy rainfall cleansing the air and swelling the river. The speed of the running water had increased by the day and she was mesmerised by the whirlpool the rushing water had created between the garden and the bank on the opposite side edging the forest. She turned her head towards the mill. Through the French windows she could see Tobias playing with his Lego, doubting anyone would ever know whether he was happy or sad. His facial expression for either emotion was the same; detached from everything around him, a steady gaze giving nothing away.

She turned back to the river. Newton's Mill was such a lovely place, but there was something melancholy about it, an atmosphere of sadness suspended like a haze across the garden and towards the river, snaking around the property like a faded ribbon, masking the hopefulness of the promised spring flowers with a pall of despondency. More raindrops fell but she stood her ground, watching the increasing rain hitting the water like stones thrown into a pool until the downpour and the fading light forced her inside. She went through the French windows, removed her boots and her parka, and shook the rain from it before closing the doors. Tobias continued to play with his Lego and didn't look up.

'It's nearly time for dinner, Tobias. Daddy won't be home until later so you and I can have whatever we want. How does pizza sound?' He nodded without looking at her. She hung her coat in the hall and threw her boots into the cupboard under the stairs. 'Do you want to help me?' she asked him, poking her head around the door. He shook his head and carried on playing.

'I'll get on with it shall I?' she said, smiling to herself.

They ate in the living room while watching television. If they'd eaten in the dining room it would have been a meal eaten in silence, so while Dan wasn't there Sarah decided to relax the unwritten rule of only eating at the table. She asked Tobias about school while they ate, what he'd done and whether he had enjoyed it. Each inquiry was answered by either a nod, or a shake of the head. Occasionally, he would say yes or no, but nothing more.

Sarah pulled out her phone. Eight o'clock and Dan still hadn't arrived. He usually came through the door at seven. Her phone buzzed.

'You okay?'

'Er, yeah. Um, I'm not going to make it back tonight.'

'Why?'

'We've got an early breakfast meeting tomorrow and I can't miss it, I've missed too many already. I have to be there or I can see them having me out on my ear.'

Sarah felt a thread of anger uncoil in her chest. She took a breath to steady her voice, to keep it reasonable and controlled. 'What's happening with Tobias? Did you manage to organise some childcare for him?'

'I'm so sorry, Sarah, I just haven't had a chance to do anything about it today. It's been hell on wheels. Something's going down here and I need to have my head on straight.'

'I see.'

'Aren't you off again tomorrow?'

'You know I am.'

'Sweetheart, I know it's a lot to ask...but could you sort him out tomorrow? I promise I'll deal with the childcare thing when our meeting is over. I might even be able to come home a bit earlier tomorrow and take you and Tobes out for afternoon tea.' As Dan spoke Sarah's hand gripped her phone tighter, resentment flooding her. She realised her hand was shaking so swapped the phone to her left ear. 'Are you there, Sarah?'

'Yeah, I'm here. What if I'd been working tomorrow? What would you have done?'

She knew his body had stiffened because she had thrown a problem in his path. She could hear it in his voice. 'I don't know what you want me to do. Shall I give up my job? What do you think would happen if I did? There'd be no beautiful mill, no decent lifestyle. Give me a break, Sarah, for Christ's sake.'

'Why didn't you organise childcare before now? And what about his counselling? Have you actually sorted anything out for him? He needs an educational statement and he's not going to get it unless you do something about it. I can't. I'm not his mum, am I? They're hardly going to listen to me. You're a little late to the party, Dan.'

'Y'know what, I haven't got time for this.'

'Now why doesn't it surprise me?' She ended the call and saw his image fade from the screen.

'Saha?'

Tobias stood at the door holding the elephant, his eyes brimming with tears. 'It's okay. You're alright,' she said wrapping her arms around him and burying her face in his soft, newly washed hair. He smelt of bubble bath, softly powdery and comforting.

'The boy had cry on his face.'

'What did you say?' she asked him.

'The boy…the boy had cry on his face.'

'Cry? What do you mean, cry?'

He raised his hand and drew a finger down her cheek. 'Cry.'

'Tears. You mean tears.' He nodded and she got to her feet, reaching for his hand. 'Where's the boy, Tobias?'

'The boy drawed a picture.'

'Did he? I'd love to see it. Do you want to show me?'

He pulled her towards the stairs and led her up to the landing. He stopped when he got to his bedroom door, let go of her hand and pointed into the room where she hesitated. Sarah laughed to convince herself there couldn't be anything there. I'm a grown up and this is ridiculous. There's nothing to be frightened of. Standing by Tobias's door, she took a deep breath and went in to the bedroom, switching on the light. On his bed were sheets of paper and crayons scattered across the duvet. Sarah went towards the bed and picked up one of the sheets. Drawn with skilled deftness was the portrait of a girl with brown bobbed hair clipped to the side of her forehead. Her eyes were green, like jade. Sarah sank down on the bed and beckoned Tobias to her, putting her arm around him.

'Did you do this, sweetie?' He shook his head. 'Are you sure?' He didn't reply, but got into bed, tucked the elephant under his arm and closed his eyes. Sarah got up and pulled the duvet over his shoulders, brushing his hair away from his face. She stood by his bed, the drawing in her hand, and watched him for a moment. He was such a little thing. A pang of conscience shot through her over her complaint to Dan about taking care of him. 'It's not you, Tobias,' she whispered. 'It's not because of you. It's because they've let you down and I know what it's like to be let down by the ones who should have put you first. I won't let it happen to you.' She bent and kissed him and switched off the light, closing the door behind her.

She wasn't sure what woke her. For a few moments she lay quite still, staring out into the darkness, waiting with breath held, wondering if Tobias had called out in his sleep. There was nothing, no sound from his room, no light apart from the glow from a new moon squeezing through the gap in the curtains.

Then she heard it, a low rumble, like thunder reverberating through the house. Sarah sat up. Even in the short time they'd lived at the mill she had come to know its night time sounds, the gnarled branch of an ancient apple tree scraping across the bedroom window, the grating of floorboards as they swelled against each other in the damp weather, the tread on the staircase, five steps up, ten steps down that creaked whenever anyone stood on it, but the sound she had heard was different and it seemed to come from underneath the mill. She waited, praying she wouldn't hear it again, but even before she'd finished her thought, there it was. Grabbing her phone from the bedside table she padded along the galleried landing to Tobias's room, putting on her bathrobe as she went. Opening the door as gently as she could she peeped around it, switching on the torch from her phone and holding it up in front of her so she could see into the bedroom. The slim beam made dark shadows in the curvature of the vaulted ceiling, grey silhouettes moving around the room as the strand of light travelled across each wall. She resisted shining it too close to the bed for fear of waking him, but as the shadow moved away her breath caught up in her throat. His bed was empty. 'Tobias,' she said softly. 'Tobias are you in here?' She flicked the light switch but no expected flood of light filled the room. Keeping the torch trained on Tobias's bed she stepped inside, circling the beam around the room. There was no sign of him except his last action before leaving his bedroom; his discarded duvet in a crumpled heap by the side of his bed. She turned and padded down the landing to the top of the stairs where she looked over the bannisters into the dark hall. As her foot reached the top step a sharp grating sound rose up from underneath the mill, jarring the walls and floor like an earthquake. Her skin prickled with fear as she held on to the handrail. 'Tobias,' she cried out. 'Tobias, answer me! Come to the stairs, sweetheart. Come to the bottom of the stairs so I can see you.' The grating juddering stopped, and she ran down the stairs calling his name. 'Tobias! Tobias! Where are you?'

She went from room to room, trying the lights and calling his name, praying she would find him playing with his Lego or in the kitchen eating biscuits, but it was as though he had been spirited away. 'Jesus,' she cried, tears making her voice break. 'Jesus, where is he?' She ran to the front door and pulled it. It was still locked and she breathed a sigh of relief. Out of the corner of her eye a shaft of pale moonlight shone through the door of the utility room. The door was open. Sarah knew she'd closed it before going to bed. They always closed it. She…always closed it. She didn't like the basement and couldn't bear the thought of it being so close, especially at night. Leaving the door open meant the gloomy and unfamiliar space was nearer to them. The rumbling sound started up again, shaking the floor and walls, the noise so overwhelmingly loud it shook her to her centre. She pushed the door open, gasping when she saw the old door to the basement was unlocked and wide open. 'Please, God,' she whispered. 'Please don't let him be down there.'

The top of the concrete steps was just visible and her blood pulsed in her ears as she went towards it. The noise from underneath her feet was horrendous, the open door allowing the rumbling to hit her with full force juddering her teeth, yet beneath the reverberation she could hear the rush of running water, hissing and gurgling, slapping against the side of the house. Her eyes widened when she realised where the noise was coming from. 'It's the wheel,' she said under her breath. 'Oh my God, it's moving.'

The beam from her phone was bright enough for her to make her way down the steps holding onto the damp walls for support, the skin on the palm of her hand picking up flakes of old paint as she felt her way down. As she got to the curve in the steps the noise was unbearable. The mill's gear lever had been pushed forward causing the waterwheel to turn, but it wasn't this that made her cry out. Tobias was sitting on the basement floor, his hands and face covered in blood, the mutilated body of a fox next to him. Sarah blinked in the poor light. She was at odds with herself, thinking she was going mad, questioning whether what she was seeing was real or imagined. Feeling her way across the wall she continued down the steps to the basement floor, shining the torch beam towards Tobias. He looked up at her, his eyes impassive.

'Tobias,' she whispered. The noise and the juddering of the waterwheel grated on her senses and it suddenly occurred to her Tobias hated loud noises yet seemed oblivious to the sickening grating of the waterwheel. She put her phone on the bottom step and made her way towards the huge wooden lever. Standing behind it she grabbed it with both hands, struggling to pull it towards her. It was so encrusted with rust it wouldn't budge. She wrapped her leg around it, then the other, using all her weight. The lever slowly began to fall towards her and the motion of the waterwheel started to slow, the wood and metal wheel creaking under its own weight, grinding blade by blade against the rusty axle as it gradually came to a halt. In the silence following the shuddering cacophony, all she could hear was her own breathing as she wiped orange rust from her hands down the sides of her bathrobe.

Tobias was gently stroking the fox's fur and murmuring something under his breath. The fox had been slit down its stomach, its entrails spilled and laid out on the floor of the basement. Sarah's heart lurched when she noticed the knife at his side. It was one of the carving knives from the block in the kitchen.

'Did you take a knife, Tobias? From the kitchen?' He shook his head without looking at her and she put a gentle hand on his arm. 'We need to go,' she said quietly.

'Doggy's sleeping,' he said. 'The boy said he's sleeping.'

'Yes, he's asleep,' she said, swallowing down the acid bile rising in her throat at the horror in front of her. 'We need to go or we might wake him.' He got up and reached for her hand and she recoiled when she saw the blood covering his fingers. Reluctantly wrapping her fingers around his hand she retrieved her phone from the bottom step and led him up to the house. When they got to the door she pushed Tobias gently into the utility room and locked the door behind them, turning it with a sharp click. Tobias watched her as she placed the key back in the old Huntley and Palmers biscuit tin where they'd first found it, pushing it on to a high shelf she knew he couldn't reach, on automatic pilot, knowing what she had to do without thinking. Grasping his hand she led him upstairs and took him into the bathroom where she removed his blood soaked pyjamas. He got into the bath without question, saying nothing as his hair was washed and his body soaped until Sarah was sure all traces of the fox's blood were gone. Wrapping him in a towel, she carried him into his bedroom, dressed him in clean pyjamas and put him to bed.

Downstairs she perched on the edge of the sofa as though she was in a waiting room. Silent tears came, running down her cheeks in rivulets and dropping off her chin. Looking down at herself she grimaced when she realised her robe was covered in rust and blood, so she took it off, flinging it away from her across the floor and grabbing a throw to put around her shoulders. She thought of Tobias, a little boy with life challenges which would make his life both wonderful and tragic—wonderful when he achieved and the world opened up to him, tragic when those achievements were unavoidably limited—sitting innocently on a filthy basement floor next to a knife and a dead fox, with the poor animal's blood on his face and hair and hands.

She remembered the look on his face and wondered if he would have it in him to kill an animal, and if he did, how? I can't say anything to you, she thought, because I don't know what to say. And if I ask you will you understand what I'm saying? Do I want to know you killed an animal because you thought it was okay? Her eyes closed and she rested her head against the back of the sofa.

Her eyes flicked open, picturing the waterwheel. There was no way Tobias could have pulled the lever to start the wheel turning. If a grown woman struggled to pull the lever into the off position because it was so rusted and old, how on earth would a child manage to start it up? It hadn't been touched for years. There was absolutely no way he could move it. She sat up, pushing her hair behind her ears, fully awake now and ready to engage with what was in her mind. When and how did he capture a fox, and why would he take a knife from the kitchen and kill it if he had? He loved animals, jumped up and down when they were on television and enjoyed watching the squirrels in the garden.

She pulled her knees up to her chin. Gradually a ribbon of consciousness wormed its way through the questions; a thread of understanding. He couldn't have started the waterwheel. And she couldn't see how at five years of age he could have caught a fox and put together a plan to kill it by stealing a knife from the kitchen. She put her head on her knees. What am I thinking? A quake of fear went through her chilling her to the bone. Perspiration ran from the nape of her neck down her spine. She pushed away the throw and began to pace the room. Nausea rose from her stomach to her throat and she heaved. She sat on her haunches, hanging on to the arm of the sofa for support waiting for her head to clear. When she felt calmer she stood by the window, looking out onto the garden and river, pressing her forehead against the cold glass and peering into the darkness. The answer to the question jostling for position with all the other questions in her mind since she'd found Tobias in the basement revealed itself.

Question: How did Tobias start the waterwheel, steal a knife from the kitchen, and capture and mutilate a fox?

Answer: He didn't.

'It was turned off at the main switch. The cables have been sheared and the fuses removed from the box.'

Sarah put her hands on her hips and frowned at the electrician. 'Sheared? What do you mean, sheared?'

'Well...it means...cut.' The young electrician had the grace to look embarrassed, looking down at his feet as he nervously shuffled them on the quarry tiles in the porch.

'Cut?' Sarah shifted her position, folding her arms and resting her weight on her other hip as she tried to compute what he'd said. 'Cut...as in...deliberately?' He nodded, and Sarah's face blanched.

He shrugged. 'A joke, maybe.'

'Right.' She pressed her lips together, thinking about the waterwheel and the dead fox in the basement. 'Not very funny though, is it?' He shook his head. 'Can it be fixed?'

'Yeah. Might take a while.'

'Can you do it now? We don't have any power and there's stuff I need to do. We take it for granted, don't we, electricity?'

He grinned. 'Everyone does.'

She went into the kitchen and heated some water on the hob. 'At least I can make a coffee,' she said out loud, shivering. The underfloor heating had gone off so Sarah had cleared the grates and lit fires in the hall and breakfast room. It had only taken the edge off the chill but it was better than nothing. There had been enough hot water left to give Tobias a shower before taking him to school, and she'd dropped him off with relief, thankful it was a school day. Sarah was still shaken after what had happened the night before and she wanted to get him out of the house. There was no way he'd been responsible for moving the waterwheel or killing the fox which meant someone else was. Shaking her head in disbelief it was almost impossible to get her head round it; someone had started the waterwheel and killed an animal in the basement of their home. And there was the knife. She hadn't noticed it was missing, but someone took it out of the block and used it to rip the animal apart. Did it mean the knife had only just been taken, or had it been gone for some time and it hadn't been noticed?

Slipping her mobile out of her back pocket she clicked it open and accessed Dan's number, clicked speed dial, changed her mind, and clicked, "End". She tapped the phone against her chin. I'll wait, she decided. After last night he might not take my call. I'll wait until he gets home, if he decides to come home.

Three hours later the electrician tapped on the porch window.

'All done,' he called through the open door.

Sarah went into the hall, smiling a smile she didn't mean. 'Difficult job?'

'Thorough job.'

'I'm sure you always do a thorough job. I wasn't quest...'

'No, I meant whoever turned off the electricity did a thorough job. The box was vandalised, main switch turned off, fuses removed...and this is the bonkers bit,' he said, frowning, getting into his subject. 'They must have used bolt cutters with insulated handles or worn insulated gloves to cut through the cables. They went to a lot of trouble to make sure there was no electricity in the place.'

Sarah's hand went to her throat and she tried to smile. 'Right, well, thanks for fixing it. What's the damage?'

'Three hundred I'm afraid.'

'For connecting some cables?'

'Well, there's the call out charge, the emergency charge, and also the new cables and the fuses. It wasn't an easy job.'

She blew out a breath. 'I'm in the wrong job. Have you got a credit card machine?'

'No cash?'

'You want cash?'

'If you've got it. It's three fifty with a credit card. Costs, y'see. I'd prefer the cash.'

'Mm,' Sarah said under her breath as she went to the safe. 'I bet you would.'

'So, there's a dead fox in the basement?'

Sarah nodded. 'Yes.'

'And you're saying Tobias found it. In the middle of the night.'

'Yes.'

'And someone cut the electricity and started the waterwheel.'

'Yes.'

Dan stared at her. 'You'd better show me.' He flicked the switch at the top of the stairs and the basement was bathed in yellow light. He turned and looked at her questioningly.

'I had it fixed.'

'That was quick.'

She shrugged. 'He charged an arm and a leg because it was an emergency. Perhaps he didn't have much work on.'

They went down the steps into the basement, Dan leading. 'So where is it?'

Sarah stepped down to the basement floor. It was clean, no blood, no knife, and no mutilated body of a fox. 'But it was here.'

He exhaled. 'Well, it's not here now.'

'I…I don't understand. There was blood everywhere. Tobias was covered in it. I had to give him a bath in the middle of the night.' She looked around the floor. 'And where's the knife?'

'What knife?'

'It was one of our knives from the knife block in the kitchen. I recognised the handle. It was what he used…to kill the fox, slashed it right down the middle. Its guts were all over the floor.'

'When you say he, who do you mean?'

She glanced at him, her mind in turmoil. 'I…I don't know. How should I know?'

'You don't meant Tobias, do you?'

'No of course not. He couldn't have done it.'

'Why not?'

'Someone started the waterwheel. He wouldn't have had the strength to push the lever for one thing. I struggled to pull the lever back to stop it. And how would he have caught a fox and killed it in such a terrible way.'

Dan shoved his hands in his jeans pockets and nodded. 'And cleaned up afterwards.'

Catching the edge to his voice her eyes widened. 'You don't believe me, do you?'

He shuffled his feet and looked uncomfortable. 'I'm not saying that.'

'So, what are you saying?'

'The fox isn't here, Sarah. The knife isn't here. The electricity is fine.'

'I told you, I had it fixed this morning.'

'Who fixed it?'

'I don't know…a young guy. It was a card he must have pushed through the door.'

'And the receipt? How much was it?'

'Three hundred quid. As I said, an emergency callout. It's why it was so expensive. And there was no receipt. He wanted cash…off the books I imagine. It's what people do, isn't it?' She watched his face. 'It was deliberate. Someone removed the fuses and cut the ca…'

'Where's the card?'

She rolled her eyes and sighed. 'He took it with him. He said they were expensive to have printed and did I mind if he took it. I've got to admit they were a bit OTT for an electrician. All glitter and gilt. I've got his number in my phone.' Dan looked intently at her and she caught the look. 'For Christ's sake, Dan. Do you think I'm making it up?'

'I'm not saying you made it up, Sarah, but I know what happens when you're stressed about something, and,' he shrugged and looked apologetic, 'the last few weeks haven't exactly been easy have they?' He made to move towards her, but she backed away and sat on the bottom step, hardly able to believe what he was suggesting. He was saying she'd either dreamt what had happened or imagined it. 'I know you've been having nightmares lately. And you're so restless when you're sleeping. Are you dreaming every night?'

She turned away and didn't answer until something occurred to her. 'The knife. The knife was down here.'

He sank to his haunches in front of her and reached for her hand, rubbing her fingers in between his and kissing the palm like he always did. 'We'll go and check upstairs, see if it's missing, then we'll pick up Tobes from school and take him out for tea. What d'you say?'

Sarah could have kicked herself, wishing she'd checked the knife block before telling him what had happened, but she'd expected it to be missing, certain the knife would be on the basement floor in a pool of blood. She stared into Dan's eyes searching for the man she'd fallen in love with. Are you still there, she wondered? Are you patronising me? *Please be there. I need you.* He was smiling. She knew the smile, it was a smile she loved, but she wasn't sure…she just wasn't sure. Her heart dropped when she understood. You actually think I dreamt all this, don't you? After everything that's happened, after all you've done, it's become my problem. She wanted to tell him if she was stressed it was because of him, but she simply agreed. 'Sounds great.'

The knife was in the block.

'It's there.'

She was stunned. 'I…I don't understand.' Her eyes met his. 'It did happen Dan. I promise you. Ask Tobias.'

'No.'

A sob caught in her throat. 'What? Why? Don't you want to know what happened?'

'I do know. I know you're traumatised, and I know when you get stressed you have nightmares and they're so real you believe they happened. I don't want you to feel bad, but I'm not going to cause Tobias any more stress than he's already had. You said yourself he's had a horrible time. Do you think I want to ask him about a dead fox that had its guts pulled out? It'll scare him.'

'He said the other boy told him it was asleep.'

Dan threw up his hands. 'Sarah! Stop this! There is no other boy, and there's no fucking fox.'

'I...didn't...dream it.'

'Okay,' He looked around the kitchen. 'Where are the clothes you and Tobias were wearing? If what you said is true they'll be covered in blood.'

As soon as the electricity had been reinstated she'd thrown them into the washing machine, desperate to get rid of the blood and the smell. Closing her eyes, she damned herself for her efficiency. 'They're in the dryer.'

He nodded and raised his eyebrows. 'I don't know what to say except we need to get going. Tobias comes out of school in fifteen minutes and we need to be there. Do you still want to take him out for tea?' She gave a small nod and his expression darkened. 'Don't say anything to him, Sarah. He's got enough to deal with.'

'What about the electrician,' she said in a small voice. 'Can't we phone him? He'll confirm what I'm saying about the electricity. And maybe we should call the police. Someone broke in here.'

'I don't care about the electricity. Did he go into the basement? Did he see the dead fox?' She stared at him and shook her head. He went into the hall and grabbed his jacket from the peg, looking worried. 'So there's not really much point is there?'

She didn't move and he went back into the kitchen, putting his arms around her and hugging her, resting his chin on top of her head. 'Let's forget about it, Sarah. Please. Let's take Tobias for a lovely tea and be a family. What d'you say?' She laid her head against his chest and closed her eyes. He didn't believe her. He thought she'd lost the plot, traumatised by Tobias's arrival and what had happened with Yelena. There was no way she could convince him about the night before.

There was only Tobias. Only Tobias knew the truth.

She tiptoed down the stairs in the dark after waiting until Dan was snoring before making her move, willing herself to stay awake, listening for the tell-tale signs of someone finally submitting to sleep. Picking up her slippers from the floor and unhooking her dressing gown from the back of the door she looked across to the bed and the motionless mound that was Dan. There was something for her to do, something to put her mind at rest. Slipping quietly out of the room she gently closed the door enough to dull any sound from the rest of the house, but not enough for it to click on the latch.

Her feet made a soft plopping sound on the galleried landing and down the stairs. The dying embers from the open fire crackled and spat, sending flashes of orange into the hall. The lingering flames intermittently illuminated the grandfather clock standing steadfastly against the wall under the stairs and the candlesticks on the mantelpiece, sending long weirdly-shaped shadows across the floor and ceiling. She derived some comfort from the warmth, but her deep apprehension of where she was going gave her a dry mouth and a rolling stomach.

Her hand went into her dressing gown pocket to retrieve her mobile phone. She'd turned down the sound and left it in the pocket before getting into bed because she knew she'd need it to carry out her plan. Flicking on the torch she made her way across the hall and into the kitchen. The utility room door was shut as always so she opened it and went through, closing the door behind her. Reaching up to the top of the cupboard she found the biscuit tin, took out the key to the basement and opened the door. The beam from the torch guided her down the steps as she held onto the dank wall, feeling the cold mildew sliding under her fingers. She shuddered at the slimy sensation but tried to concentrate on her footing. If she fell down the stone steps she'd probably get hurt at the very least, at worst Dan would want to know what on earth she was doing creeping about the basement in the dead of night, fuelling his concerns about her.

At the bottom her foot came to rest on something spongy making it uneven underfoot. Shining her torch across the floor she cried out in horror when she realised what was beneath her feet. Her phone slipped out of her hand as she fell back against the steps, clattering to the floor and breaking up against the bottom step. 'Shit,' she cried, pulling her dressing gown up to her waist and going gingerly back up the steps on her hands and knees. 'Shit, shit, shit,' she cursed under her breath. When she got to the basement door she stopped and switched on the light, turning on the top step to look down to the floor. What she saw below her took her breath away.

Dozens of dead magpies were piled up around the waterwheel lever and against the walls. Blood oozed from their necks because each one had been decapitated, and maggots were beginning to multiply in the wounds. She put her hand across her mouth to stop herself from crying out, thinking maybe Dan had been right when he said she'd dreamt or imagined the dead fox. He'd been patronising about her claims, patting her down as though she were a child to be placated. She'd come down to the basement to check for evidence. It had been her plan to find what she needed to prove the mutilated fox had been there, to uncover any remnants of the blood that had covered the floor in a red sticky mess, determined to find something, anything, to prove she hadn't imagined or dreamt it. Now she couldn't because what was on the basement floor was far worse.

She wanted to see if the door leading into the garden was locked, so retraced her way down the steps, holding onto the wall with both hands. At the bottom she picked her way through the now stiff black and white bodies to try the handle expecting it to be unlocked, but it wasn't. She frowned. Someone must have got into the basement to do all of this. How could it be locked? They had the only key other and she knew where it was...on Dan's keyring. Pivoting on her toes, trying not to touch any of the birds and leaning against the wall as she went, she glimpsed her phone lying in three pieces at the bottom of the stone steps and stooped to pick them up, her eyes on the grizzly scene across the floor. Back at the top of the steps she flicked off the light and went into the utility room, shutting the door behind her. Taking the key from her pocket she locked the door and replaced it in the biscuit tin, sliding it on top of the cupboard and went into the kitchen, shutting the door as she always did, her nightly routine.

After wiping the pieces of phone on kitchen paper she washed her hands at the sink and took the pieces over to the window, not wanting to switch on the lamps over the island which would light up the garden. The moon shone like an orb in a cloudless sky sending a shaft of light through the window, illuminating the pieces enough for her to see them. The screen was smashed, but when she fixed the battery in to the casing and replaced the back, the phone switched on. It wasn't perfect but good enough for her to use. A headache had settled over her eyes and she rubbed them trying to work out what to do next. I could wake Dan now and tell him what's in the basement, but if they've disappeared by the time we get down there he'll take control. He'll want me to see someone, convince me I'm distressed by what's happened and expect me to have treatment. I won't do it. I know what I saw and I didn't imagine it. There are dead magpies in the basement and I daren't tell him. We used to have faith in each other. We were each other's best friend, but now...now we seem to be suspicious of each other, like people who don't know each other enough to trust each other. Nothing is the same as it was and I don't know if I can count on Dan to be on my side. I always assumed he would be. Maybe this is how the problem developed. I assumed he would always be there for me because I never gave him reason not to be. I was wrong, so very wrong. Maybe I was lulled into believing we had the perfect relationship when all the time he was living a life so very different from the one I thought we had.

And I can't be sure he'll believe me when I tell him what's happening here, because... *something* is happening here, I'm sure of it. He won't believe me because deep down, he doesn't want to. Dan's life has always gone perfectly until now. And even though he has lied and made me question our life together I seem to be the one manifesting the fallout, the one who is out of step because he can't accept responsibility for his mistake and wants to pretend things are the same as they were and wants me to do the same.

I daren't tell him I know something isn't right in this place, that I'm convinced something very bad is happening here, to me, only to me, because not only do I not trust him to believe me, I'm not even sure I trust myself.

Slaughter's Wood
16th December 1999

17

Lacey stayed with him until morning. She laid down on the dry curled up leaves and the bits of twig they'd used for a floor in the den, and waited for him to say something. She shivered as she watched him in case he moved, her eyes on his face. He was Aaron, and yet…this was an Aaron she didn't know. Her family hadn't known a moment of peace since he could walk and talk because he was never still and never silent, and she knew he was still awake because his eyes were open and he was watching her as closely as she watched him. Occasionally she would whisper to him, 'Aaron. Aaron, this joke isn't funny. Please stop pretending. You're frightening me,' but Aaron hadn't answered. The blank expression on his face hadn't changed, not once. He just stared at her until she fell into a troubled sleep. Throughout the night she woke momentarily, had reached out to touch him. His hands were stone cold and she worried he wasn't warm enough, so she shuffled closer to him and lay next to him to warm him, laying her arm across his lap.

She was woken by someone dragging her out of the den by her arm. It hurt her and she cried out in shock. She saw her mum and dad standing outside the den, their faces pale, waxen, lips blue with shock, the sound of screaming; her mum falling to her knees in the mud, her hair like rats' tails as she opened her mouth allowing the sound to fall out of her face as if it would never stop. She'd put trembling hands over her ears, not comprehending what had happened, looking up at her dad pleadingly, hoping he would let her stand next to him until he pushed her away from him with such savagery, and staring at her with such hatred she could hardly draw breath. He called her a bitch, a jealous little cow. He said he hated her, would always hate her for what she'd done and he hoped someone would lock her up and throw away the key. And all the time, all the time when she needed someone, someone to tell her…she didn't know what she'd done.

They kept her in a strange place, the people who had taken her away, somewhere so unlike her house, so different to what she was used to she felt like an alien. Everything was hard, uncomfortable, the chairs were plastic, walls white; the room pristine and straight edged, and everywhere smelt of disinfectant. Grownups she didn't know with hard faces questioned her for hours and hours until the accusations came and she wanted to be sick and lie down on the floor so she could sleep. She wanted to go home. She wanted them to leave her alone.

They said she killed Aaron, had hit him with a branch over and over and over until he was dead. They asked her why, why had she killed her brother? Why did she hate him? Was she jealous of him? Had she planned it? She shook her head and said no; no she hadn't killed him, no she didn't hate him, but they weren't listening, wouldn't listen, their faces screwed up in anger as they pointed their fingers at her. When the grownups were talking to each other they kept saying the words, Lacey Murphy, child killer; child killing a child. Could it get any worse?

They asked her if she wanted to see her mum and dad and she said yes because she was desperate to see her mum, but through the glass in the door she saw her father shake his head, heard her mum say, 'Let me see her, Len. Please let me see her, she's my daughter,' and heard him shout at her, 'No way, no fucking way. She's nothing to do with us. We've got to bury our son because of her,' and a policeman in uniform struggled to restrain him, telling him he wasn't helping matters by shouting, and was he sure he didn't want to see her. Her dad looked through the glass with narrowed eyes and a sneer on his lips. 'Never. Never again.', and turned away. Her mum followed him compliantly without turning her head to look at her, and when she tried to get up to run after them the child liaison officer stopped her and said, 'No. You're not to leave this room, Lacey Murphy. The police aren't finished with you yet. Stay where you are. Stay right where you are.'

The City
May 2019
18

The coffee shop was nearly empty. A smartly dressed man wearing a grey trilby hat sat at a table in an alcove in the far corner, an elderly Schnauzer at his feet. Dan had pulled a grin when the old boy had ordered a Vienna. He pushed his finger into the whipped cream on top of the ultra-strong espresso and let the dog lick the cream from his finger. The man had ruffled the dog's head and sighed with pleasure, and the dog had looked up at him with complete love in his eyes.

A university student sat in the middle of the cafe occupying a table for four, an open laptop and a pile of books in front of him, a cappuccino cup rimmed with the last dregs of coffee-coloured froth by his hand. Dan watched from his place at the counter as a young waitress with flaming red hair and a short skirt and Doc Martens filled the student's cup from a pot after making sure the owner wasn't around. The student glanced up and winked at her and the waitress pulled a flirty smile and returned behind the counter.

Dan took a deep breath and shoved his hands in his pockets. He was late for work—deliberately—reluctant to face the day ahead. The waitress pushed a cappuccino towards him without making eye-contact.

'Three-fifty please.'

He searched the pocket of his jeans and found two two-pound coins. 'Keep the change.'

'Gee, thanks,' the waitress said under her breath. Dan rolled his eyes at her rudeness but couldn't be bothered to say anything. He pulled a chair out and sat with his elbows on the table and his back to the counter, staring out of the window, his eyes trained on the entrance of the building where Southgate-Torrance had their offices. He furrowed his brow, wondering how he would get through it all.

The impressive building with its facade of glass and chrome dissolved and Sarah's image replaced it. She was everything he had ever hoped for in a partner, warm, kind, loving…and so beautiful, though she had no idea how beautiful to him she was. It was what he loved about her. Whenever he told her she was beautiful her fingers would immediately go to her scar, like a reflex action. It wasn't just the way she looked. It was her quirkiness, the funny things she said, her wonderful intelligence and knowledge of her subject. He was proud of her, but...there was something he couldn't put his finger on, a trace of something insidious undermining the connection they had. And it wasn't just the mistakes he'd made. There was something else, a sense all wasn't right with her.

He hated what he'd done, disgusted with himself, not only for sleeping with someone else, but for lying. He was well aware his parents could be difficult. Coral in particular needed careful handling, but they'd raised him with good values; decency, trustworthiness and honesty. And yet...he'd broken every single one. He hadn't set out to have sex with another woman. He'd always enjoyed the trips to other countries, it was part of his job to liaise with foreign businesses, but in Prague it had gone horribly wrong. He'd got mind-numbingly drunk, couldn't even remember any of the evening and was unaware he wasn't alone in his hotel room until he'd rolled over and found Yelena next to him. It was one of the most surreal experiences he'd ever had, expecting to see Sarah's brown hair fanned out across the pillow, her gentle face relaxed in sleep, and instead find a blonde, her face exhibiting the faded remnants of the makeup she'd worn the night before. He'd been horrified and jumped out of bed to throw up in the en-suite. He'd sat on the cold tiled floor trying to get his head around it, showered and returned to the bedroom, hurriedly dressing.

To his shame he had asked her how much she wanted and demanded she get dressed and leave as soon as was humanly possible. He'd panicked, desperate to get her out of his room before anyone discovered them together. She'd pulled on her dress and left the room in a temper, and he'd wondered if anyone had realised she'd spent the night in his room. He'd hoped not. He'd just wanted to forget it, to push it to the back of his mind and pretend it hadn't happened.

Six weeks later he discovered he wasn't going to be allowed to forget it. Yelena contacted him at his office. She was pregnant and the baby was his. The DNA test he'd insisted upon proved it, and he remembered with a sickness in his stomach the utter turmoil he had felt. He and Sarah hadn't been together long, but she was the one, the one he'd been waiting for. The situation had turned into a nightmare. Yelena had taken the whole thing up a gear. She pestered him to tell Sarah about her and Tobias, tried to blackmail him into it by threatening to tell her herself. He'd delayed it as much as he could, giving her money and trying to placate her, but Yelena was streetwise and she wasn't about to be taken in. He knew what she wanted, and by leaving Tobias at the mill without telling him what she was planning she'd made it clear she wasn't going to give up until she got it.

He looked down at his coffee. He hadn't touched it and it had gone cold. He glanced over his shoulder and around the coffee shop. Just the old boy and his dog remained, snoring gently by his master's feet. He looked across to Southgate-Torrance then his phone. Ten-thirty. He had a meeting at eleven. He pushed back his chair and it scraped noisily against the fashionable light oak flooring, pulled the door open and stepped out onto the grey flagstones of the courtyard.

The waitress sauntered around the tables, flicking a damp cloth across them. When she got to the table where Dan had sat she stared at the lonely cold coffee and tutted. She watched him out of the window as he walked across the courtyard.

'Wasteful bastard,' she muttered.

'You alright, mate?' Jed was standing beside Dan's desk, hands in pockets, looking at him with a frown. 'You seem a bit distracted.'

'Yeah, sorry.' He looked up at Jed and made a grin which slipped from his face. He was horrified when he felt his eyes tear up. Fuck, he thought. Don't cry, for Christ's sake.

'Problems?'

Dan smiled again, wanting to reassure his colleague he was on the ball and nothing would get in the way of the project. 'No, no, just trying to make sure we do the best job for Southgate-Torrance. We won't get another chance like this, will we?'

Jed shook his head and dragged a chair over to the desk, sitting on it back to front, legs apart and leaned his elbow on the back. 'Is that all it is? You've seemed a bit distant since...well, since you moved into your new place. I know things have been a bit rough for you.' Dan leaned back in his chair and closed his eyes. When he opened them Jed was staring at him. 'Not just the project, is it? Is it Sarah?'

'Why d'you ask?'

'She's your partner and if it's not work bugging us it's usually something to do with home. Has she not taken to Tobias?'

Dan shook his head. 'No, no, she's great with him and he loves her, more than me I reckon.'

'So...'

'I'm worried about her...about her emotional state.'

'Oh.' Jed frowned. 'Why?'

'Since all of this stuff with Yelena and Tobias she's been different. It's like she's unravelling and it's freaking me out.'

'Well she would be different wouldn't she? You fucked someone else while you were with her.' Jed had a chuckle in his voice, his Australian accent becoming even more pronounced. 'What d'you expect?'

'No, I know, and she has every reason to feel insecure. I didn't handle it well, did I?'

'Bit of an understatement, mate. I told Claudia about it.'

Dan rolled his eyes. 'Oh, great. Now she hates me too.'

'Let's just say you've gone from top of her Christmas list to the bottom. She said she would have kicked your arse out the door, never to darken the doorstep again.'

'Right, well, I guess that's fair enough.'

'Yeah, but she's the feistiest, most vindictive woman I've ever known so I don't think we can go by her estimation of events, but I don't think she understands why Sarah hasn't done something similar.'

'Sarah's a lovely person, but I'm still not sure how well I know her. I mean, really know her. On the surface she's as calm as a millpond, but underneath…I think she's as turbulent and raging as the river at the bottom of our garden.'

'You can't blame her for being angry, Dan. What you did…hiding the existence of a kid while telling her you didn't want any with her. It must have hurt like hell. Even I'm shocked at your front.'

'It wasn't front, Jed. I didn't know what to do. Yelena was threatening me with all sorts and I made a decision, a really bad one as it turns out, not to tell Sarah. I just thought telling her would compound the problem, and in a way by keeping it away from her and everyone else I could almost pretend it wasn't really happening.'

He stood and went to the window. His office was glass, towering above the buildings around it and affording a stunning view across the city, one he loved and never wanted to give up. The glass office and the amazing view from it was the physical symbol of his success, heralding his business acumen and his knife sharp negotiation skills to his colleagues and his clients. He rubbed his chin, deep in thought. 'Strange how I'm so confident in my working life but seem to have got it so bloody wrong in my private life. I'll hold up my hands and admit I got it wrong. I mean, I've really fucked up. To be honest it would have been easier if she had thrown me out, kicked my arse, thrown things, slashed my tyres, I dunno. I could have understood it if she had.' He turned to face Jed. 'I'm not saying she wasn't angry. She was madder than I've ever seen her. I mean…she lost it. The thing about Sarah is she's good with words and she doesn't take prisoners, but….'

'But she's doing something, right?'

Dan nodded. 'Yeah.'

'What?'

'I wish I could nail it. I'm not sure. It's since we moved to Newton's Mill. It's like…' He looked at the floor, his lips a straight line. He turned to Jed and laughed. 'I can hardly believe I'm saying this but she thinks the place is haunted. It's this thing with Tobias. He keeps saying there's another boy living in the mill. And…' He sighed. 'I think Sarah believes him. It's like a cloud hanging over us, a presence we can't see but is having a really negative effect on our life there. And she's struggling. She doesn't want to frighten Tobias, but I'm sure she's internalising whatever it is she's scared of. I'm concerned about her.' His brow furrowed. 'I've always known she suffers from nightmares. Whenever things get difficult they seem to plague her, but…it seems to have gone into overdrive.'

'Maybe you should leave. Give her some space?'

'Yeah, I've thought about it, in fact she suggested it. But…there's Tobias. If I stay in the company flat I can't have him with me, and I don't want to leave him with Sarah.' He turned to Jed and pulled a face. 'I think it would be pushing my luck too far, wouldn't it, leaving the child I had with another woman with my partner who didn't even know he existed until a few weeks ago?'

'Are you in contact with Yelena?'

He went back to his seat and sighed. 'Yeah, I am.'

'How often?'

Dan's jaw hardened. 'Every day. Emails. Lots of 'em.'

Jed's eyes widened. 'Wow. Not giving up, is she? Surely she can't think there's a future for you and her?'

'It's what she wants.'

'You're kidding me. She wants you to be a family?' Dan nodded. 'And does Sarah know?'

'No…and I'm not going to tell her.'

'Something else you're not telling her.' Jed went across to the water cooler, filled two plastic cups and handed one to Dan. 'So…if she wants you to be a family why has she dumped the kid on you and Sarah? Surely she should have hung on to him? Seems the logical thing to do.'

'She said she had to go back to Russia and couldn't take Tobias. I don't know why she's gone back, some work thing I think. Sometimes her boss sends her abroad to ease the way for certain business deals.' He looked sheepish. 'Well, we know how it works, don't we? She said when she comes back she and I have to talk about Tobias and what we're going to do about him. He's about to see a specialist because we believe he's on the autistic spectrum?' Jed nodded. 'She says we're his parents and we need to be together for him. She wants me to tell Sarah.'

'Just like that? What planet's she on?'

'Planet Yelena. All she cares about is herself.' He held up his hand, rubbing his thumb against the inside of his fingers and Jed nodded. Dan reflected on the sachets of cocaine Yelena had hidden in Tobias's elephant and decided not to mention it. 'I'm not even sure she cares much about Tobias. He's just another money making opportunity.'

'You're paying her?'

'It's the law, Jed. It's meant to be for Tobias.'

'And?'

'I'm not sure how much of it he actually gets. By the look of him none of it.'

Jed shook his head in disbelief. 'She turned up with the boy, didn't she? When you were away from the house?'

'Yeah, fucking bitch.'

'Deliberate?'

'She knew I hadn't told Sarah about her and Tobias. She'd also worked out the longer it took for me to tell Sarah the longer she would have to wait for me to make the decision. She went for it, took steps to hurry up the process by turning up at the mill unannounced.'

'Did she know you weren't going to be there?'

'Course she did. I'd spoken to her about Tobias that afternoon and I'd told her I'd had to come in to work. What I didn't know was that she was already staying in a bed and breakfast with Tobias in the next village to Newton Denham. It's how she got to the mill through all that snow we had. She had it planned right down to the last nth. You can imagine what it did to Sarah. I'm gutted. Christ knows what it did to her.'

'So what now?'

Dan threw back the last of his water and wiped his mouth on the back of his hand. He glanced up at Jed and shook his head. 'I dunno.' He puckered his brow again and glanced up at Jed. 'Honestly, I don't know.'

Sarah closed her diary and tidied her desk. Marcus came out of his office and took his jacket off the coat stand. She looked up as he came into the room.

'How did it go? I haven't had a chance to talk to you today. I was thinking about you.'

'Thanks, Sarah. Yes…it was fine. I think Dad would have been pleased. Limiting the mourners to family was the right thing to do. We're quite a big family.'

'You seem okay, Marcus. To be honest I'm surprised you're in today. Don't you want to take some time off, maybe a holiday somewhere warm and sunny?'

'Yeah, we thought about it. Dad left me and sis some money in his will…for fun he said.' Marcus grinned sadly and raised his eyebrows as if asking a question, inclining his head towards her. 'And how is it in your neck of the woods? Have you come to terms with having a readymade family yet?'

'Tobias is a sweetheart. I just wish he didn't have so many challenges.' She looked away and took a deep breath. 'Anyway, it is what it is. We'll manage…somehow.'

He strolled across to her desk and put his hand on her shoulder. 'Do you need some time off?' She looked up at him. Her eyes met his and she blushed when tears ran down her cheeks. 'Oh, Sarah.'

'Sorry.'

'What is it?' He drew up a chair next to hers.

She blew out a breath. 'I don't know, Marcus. Something's…happening. At the mill. Tobias keeps talking about this other boy he says is living there. Dan's adamant he's making him up. And of course there's no one else living there, but…why does Tobias think there is? And now Dan thinks I'm having nightmares and imagining things. I don't know if I'm coming or going.'

'I take it Dan doesn't believe in the afterlife.'

'No, not at all. It's something we've spoken about in the past and he says its rubbish and absolutely convinced Tobias is making it up and there couldn't possibly be anything. As far as he's concerned it's out of the question. He won't even listen to it.'

'Hmm, people often vehemently dispute something if they're scared of it. They'd rather dismiss it than confront it. And *are* you? Having nightmares and imagining things, I mean. You've taken on an awful lot lately.'

She absentmindedly played with the pencils in the holder. 'Well, I have nightmares, but I've had them before. It's nothing new.'

'What does he think you're imagining?' She told him about the waterwheel and finding Tobias in the basement with the dead fox. He frowned. 'But you know what you saw. You're not an idiot,

Sarah. You're one of the most level-headed people I know. Why doesn't he ask Tobias?'

'*I* wanted to. I wanted him to explain to Dan what happened but Dan wouldn't hear of it. He said no way. And I get it, Marcus, I really do. Tobias has had so much to deal with, but he was the only person there apart from me, although Tobias felt he wasn't alone. He said the other boy told him the fox was asleep.'

'Crikey.'

'I know. I know how it must sound. It's just crazy.'

'It sounds like you need some breathing space. Take some time, Sarah. Look, I tell you what, work from home for the next couple of weeks. If a client asks for you and will only deal with you I'll call you in. How does that sound?'

Sarah leant towards him and kissed him on both cheeks. 'Thank you so much, Marcus. You're a star.'

He grinned. 'I know, darling. It just comes naturally. Just be sure to tell Fliss the next time you see her. I'm going to ask her to marry me. Perhaps the holiday you mentioned will be our honeymoon.'

'Oh, Marcus, how lovely. She'll say yes, she adores you.'

Marcus nodded and grinned again. 'And who could blame her?'

Sarah held Tobias's hand as they walked down the lane. She peered down at him as he bobbed along beside her, feeling his fingers in hers. Her heart jumped and she shook her head, laughing at herself. He glanced up, his dark brown eyes steady, holding hers for a long moment. Then he smiled. Her heart soared. Tobias had smiled at her. It was the first time he had smiled just for her. She wanted to jump up and down, fist-pump, even crowd surf if they'd been in a crowd, and she laughed again. It was a momentous event; such a natural thing for other children, to smile at someone, to connect with another in such a small way, yet for Tobias it was huge. He'd smiled because he felt something for her. She hoped with all her heart it was because he was happy.

All around them spring was coming into its own as nature turned what was dull and weather-beaten into the splendour of the season. The unfurling pale green leaves were almost translucent and the hedgerows were bursting with buds and blossom. Sarah felt her spirits rise. She was glad the winter was over. It had brought uncertainty and tears, not the joy she had hoped for, and she was happy to see it slide away for another year. She breathed deeply. After all the rain in April, Late May had ushered in a comfortable warmth and blue skies. All she could hear was birdsong and fluttering in the hedgerows as they made their nests for their impending young. This is how I imagined it, she thought, relishing the peace and stillness.

As they got further down the lane the grass was longer, uncut and allowed to have its head. Through the trees and edging the lane were patches of bluebells. Tobias stretched out his arm, brushing the long grass as they walked, pulling his hand back as it tickled his skin. She wanted to ask him if he was enjoying himself but thought better of it. In the distance was a gate.

'We'll walk as far as the gate,' she said quietly. 'When we get there we'll turn around and go back the way we came.'

The closer they got to the gate the neater the hedges on the left-hand side of the lane became. They were clipped, some beautifully laid and bound, and beyond the hedge a garden, laid out with round flowerbeds, topiary and water features. There were garden gnomes everywhere, in every colour and every position. They were by a pond with fishing rods, under shrubs, lining the path to the house, and even in a circle on a blanket as though they were having a picnic. There must have been at least a hundred and Sarah couldn't help smiling. She stopped and peeped over the hedge at a garden which was so unlike theirs at Newton's Mill, then realised Tobias couldn't see it.

'Do you want to see the gnomes, Tobias?'

He stared at her and she understood he probably didn't know what a gnome was. 'Will you let me lift you up so you can see them?' His eyes went to the left which Sarah had learnt meant he was giving some thought about her offer. He stuck his finger in his mouth and nodded. She put her hands under his arms and held him up so he could see over the hedge. His face broke into a broad smile.

'Hello.' A voice startled them and Sarah stepped back onto the lane. 'Did the little boy want to come and see the gnomes?' A straw sunhat decorated with bright red silk poppies gradually rose above the top of the hedge. Underneath it was a woman with dyed jet black hair and wearing orange cat's eye sunglasses. Her mahogany tanned skin was mottled by age spots. Around her neck were rows and rows of colourful glass beads. Sarah noticed with astonishment the garment she was wearing wasn't actually a sundress, but a pale pink flannelette petticoat.

'I'm so sorry,' Sarah said, hardly able to drag her eyes away from the flannelette petticoat. 'I didn't realise there was anyone in the garden. We didn't mean to be nosy. It's just…well, the gnomes. You have so many. I wanted Tobias to see them.'

'Oh, don't worry, dear. We love it when people see them. Bring the little boy in. He'll see them better from in here.' She pointed towards the gate at the end of the lane. 'Go through the gate and it will bring you right into the garden.' Sarah nodded, and putting Tobias down led him towards the gate.

The garden was huge. There was an orchard which separated Newton's Mill from the garden, and a copse of oak, ash and sycamore trees. Beyond the copse the garden was formal, with hardly a space without something in it. Fairy lights were strung from tree to tree, bird feeders hung from branches, and wind chimes clinked together in the light breeze. The sound of flowing water was everywhere and it was very calming. A Japanese garden with a little stream and a wooden bridge over it broke the garden into two areas, and at the far end was a huge green pagoda. Sarah's eyes grew wide as she looked around what was more like a fairy grotto than a garden.

'Wow.'

The elderly woman walked slowly towards her leaning on a walking stick. 'I'm Mrs. Locke,' she smiled. 'You're from Newton's

Mill aren't you? I heard it had been sold to a young couple. I haven't had neighbours for years. It'll take some getting used to I can tell you. The mill has often been empty. I thought the other family would stay, the ones who were there a few years back, but they went very quickly, left in such a hurry we didn't even realise they'd gone. Moved abroad I hear. From London, aren't you? High flyers I understand.'

Sarah's lips twitched into a smile. The gossipmongers had clearly gone into overdrive, and she remembered the taxi driver's warning. 'We moved in just before Christmas.'

'And who's this young man? Hello,' she said to Tobias who ignored her. Mrs Locke's eyes met Sarah's and Sarah changed the subject.

'Your garden is amazing. It must have taken a lot of work.'

Mrs Locke looked pleased. 'This garden is my pride and joy,' she said. 'My late husband, Johnny and I used to work on it from breakfast until dinner. It was such a mess, you know, when we moved in thirty years ago. Rocks everywhere and completely overgrown. Johnny said it was a jungle, and do you know, it was. It took us months of hard work to clear it. We finished it just before my Johnny died. Heart attack. I do miss him. Even now after all these years.' She took a folded tissue from underneath one of the many gold bangles she wore around her wrist and wiped her eyes underneath her sunglasses.

'I'm so sorry,' said Sarah, ready to leave. 'Perhaps we should go.'

Mrs Locke quickly recovered. 'Oh, no, you must see all the garden now you're here. We love having visitors, don't we boys?' Sarah looked around thinking someone else had joined them. 'My boys and I spend all our time in the garden. It's our own little world. Look at Raymond over there by the pond. He loves to fish but never seems to catch anything. Would your little boy like to go over and say hello?'

Sarah suddenly realised Mrs Locke was talking about the gnomes. 'Er, yes...yes, why not?'

The old lady leant on her stick and ambled over to the pond. Sarah and Tobias followed her. 'This is Raymond,' she said, looking at Tobias. 'Say hello. He loves it when people talk to him.'

Sarah glanced down at Tobias thinking if Mrs. Locke managed to get him to say hello to the gnome it would be a miracle. Tobias stood stock still, his hand still in Sarah's.

'Lo, man,' he said. Sarah's eyes widened with surprise

'His name is Raymond,' Mrs Locke corrected him. 'Say Ray....mond.' She enunciated the name, pursing her lips on the "mond" which accentuated the deeply ingrained lines around her mouth. Tobias said nothing and Mrs. Locke shrugged. 'Does he not like the name Raymond?' asked the old lady, frowning. It's such a nice English name. 'We also have Arthur, Ted, Robert, Gerald, Samuel, Harold and lots of others. We even brought Giovani back from Italy with us. He loves the hot weather. And there's Itsuki who Johnny found in Tokyo when he was there on business,' she said pointing across the garden. 'He's on the Japanese bridge. I think he's a bit homesick.'

Sarah smiled and bit her lip, desperate to find a way to leave without seeming rude.

'Thank you so much for showing us around,' she said. 'You have a beautiful garden and it's been lovely to meet our near neighbour. We should go now. I'm working from home at the moment and I've got so much to do.' She tightened her grip on Tobias's hand and went to leave. As she turned she bumped into someone standing behind her, a man, standing so close he almost touched her. Sarah's hand flew to her mouth. 'Oh!'

He was very overweight and wearing a pair of old jeans bagging at the knees which were fastened at the waist with a length of string. He wore a once white vest tucked into his jeans and no shirt. On his left arm was a tattoo of an ornate crown with God Save the Queen in script underneath. His head was shaved and his fingers were yellow with nicotine stains. He stared intently at Sarah and Tobias. Sarah drew in a breath and Tobias shuffled behind her, wary of the man who had seemingly appeared out of nowhere. Mrs Locke laughed. 'Ah, and now you've met another of my boys. This is my son, Vernon Locke. Vernon, this is…oh, I'm sorry, my dear. I didn't catch your name, or the little boy's.

Sarah kept her eyes on Vernon. 'I'm Sarah, and this is Tobias.' She turned to Mrs Locke. 'We should go now. We've outstayed our welcome.' Bringing Tobias back round to her side and holding tightly onto his hand she sidestepped Vernon and almost ran across the lawn to get to the gate at the end of the lane.

'Come again, dear,' Mrs Locke called after her, 'and bring the little boy.'

'Not if I have anything to do with it,' Sarah said under her breath. She opened the gate and pushed Tobias through before shutting it behind them with a comforting click. As they walked back down the lane she could feel Vernon's eyes following her. She tried not to look over the hedge but she couldn't help herself. Sure enough, Vernon was standing in the middle of the lawn, a cigarette in his hand, watching them intently as they retraced their steps. Sarah shivered and walked even faster. Tobias was doing his best to keep up and when they got to the end Sarah breathed a sigh of relief.

'Whoa, I'm glad to be out of there. What do you think, Tobias?'

'The man is sorry.'

She laughed and gazed down at him. 'Why would the man be sorry? We don't know him, sweetheart. What could the man be sorry about?'

'The other boy said man is sorry.'

Sarah closed her eyes and slowed her walk. 'When did the other boy say that?'

He raised his head. 'The other boy said. Man. Sorry.'

They carried on towards the mill. Sarah wanted to talk to Tobias about the other boy. She knew Dan wouldn't broach the subject with him so it looked like it was down to her. I have to know, she thought as she weighed up the wisdom of mentioning it to Tobias again. Something's going through his mind and we need to know what...and why.

Back at the mill Sarah made sandwiches and put Tobias's favourite cakes on a plate, taking them into the garden where she'd laid out a blanket on the lawn. Tobias was in the living room, drawing.

'Tobias, come and have a picnic.' She watched him through the French windows. 'Tobias, come on,' she called, holding up a plate. 'I've got your cakes, you love these, don't you?' She held one up. Again he ignored her. Sighing, she went to the French windows and was about to ask him to come into the garden until she looked into the room. Tobias had placed his crayons on end, lining them up in colour and size order. The sheets of drawing paper were carefully placed one on top of the other as if they'd just been taken out of the packet, apart from one which he'd placed in front of him. Kneeling beside him she picked up the sheet of paper on which was a faithful image of Vernon Locke, right down to his tattoo. 'What's this, sweetie? Why did you draw a picture of this man?' He turned away. 'Tobias. It's okay,' she said softly. 'You can draw what you like. Sarah's just wondering. Why did you draw this man?'

'Other boy drawed it.'

'The other boy?' He nodded. 'When? When did he do it?' He stared at her, saying nothing. 'Didn't Tobias draw it?'

He shook his head frantically and started to scream. 'Other boy, other boy, other boy.' He got up and kicked the carefully lined up crayons and perfectly organised sheets of paper across the floor. Sarah reached for him and caught his arm, trying to hold onto him, but he wriggled out of her grasp, bent his head and sank his teeth into her shoulder. She screamed, more in shock than pain as a blood stain grew on her shirt. When Tobias saw what he'd done he began to walk backwards, away from her, his hands across his mouth, then burst into tears and ran from the living room into the hall. She heard him grabbing at the handle on the front door as if trying to get out and she got to her feet and ran into the hall. Tobias stood by the door sobbing.

'Tobias, it's okay,' she whispered, kneeling in front of him. 'Please, sweetheart, calm down. You're not in trouble.' She pulled his hand away from his face. 'Would you like a cuddle? Sarah needs a hug.'

To her surprise he nodded and went willingly into her arms. 'Sorry, Saha,' he said between sobs. 'Mustn't hurt Saha. Tobias bad boy.'

Stroking his hair, she held him close. 'No, darling, please don't. Tobias is a lovely boy. You're Sarah's lovely boy.'

She watched him through the little window in the classroom door. He sat very still on the mat with the other children in his class as the teacher called out their names from the register. Sarah waited, hoping Tobias would put his hand up when his name was called. He didn't. The teacher glanced up, noted he was in class, and put a mark against his name. She looked through the door and her eyes met Sarah's. They both shrugged, and Sarah sadly shook her head and walked away. Tobias had never answered his name at school, had not said one word.

Back at the mill she tidied everywhere, stacked the dishwasher and made the beds. This had become her daily routine since she'd agreed to work from home and she couldn't help laughing to herself.

'Who'd have thought it,' she said under her breath. 'Sarah, you've become a housewife.'

She made a coffee and went into the study. It was a beautiful day, sunny and warm, tempting her to lie with her diary and mobile on the hammock they had strung between two of the trees in the garden, but she knew this was the road to hell. She had to work; make phone calls and arrange appointments for the gallery. The last thing she wanted was to let Marcus down and shake his faith in her. He had been so understanding, totally accepting of her situation, so she cleared Dan's papers from the desk and opened her diary. She was about to make a phone call when she noticed the computer had been left on. Dan had become obsessively vigilant about turning appliances off and recycling, so discovering he'd left the computer on felt like a small triumph. 'Ha,' she said under her breath. 'Got you.'

She clicked the mouse and the screen sprang into life. Displayed in front of her was Dan's email account. She froze. It was a long list of emails, all from yelena.kashirina@yandex.ru. Her stomach flipped and she shut her eyes briefly, praying she'd made a mistake. She got up and went to the window, leaning against the frame and staring sightlessly at the garden. This was Dan's email account, and in the six or so years they had been together she had never checked his email accounts or his phone. She didn't think it was something she would ever need to do, and when Eve had told her she checked her husband's phone and email accounts regularly Sarah had thought it was an invasion of his privacy.

'Have you ever found anything?' she'd asked her.

Eve had grinned at her over her computer screen. 'His secretary had been emailing him out of work hours. I checked his phone and read some of the texts they'd sent each other. They were about work, a little flippant and over friendly. Banter, he said. You know the sort of thing. These things can escalate. I let him know in no uncertain terms I would never accept him having email or text relationships with anyone from work out of regular work hours, particularly if they were female.'

'What did he say?'

'He didn't say anything. He just nodded and I checked again over the following days.'

'And?'

'Nothing.'

'He might have deleted them.'

Eve shook her head. 'No, he hadn't. I checked.'

Sarah rolled her eyes when she recalled the conversation. Hiding things from her was all Dan had done over recent months. She glanced at the computer and reluctantly went back to it, knowing once she opened the emails there was no going back. What was read could not be unread. She also knew there was a good chance she was about to find out some things she might wish she hadn't. Her hand hovered over the mouse. She grabbed it and clicked on the first one. It had been sent that afternoon. Dan had opened it, at work Sarah assumed.

"Dan. You must tell her. You are his father. I don't care what she does for him. You must tell her."

Sarah frowned. Who was Yelena referring to when she said "she"? She opened the email she'd sent to Dan half an hour earlier.

"You must do what best for him. I am his mother and I live in shit in old rental house with other people. She not have child but she live in comfort in huge house. This how your son should live. When Tobias come back to me he will live in shit. You think this okay? You think it okay your son live in shit like his mother live?"

Sarah's jaw hardened and it suddenly hit her. From the very first day when Yelena had turned up on the doorstep it hadn't seemed right. What mother would take her child to a strange house and simply dump him on a woman she had never met; a complete stranger to her and her son. Okay, she knew it was Dan's house and he was Tobias's father, but it explained why Yelena had turned up at the mill without telling Dan what she planned to do, turned her back on her son and left without waiting for an argument. She wanted Dan to fall in love with his son, so deeply in love he couldn't bear to be parted from him. And now Yelena had made her move, the one she had likely planned from the very beginning, demanding Dan give up Sarah so she and Dan could raise him together. Sarah shook her head at the lengths Yelena would attempt to get what she wanted, which was certainly not Tobias. What she wanted was what Sarah had; the house, the money, the life. And Dan.

Sarah leant back. I need to start thinking like Yelena, she thought. What would I do if I was in her position, with a child by a man I wasn't in a relationship with and having to fend for myself? But I'm not in her position. I don't have the faintest idea what I would do. I have a job, a good one, and if I was on my own I could easily manage financially. She sat up, more alert to the theories pressing her. Maybe that's the point. Yelena's not in my position. Her appearance had given it away. Was all of this something Yelena had planned before she'd even met Dan, to sleep with an unsuspecting guy, get pregnant, insist on having the child and demand they not only accept her into their life, but bankroll her and provide her with everything she and her child needed? It occurred to her she hadn't read any of Dan's replies. Scrolling through the folders she accessed his Sent folder and read his last message to Yelena.

"Of course it's not what I want. I want my son to be safe and secure and well looked after and right now he is. I don't know what will happen in the future. You ask too much. Threatening me with taking Tobias to Russia isn't helping. Stop making threats and we'll talk."

The doorbell rang and she shook her head with frustration, irritated at the interruption. In the hall, the daylight from outside filtering through the stained glass window was completely blocked by a person standing the other side. Sarah hesitated, trying to work out who it could be, hoping whoever it was couldn't see her through the stained glass.

'Shit,' she said under her breath. 'Please don't let it be Vernon Locke.' She opened the door a fraction and peered through the gap. It wasn't Vernon.

A heavyset man stood in the porch. Sarah could smell his aftershave, expensive, attractive, the same one Dan used. He was well-dressed, casually smart in designer jeans and a pristine white shirt. His navy jacket was beautifully cut and fitted his huge frame like a glove. The first six seconds, she thought. It takes the first six seconds to make an impression on someone. You smell gorgeous and you look okay but your body language says trouble. Why do I always feel I have to open the door when someone knocks as if it's some unbreakable social obligation? He wouldn't have known I was here. Idiot! She smiled nervously and couldn't ignore the thumping of her heart.

'Can I help?'

He gave a sure smile Sarah was certain he didn't mean. 'I want to speak with Yelena Kashirina,' he said, his voice infused with a broad Russian accent.

'Yelena isn't here. She doesn't live here.'

'You know her?'

'I know of her.'

He nodded while staring at her, his eyes narrowing slightly. The slow patronising way he bobbed his head sent shots of fear through her and she knew instinctively there would be a problem. It was a slow measured action indicating he didn't believe her. He pursed his lips, daring her to contradict him. 'This is where she said she would be. If she is hiding you tell her I know what she is doing and I will find her. You tell her.'

'I've just told you, she's not here. She's not hiding, at least not here. Anyway, why should she be in hiding? She told us she was going home, to Russia, so if you want to see her I'm afraid you've got a long journey ahead of you.'

'What I want is to see the boy.'

Sarah froze. 'What boy?'

'Tobias Kashirina. I want to see him.'

'Why?'

He glowered at her and she took a step back. 'It is not for you to ask. They are here, yes?'

She shook her head. 'No, they are not here. I just told you. I've told you the truth. They are not here and I don't know why you think they are.' He put his forearm against the front door and pushed, placing one shiny brogue on the step, ramming his knee up against the bottom of the door. Sarah was forced back into the hall, struggling to keep herself upright, but slipping on the parquet floor. He pushed the door wide open and the edge hit her in the face. She felt her cheekbone and forehead go numb before excruciating pain set in. Shock took her breath away and for a moment she couldn't speak. 'You can't just force your way in here. I've told you, they're not here.'

'They are here, and I will see them.'

He stood in the hall, squinting up at the galleried landing. Sarah hauled herself off the floor and ran into the kitchen, grabbing her phone off the island. As she keyed in the emergency number he went from room to room, hollering for Tobias. When he realised

Yelena and Tobias weren't downstairs he ran across the hall, and with amazing agility for such a big man he dashed up the stairs two at a time. Sarah was terrified, realising she couldn't stop him now, that he would have time to search the mill and disappear before the police arrived. By the time her call was answered Sarah was hyperventilating. She screamed into the phone, 'I need someone here now. Newton's Mill. There's an intruder. He's pushed his way into my house. Please hurry. Please help me.'

'Your name, Miss.'

'Sarah Anders. Please hurry.'

'Can you get to safety? A place where you can protect yourself? Keep your mobile connected. Do not end this call.'

She ran into the kitchen and shut the door, dragging one of the leather chairs to push in front of it, doubting it would stop him from forcing his way into the room if he made up his mind to get in, but knowing she had to try, to do something to prevent him from getting to her. She considered escaping into the garden but just thinking about it made her angry. Why the hell should I? This is my house and he has no right to be here. Why should I be the one to leave? Running behind the island she pulled a carving knife out of the block on the counter. It was probably the most dangerous thing she had ever done, maybe the worst decision she had ever made, but she had to protect herself somehow.

Her breath was stagnant in her chest, not daring to breath. Above her she could hear him in Tobias's room, his footsteps heavy on the wooden floorboards. She glanced up at the ceiling. Tobias's bedroom was a little boy's room, full of toys and cars; all the paraphernalia one would expect. Would the intruder put two and two together and work out whose room it was? Her mind took a tour of Tobias's room. Were there any photos in there of Tobias and Dan together? I can't remember. Why can't I remember? She heard the flinging open of wardrobe doors, the shattering of glass bottles in the bathroom and the clattering of his shoes on the wooden treads of the staircase as he made his way downstairs. Trembling, she went to the kitchen door and put her ear against it. There was no sound from the hall. Her throat was parched with fear and it took all her effort to stop herself from coughing. She held the carving knife up in front of her. If he was planning to come into the kitchen she would be ready for him.

The chair began to move very slowly into the room as the kitchen door was gradually pushed open. Her body shuddered with terror and she raised the knife to her shoulder ready to plunge it into him.

'Ms Anders?'

Sarah closed her eyes and her knees almost gave way as she sank to her haunches. She laid the knife on the seat, resting one hand on her stomach, the other holding onto the arm of the chair.

'Yes, I'm Sarah Anders,' she answered, her voice almost a squeak. A police officer put his head around the door. Sarah stood shakily and the officer pushed the door open wider. 'It looks like the assailant has gone, Ms Anders. I've got men searching the gardens and the lane but it's so easy to get away here. All he had to do was go across the bridge and disappear into the woods. Slaughter's Wood leads into the Newton Denham council estate but he might not have gone there. To be honest he could be anywhere.' He led her to the chair and encouraged her to sit, peering at the cut on her head. 'Your forehead looks bad. Is there anyone we can call for you?' She closed her eyes and rested her forehead on her knees, feeling faint. The police officer sank to his haunches at her side and handed her a wad of kitchen towel which she held against her forehead. 'Did you know him?'

'No.'

'Did he say anything?'

'He was looking for my partner's son, Tobias, and Tobias's mother. For some reason he thought they were living here.'

'I take it they're not.'

She glanced up at him. 'Tobias lives here. His mother left him here on Christmas Eve and we've been taking care of him.'

'And your partner is definitely Tobias's father?'

'Yes, why?'

'We have to be sure the boy is safe. We have a duty of care. If this guy is looking for him he might come back. Did he say why he was looking for him?'

'No.'

Dan poured a glass of brandy and handed it to Sarah who was laying on the sofa. Tobias lay next to her snuggled into the crease of the sofa, his arm across her stomach and his head on her chest.

'Drink this. You should have gone to hospital, Sarah.'

Sarah took the glass from him, shaking her head. 'It's not deep. I think it looks worse than it is. To be honest it's my cheekbone that hurts more. It's throbbing like the devil.'

'What was he like?'

'Big and Russian...or something similar.' She sipped her brandy.

'Right. Did he say anything?'

'He was looking for you know who and...' She inclined her head towards Tobias.

'Right.' Dan cleared his throat. 'Well, I'm glad they called me, although they said you'd asked them not to. I couldn't believe what they were telling me. I thought it was a joke at first, some prat at work. You shouldn't have been left on your own.'

She shrugged, thinking about the emails Dan and Yelena had sent to each other. At some point she would have to tell Dan she'd read them, but it wasn't the right time. Before he'd arrived home she'd closed down his email program and replaced it with her own. It was something she wanted to keep to herself, at least until she could work out whether Dan was taking Yelena's demands seriously, or whether he was stalling for time. In her email Yelena had said Tobias would go back to her. Surely Dan wouldn't let it happen, regardless of where she was living. They'd found her stash of cocaine in Tobias's elephant. There was no way he could go back to her. 'So what now,' she asked him.

Dan sat in front of the sofa, leaning against the arm, his head close to hers. He pushed her hair away from her face, careful not to touch the wound, her skin caressed by the warmth of his breath. 'What do you mean, what now?' he said quietly.

'The man who got into the mill said he was looking for Yelena,' she whispered. 'Don't you want to find out who it was and why he was looking for her?'

'How am I supposed to do that?'

'Try asking her?'

'She's in Russia, Sarah. Like she cares. And I don't suppose she'd tell me anyway.'

Sarah pushed harder. 'You can get hold of her though, right?'

'I have her phone number. You know I have it. We're in phone contact. We have to be because of Tobias. She phoned me don't forget.'

Sarah looked away. He didn't mention her email address like she'd hoped. 'So text her and ask her who the hell it was, why he thought she was here, and what gives him the right to force his way into our home and threaten me.'

'Okay, I'll text her.'

'Now?'

He looked at his mobile. 'It's late in Vladivostok. She'll be working I expect. I'll text her tomorrow morning.'

Sarah looked at him, waiting for him to realise what he'd said. 'How do you know she's in Vladivostok?'

He raised his eyebrows and his mouth dropped open as he grasped what he'd carelessly let slip. Sarah didn't know Yelena was in Vladivostok. How could she? He flushed slightly and looked uncomfortable, conscious he was on the back foot. 'I'm assuming it's where she'll be.'

'Why?'

'Because she told me it's where she comes from, and didn't she say she was going home? It's what she told you, and it's what she said in her phone call. It's why I assumed she'd be there. It'll be late there anyway. Vladivostock is nine or ten hours ahead of us.'

Sarah narrowed her eyes as he turned away, and she nodded to herself, her lips a straight line.

'Oh.'

'Will you be alright?' he asked her with a quick kiss.

She gave a humourless smile. 'I'll be fine, Dan, don't worry.'

'Of course I'm worried, Sarah. I'm concerned the guy will come back. Promise me you won't answer the door, or at least ask who it is before opening it. If things weren't so manic at work I'd stay home.' She didn't say anything. 'You could go and stay at Mum and Dad's for a few days, so you're not on your own.'

She threw him a look. 'What have the police said?'

'They're going to swing by a few times. At least if he intends a return visit he'll see them and hopefully change his mind. The last thing he'll want is to be caught out. They won't knock, just keep an eye on things. To be on the safe side.'

'What about Tobias?'

'The school know. To be honest I think he's safer there. Unless the guy's been watching us. The police don't think he's had a chance to work out we have Tobias yet. If he had he would have gone to the school yesterday instead of here.'

'Am I to pick him up?'

'The police said they will.'

'But won't it draw attention to him?'

'It might, but it'll also be safer.'

'I don't know, Dan. I think we should keep everything as normal as we can for him. You know what he's like. If he has a meltdown while he's with them they won't know what to do.'

'Are you up to picking him up? Please don't say you are if you're not sure. I'll worry even more.'

'I'll drive. It'll take me ten minutes.'

'Okay. I'll let the police know you're going.' He bent his head and looked at her. 'You're sure, Sarah? Really sure?'

'It'll be fine.'

Sarah was glad when Dan left for work. She needed time to think, some breathing space to consider what was happening, and even though Dan had been lovingly attentive to her since the day before, there was still an undercurrent. And it wasn't just because of the emails. There were questions she needed to ask herself, difficult questions, mostly about Dan, and also about why she had an uncomfortable feeling worming into her psyche that someone had set out to frighten her.

She tried to keep to the routine she had slipped into while working at home, the bed making, the tidying; the constant drip, drip of the coffee machine as she worked out her day and who she needed to contact for gallery business, aware all she was doing was putting off sitting in front of the computer. At least she wouldn't be able to access Dan's emails so there would be no chance of checking them again. I don't want to see them, she thought. All they've done is make me doubt him again.

In the bedroom she sat at her dressing table, peering into the mirror, gently pressing her finger against the cut on her head. The soreness made her wince. She squeezed some of the medicated cream she used for the scar on her cheek into her hand and dabbed it onto the wound, recoiling at the pain. A dull headache had settled over her eyes, but she was more cross than hurt.

'Another scar for my collection,' she murmured, peering into the mirror.

Taking her coffee into the living room she sat looking out of the French windows. It was warm enough to keep them open, and the sight of the blossoming garden and the sound of the river as it snaked past the mill and under the old bridge relaxed her and stilled the thoughts zipping around her head like racing cars on a chicane. She left the sofa and wandered into the garden, sitting on the swing seat and leaning back against the huge stripy cushions. Her foot resting on the grass rocked her gently back and forth and she took a calming breath. The squeaking of the chain scraping against the swing's wooden frame was strangely comforting, and for the first time in two days she felt peaceful. A thread of guilt went through her, aware she was prevaricating about starting work. Her misgivings about Dan and whether his hidden contact with Yelena was the last straw and sounded the death knell for their life together had to be confronted, regardless of how painful it would be. I'll mull it all over later. I know I must face it and be honest with myself, but right now…right now I just want to be quiet.

Someone called her name and the voice startled her awake. Mary peered through the wrought iron double gates, a bunch of flowers in her hand, the sun glinting off the lenses in her glasses.

'Hi, Sarah. Oh, I'm sorry, lovely. I woke you. Shall I go? I can come back another time.'

'No, Mary, please, come through. It'll be nice to have someone to talk to. Come in and have a cuppa.'

Mary pushed open one of the gates and followed the path to the garden behind the house where Sarah was still sitting on the swing.

'Lovely day,' Mary said as she joined her. 'How are you feeling? Hear you had a bit of excitement yesterday.'

She followed Sarah into the kitchen and sat on one of the stools behind the island.

'These are for you,' she said, handing the flowers to Sarah. 'Thought you might need cheering up.'

Sarah was touched by her kindness. 'Oh, Mary, thank you so much. They're beautiful.' She filled the kettle and lit the hob, and while she waited for the kettle to boil she found a vase and arranged the flowers. 'Not in the shop today?'

'As it's such a lovely day I decided to have some time off. It doesn't happen very often. My son's covering for me. Luke. He's a good lad. Hardworking. Doesn't mind what he takes on. Always willing to lend a hand to anyone who needs it.'

'Is he your only child?'

'No, we have a daughter, Rebecca. She lives in Australia with her husband and children.'

Sarah looked at her with sadness. 'You must miss her, Mary. Mothers and daughters…have a bond, don't they? What a shame.'

'Yes, I do miss them, especially the grandkids. They have a wonderful life there though. I don't begrudge them leaving here. They're happy enough.'

Sarah looked up from arranging the flowers, wondering at the gloomy inflection in Mary's voice. 'I'll make some tea.'

They sat in the garden. Sarah thought about the work she should have been doing but put it out of her mind as she listened to Mary talking about her family and the shop, and became aware there wasn't much going on in Newton Denham Mary didn't know about.

'I hear you met Mrs Locke and Vernon,' Mary said as she splashed more tea into her mug. 'They're our resident weirdos. What did you make of them?'

Sarah laughed, although she felt a bit guilty. Mrs Locke had made her welcome even if her son had frightened her and Tobias half to death. 'They're certainly unusual. Mrs. Locke's way of dressing is a little…avant-garde to say the least.'

Mary's eyes widened. 'Avant-garde? I don't know about that. If you want to know what I think it's more like bloody bonkers. And what about all those damned gnomes. What are they all about?'

'Maybe they bring her some comfort in her loss.'

'Did she tell you her husband had died? Her Johnny?'

'Yes, poor old lady. She was so upset, cried actually when she was talking about him and how much she missed him. A heart attack, wasn't it?'

Mary threw her head back and chuckled. 'A heart attack, my eye. He's been residing in one of Her Majesty's hotels for embezzlement since 2001. Johnny Locke is one of the biggest criminals we've ever had around here. He's notorious. A swindler. An out and out criminal. He'd sell his own grandmother if he thought he could get away with it. He probably did. Sylvia Locke's lucky he didn't try to sell her.' She placed her mug carefully on the table. 'And embezzlement's not the only thing he was accused of, either.'

'Really? What else did he do?'

Mary leaned forward, warming to her subject. She had a glint in her eye, clearly enjoying knowing something Sarah didn't.

'Some years ago he was accused of attempting to rape a young woman from the Newton Denham estate, the one the other side of the woods where the school is. Got across the river in one of them canoe things so he wouldn't be seen, then went through the woods and attacked her.'

Sarah's mouth dropped open. 'No. Oh my God. What happened?'

'She fought him off. He said she'd come on to him and was asking for it. Unfortunately she had a bit of a reputation for being flighty and it went against her. No one came out of it well, but to all intents and purposes he got away with it.'

'How?'

Mary shrugged. 'I dunno. Maybe he had someone in his pocket. He wasn't sent to prison but he was fined a lot of money though, for those days anyway, and he paid it on the day of his trial. Pulled an old grey sock out of his pocket. It was where he kept his money. Wads and wads of it. He just peeled it off, note by note and slammed it on the table one by one in front of the judge. Can you believe it?'

'A sock? Why would he keep it in a sock?'

'You tell me. I told you they were odd. And I'd love to get into the Locke's garden. We all thought Johnny Locke's ill-gotten gains were hidden in those gnomes. I'd give anything to have a good old nose around in there. Don't have a mortgage y'know. S'pose all his victims paid for their house by the river. All right for some.'

She retrieved her mug and took a gulp of tea.

'That bloody family. All criminals. Sylvia's family were as rotten to the core as Johnny by all accounts, so I suppose she must have been used to all his carrying on. People don't change. The apple never falls far from the tree. And Vernon's not much better. I don't think he's quite the ticket either. Fifty-six years of age and never done a days' work in his life, but I suppose he didn't have to with all the money his father screwed out of other people. He takes a strange interest in the kids from the estate too. I've heard he watches them from the slope at the bottom of the garden when they're playing in the wood across the river from the Locke property. Just stares at them for hours. Their parents come in the shop. They've all said he scares them witless and a lot of them have stopped their children going there. It's such a shame. Kids should be allowed some freedom. You want to keep your Tobias away from him. I know they're your neighbours but I wouldn't get too friendly with them if I were you. They're not good people. Criminals, the lot of 'em. And Vernon. Not right in the head if you ask me. I'm not one to judge people, live and let live is what I say, and heaven knows it takes all sorts to make a world, I'm the first to admit it, but you can't help wondering can you? Goodness knows what sort of things he's got up to in the past.'

'He *is* a bit creepy.'

Mary nodded. 'Mm. That's one word for it.' They both went quiet. 'And what about you?'

Sarah stared at her. 'Me?'

'You had a terrible day yesterday, so I hear. You were attacked weren't you? It's what we all heard anyway.'

Sarah inhaled a deep breath. She had a feeling this was coming and wondered if this was why Mary had visited her. She couldn't think of a reason not to tell her. Evading the question would mean lying and she didn't have the energy for it. She told her everything.

'So the little boy you've got up at the school isn't yours?'

'No.'

'But he's your husbands?'

'My partner's.'

'So where's the mother?'

'Gone back to Russia.'

Mary looked thoughtful and drained her mug. 'He was seen in Newton Denham, y'know, the man who attacked you.'

Sarah was horrified. 'When?'

'He was asking questions about a woman, saying she was living with someone called Dan and he wanted to know where he could find them. He came into the shop, and went across to TipTop Cars and spoke to Craig, the young taxi driver who took you home the other day. He told him you and Dan were here and gave him directions to the mill. It's the talk of the village.'

Sarah rolled her eyes. 'Oh, great.'

'He didn't know what he was after, did he? I'm sure if he'd have known he wouldn't have said anything.'

'No. No, of course he didn't know.'

There was a lull in the conversation. 'He wasn't after you?' Sarah shook her head and Mary sniffed, gearing up for an inquisition. 'I'd have thought your mum would have come over to make sure you were alright, y'know, helped out a bit while you were laid up. Does she live local?'

'No.' Mary waited for Sarah to open up. She knew if she waited long enough she'd get the information she wanted. She could give a masterclass in digging for information. It worked every time. 'I…didn't live with my parents. I was raised in a children's home.'

Mary nodded. 'Oh, right. Sorry, Sarah. I shouldn't have asked.' Mary waited again but Sarah had clammed up and didn't look like she was going to take the conversation further. 'So, did they die, your parents, when you were a child? And what about your brothers and sisters? Were you with them?' Sarah felt trapped. It was like she had a pair of hands around her throat, squeezing the life out of her. Her chest tightened up and she could hardly breathe. 'Sarah? Are you okay? Is your head bothering you? It looks very sore?'

'No, no, I'm alright. Just feel a little lightheaded.'

'Should I call your Dan? Get him home from work.'

'No, I'm fine now.' She took a deep breath and another mouthful of tea. 'My parents are still alive as far as I know. I haven't heard anything different. I don't know what happened to them. They left me in a children's home and I never saw them again. They could be anywhere.' She paused, her eyes shaded with sadness. 'Or they could be dead I suppose.'

Mary pulled a face, but said nothing. She watched Sarah closely, mentally recording her struggle with talking about her past, but wasn't about to give up. 'And do you remember them?'

Sarah stared off into the distance. 'No.'

'How sad. What an awful thing for a child to go through, to be abandoned by your parents. And you don't have any memory of them? Or where you lived before the children's home?'

Sarah chewed the inside of her mouth and closed her eyes. The wound on her head was aching and her cheekbone felt even more swollen. She could see it at the corner of her vision, protruding beyond the edge of her eye line. 'Er, no. No, I've tried…tried to remember their faces, but I can't.' Mary pursed her lips as Sarah raised her hand to her head. 'I'm sorry, Mary. It's time I took some more painkillers. My head's thumping. Do you mind?'

Mary stood and gathered up the mugs and plates and put them on the tray. 'Let me take these in for you. You can get some rest.' Sarah nodded and winced. 'And I'll visit again. You need someone, Sarah, a friend in the community. Everyone needs a friend, someone they can confide in. You know it won't go any further, whatever you tell me. If anything else happens you call me, right. Anything at all.' She fished about in her huge embroidered cross body bag and found a pen and a scrap of paper. 'Here's my number. Call me day or night. Understand?' She laid the paper purposefully on Sarah's lap. 'Day or night.'

Sarah looked up at her and gave a watery smile. 'Okay.'

The delicious smell from the slow cooker made her mouth water. Slow cooking was her new discovery and right up her street; the best results with minimum effort. The instructions said not to take the lid off until thirty minutes before the end of cooking, but she couldn't resist lifting the lid and giving it a stir. By the time Dan walked in the door it would be ready; fragrant chicken curry and basmati rice, one of his favourites. Tobias loved it too.

Sarah had convinced herself the nurturing thing was what mothers did, even if she wasn't a "real mother". The intention was there, the need was there, and more than anything she had discovered an instinctive love she hadn't known she possessed. Tobias had become her world, so much so she could weep at the thought of him. His bright eyes or a rare smile on his round face meant so much to her it could melt her heart. Sarah wanted to please him, to teach him things and make him happy. She was also aware her nurturing of him, cooking, and building her nest had become the most efficient way of filling up the gaps in her mind, the dangerous spaces where destructive thoughts of Dan and Yelena and what happened between them became living, breathing, moving images; Dan and Yelena writhing together on a bed, their bodies glistening with droplets of sweat, whispering, kissing, thrusting. It was like a movie on a loop. Sometimes they were so vivid and so real it was like a punch to her stomach, winding her and making her gasp, setting her teeth on edge with incandescent anger and feelings of betrayal.

She pottered about the kitchen, setting the table and warming the plates, then went into the living room and stepped out of the French windows to pick some blossom for the table. Back in the kitchen she found a jar of almost used up jam and rinsed it clean, arranging the stems so the blousy heads of pink and white cascaded over the rim. She stood back and admired her handiwork.

'Mm.' She folded her arms with a smile and inclined her head to one side. 'Not bad, Sarah, if I do say so myself.' She remembered the length of pale blue ribbon fastened around the flowers Mary had given her the previous week and found it in the bits and pieces drawer, knotting it around the middle of the jar and placing it in the centre of the table.

As she went behind the island she glanced at her reflection in the smoky glass of the microwave. The tender area on her cheekbone had disappeared, apart from a sickly yellow bruise which had faded from black to purple to yellow as the days had passed. The cut on her forehead sported a red and brown scab, but the tell-tale signs of healing were evident because it itched like crazy and she'd had to stop herself from picking at it.

'Right,' she said, rubbing her hands together. 'Chapattis. How on earth do you make a chapatti?' She reached up to one of the cupboards above the worktop and opened it. Inside were lots of recipe books, some of them unopened, all certainly never used. 'There must be a recipe for them in one of these.' She pulled one of the books towards her. 'Indian Cuisine for the Beginner'. Her laughter echoed around the kitchen. 'Well, I'm definitely that,' and looked down the index for chapattis, finding two recipes, one simple, one a little more complicated. 'Simple's always best,' she said under her breath. Running her finger down the list of ingredients and finding the flour, salt and olive oil in the cupboard as she went, she suddenly stopped, her hand in mid-air as she reached into the cupboard. Lowering her hand she leant against the counter and listened.

Tobias was playing in his room. The window in his bedroom was open as was the one in the kitchen and Sarah was sure she could hear him talking. A flock of birds with spring fever was singing at full pelt in the garden and she frowned as the shrill sound drowned out Tobias's voice. She waited for a few moments to see if she could make out what he was saying but his voice wasn't clear enough for her to discern any words so she went into the hall and stood at the bottom of the stairs.

There was no sound. Maybe I imagined it, she thought. As she turned away she heard Tobias's voice again, and went softly up the stairs, following the sound, stepping over the creaky tread and up onto the galleried landing, standing silently at the top. Listening.

'I not come to Secret Club. Saha will know and she be sad,' Tobias said firmly. 'I not know the Wishing Tree. I not know the den.' Sarah crept forward on the landing, edging closer to Tobias's bedroom. 'I not allowed in the woods. Saha says. Not allowed just Tobias. Never just Tobias. Must stay with Saha. The big man came. The big man hurt Saha.' Sarah stopped just short of Tobias's door and peered into the room.

He was sitting on the floor, his Lego lined up in chunks of colour and size, all in perfect formation. The Lego men were also lined up in a perfect arrangement as were his cars. He was staring at an area in front of him, talking to the space between him and the bed. 'We play. You drawed pictures. You drawed pictures, Tobias colour.

With crayons.' He took a crayon from the end, very carefully with forefinger and thumb so as not to disturb the uniformity of the meticulous line, the smallest crayon; the one he had used most, and held it up. 'I colour pictures you drawed. See, Aaron. We friends. We best friends.'

Sarah's breath caught up in her throat. Everything around her spun out of control, the walls, the windows, the stairs revolving around her like a cyclone as though she was caught up in its funnel. Her knees buckled underneath her and she fell to the floor, landing so hard on her stomach all the breath was knocked out of her.

A wave of intense nausea picked up speed at the base of her solar plexus and rose up through her chest to her throat. Her temperature shot up making her head swim and she lost control of her bladder, a warm puddle spreading out underneath her and across the wooden floor. Face down on the floor she began to retch as sweat soaked the roots of her hair and trickled off her forehead. She put her cheek down onto the boards, praying it would cool her down. The intense heat was overwhelming; her brain and the inside of her head was at boiling point. Her heart pummelled the inside of her chest, beating out of rhythm like a drummer gone crazy. The blood running through her veins pulsed like a siren in her ears. Her breath left her in short gasps, and when she tried to swallow her throat was gravel.

'I'm dying,' she breathed. 'Am I going to die?'

A thin trail of decision went through her mind to call Tobias but she knew he would be frightened to see her the way she was, so she stayed on the floorboards and waited for whatever sickness had overtaken her body to pass. It was the name, the name Tobias had said.

Aaron.

He said Aaron.

An uncontrollable sob left her, and she retched again, heaving so hard it hurt her ribs. She dragged herself across the landing into the bathroom and lay her cheek against the cold tiles. Closing her eyes she tried to slow down her breathing, and gradually the overwhelming nausea dissolved and she lay on her side, thankful for the cool hardness of the floor...

There was something about Aaron. He was such a pain, but she loved him even though he often got her into trouble. He was a funny little thing, skinny to the point of emaciated; his elbows and knees bony and sharp yet his face was round with chubbiness and his cheeks were always red and usually dirty. He loved digging his elbows into her when she was trying to sleep.

He'd slide down off his bunkbed—there wasn't a ladder because he'd broken it by using it as a bridge between his bed and the wardrobe and it had shattered underneath him—and deliberately ram his elbows into her. He didn't care if she was awake or asleep, the result was always the same. She'd holler at the top of her voice and he'd scramble back up to his bunk and pretend to be asleep. When her mum or dad came in to the room to investigate it was always her who got the thick ear, particularly off her dad. Her mum said Aaron had issues and wasn't right in the head, but he was capable of much more than they knew. He meant so much more to her.

They never saw the pictures he drew, the portraits so absolute they were like photographs. They weren't interested in what Aaron could or couldn't do, or what she could do either. Her dad was only happy when he had his fags and enough money to go down the pub to see his mates, and her mum was only happy when he went.

Sometimes, when she and Aaron went to the woods and played Secret Club, they were friends. Aaron was a joker, so funny, even at six. He used to say things which made him seem much older, and the first time she'd seen him smoke a cigarette from a packet they'd nicked from the kitchen drawer she'd laughed so much she'd nearly wet herself. He'd done an impression of their dad, copied his every move as he lit and smoked his roll-ups. First, he'd rolled the cigarette around in his fingers to smooth down any bumps, then he peered at the end to see if there was any tobacco sticking out. He'd picked bits out like their dad did, put it in his mouth and lit it with a match, cupping his hand around it so the flare from the match made an orange glow against his cheeks. He held it between two fingers and a thumb.

'This is how blokes smoke,' he'd said, and when he'd smoked it down to the end he narrowed his eyes like their dad did, squinting through the smoke. She and her friends had laughed and laughed, rolling around on the ground at his perfect impersonation. She'd been proud of him. He was her little brother, her best friend, the person she knew better than anyone else.

Then the darkness had come.

Sarah frowned as her mind went into the shadows, a place of mist and memories so dark, so overwhelming she felt every muscle in her body tense with fear. This was the place she had pushed away, the one she'd hidden from herself for so long, knowing if she visited it again it could be the end of her. Nothing could have prepared her for the judgment they made about Lacey Murphy, the ones who wouldn't listen when she told them it wasn't her, and they'd sent her away from everyone and everything she knew. The decision to imprison her had sent her to hell. She was just a child, only ten, and she had been convicted as a killer.

Anxiety made Sarah sweat. Perspiration drenched her face and ran down her back and she was scared the heat and the sickness would overtake her again. She tried to stop her mind from going to a murky street, myriad snowflakes highlighted in sickly yellow beams, the gloomy woods shadowed with silhouettes of cold terror, but she was dragged there by her memory, now free from the constraints she had placed on it, that defining moment when everything had changed…

Her stomach had rolled over and over when she knew he'd left the house. She was frightened for him. My little brother, she thought. He's outside in the dark by himself. Even though she knew Aaron wasn't scared of the dark, she was. She hated it when they were made to switch their light off at night before they went to sleep, and she'd been grateful Aaron was in the bunk above her. It made her feel safe. He didn't see faces in the patterns on the curtains or hear the creaking of the bedroom floorboards as though someone was walking across them, or flinch at the scraping of branches on the window when the wind got up, but these were the things that frightened her.

Nothing frightened Aaron, yet she was scared of everything. He'd just laugh at her and call her a plonker and say he would tell everyone in Secret Club what a wuss she was, but she hadn't cared. At least he was there. With her.

When their Nana died and Aaron had been moved to her old room he hadn't cared, even though she'd died in there, passed away in the bed he inherited. She'd shivered thinking she was glad it was Aaron who got Nana's room and not her, but she wanted him to stay in their room even if he did make trouble for her. She'd remembered what they'd told them in school about stranger danger and safety in numbers. They were a two, but when Aaron moved rooms she was a one. She hadn't liked it. Not one bit. She'd asked him about it.

'Aren't you scared of ghosts?' she'd asked him.

'I don't care,' he'd replied.

And she'd repeated the rhyme her Nana always said to him when he said he didn't care about anything…

'Don't care was made to care.

Don't care was hung,

Don't care was put in a pot and boiled 'til he was done.'

Aaron had roared with laughter and said, 'So boil me. Go on then, put me in a pot and boil me. It would be so funny.'

The wood was their place. It meant they could get away from home, the arguments, the accusations, the poverty so ingrained in everything about their lives you could smell it. And Aaron, jumping from tree to tree, making silly noises, calling her names everyone laughed at which made her feel small. Aaron running around the house making whooping noises and laughing as though he would never stop.

Aaron vanishing into a night so dark it was as dense as outer space.

Aaron. In the den they had made together.

Aaron. Covered in blood.

Then…

After a while Sarah pulled herself into a sitting position, her knees pulled up in front of her. Leaning against the doorframe she wiped the perspiration from her face with the bottom of her sleeve. She closed her eyes and rested her head against the door. Aaron was in her mind's eye, the mop-headed boy with the snotty nose and the cheeky grin, and heard his raucous laugh ring out, the one that sounded as though he smoked twenty cigarettes a day.

Sarah recalled the night he went missing and trembled, pulling her legs closer and wrapping her arms around them, resting her forehead on her knees.

'Oh, Aaron,' she cried, and began to sob, convulsions of grief shaking her body so violently and engulfing her so completely she frightened herself.

After a while the sobs subsided, and she raised her head to find Tobias in front of her, his elephant under his arm, his eyes focussed on her face. She drew in a breath of dismay as he stared at the tears and snot on her face. He reached out a finger and pressed it against her skin, stopping a tear from under her eye threatening to run down her cheek.

'Saha? Saha got cry on her face.' Sarah reached forward and pulled him towards her, enfolding him in her arms. He didn't flinch or try to pull away, but relaxed into her, laying his head against her shoulder, his arm around her side. She lay her cheek against his thick curls and breathed in his little boy smell of biscuits and wax crayons and school, a scent so familiar it transported her back to the primary school at the top of the hill where she and Aaron had been pupils.

'Sarah stubbed her toe on the door. Aren't I silly?' She put a finger under his chin and smiled at him. 'I really hurt my poor foot but I'm okay now.'

'It made Saha have cry on her face.'

'Yes, it did. Remember when you fell over in the playground at school? You hurt your knee didn't you? And the nurse, Mrs Brown put a Mickey Mouse plaster on it to make it feel better.'

His eyes suddenly brightened. 'Saha can have Mickey Mouse plaster. Mrs Brown put it on, make it better.'

She laughed quietly so he could see she was alright, her swollen eyes creasing at the corners. 'Yes. I'll tell her I hurt my toe and ask her for a Mickey Mouse plaster.' She released a breath and got to her feet. 'Are you hungry, sweetheart?'

He nodded. 'Pizza and Barney Bear.'

'You can't have pizza and Barney Bear cake every day. They're a treat, for special days, like when you get a gold star in your book.' He looked so crestfallen she knelt on her haunches and pushed the hair out of his eyes. 'Okay,' she whispered. 'But it's our secret. Don't tell Daddy or Sarah will be in trouble.' She winked at him to let him know it wasn't a serious secret, and he nodded.

After Sarah had showered they went downstairs hand in hand. She glanced down at his tiny fingers with the pink shell-like nails, clasped so tightly around hers the colour had left them and turned them white. Her heart lurched with sorrow. Tobias was almost the same age as Aaron when he was killed. He had been such a little boy, a skinny, mischievous urchin so very different from how six-year-olds were expected to be. Just like Tobias, really. A child who needed the understanding of others, who couldn't help who or what he was.

Like Tobias he didn't have any control over his behaviour or have a choice about the things he could or could not do. He was a pickle, that was all, and who knows what he would have achieved. Whatever the reason he was killed, someone made a decision to take the life of a little boy who couldn't fight back, and dumped him in the den to rot. Someone made a choice all those years ago. They decided he shouldn't live and allowed me to take the blame, she thought, a child who had no one on her side and who couldn't defend herself, a young girl at the beginning of her life who was shut away from everyone and everything she knew, imprisoned in an institution and labelled a murderer.

Scarred for life.

Changed forever.

And I'm going to find out who that someone was.

'You okay?'

Sarah glanced up from the laptop and raised her eyebrows. 'Yeah, why?' She'd been waiting for him to ask her because he kept looking at her as if he wanted to say something but wasn't sure if he should. She wondered what he was thinking, whether he thought she was fragile. If she could have told him the truth she would have told him she was so fragile and so brittle, if she heard Aaron's name on anyone's lips she would surely shatter like imploding glass, and would never have the strength to reconstruct herself.

There had been tears of remorse and loss when she found herself alone, wracked with guilt, wondering how she would ever come to terms with hearing Aaron's name again. She had been masterful in hiding it all away, enfolding Aaron in her heart with such precision no one could find him. Not even Sarah. They had questioned her over and over on the night he was murdered. They'd refused to believe her when she'd denied it, accused her of lying to save her own skin. So she stopped speaking. For months.

The questions had continued. They'd taken her into a special room painted in bright colours with pretty pictures on the walls and dolls for her to play with so she could demonstrate what had happened, and still she had refused to speak. The psychiatrists at the unit had used every trick in the book, a soft word here, a censure there, encouraged her to say something…anything, and when she hadn't responded had sat silently with her, waiting for her to break down and admit everything. She heard them say she had a personality disorder, a direct result of the environment in which she'd been raised; the violence of her father and the subservience of her mother. They'd grown tired of her refusal to co-operate and they'd let her be. And she'd been thankful, because it meant she could forget the awful night when she'd found Aaron in the den, thinking he was playing games like he always did. She could forget trying to get him to talk, nudging him and holding his hand, begging him to get up so they could go home. Forget he'd been killed, the image of which she'd folded into a tiny little piece and pushed to the back of a cupboard in her mind, padlocking it and throwing the key into a dark void.

She had never spoken of it again. Aaron's name had never left her lips because to say it would have taken her somewhere where she would have been irretrievable. She'd pushed it away so well her mind had dissolved it into nothing, as if it had happened to someone else. Not to Aaron, and not to Lacey Murphy.

She remembered him so clearly now. And even when she was sobbing and his round, grimy little face was in front of hers she'd felt herself smile, because Aaron had smiled all the time. She had loved him because his parents were the same as hers, because he knew how she felt when things were difficult at home, and because they both had dreams of something better. He told her he wanted to be a pilot so he could be up in the air with the birds, above the clouds and away from the world, and she understood. How well she understood. Yes, he was trouble on two legs, and yes, he annoyed her like no one else could, but when Aaron was around there was always fun, always laughter, and she hoped and prayed he'd known how much she loved him, because she'd never had the chance to tell him.

'You seem…different today.'

'Different, how?'

He shrugged. 'I dunno. A bit distant, maybe?'

She glanced back at the screen. 'Do I? Sorry.'

He pulled a chair near hers and sat with his elbow on the desk, reaching for her hand. 'Shall we do something today? I thought we could take Tobias to the lavender farm. They've got a really nice restaurant there and Tobias can cut his own bunch of lavender after we've eaten.'

'I think he'd like that.' Dan nodded and seemed to relax. 'How's Tobias with you now? Any better, d'you think?'

'Yeah. Yeah, I think there's been an improvement. He sat next to me on the sofa yesterday and rested his head on my arm when we were watching television. He wouldn't have done it before.'

'I'm so glad, Dan. It's nice for both of you.'

'You've worked your magic on him, Sarah.'

'Me? I don't think it's got anything to do with me.'

He got up and strolled around the room, looking at her art books, picking one off the shelf, flicking through it and replacing it, examining another. 'I think it's got everything to do with you. You're amazing with him. He really loves you, you know.'

A warm curl of pleasure unfolded down her spine. 'Well, I love him. He's a lovely little boy. And I think the sessions with the counsellor are helping too, don't you?'

Dan nodded. 'Yes, he's definitely making progress. He's saying a few more words too, isn't he?'

Sarah cleared her throat. 'He's certainly saying more.'

'Has he said anymore about the other boy? I was hoping the counselling sessions would put paid to it.' She felt a cold frisson of irritation replace the warmth she'd felt earlier. What Tobias is saying is true, she thought, no matter what you may think or believe. I know the other boy exists because I know who he is, but how on earth am I going to make you understand. If I tell you what I heard you'll have us both in the psychiatrist's chair. She fixed him with a stare and he felt it because he turned to face her. 'What is it, Sarah.'

'I need to talk to you.' He ran his hand through his hair and she noticed his skin was mottled, out-of-condition looking, a rarity for Dan. He had dark semicircles under his eyes making his face look gaunt. She didn't want to add to his woes but this was something she couldn't, shouldn't keep to herself. There had been too many lies and she didn't want to compound it with another. What should I tell you, she thought? How much will you take? 'Can we go into the garden and sit on the swing? Tobias has the little barrel filled with water out there. He's watching the pond skaters skim along the surface. He's been doing it all morning. His powers of concentration are amazing. He never seems to get bored with it.'

'Sure. We'll take some iced lemonade and the chocolate cake you made.'

She followed him out into the garden carrying the cake. Dan put the lemonade on the blue wrought iron garden table and sat in the swing seat. Tobias looked up to acknowledge their arrival and Sarah realised it was a first.

'Want some lemonade and cake, mate,' Dan asked him. Tobias nodded, and leaving the pond skaters to skim across the barrel by themselves ran over to them. Sarah willed him to smile at Dan. Just smile, Tobias, she thought. Please, just one smile. Dan passed him his special beaker, a plastic picnic cup with pink flamingos around the outside and put a slice of cake on the matching plate. Tobias bit a huge chunk out of the cake and smiled. Sarah's heart soared. It was the first time he had actually shown any pleasure in anything.

'Did you see him smile?' Dan whispered as Tobias went back to kneel by the barrel. 'He did smile, didn't he? I wasn't imagining it.'

'He definitely smiled. It couldn't have been the cake. I haven't mastered baking yet.'

'It's so brilliant. Do you think he was smiling at me because I gave him the cake and the lemonade?'

'Yes, I do.' She saw his throat move as he swallowed, the pools in his eyes. 'Oh, Dan.' She put her hand on his arm.

He wiped the tears away from his eyelashes with his fingers, looking embarrassed. 'Sorry. It's been hard.' A look of contrition crossed his face. 'For you too. Sorry. I'm just feeling sorry for myself. Bet you want to kick me up the arse.'

'I know it's been hard, Dan. You've had stuff to come to terms with too.'

'So,' he said sighing. 'What was it you wanted to talk about?'

She shook her head and took a bite of cake, trying to appear casual. 'Oh, nothing. Nothing important anyway. It'll keep. Let's just enjoy today.'

Dan nodded and seemed happy to leave it. He didn't force the issue and she was relieved when he didn't seem bothered. He left the swing and picked up a colourful ball, rolling it to Tobias. It rolled up against his leg and he glanced up at his dad when he felt it. 'Roll it back, Tobes. Roll it back, and we'll roll it to Sarah.' Tobias looked towards Sarah, and she raised her eyebrows and smiled at him to encourage him.

'Go on, Tobias. Let's have a game of roll the ball.' Tobias picked up the ball and looked at it, his eyes on Sarah and Dan as if deciding who to roll it to. Roll it to Dan, she prayed. Tobias, please, please, roll it to your dad. Tobias put the ball on the grass, pushed it around a little with his finger and rolled it towards Dan. Thank you, she said silently, raising her eyes to the heavens. Dan's face lit up. He looked across at Sarah and grinned. 'He chose me,' he said. 'I didn't think he would.'

'Of course he chose you. You're his Dad.'

'Got another difficult day today.' Dan piled documents into his briefcase, and filled a plastic bottle with water from the fridge watercooler. 'It's so bloody hot. Thank God our building's got air-con. I've got a feeling everyone's gonna get hot under the collar.'

'Why?' Sarah straightened Tobias's school tie, then took his hand and led him to the table where his favourite Coco Pops were waiting.

'Because the shareholders don't agree. Some are happy to let the hostile takeover take place because they're willing to sell their shares, but there are others who want to hang on. It's going to be an interesting few days.' He put the water bottle into his bag. 'And it looks like I might have to stay over again.' She glanced up quickly. 'Sorry, Sarah. I know after what happened you're nervous to be here on your own at night. I just don't know what I can do about it. If I'm needed…'

'It is what it is. We knew this would happen sometimes. It's the penalty we pay for your ridiculous salary.' She smiled. 'It's okay. I've got loads to do, and I've got my protector with me.' She ruffled Tobias's hair. 'He'll look after me, won't you, Tobias?'

Tobias looked up again. 'Boy wants Coco Pops.'

'Darling, you've got your Coco Pops. You can't have any more or *you'll* go off pop.'

He slammed his spoon down onto the table. 'No... Boy...wants...Coco Pops,' he shouted. 'Boy...wants...Coco Pops.' He picked up the spoon and threw it, tipping the bowl and spilling its contents like a brown, rice studded puddle across the table.

'Shit,' said Dan under his breath. 'What the hell caused that?'

Sarah shook her head and waved him away. 'I don't know. You go, or you'll be late. I'll sort it.'

'Are you sure?'

She closed her eyes momentarily, inwardly willing Tobias not to say Aaron. When she opened them Dan was staring at her. 'Yeah, yes, it's fine. Go on. It'll be okay.'

He kissed her cheek and pulled her towards him. 'Thank you for being so understanding. I don't know how I'd have got through this without you.' He gently pushed her away from him and looked into her eyes. 'Not back with me yet though are you? Even after all these months. I know you're staying for Tobias, but I wish you'd come back to me, Sarah. I really wish you would. I miss you.'

It was on the tip of her tongue to say, 'But Yelena would push me aside and take my place in a heartbeat, and you know it,' but she thought better of it. She held her breath, wishing she had the bottle to say something, but gritted her teeth and made herself let it go. When the time is right, she thought. And this isn't the time.

Sarah opened the front door and picked up the post from the mat, tutting when she saw the colour of the envelopes, all buff containing the latest bills. She threw them on the counter. There was another caught up in between them, a smaller white envelope. She raised her eyebrows thinking they'd received an invitation, and she eagerly ripped it open. There was a small card inside, folded over like a greetings card. On the front, written in solid blank ink were the words, "WHY ARE YOU STILL HERE?" She opened the card and three feathers fell out, two black and one white. Gasping, her fingers released them onto the kitchen floor. She stared at them for what seemed an age, mesmerised by them.

Pushing the feathers and the card back in the envelope she threw it in the kitchen bin and her thoughts went to the basement. There hadn't been an opportunity to check it since the night she'd found the dead magpies, and Dan had had no reason to go down there.

In the utility room she retrieved the key from the biscuit tin and unlocked the door. A sick feeling flooded over her when she remembered the night she had found the magpies and she hesitated before flicking on the light. Standing on the top step she looked down. It was like an electric shock going through her.

The basement floor was clean. There wasn't even a stray feather. Her hand shook as she pushed her fingers through her hair. Whoever had left the magpies in the basement and sent her the black and white feathers knew she had a magpie phobia, one she'd had since childhood, a loathing of the stark black and white of their plumage, the clicking nose they made and the way they strutted around the garden and nestled like grim reapers in the trees in Slaughter's Wood.

'Why are you doing this?' she said aloud. 'What have I ever done to you?'

What she was planning to do felt like madness, so far out of her comfort zone she could hardly believe she was about to attempt it. I have to know, she thought, because until I do I'll go nuts wondering.

Instead of switching on the light in the basement she was content to let the pale slivers of daylight coming in through the gaps in the garden door making narrow spikey shapes across the floor light her way. It was enough for her to see whatever it was she would see.

If there was anything. To see.

Her pumps crunched against the silt on the steps as she felt her way down the wall and sat on the last step. She wondered what she could have done to bring a semblance of normality to her task; to sit alone in a damp old basement covered in cobwebs and mildew was anyone's guess. It just felt right to do it here and not up in the house. She didn't know why.

Her heart trembled and she wasn't sure if it was with fear or excitement at what might happen, or the anticipation of disappointment if nothing did. Looking around the basement she said a silent prayer, grateful she was on her own. Some things had to be faced alone.

What she was about to do was out of love, a love she'd held for a long time but mislaid for a while. She thought about love. People spoke about nursing a broken heart when things went wrong with their loved ones, but was it really the heart cleaved in two or the mind with its electrical impulses and neurons and memories?

The brain was clever. When it wanted to heal itself it blocked things out, as though the grief-stricken part of it somehow shut down and denied whatever it was that had ripped it apart. Something profound would shake it awake again, forcing it to face up to things. The heart would still be a fully functioning beating heart, but the mind would never look the same, could never be the same. Just like the jagged scar on the side of her face. Its presence had changed everything, had marked her for life. Labelled her. She couldn't forget it was there or why. In a strange way, she didn't want to.

'Aaron,' she said, quietly into the musty, dust-laden air. 'Aaron, it's Lacey.' She waited, her breath held like a heavy weight in her chest. 'Do you remember, Aaron, when we were together? We were such good friends. Can you show yourself to me like you do to Tobias? I want to see you, Aaron.' She waited, for something...anything. 'Aaron I know you and Tobias are friends,' she whispered. 'He...talks about you, all the time. Please, sweetheart. I need to see you. Please come back to me.'

At the far end of the basement, in the gloom and dust motes he gradually appeared like a pale shadow, a soft, mercurial haze in the muted light. Her breath caught in her throat as tears threatened to engulf her, to release the grief she carried in her still. She swallowed and blew out small puffs of air to steady herself. She didn't want to frighten him, would have been mortified if she scared him away. Trying to remain still and calm she smiled gently, her voice soothing and tender.

'Hello, Aaron.' He grinned at her and lifted his hand in a wave. 'Do you know me?' He nodded once. 'You know I love you don't you? You know I miss you? Someone hurt you but it wasn't me. I would never hurt you, sweetheart.' He hopped up onto one of the packing boxes they'd stored in the basement after the move and hung his legs over the edge, swinging them backwards and forwards. 'You've been so good to Tobias. He needed a friend.' He stared at her. 'Did you teach him to draw?' He grinned again and thumbed his chest. She laughed. He'd always thumbed his chest when he was showing off.

There was a reason she'd gone to the basement, even though it would break her heart. Dan had mentioned exorcism if Tobias didn't stop talking about the other boy. It had horrified her, and told her something important about Dan. He wasn't as sure of his assertions as he would have her believe. To him it was just the next step to getting rid of a problem. She couldn't allow it, couldn't stand by and watch as Aaron was flung out into the ether to who knows where. It would be like his dying all over again. She was frightened for Aaron and wanted to protect him. Surely there was somewhere else he should be? Maybe he didn't know. He was just a little boy, so very young. Maybe he didn't realise he was supposed to go to the other place.

'Don't you want to leave the mill, Aaron? Is there something I can do to help you to go to the other place?' The grin left his face and he shook his head, scowling, looking troubled, as if leaving was the last thing he wanted.

'Who did this to you? Can you tell me who it was who hurt you?' It wasn't me, Aaron. I promise you, it wasn't me, but it's not safe for you here,' she said. 'I don't want you to be sent somewhere you don't want to be, or to be hurt again. You've been hurt enough already.' He gently raised his eyes and looked hard at her, his chuckle enfolding her, echoing around the walls, then by degrees he faded away and the air was still again.

Sarah held her breath as he disappeared into the air, wanting him to stay, wishing she could bring him back. She was alone in the basement again. Lonely without him, without Aaron. She put her arms around her legs and laid her head on her knees, closing her eyes.

'Oh, sweet Jesus,' she said under her breath. 'He's still here. Aaron's really here.' She raised her head and opened her eyes, looking through the thin shafts of light and the dust motes, searching for him, needing desperately to see him again.

'But why? Why hasn't he left the place where he was killed? What is it that's keeping him here?'

She hadn't slept the previous night. It was as though the ability to sleep had deserted her. Part of her thought it was what she wanted. If she'd slept she would have been at the mercy of her dreams. It wouldn't have been real. And she needed real. Her mind wouldn't or couldn't stop working, running repeatedly through those moments in the basement when she had seen Aaron again.

She'd gone up into the house afterwards and hugged it to herself, had repeated it again and again…Aaron's here…Aaron's here. This was something no one else—apart from Tobias—knew about, and now she and the little boy who had been hurtled so unexpectedly into her life had even more in common.

Sitting at the desk in the study she opened her diary. She had a few calls to make, organising visits to the gallery, one from an art school. She loved thinking they might find a superstar artist amongst all the youngsters who visited them. Fuelling the dreams and aspirations of young artists gave her a real sense of making a difference. The art world had saved her during some of her most difficult times and if it had helped her it could help someone else.

She thought about Tobias and his growing talent for drawing. Even with the challenges he would face during his life he could have a promising career as an artist, yet every time she found a picture she was sure he'd drawn, he'd said it was the other boy who had drawn it. She wondered why. She had seen Tobias draw. His movements with the pencil were deft and confident.

Later, she picked Tobias up from school. He wasn't waiting in the playground with his teacher like on other days and anxiety shot through her. She found him in the classroom, sobbing. His teacher, Ms. Roberts looked upset.

'What happened?'

'One of the girls wasn't very nice to him. She called him an unkind name and he clearly understood what it meant.'

'What was it?'

'I'll write it down for you.' She wrote the word, "weirdo" on a scrap of paper.

Sarah felt only sadness. 'It's probably not her fault. They're only five. It's tempting to get cross but…maybe she heard someone else say it. An adult?'

'Have you ever thought about inviting one of the children in the class for tea, Ms. Anders? It might help Tobias connect with them.'

'Tobias's dad and I have talked about it, but let's be honest,' she smiled ironically at her, 'they'd probably refuse. Unfortunately I haven't connected with the other parents because of the difficulties Tobias has, so I think it's unlikely they'd agree. They don't know me either, do they?'

Back at the mill Sarah let Tobias choose his own dinner. He asked for chicken nuggets which had made her wince but let him have them anyway. Afterwards, an ice lolly seemed to cheer him up.

'What do you want to do, Tobias? Would you like to go out, maybe a walk by the river?' He shook his head. 'Okay, perhaps some telly, and when I've prepared dinner for Daddy and me, you and I can play a game. Would you like to choose one?'

Tobias didn't answer, simply went into the living room and switched the television to his favourite channel. This was one of the worst parts of Tobias's condition; the lack of social interaction. At a crucial point in Sarah's life she'd also lost the ability to connect with others, and a shudder of regret ran through her. She couldn't blame Dan for Tobias not having friends back to tea, certain that if he was the one taking him to and from school he would have already sorted it. He had a charm people found difficult to resist. Dan was gregarious, a people person, while Sarah was only comfortable with like-minded people, and this shyness had caused her problems in the past. It dawned on her she identified with Tobias more than she'd realised.

The gorgeous exotic smells she'd created in the kitchen after putting together a complicated dish with the help of a recipe from a magazine comforted Sarah, and without mentioning it to Dan had armed herself with every conceivable spice and herb. The array of jars on the worktop looked impressive.

'This had better work or it's a secret trip down to the local Indian restaurant,' then realised they hadn't ordered an Indian takeaway since they'd been at the mill. Turning the concoction down to a simmer she went to check on Tobias, thinking how quiet he was, poking her head around the living room door expecting to see him in his usual place, the tatty elephant by his side. The children's channel was nearly at shutdown—the bedtime story being read by Tom Hardy—but there was no Tobias. He'd never taken himself off to bed before. There was always a first time of course, but he wasn't there either. Searching all the other rooms off the landing, she retraced her steps, returning to the kitchen. Her eyes widened when she saw the utility room door open and her heart sank.

'Oh, no. Not again. Please don't let him be down there.'

A draft of damp air cooled her skin, and a pungent, mildewy smell hung around her like a cloud. The urge to go down the steps was overwhelming, but she stopped when she got to the door, willing herself to be rational, insisting it was probably nothing. As she turned to go back into the kitchen she noticed the kitchen steps against the worktop and the biscuit tin shoved haphazardly into a cupboard, its door partially open as if the tin had been hurriedly pushed in. She tiptoed back to the top of the steps and heard a voice, a male voice, its timbre low and secretive. She went back to the kitchen and pulled a knife from the knife block, hoping she was overreacting. She went back to the top of the basement steps and began to step down, silent, cautious, sliding down the wall to give her support. Halfway down she could see exactly who it was; the man who had forced his way into the mill. He glanced up at the sound of grit falling from the steps onto the flagstones below, and when he saw her got up from his haunches and faced her.

'What the fuck...! Get away from him. Get away from him now!' she screamed. 'I'll use this.' She held the carving knife up in front of her like a lightsabre, hoping she looked more confident and capable than she felt. 'Let him go, or else.'

He held up a hand to stop her, looking nervous and frantically shaking his head. 'No, no, please, I will not hurt him. I will not hurt him. He can go, look. He can go.' He pushed Tobias gently towards her. She jumped down the remaining steps and took Tobias's hand, pulling him behind her.

'You hurt me. Look,' she swept her hair away from her forehead, showing him the wound, now a jagged silver thread. 'This is what you did so don't give me any of your shit about not wanting to hurt anyone.'

He pulled his hand down to his side looking contrite and spoke very carefully. 'Please forgive me for what I did. I'm very sorry. I am so sorry. Please. I did not mean to hurt you, but...I was...desperate. It's what you say, isn't it? The correct word. Desperate? It's no excuse, I know. I hurt you...and it was wrong. I hope you will forgive.'

'How the hell did you get in here?'

'The door.' He pointed to the garden door. 'I tried it and it was unlocked.'

Sarah frowned. How was it unlocked? 'Why would you be desperate? Why are you here? I'm not buying this. If you don't leave

I'll call the police. They know who you are. They can be here in seconds.'

He pressed his hands together in front of him as if in prayer. 'Let me explain. Please, let me explain. I won't hurt you. I haven't come here to hurt anyone. I just wanted to see Tobias.'

'Why do you want to see him? What's he got to do with you?'

His eyes met hers. 'Yelena…'

'Oh, I might have known. What is she to you?'

'I was her…'

'Pimp?' she interrupted, scowling with anger

He looked horrified. 'No. No. I love Yelena. We were together. We came over to UK from Russia together. She is nice girl.'

'Oh, really. A nice girl. What about the drugs?'

'You know…'

'Yes, we know. Dan will never let her have Tobias. She hid them in his elephant.'

He blushed and had the grace to look embarrassed. 'She does silly things, but I didn't know that. It is unforgiveable. It's not how we are. She was selling them to make money. This a crime I know, but…for a while…she was desperate. We…were desperate.'

Sarah lowered the knife and stared at him for a moment, weighing up what she should do. She wasn't the type to be a sucker for a sob story; living in a London plagued by fake beggars had taught her that, but it was the look in his eyes. The huge man standing in front of her like an about to be punished schoolboy seemed genuinely distressed.

'A nice girl…who slept with my partner.'

'She made mistake.'

'Yeah, she did, a huge mistake. It's messed up all our lives.' She sighed, then it occurred to her what he might have done. 'Just tell me one thing. Did you leave a dead fox here, in the basement?'

His face puckered into a grimace as though not understanding what she was saying. 'What? A dead fox? What are you talking about, dead fox? Why would I leave a dead fox here? How would I do this?'

'Someone did. Someone mutilated a fox and left it down here. Tobias found it.'

'No,' he chuckled nervously. 'No.'

'Why do you laugh? It wasn't funny. It wasn't funny for Tobias.'

'No, I would never do something so crazy. It is madness. It is shocking. Was Tobias okay? Did he cry?'

'No. If you knew Tobias you'd know he is different.'

'Yes. Yes he is. He is special boy.'

'And the waterwheel? What about the waterwheel? Did you start it up?'

'No. How could I? I wouldn't know... I don't know,' he shook his head, frowning, 'waterwheel.'

'And did you follow me and Tobias down the lane by the side of the mill one evening? Did you stand on the bridge at the end of the garden and watch us?'

'No.'

She thought again. 'Do you smoke?'

He nodded and held out his hands in protest. 'So many questions. Yes, sometimes I smoke.'

She breathed deeply, wondering if she was about to do the most stupid thing she'd ever done in her life. 'If I let you come into the house do you promise you won't try to take Tobias?'

He looked relieved. 'I didn't come here to take Tobias from you,' he said quietly. 'I came to find Yelena, and to make sure Tobias is okay. It is all I wanted. I was worried about him. Sometimes Yelena...' He looked down as if trying to find the right words, treading carefully so as not to make things worse. 'Sometimes Yelena did not take the best care of Tobias.'

'What do you mean?'

'She did her best, but...she had to work. There was no one to take care of him.'

'So what happened to him when she had to work?'

She saw him swallow, his throat moving up and down in his huge neck. He looked uncomfortable and he wiped his mouth with the back of his hand. 'He was left.'

Her eyes widened. 'Left? On his own?' He made one nod. 'Jesus.' She shook her head. 'At night?' Another nod. 'Where?'

'In a rent house. In one room.' He held his hand up again to confirm his words. 'Please believe, I was not happy, very unhappy when I knew. I told her it was wrong, but she said not to judge her and what was she supposed to do with him. There was no one to help and she had to earn money.'

Sarah bit her lip and blew out a breath of frustration. All she could think about was Tobias, left on his own at night with God knew who in the other rooms. Anything could have happened to him. Perhaps it did. She glanced at the man whose expression revealed everything he was feeling. 'What's your name?'

'Andrei. Andrei Kuznetsov.'

She stepped back and pointed to the steps leading up to the house. 'Those steps go up to the inside of the mill. I don't want to stay down here any longer than I have to. I'm going to back up the stairs and you can follow. Then we'll talk. Agreed?'

Andrei nodded, his mouth forming an upside down crescent. 'Agreed.'

She pushed Tobias up the steps behind her, ascending them backwards holding onto the wall for support, the knife held firmly in her other hand and her eyes fixed on Andrei. When Tobias reached the basement door she pushed him through, and indicated for Andrei to follow them into the utility room. She shut the basement door behind him and locked it, pocketing the key.

'Go into the kitchen, Andrei. Please wait there.' She watched his retreating back as he complied. She released a breath of relief and sat on her haunches in front of Tobias.

'Do you know Andrei?' she whispered. His eyes slid to the left. 'Is he good to you or is he a bad man?'

'Not bad man,' he said softly. 'Boy say Andrei not bad man, Saha. Boy say Andrei here. Down there.' He pointed at the basement door.

She put her hand gently under his chin. 'The boy's not here, Tobias.'

He smiled and pointed behind her. 'There.'

Swivelling on the balls of her feet she lost her balance, and as she landed heavily on her backside she heard a peel of throaty laughter from above their heads. She looked up hoping to catch a glimpse of Aaron floating above them, but he wasn't there. She glanced at Tobias who was grinning with amusement and she smiled.

'He's cheeky…isn't he?'

Tobias looked at her, still grinning with delight, his eyes sparkling, and nodded his head.

Sarah took his hand, and led him into the kitchen where Andrei was waiting.

'Would you like something to drink, Andrei?'

'Yes, thank you.'

They sat in the armchairs, Tobias on a footstool. Sarah wondered at the wisdom of what she was doing—casually drinking tea with the man who had pushed his way into her home and caused her injury—aware it was probably the only way she would get the information she needed. Andrei filled the chair with his huge body, and Sarah speculated on what he did for a living.

'Do you work with Yelena?' she asked him.

'I work the nightclubs. In London. We get famous people there. It is funny to see them. Sometimes they don't look like they do in the photographs in the magazines.'

She couldn't help smiling. 'I bet. So what's your job?'

'Security. No one gets past Andrei Kuznetsov.'

'No, I know.'

He closed his eyes and bent his head. 'It was unforgiveable of me. Are you okay now?' She nodded. 'I'm so sorry. I felt guilty because of you. I think you are nice lady and I hurt you. I never hurt a woman. I was...so worried about Tobias. I suppose...I love him...in a way and I didn't know where he was.'

'Yelena got past you, didn't she?' He stared at her. His eyes were shadowed with sadness and it wasn't lost on Sarah that she and Andrei were in the same position; in love with someone who had betrayed them. 'I don't know what to do. I tell her I love her, I will give her everything but she wants more. Love is not enough. She says she can have big house and money. And she can look after Tobias with father.'

A shot of anger went through Sarah but she gritted her teeth. She would only find out what was happening between Yelena and Dan if she kept her cool. 'Has she mentioned me?'

'She says you don't have child with him. He wants the child. He tells her he wants the boy. She says if he wants the boy he must have her too.'

'And what about you?'

'Not important.' He shrugged and sipped his tea, his meaty hand surrounding the mug. 'I have nothing to offer. She had child with another man and broke my heart. She did not need to have the child.' When Sarah looked horrified he held up his hand to silence her. 'Please, do not think badly of me. You and I...our partners have child with someone else. I have come to love Tobias but it has changed my life. Can you say it hasn't changed yours?'

Sarah purposely avoided the question. 'Do you know why Yelena has gone back to Russia?'

He looked at her quizzically and shook his head. 'No, she is not in Russia.'

Sarah blanched. 'Yes, she's gone back. She told me she was going back to Russia. It was why she left Tobias with us.'

He drained his mug and put it on the coffee table. 'No. She has been in London, working in nightclub. One of the big clubs where I work. She is a hostess.'

Sarah bit her lip. Something was unfolding and she was getting an unsettling feeling she wasn't going to like it.

'So, you've seen her?'

'Yes.'

'When?'

'Four nights ago. She had been away before, working in Europe as a dancer since January. She came back to UK beginning of last month but she keeps disappearing. I just want to know where she is.' He looked surprised. 'This is why I came to look for her here. She said she was coming here...to see Tobias. I wanted to make sure he was safe...safe with you. She is angry with me because I think he should stay here...with you and his father. I don't want her to bring him back to London to be left in old house while she works. This is not right.'

'Dan thinks she's in Russia. He'll be furious when he finds out. He needs to know where she is.'

'No,' Andrei said, shaking his head again. 'Don't worry, it's okay. He knows she is here.'

'What d'you mean? How can he know?'

'He came to see her...at club.'

A tremor went down Sarah's spine. 'What? When?'

'Mm, maybe two weeks ago.'

Tobias stood quietly by Ms. Roberts waiting for Sarah to pick him up. He clutched some drawings in one hand and hung onto her hand with the other. All around him the children from his class were putting on their coats, chatting, laughing, and screeching with excitement. He didn't flinch or even acknowledge they were in his sphere. It was as though they were like insects buzzing around him, minor irritations to be ignored.

He stared at the gate. Sarah would be with him soon, and until he saw her he would stand totally still because it was all he needed to do. He didn't want anything else but to wait for her. He heard Ms. Roberts sigh and admonish his classmates for making too much noise.

'Quiet now, for goodness sake. You sound like banshees. Keep the noise down, please,' he heard her say. He wondered what a banshee was. He liked the word and he said it to himself in his head over and over as he waited for Sarah, banshee, banshee, banshee. He could hear his own voice as if it existed outside of his body and it satisfied him. He wondered if Ms. Roberts could hear his voice too. He hoped she could.

Ms. Roberts smiled to herself. Part of a teacher's job was to remember what it was like to be a child and she knew why they were so excited. They'd all received a party invitation for the weekend; a trip to a bowling alley with burgers and chips afterwards and a goody bag to take home. Everyone in the class had one. Everyone apart from Tobias. She glanced down at him wondering whether he knew he had been left off the invitation list. It occurred to her he probably didn't know what an invitation was, assumed the social mores of his classmates were lost on him because he didn't understand the connections children made with each other. He certainly hadn't connected with any child in his class. He arrived in the morning, every morning without fail; the patchwork elephant either in his backpack or under his arm. He was present during lessons and wasn't disruptive apart from once when a child had thought his lunchbox was hers and had tried to take it from the table. He had thrown himself on the ground, kicking and screaming, and growling at anyone who tried to approach him because he didn't have the speech to tell them a mistake had been made. The other children had run en-masse to the classroom door, some of them crying, and she'd had to calm them down and explain to them he was different from them, but she knew they hadn't understood. Why would they understand? They were five, and when you're five you expect everyone to be like you and everything to stay the same. If someone deviates from those expectations they're marked out, and this initial judgement made by the youngest members of the school would stay with the conspicuous child, probably for the rest of their life.

Those early feelings of abandonment or rejection would never be forgotten and it was difficult for an educator to change that trajectory, particularly when the parents of the other children sent letters to the school complaining about a pupil who had disrupted the class, one whom had growled at their child and was therefore not only disrupting the child's education but was a danger to others. Ms. Roberts was aware Tobias was a pleasant little boy underneath the impermeable shell he'd built around himself, and she wished the other children and the parents could see it. She shook her head sadly, tutting to herself, wondering how any parent who knew how much it would hurt a child could deliberately leave out one child in a whole class of party invitees.

Tobias saw Sarah as she arrived at the playground through the school gate. He had kept his eyes on the path waiting for her arrival, and his heart jumped a little when he saw her. She was wearing the scarf he liked, the one with big red flowers on it. It made her look happy and more than anything he wanted Sarah to be happy.

'Hi, Tobias,' she said, smiling at him and Ms Roberts. The teacher took her to one side, and Tobias watched them as Ms Roberts spoke with her mouth very close to Sarah's ear. Sarah nodded and said, 'Oh, okay. What a shame,' and Ms Roberts said, 'They're so shortsighted. I'm sure he would have loved it.'

'I'm not sure how he would have reacted but it would have been nice for him to be included. We just want him to feel part of life in Newton Denham, and if he's always going to be excluded he doesn't stand a chance.'

Ms Roberts put a hand on her arm. 'Do you want me to say something?'

'No, no. Thanks, it's fine. It's not worth it and I don't want to put anyone on the spot. He…he probably doesn't realise or understand anyway. Hopefully he'll be invited to the next one.' Ms Roberts nodded desolately and Sarah held her hand out to Tobias. They walked across the now deserted playground and out through the gate towards the car parked on the hill. Tobias waited for Sarah to ask him about his day like she did every afternoon, but she didn't.

In the car Tobias watched Sarah in the rear view mirror. She had a sad face, or was it a cross face? He could see her eyebrows had almost joined together at the top of her head near where her hair was, and there was a deep line in the middle of them. Her eyes were all shiny and she kept sniffing. She didn't say anything to him in the car either.

The space in the car felt different, was different. Usually Sarah would sing a song as she was driving them home, like Wind the Bobbin Up or Twinkle, Twinkle, Little Star. His favourite was 1, 2, 3, 4, 5. Once I Caught a Fish Alive because he liked fish and it reminded him of the barrel in the garden where the insects skated across the water and made shapes on the surface. His dad said he'd get some fish for the barrel, and he'd looked every day to see if the fish were in there, but they weren't.

Once there had been a frog in the barrel. The boy with the dirty face who came to the house said he liked frogs and he said Tobias should be its friend, so Tobias decided to be a friend to the frog because the boy told him to. It kept swimming around the edge as if it was looking for a way out. Tobias was sure it couldn't get out by itself and he thought it would be upset because it was stuck in the barrel without its mummy, so he'd helped it out with a stick. The boy with the dirty face had clapped his hands and jumped around like a frog and Tobias had laughed and laughed. The frog had leapt off the stick and Tobias had sat quietly and watched it hop across the grass until it disappeared amongst the shrubs in the flowerbeds.

He'd smiled and said, 'Bye, frog.'

When they got to the mill, Sarah didn't say, 'Out you get, little man,' like she always did, and when he looked into her face it seemed like she was somewhere else because her eyes had a faraway look in them, as though she wasn't really with him at all. He stood on the gravel and waited for her to lock the car doors then followed her up the steps into the hall. She helped him take his coat off and hung his bag in the cupboard under the stairs.

'Did you eat all your lunch today, Tobias?' she asked him, opening the lid of his lunchbox. He hoped she wouldn't notice the half-eaten ham sandwich he'd hidden at the bottom of the box under a piece of kitchen paper. She'd told him to eat the ham sandwich and the carrot sticks first, then the tube of yoghurt, and the little sponge finger last, but he'd eaten the sponge finger as soon as he'd opened his lunchbox washing it down with a box of Ribena, and drunk half the yoghurt tube. By the time he got to the ham sandwich he wasn't hungry anymore. She glanced at him and raised one eyebrow. He noticed her eyes were pink and a bit puffed up and she wasn't happy, because when she was happy she had little lines on her face at the side of her eyes.

'I don't know,' he heard her say in a voice he didn't know, and she sighed and turned away. He thought it was a sign of dismissal and time for him to do the things he liked to do, like drawing and lining up his cars in order of size and colour, and investigating his barrel pond in the garden.

He went outside. It was sunny and warm and he managed to take his arms out of the sleeves of his school jumper and pull it over his head like he'd been taught at school. He laid the jumper on the garden swing and went over to the barrel pond. The pond skaters were skimming across the pond and there were two blue damsel flies hovering over it as though they were suspended on springs. He put out his hands and tried to catch them but they were too fast for him and flew off towards the river at the bottom of the garden. He stuck his finger into the barrel and whirled the water around, which was when he saw it; a flash of silver and orange swimming at the bottom under the weed Sarah had planted for him. It was a fish, he was sure of it.

He swirled the water again and a goldfish darted into the shadows as though hiding from a threatened foe, and Tobias was sure the fish knew he was there. He looked up to the kitchen window and saw Sarah watching him. She was smiling and his heart jumped. Sarah was happy again, and he was happy because he'd got a fish in his barrel pond.

He sat and watched it swimming round and round and round. He wanted Sarah to see it but when he looked up at the kitchen window again Sarah wasn't there. He wondered where she was and he got up and looked in the French windows, pushing his face in between his hands and making the glass mist over with the warmth of his breath. She wasn't in the living room so he decided to go back to the barrel pond to see his fish.

When he turned from the windows and looked across the lawn, there was someone standing next to the barrel pond. He hesitated at first but he'd seen the man before, so retraced his steps and went back to the barrel. Tobias knelt by the barrel and swirled his finger in the water and the man watched him. The fish swam frantically around the edge and Tobias glanced up at the man, feeling proud of his fish, hoping he was as impressed by it as Tobias was. The man didn't say anything but took a cigarette from his pocket and lit it with a red plastic lighter. He puffed on it making the tip glow bright red and held his hand out to Tobias.

Tobias stared at the man's hand. It wasn't like his dad's hand, it was a big, meaty hand covered in brown leathery skin. The fingers were stout and there were coarse black hairs on them, stopping just short of the knuckles, and under the bits at the end was what looked like mud. Tobias noticed some of the fingers were coloured an orangey-yellow, like one of the wax crayons he had in his crayon box. He didn't like the colour and he'd thought about throwing the crayon down the toilet but hadn't got around to it. He wondered why the man had painted his fingers such a horrid colour when he could have chosen his favourite colour, blue, the crayon he used the most, the one worn down to a little stump and was the shortest of all his crayons and always at the end of the line when he stood them all together.

Tobias looked across the barrel, and there was the boy with the dirty face. He had his hands on his hips and was nodding and grinning, so Tobias stood and put his little hand into the man's big one and they walked towards the gate behind the summer house, leading to the lane. The man's hand felt rough, and Tobias could feel callouses on the cushiony areas of the palm, like little circles of grit.

The man walked with a slow gait but Tobias had to run to keep up with him. He had a long stride, and as Tobias ran beside him his eyes were on the man's lower legs, encased in jeans with turn-ups at the ankles, and brown boots with mud on them. Tobias thought the man must have spent a lot of time jumping in the puddles down the lane. He looked for the pools of water on the uneven path but they weren't there anymore. Sarah had washed their wellie boots under the hose in the garden and he wondered why the man hadn't cleaned his own boots. Tobias thought he must be very naughty, and if he lived in their house Sarah would make him wash them, and wash his hands before tea. He always had to wash his hands before tea, although he didn't know why.

They walked down the lane past some tall hedges. Tobias recognised it as the place where Sarah had shown him the lady's dolls. The man didn't lift him up to look in the garden like Sarah had, but carried on walking towards the wooden gate at the end of the lane. He opened the gate and gently pushed Tobias through onto the lawn. Before he shut the gate the man dropped his cigarette on the ground and stood on it, grinding it into the dirt with his heel.

'Can't be too careful,' Tobias heard him say. 'Don't drop your cigarette ends onto the lawn. It burns the grass. We know better, don't we?'

Tobias stood as still as he could, waiting as the man muttered under his breath. He took Tobias's hand and led him towards the pagoda at the end of the garden. As they walked across the neatly clipped lawn Tobias saw the gnomes lined up by the side of the path.

A waterfall tumbled down some big grey stones making a splashy sound like when he was in the bath with his toys, and a little green bridge went across the pond from one side to the other. There was a doll on the bridge. He wore a white dress with random splashes of red like the dollops of tomato sauce Tobias had accidently dropped on the kitchen floor a few days before. The doll's painted black hair was pulled off his face, making a bump at the back of his head like how Sarah sometimes wore her hair when she was rubbing the television with a cloth, or pushing the noisy thing across the floor. Tobias wanted to ask the man if the dolls ever went inside, but he didn't know how, so he looked up at him, waiting for him to say something.

The man was still muttering as they went across the lawn, and when they got to the pale green pagoda with the red and gold front he released Tobias's hand and opened the door to the storeroom underneath. He reached into his pocket and took out a bar of chocolate which he broke in two, giving Tobias one half and keeping the other. Tobias tore off the wrapper and dropped it on the grass. The man tutted.

'Don't drop rubbish on the grass. It'll only make more work. We know better, don't we?' He put his half of the chocolate bar into his mouth and retrieved the paper and foil from the grass, putting it in his pocket.

'In you go,' he said to Tobias as he ate his chocolate, indicating the door under the pagoda. 'I've got something to show you. We can play a game.'

Tobias stared at him for a few moments and went through the door. The man followed closely behind.

Sarah swirled spaghetti into a bowl glancing through the kitchen window.

'Tobias,' she called. 'Dinner's ready. It's your favourite. Come in now and wash your hands.' Into another bowl, the same design as the bowl holding the spaghetti—a ceramic bowl with pictures of owls on the outside—she spooned bolognaise sauce, and in another bowl—a smaller version of the first two—she grated a small mound of cheese. Spaghetti bolognaise was a meal Sarah knew Tobias would eat as long as all the components were kept separate and not touching each other. If the sauce coloured the spaghetti with a tomatoey, herby glow, or the cheese made its way into the wrong bowl and got muddled with the sauce, as far as Tobias was concerned it was rendered inedible.

As she prepared his multi-bowled dinner she thought again about what Ms Roberts had told her. She sighed, wondering what she could do to change people's perceptions. When she'd collected Tobias from school and seen the other children from his class running to their respective parents clutching party invitations her blood had almost boiled over. She wanted to march back to the gate where the parents stood in a cliquey huddle in the playground and ask them what they thought they were teaching their children about acceptance and compassion by so blatantly ignoring Tobias and leaving him out of birthday parties. Every child had an invitation apart from him. It was the third time since the term had begun. And she knew why. It was because of one incident which had been blown out of proportion by the gossipy Queen Bee of the playground who had labelled Tobias an aggressive child, which was so wide of the mark it would have been funny if it hadn't so badly affected his life.

Thanks to the gossipmongers Tobias had no friends and was unlikely to make any, considering the pupils stayed together in the same class until they went up to high school.

She was glad he had something to take his mind off school. The barrel pond had been a great success and he loved it, spending most of his time watching as life unfolded in the watery world. He seemed to derive far more pleasure from it than anything she and Dan had bought from The Toy Box. Even the trampoline had been stowed in the summer house because he didn't seem interested in it anymore.

She called him again, and when he didn't come running into the kitchen she went around the island into the breakfast room and looked out of the door. The barrel pond was there but Tobias wasn't. A tiny bud of panic bloomed in her chest.

'Tobias, can you come in now please, sweetheart?' She waited but there was no sign of him. The garden seemed deathly quiet and her gut instinct told her he wasn't there. She ran into the hall and called up the stairs. 'Tobias, come down now,' hoping he was hiding, but the concept of hiding away until you were found a few seconds later would have been lost on him.

Sarah ran into the garden and stood by the barrel pond, looking frantically around the garden trying to spot his bright red jumper in all the green until she saw it neatly folded on the garden swing. She picked it up, holding it up to her face. It smelt of fabric conditioner and something else Sarah couldn't define, but it was Tobias's smell.

Swallowing down her panic she assured herself there was bound to be a reasonable explanation, deciding to search the garden bit by bit until she found him. He knew never to try and go through the gate edging the slope leading down to the river. In any case they kept it locked and bolted and there was no way he could get through it. Flinging the jumper back onto the swing seat she followed the path around the house. The side gate leading onto the front garden was also locked, so she doubled back and went round the other side past the French windows, peering in as she went in case he'd gone inside, and around the back of the conservatory, calling him again, waiting for him to run up to her out of breath, with some poor pond creature in his hand.

The bloom of panic had now blossomed into an anxiety attack and she ran back across the lawn towards the summer house. He must be in there, she thought. It's the only place I haven't looked. He must be in there.

The summer house looked benign and welcoming, a pretty blue structure with a veranda and a pointed fascia covered in honeysuckle and wisteria. 'Please be in there,' she pleaded. 'Please be in there. Please be in there.' She looked through the windows first, and when she could see Tobias wasn't inside followed the path around the summer house to the gate at the back which opened onto the lane; always closed, always bolted.

It was open.

The lane was empty. She looked left and right and did it again, not really knowing what she expected to see, praying Tobias was playing on the verges amongst the grasses and flowers not realising he'd put the fear of God in to her.

The feeling of hollowness, the quiet expanse of space around her, the not knowing which way to turn, the unbearable fear if she went one way to find him it would be the wrong decision and the wishing she'd gone the other way came flowing back. Yet again the sensation of déjà vu made her skin prickle. It doesn't matter what I do, it'll be wrong. I'll get it wrong and it will be too late. How can this happen again? Why is it happening again?

Tears welled up misting her vision and she wiped her eyes with the back of her hand, suddenly feeling like a child, not just any child, but a child accused of murder standing outside the den of branches where Aaron's body lay motionless, as though he was thumbing his nose to the rest of the world, and saying, 'You see, arseholes. I can keep still if I really want to and not because you've told me to.'

The force of the dread flowing through her shook her to her core. Those memories would never leave her no matter how much therapy she underwent or how much life moved on. She was still Lacey Murphy whose childhood had been snatched from her, who had been incarcerated because they believed she could take her brother's life without empathy and sit with him until they were found. In court she remembered someone had used the word "arrogance", saying she was so confident she wouldn't be accused and convicted she hadn't even made an attempt to run away. She'd wanted to scream at all those stony-faced people who, when they looked at her with revulsion, seemed to want her to disappear, or worse. Her parents had prevented her from getting near them, and at the time she thought it was because the judge wouldn't allow her to speak with them, but when they had not visited her once in the detention centre she'd realised it was because they'd chosen to stay away. They'd abandoned her, turned their backs to her and left her fate in the hands of strangers.

She ran past the mill to the road end of the lane to make sure he wasn't there, then turned and ran in the other direction, panic-stricken, her hair sticking to the perspiration running down her cheeks and flying into her mouth as she ran calling out his name, searching every hedge and patch of long grass.

When she got to the apple orchard she bent over from the waist to catch her breath. After a few moments she straightened up and leant against a tree, closing her eyes, wondering what would happen when she called the police to tell them a little boy had gone missing whilst in her care. They would find out who she was and the whole sorry story would come out, and yet again she wouldn't be able to control the damage it would do.

She ran up and down the lanes of fruit trees, squinting into the shadows in the undergrowth, nausea hitting her throat when she realised he wasn't there. Returning to the lane she took her phone out of her back pocket and called the police, and Dan who was already on the train back to St. Denys Station. He told her to stay calm and to try and think of anywhere he would have gone on his own.

'He doesn't know anywhere around here,' she said, looking over the gate at the end of the lane, 'apart from the Locke's, y'know the woman with all the gnomes, and Vernon her son, the one Mary said stares at the kids when they're playing in the woods. He doesn't exactly know them but he met them a few weeks ago.'

She heard a rustling behind her. Peering into the orchard she looked for Tobias amongst the trees. She saw a shadow, flitting from behind one tree to another, a silhouette, hopping from one foot to the other, then darting into hiding. It was so gloomy in the orchard, the trees so densely planted, she couldn't see anything but flickers of light and shade as the trees swayed in the breeze.

'Tobias. You can come out now. Please don't hide, sweetheart. You're scaring Sarah. Tobias?'

She heard a raucous chuckle and she turned towards it. Her heart's rhythm faltered. There was Aaron, bathed in sunlight, appearing and disappearing as the sun went behind a cloud, then came out again. His face and hands were filthy and he kept scratching his head like he used to when they were kids.

'Aaron. Where is he? Please. Do you know?'

He grinned and ran behind a tree, then stuck his head out, then his tongue. This was Aaron as he was, she reminded herself. He hadn't grown into adulthood as she had. His life had ended when he was six. He was still the little boy he was then, naughty, bold, irreverent.

'Aaron, I'm still Lacey. I know I look different but I am Lacey. Can you help me? You like Tobias, don't you? Did you see where he went?' Aaron stepped out from behind an apple tree, his face a picture of cheeky impudence, and pointed towards the Locke house. Sarah's throat went dry and she sank to her knees. 'Oh, God, no. Not there. Please not there.'

The gate squeaked as she pushed through it. She walked across the lawn to the back door and rapped on it with a swift knock. There was shuffling from the other side of the door, and the sound of a security chain being fixed into place. The door opened a little and Sylvia Locke stood in the shadow of the narrow hall.

'Mrs Locke. It's Sarah, Sarah Anders from the mill.'

Sylvia Locke opened the door a little wider. 'Oh, hello, dear. You were the last person I was expecting. I thought it was naughty Vernon trying to get back into the house before he'd finished his chores. It's why I keep the chain on, to make sure he does what he's meant to do. I don't like slacking. Is everything alright?'

'My little boy's gone missing. I wondered if you'd seen him.'

'The little boy who was with you the other day?'

'Yes. Tobias.'

'I haven't, but Vernon might have. He's been in the garden all day.'

A chill went through Sarah and she wasn't sure if she hoped Vernon knew where he was or whether she hoped he didn't. 'Could we ask him?'

'He's probably in the pagoda. I know he hides in there when he's meant to be working. Just give me a moment to get my stick.'

As the old lady went into the house a police car pulled up in the lane. Two officers got out and Sarah met them at the gate.

'Ms Anders?'

'Yes.'

'It's your son who's missing, is it?'

'Actually, my partner's little boy. Mrs Locke thinks her son, Vernon might have seen him.'

'Right.' The police officer nodded. 'Let's go and ask him, shall we?'

They walked across the lawn towards the pagoda and the officer pulled on the door. It was locked.

'Does he always lock the door when he's in here?' he asked Sylvia Locke.

'I...I don't know. There's not really any reason for him to lock it. I rarely go into the storeroom underneath. It's Vernon's place.'

The officer banged on the door. 'Vernon Locke, it's the County Police. Can you open up please?'

After waiting for what seemed an age, Sarah heard a key being turned in the lock and watched as Vernon Locke appeared. He looked even bigger than he did before and Sarah shuddered when she thought of what he could be capable of. He gazed at them all as if he were in a dreamlike state until his eyes rested on Sarah. He stared at her without blinking and she felt so uncomfortable she had to look away. Is it you, she wondered? Are you the person who's making my life a misery? What would you do if you thought you could get away with it?

'Mr Locke, are you alone?' the officer asked him. Vernon shook his head. 'Who's in there with you?'

Tobias appeared at the door and pushed past Vernon's legs. Sarah put her arms around him, clutching him to her, the relief almost melting her. 'Oh, my God, Tobias. Thank goodness you're okay.' She glanced up at Vernon Locke, then stood and faced him. 'What the hell were you thinking?' she shouted. 'Did you take him from our garden? You must have done because he wouldn't have left by himself? Answer me. Why did you take him?'

The other police officer put her hand on Sarah's shoulder. 'Ms Anders, we'll deal with this now. My colleague will investigate what happened and why Mr Locke took Tobias into the pagoda.'

Sarah watched as the first officer went through the door and up some steps. 'Will you, though? No one would take a child from their own garden unless they were up to no good. What was he doing in there and why was Tobias with him?'

'We'll find out soon enough,' she said gently. 'Tobias looks unharmed, but if you want him to be examined by a doctor I suggest you take him to A and E and tell them what's happened. Any report will be sent to us to be actioned. If it's urgent we'll receive it immediately.'

Sarah pulled her hair across the left side of her face. She didn't want the police to see her scar so she made sure her right cheek was facing the officer. 'I don't know, it's up to his dad. He'll be home soon.'

The officer came out of the pagoda, his cap under his arm, a slight smile on his lips.

'It's a train set.'

Sarah stared at him. 'What?'

'He's got a train set up there, actually more than a train set. It's more like a whole station, and a village, with houses and cars and people. He built it apparently. Vernon Locke. It's his hobby.' The officer scratched his head, a look of rapt admiration on his face. 'It's beautifully put together, a real work of art. It's Newton Denham in miniature.'

Dan joined Sarah in the kitchen. He leaned against the island and watched her silently as she cut Tobias's pizza into little squares, the only way he would eat it.

'I've got something to tell you.'

Her head snapped up. 'What?'

'Vernon Locke has been released.'

'Why?'

'He's been bailed because they're not sure they have a case against him. There are conditions though. He's not allowed to come near the mill or attempt to speak to Tobias.'

'But what if he does it again? He didn't seem to understand you can't just take a boy from his garden.'

'I don't think the police see it the same way. They're saying there's nothing to prove he actually took Tobias out of the garden.'

She thought for a moment. 'Well, what about the gate to the lane. It was unbolted. There's no way Tobias could have pushed the bolt across.' She ran a hand across her forehead. 'How *do* the police see it anyway?'

'There's nothing to prove we didn't accidently leave it unbolted, and he's a close neighbour who Tobias had met before. No one saw Vernon take Tobias from the garden.'

Sarah's heart sank. After Vernon Locke's arrest she'd hoped their troubles were over. She was sure he was behind the envelopes with the twig figures and the magpie feathers. He was clearly a man with complexities, and when she'd discovered he'd taken Tobias she had convinced herself he was more than capable of mutilating a fox and ripping the heads off magpies.

'Tobias wouldn't have gone on his own. He doesn't have it in him to wander off. Our garden is his sanctuary and he wouldn't have left his barrel pond willingly.'

'I'm not sure it will stand up. They're saying Tobias could have left the garden through the gate, wandered down the lane and gone into Locke's garden. Their garden gate isn't bolted. Vernon assumed it was okay so he took him to the pagoda to play with the train set. The police think he's harmless.'

'Completely opposite of what Mary says.'

'Mary's a gossip. Vernon doesn't have a police record, unlike his father. They don't have anything on him apart from being a bit odd and they can't keep him in a cell for being odd.'

'There's a first time for everything. How do they know what he's done in the past? It doesn't mean he's never done anything he shouldn't have. Maybe he was never caught.'

'What d'you mean?'

She shook her head dismissively. 'Oh, nothing,' she sighed. 'Just ignore me. I'm just upset about today. The feeling of utter panic, I don't ever want to feel like that again. Everything was so silent, Dan, like I was in a bubble, as though the only place existing in the Universe was the mill and the garden and the world outside of it had disappeared. It was the strangest, most frightening feeling I've ever had. The thought of Tobias being out there on his own, fending for himself was...was awful.' She glanced at him and took a breath. 'And it felt like it was my fault, and if only I'd watched him better...'

He went round the island and put his arms around her. 'Sarah, it's okay. Don't get upset. Tobias is alright. To be honest he seemed to love the train set. I was astonished when the police took me into the pagoda and showed me. It's quite something and I can imagine any little boy would be bowled over by it.'

He kissed her forehead and hugged her. 'We thought we'd taken every precaution to keep him safe, but...well, Tobias is different isn't he? Maybe another child would have run in to you if someone was in the garden. Tobias takes things on face value and only gets upset if it's something he doesn't want to do. He didn't seem scared of Vernon.' He looked at her and shrugged. 'Maybe he didn't feel threatened. It could be he felt Vernon wouldn't do him any harm.'

'Do you think I overreacted?'

'Absolutely not. He wasn't where he should have been. And let's face it life hasn't been easy since we moved here. I know we're both on edge but anyone would have been worried.'

'I won't leave him in the garden on his own again. I know what the police think and I get the feeling you have some sympathy with him and I get it, I really do, and maybe I'm judging him too harshly, but I don't trust Vernon Locke.'

The dream filled her sleeping hours again, and she wasn't really surprised after what had happened the day before. Tobias going missing was a tortuous reminder of the excruciating fear she'd felt after discovering Aaron had left the house in the dark and when she'd been sent away from her parents. At least now she knew why it came back to her again and again. The dream was different this time though, because unlike the previous dreams she saw who the person was who stood under the muddy yellow pools of light from the streetlamps, the man she was sure would do her harm.

Vernon Locke.

Dan had had to wake her. He'd been startled awake when she'd called out, no names, he'd said, nothing he could make sense of, gibberish really, but she'd sobbed in her sleep, her face pressed into the crook of her arm.

'Do you think it's time for you to see someone,' he asked her. She looked horrified and he held her close to stop her protesting. 'It's just to protect you,' he said softly. 'I want to help you and end whatever it is you're going through.'

'I don't need a shrink, Dan. It's the last thing I need. It will pass, I'm sure it will. Please listen. I really need you to listen to me.'

'You look exhausted, Sarah. You're done in. I'm so worried for you.'

She pushed him away, and threw him a look that any sharper would have killed him.

'Exhausted? You think I'm exhausted? I'm fucking terrified, Dan, never mind exhausted.'

He looked shocked. 'Why would you be terrified?'

'Where shall I start? Because someone's been trying to scare the shit out of me since we've been at the mill and I don't know why, and because you've been seeing Yelena. She's in the UK isn't she, something you failed to mention. Why, Dan? Why didn't you tell me? And I know you've been emailing each other. Your ecowarrior status let you down I'm afraid. You forgot to turn off the laptop. Your email account was on the screen and I read the messages. All of them.'

He looked shocked. 'Yes, Dan. I took Eve's advice and checked you out and I found out plenty. I found out you're a liar and a cheat, and I found out Yelena has been back in the UK for weeks. Why didn't you tell me?'

He looked shocked, caught out. 'How did you find out?'

'Andrei Kuznetsov.' Dan blanched. 'Ah, yes, you know him too, don't you? And you knew it was him the first time he came here but you didn't say anything.' She threw her hands up. 'Why, Dan? Why would you not say anything? I...I can't get my head around it.'

'The first time? What do you mean?'

'He came here, to see Tobias. The other day. And yes, he hurt me and scared me half to death, and yes he shouldn't have done what he did, but he seems to be the only person who genuinely has Tobias's interests at heart. He apologised about what he did and told me exactly what's going on.'

She stared at him, her expression sharp, her eyes sparkling like glass 'Do you not care how much he scared me. You didn't mention you knew him when I told you what happened.'

'Yes, I care. Of course I care.' He ran his hands through his hair in exasperation. 'Do you think I want this to happen?'

'So why didn't you tell the police who he was?'

'Because if they get their claws into us they'll tell Social Services and I'll lose him. Tobias. I'll lose him, won't I? We'll all lose him. You know how it is these days. They won't let it go and it won't matter if we've done our best for him. They'll put his wellbeing first and the next time we'll see him will be under supervision through plate glass. Imagine it, Sarah, if they took him away from us.' He glanced at her with troubled eyes, praying she would understand why he hadn't told her. 'How did you get to speak to Andrei?'

'The garden door was open in the basement. It was unlocked.' She watched his face for any sign he knew.

'How the hell...? It's never unlocked. There's no need for it to be.'

'How should I know? You have the key.'

He leaned across to his bedside table, grabbed his keys and inspected them. 'It's here.' He held it up. 'And I haven't opened the door since we've been here.'

'It's how he got in. He told me Yelena was here, in London, and that you'd been to see her. Was it for seconds?' He looked uncomfortable. 'Oh, not seconds. Thirds? Fourths? Exactly how much dirty sex have you had with Yelena Kashirina? Yes, Dan, I know her name.'

'It's not what you think'

'Oh, and you know what I think, do you? Well just so we're not in any doubt, I think you're fucking her brains out whenever you get the chance, that's what I think.'

'It's not what I'm doing.'

'So what are you doing exactly?'

'I'm trying to protect you, Sarah.'

She got out of bed and pulled on her robe. 'Aw, how thoughtful. By having sex with her?'

'For Christ's sake, I'm not having sex with her. I slept with her once, which was when she got pregnant with Tobias. I've told you this already.'

An edgy silence settled over the bedroom. Sarah sat on the window seat and looked across the garden to the river, wanting to cry without limits like the child she once was.

'I don't know what to believe anymore.' She pressed her head against the glass, turning to look at Dan as he stared up at the ceiling. 'And I don't think you believe *me* either.'

She stared out of the window.

'There's something not right here and I'm not talking about Tobias and the other boy. I mean what's happened to me since we moved in to Newton's Mill, the feeling I'm being watched, the fact...yes, Dan...*the fact* someone followed us a few weeks ago when we went for a walk down the lane. I was so scared, for me and for Tobias. And the dead fox in the basement you're so sure was a figment of my imagination, yet all you had to do was ask Tobias and he would have confirmed it. I know he has a lot to deal with, but...why aren't you on my side?'

'I am on your side.'

'Oh, really? It doesn't feel like it. And there have been other things.'

'What things?'

'Envelopes, one with a little figure made of twigs with one poked through the stomach like a spear, and notes asking, "Why are you still here?" with black and white feathers pushed inside. And in the basement I found dead birds, piles of dead magpies, all with their heads ripped off. I hate magpies, you know I do. I'm utterly terrified of them. Someone is trying to frighten me.'

'I don't get it. Why didn't you tell me?'

Their eyes locked and she couldn't help an ironic smile. 'Why would I? You don't believe me do you? You think I'm imagining these things, yet ever since we've been here I've felt as if I'm being got at. Someone is trying to frighten me. Is it you? Are you gaslighting me, Dan, because you seem to find it very easy not to believe anything I tell you?' She shook her head. 'And that I don't understand.'

'How could you think I would do something like that to you?'

She turned on him. 'How could you think I'm imagining a dead fox in the basement, and Tobias sitting next to it covered in its blood?

Why wouldn't you believe me? What kind of mind do you think I have to come up with a lie like that?'

She looked out onto the garden again. 'I'm the one they want. I'm the one they're trying to frighten. I know it. I can feel it. Every time I go into the garden…I know they're there. My instinct shouts loud and clear. I'm being stalked.'

He sat up and rested his elbows on his knees, perturbed, a flush of guilt across his face.

'Why do you think it's you they're trying to scare? Why not me?'

'Because you're never here when it happens. They know. They know when you're not here.'

'How?'

'Because when I'm alone and I feel the mill is being watched I'm certain it is. Someone is actually out there watching our every move. I'm not imagining it, I know I'm not. Since we've been here it's as though I'm living in the middle of a nightmare, never mind the ones I have when I'm asleep. Someone is trying to get rid of me. Someone doesn't want me here, I can feel it. I just don't know why.'

There was silence, heavy, uncomfortable, each waiting for the other.

'Is there anything else, Sarah? Anything you want to tell me? We've plumbed the depths, mostly my doing I admit, but if there's anything else…. Could there be anything, something you need to tell me? A reason why someone would do this. An explanation.'

'You said you're on my side.'

'I am on your side.'

He got out of bed and sat next to her on the window seat, putting his finger under her chin and raising her face.

'And I always will be. I've done some stupid things and made some bloody stupid decisions, and I've hurt you so badly, but I never stopped loving you. I never will. If there's something you need to tell me just say it. I don't care what it is or how bad it is. It won't change the way I feel about you.' He placed his lips tenderly against hers and as he kissed her tears pooled in her eyes and rolled down her cheeks. He pushed her gently away from him. 'Sarah?' he said softly, his eyes questioning.

She hung her head. Now was the time. She'd wondered when it would be and it had to be now. She'd begun to feel her life was in danger, out of her control, and if anything happened to her she wanted him to know everything about her, everything she'd been through. It was like putting what he'd said to her to the test. Now she would discover how much he meant it when he said he would never stop loving her no matter what. This was it. The moment of no return. Dan was about to discover who Sarah Anders really was.

That in another life her name was Lacey Murphy, a girl branded a child killer.

She collapsed against him and he held her body close to his to quieten the trembling that had overtaken her. The rigidity had gone, her tenseness had evaporated, and the anxiety he'd witnessed since they'd lived at the mill was suddenly released and she became Sarah again...his Sarah.

While he held her he knew he must keep the overwhelming shock surging through him in check. Her cheek was pressed against his chest, her copious tears soaking his skin, and he stared into the distance over the top of her head, his mind in a whirl of disbelief. Could this be real? Had his beloved Sarah, this beautiful, loving, caring woman really have been in a place of detention for killing her brother and not in a children's' home?

When he'd discovered she'd been separated from her family and abandoned his heart had broken for her, but he also knew he hadn't shown her the love and support he should have. Yet again he'd put his own feelings first and the guilt was almost more than he could bear. His parents had always been there for him. He could hardly imagine what it must have been like for Sarah to have parents who cared so little about her they left her to rot. Now he knew why. It was because of Aaron, a little boy who had been brutally killed in the garden of the home they'd chosen together.

And yet...she had been so traumatised by what had happened to her, her mind had refused to recognise the mill, The Big House as she called it, and the village where she had been raised until the age of ten. How much damage would it do to be locked up, kept from your family and friends and everything you knew for ten years for something you didn't do?

She'd pleaded with them, she said. Begged them to listen to her, to understand she loved Aaron and would never hurt him. She hadn't known he was already dead. She hadn't really known what "dead" meant. Her Nana had died but she was old. She hadn't known it could happen to a little boy. She told him the courts had allowed her to be released on licence with a new name and identity to protect her. Dan wondered how much protection could be afforded to her bearing in mind they were now living amongst the very people who had been so ready to accuse her.

She'd begged him for forgiveness and he'd held her shoulders and looked into her eyes and told her there was nothing to forgive. She asked him if he believed her and he'd assured her he believed her utterly, and there was no way he could ever accept she was capable of something so terrible as to take someone's life. She kissed him and thanked him and told him how much she needed him. When she had no more tears they lay on the bed, arms around one another, the only sound the hushed tones of their breathing and his gentle murmurings to her, assuring her everything would be alright.

Dan drifted into sleep and Sarah lay in the dark, watching him as he slept, knowing she could never tell him Aaron had never left the mill, was there with them still and she didn't know why. He would never accept Aaron was a restless spirit whom Tobias saw every day, and until Aaron finally found a resting place and went to sleep forever, she could never, ever be at peace.

The High Street in Newton Denham heaved with shoppers. Tobias skipped alongside Sarah, jumping over the cracks in the pavement. He held onto her hand until they approached a lamppost when he would drag her across the pavement so he could touch it. This was a new habit.

'Do you like lampposts?' she asked him.

'Tobias must touch,' he said.

She accepted it. This was the most recent tick he'd developed, an action which made him feel secure. She had her own after all, in a way. Every time she saw a single magpie in the garden she saluted it. "One for sorrow" scared her, and she always looked around for another to make the pair.

"Two for joy".

'Would you like to go to The Toy Box? You can buy some new crayons and some of the coloured paper you like?' He glanced up at her without smiling and nodded.

The centre of Newton Denham was always at its busiest on Saturday mornings. The High Street where The Toy Box was nestled between a jewellers and a book shop was narrow, just a slim road wide enough for one vehicle to pass through at a time, with a walkway for a pedestrian either side. Artisan shops lined the street; there was always a queue outside the bakers which made negotiating the street even more difficult, but the wonderful sweet yeasty smell which came out of the ever-open door was enough to tempt anyone and was hard to resist. Sarah's mouth watered as they went by, stepping out onto the road because there wasn't enough room on the path.

'We'll go to the bakers afterwards,' Sarah said. 'When we've been to The Toy Box we'll be naughty and get some cakes for our lunch, and some of the lovely Italian bread your dad likes.' She waited for a reply but Tobias didn't answer. Some days he chose not to speak. This was one of those days.

Groups of people gathered on the tiled street, mums with buggies, teenagers with pink or purple or blue hair showing off their latest tattoos, and trios of old women with pull along shopping trollies and wicker baskets, whispering behind their hands and speaking in low monotones as they imparted the latest gossip, vying for who could deliver the juiciest piece of tittle-tattle, like Dangerous Liaisons,

Sarah thought. She was sure they were the gossips the driver from TipTop Cars had told her about, and as she and Tobias passed them she was aware of the conversation coming to a halt and three sideways glances in her direction. She felt a shiver go through her. Is this how they make all newcomers feel? Is it why the previous occupants of the mill left in such a hurry, because they were intimidated by the grande-dames of Newton Denham? Or was it because the mill hadn't welcomed them? Was Aaron causing mayhem for them even then?

His face loomed up in her mind's eye and her mouth automatically pulled into a grin. This was what he did to you, made you smile, and she remembered rolling around the floor clutching her stomach as she laughed and laughed at him. He was such an imp. Such a scrawny little imp.

The tinkling bell welcomed them into The Toy Box as Sarah pushed the door open. Mary was down one of the aisles with Dave Crowther and another man. Mary glanced up when the bell jingled, a hopeful look on her face disappearing when she saw Sarah. Sarah was surprised when she didn't look very welcoming, but her expression changed as though she was aware of the impression it gave and her face suddenly broke into a false smile.

'Sarah,' she cried, walking towards her. 'How lovely to see you. You're looking a lot better than the last time. How's your head?'

'Yes, it's okay. No more pain and the marks almost gone.'

'You didn't see him again?'

Sarah frowned. 'Who?'

Mary indicated with a nod to Sarah's forehead. 'The one who did that. You must have been a bit worried he'd come back.'

'Er, yeah. I think the police were, but, no, nothing to report there.' She smiled at Dave and the other man.

'Oh, Sarah, I'm sorry,' Mary said. 'You haven't met my husband have you? This is Ray, Luke's dad. Ray, this is Sarah Anders from Newton's Mill. You know, I told you about her and her partner, Dan, and little Tobias here.'

Ray greeted Sarah with a handshake. 'Nice to meet you at last, Sarah. Mary's told me all about you.'

Sarah's stomach rolled and her heartbeat picked up pace. The years hadn't been kind to Ray Duffield. He was almost unrecognisable, but she knew she must play the game if she was to keep her identity protected. She pulled a face. 'I think I'm supposed to say, "All good I hope."'

Ray nodded and glanced at Mary without confirming it. Mary didn't return his look but glanced away. 'Yeah, you're from London, aren't you? You must be finding things very different here in Newton Denham?'

'Just a bit.' They laughed in unison. 'You can be anonymous in London. No one really bothers you. Everyone just gets on with their lives but I have a feeling it doesn't happen so easily here.' She stepped back and glanced out of the shop window at the three elderly ladies who were still gossiping, standing around their trollies like witches around a cauldron.

Ray tutted. 'Oh you don't want to take any notice of those old biddies. They'll only go for you if they think you've got something to hide.' He looked steadily at her, his eyebrows raised high on his forehead. 'Don't have anything to hide, do you Sarah?' He waited for her to answer, breaking into a guffaw. Sarah didn't say anything. 'You should see your face,' he cried. Dave Crowther tutted and shook his head, looking embarrassed, and Sarah pulled a small smile she didn't feel. She got the distinct impression Ray Duffield was a bully, covering up his aggression by turning it into a joke, usually at someone else's expense, the type of person with whom you never knew where you were. No wonder Mary looked so morose most of the time.

Mary smacked him on the arm in a kind of playful slap.

'Oh, Ray, leave the poor girl alone.'

Ray stopped laughing and his expression changed, his annoyance with Mary obvious. 'Ah, she knows I'm only joking, don't you, Sarah? Anyone can see I'm having a joke. Got to have a sense of humour. Can't go about being miserable all the time. Welcome to Newton Denham, Sarah. I hope you'll be very happy here as part of our community. If you need anything you know where to come. It must be difficult trying to integrate into village life. Me and Mary are always here for you. We all need a friend.'

He thumbed behind him at Tobias who was looking at the toys on the shelves down the aisle over which Mary had hung a new sign, LITTLE GIFTS FOR LITTLE PRINCES. 'Bet that little bugger keeps you on your toes, eh?'

'He has his moments. I suppose they all do.'

'Yeah, I bet he does,' he replied. 'Little sods, all of 'em. Except my Lukey. He's a good boy. Smart, intelligent, always willing to help. Takes after his dad, see.'

As he broke into another loud laugh Mary took the opportunity to jump into the conversation, determined to make a sale and retrieve something from the so far unsuccessful morning. 'Were you looking for something in particular, Sarah? For Tobias, was it?'

Sarah eyed the three of them. She had been confident they wouldn't recognise her. A twenty year gap and a stay in a young offenders' institution had changed everything about Lacy Murphy, her looks, her manner, and the way she spoke. The long scar on the left side of her face slightly stretched her eye and mouth distorting her appearance. And she was no longer Lacey Murphy. She had been tutored in speech and body language, received an extensive education which had shown her to be a prodigious student, and a new identity as Sarah Anders to enable her to begin a new life when she left the detention centre. She had the paperwork to prove who she was, and a passport which was her pride and joy because it meant Lacey Murphy and what she had been accused of and imprisoned for no longer existed.

It had been her plan to tell Mary she knew about the child whose body had been found in the garden of Newton's Mill, and had discovered it was a boy, not a girl who had been killed, and that his ten year old sister had been detained for his murder.

When she'd heard Tobias say Aaron's name and everything she'd buried had come flooding back she'd resumed her search on the net, uncovering old newspaper articles about Aaron and what had happened to him. There was even an interview with Mary Duffield and one with Dave Crowther, and interviews with other residents who couldn't wait to get their fifteen minutes of fame and their claws into the Murphys. They'd all known the notorious Murphy family. They had a reputation in the village for their behaviour, none of it good, and were damned by the residents of Newton Denham even though the family had lost a little boy in the most appalling circumstances. No one had held back. Not Mary. Not Dave Crowther. And not the myriad people who had come forward to give their opinions. She'd struggled to remember the names of the people who had been their neighbours when they'd lived on the estate, but there were a few she recognised. They had been old when she was a child and she assumed they were probably dead.

Well, *they're* here, she thought. And I'm here. Mary wasn't straightforward with me about the body found at the mill, and if I confront them she won't be able to hide behind what she pretended not to know.

'Actually I wanted to talk to you about what happened at the mill, twenty years ago. The child whose body was left in the garden?' No one said anything and Sarah felt her throat go dry. 'I've been doing some digging on the internet. Apparently it was a little boy who was murdered, not a girl.' She glanced at Mary. 'He was just six. Aaron Murphy?'

She paused again and Dave cleared his throat. 'It was a bad business.'

Sarah's heart thumped. 'You remember it?'

'Course I remember it. Everyone remembers it.' He coughed, rotating his shoulders, visibly shivering, shoving his hands in his jacket pocket. 'Feels like it was yesterday. That murder was why me and the missus moved out of the village. And we weren't the only ones. Couldn't stand the way the papers were treating us, saying we were all hillbillies, interbreeding and killing each other. All lies but they made the most of it. The Village of the Damned, one rag called us. It was awful and the missus was on the edge of a breakdown.' He seemed miles away, his face stony with unwanted memories. 'My Sheila suffered, we all did, so I got her out of here. I only come back because of my job.

'The last company I taxied for went under. Drive Time Cars. Been in the village for donkeys' years but they couldn't ride it out. No punters see. No punters, no money coming in. We were on our uppers me and Sheila, with four kids to feed and clothe. That family caused us hell. They were to blame for everything that happened to us. Sheila's never been the same, never returned to the person she was before.' He looked around at them, almost surprised they were there where his thoughts had led him, suddenly dragged back to the present. 'I feel for 'em, course I do, but it's hard to feel sorry for people when your own life's going tits up.'

Mary went behind the counter and picked up a pricing gun.

'I told you, Sarah. There's no point in bringing it all up again. It was awful and best forgotten.'

Ray Duffield said nothing, just stared out of the window with a faraway look in his eyes. Sarah detected sadness, but he seemed distracted. 'But a child was convicted of his murder and some of what I've read says the conviction was wrong, articles saying she didn't do it. There are special sites set up for miscarriages of justice, and Lacey Murphy is often on them. There must be a reason.'

'She done it,' said Ray. 'No doubt about it. She was a strange kid. Sullen. Always got her nose in a book. A bit of a loner. Too grown up for her own good. And there was more to her than met the eye. She was capable and she done it.'

'Don't think she had a choice did she,' said Dave. His face was shaded with sadness and Sarah glanced at him. Was there also guilt there, as well as anger? 'Look at the family she came from, rough as 'ouses, the worst family on the estate. The father was always out of it, drink, drugs, you name it, and everyone said he knocked her about...what was her name?' he pondered, rubbing his chin.

'Vonnie,' said Mary sullenly. 'Her name was Yvonne.'

'That's it,' said Dave, pointing at her. 'You've got it. Yvonne Murphy, Vonnie Lawton as was. She was in my class at school. She was alright was Vonnie, till she met him. Quiet, didn't have much to say for herself.'

Sarah listened without interrupting. You've got no idea have you? The people whose lives you're pulling apart, the ones you're running into the ground and calling dirt were...are my parents.

'Where are they now?'

'Nobody knows,' said Ray. 'And nobody wants to know. They pulled this village into the gutter. It's only luck we've recovered from it. If they'd watched their kids better the boy would still be alive. Instead they went down the pub and left them on their own. She was too young to be left in charge of a boy like Aaron Murphy. There was something wrong with him. He was like a feral cat...uncontrollable, always in bloody trouble. Me and the missus did our best to keep our Luke away from him because whatever trouble Aaron Murphy was in he'd drag one of the other kids from the estate into it. Everyone did the same around here, did their best to keep their kids away from him. Proper pain in the arse.'

Dave looked ill at ease as he remembered. 'He was a little git. Got my Liam in trouble once, nearly got him expelled for setting light to a bike shed. How a kid of that age can cause so much trouble is anyone's guess. The other kids thought he was great because he didn't care what he did. Into everything he was, smoking, causing havoc, nicking anything that wasn't screwed down. Like the flippin' Pied Piper, he was, although I'm not sure we should be running the lad down. The kid's dead after all.'

Ray nodded looking contrite. 'Yeah, yeah, I know, they lost their son and it must have been terrible, but because of the Murphys everyone who lived here suffered, especially those with businesses relying on tourist money.' He directed what he said to Sarah. 'Stopped coming, see. Holidaymakers didn't want to come to a place where a kid had been murdered. And there was all the talk about it not being the girl what killed him so people were saying, "Well if she didn't kill him, who did?", thinking they could be in danger because the killer was still out there. The only people what came here were reporters and rubber-neckers. No one brought their kids here and no one spent any money. We nearly folded, didn't we, Mary?' Mary nodded without looking at them. 'It's a load of bullshit, anyway. Course she killed him. I saw her. Spitting chips she was because Aaron had gone walkabout again. I heard her screaming his name and using foul language. Course it was her. She battered him with a log over and over and hid his body. Got everything she deserved, I reckon.'

It went quiet. Tobias quietly slipped his hand into Sarah's and she pulled him close. Her eyes went to Mary who said nothing. She was pale and seemed to be looking everywhere but at the others.

'Well, I've got to go,' said Dave. 'I've spent far too long gabbing to you lot. Need to get some fares or my Sheila will be on at me for not earning anything and she wants a holiday. Haven't had one for the last five years.' He patted Sarah on the arm. 'Forget about it, lass. It was years ago. No point in dragging it all up again.' He opened the door to go out, pausing on the step. 'It's unpleasant ancient history for the village y'see, something we all want to forget. No one will thank you for raking it up again, Sarah. You mark my words.'

He shut the door behind him and Mary raised her face, her eyes glassy and emotionless.

'You should listen to him, Sarah. If you want to be part of the community in Newton Denham you'll leave it alone. We had enough trouble when the child was murdered. It's done and dusted and you've got enough on your plate.' She looked pointedly at Tobias. 'I'd forget it if I were you.'

The green in the centre of Newton Denham was deserted. Rain had fallen steadily for fifteen minutes and the children who had been playing their ball games and shrieking with excitement had deserted it. Sarah sat on a bench next to the path which traced the perimeter of the green, her hair hanging in soaking wet ribbons around her face. Her cheeks were pale but her eyes were ringed with red.

She gazed out over the grass to the maypole in the middle of the green and thought how different everything was since the day she and Dan had brought Tobias to the green and watched children from the local schools dance around it, weaving plaits and chains with long coloured ribbons. The girls had worn white dresses and the boys white shirts and black trousers, and Dan asked her if she thought Tobias would ever be able to join in, and she'd said, 'Of course he will.' Her assurance had been to please him because it had been one of their happiest days in Newton Denham, their troubles temporarily forgotten, but in her heart she hadn't been sure.

Tobias sat next to her on the bench eating an iced bun from the bakers, oblivious to the desolation and sorrow Sarah felt. It had taken everything she had, every ounce of willpower, not to speak out and defend herself and her family when she'd stood in The Toy

Box listening to Mary, Ray and Dave talking about what had happened twenty years before, making a judgement on them, particularly her mother who Sarah knew had struggled with the life she'd found herself living with her father. She had remained silent and watched Mary as Ray and Dave had talked about the Murphy family as though they were the devil's spawn, running them into the ground and painting them like the worst family that had ever drawn breath. Dave's face was a picture of intense dislike, hatred almost, as though he could smell something rotten, and Mary seemed uncomfortable, embarrassed even. So she should, thought Sarah wiping the rain off her face with her sleeve, for lying to me in the first place and being so judgemental. As a mother herself she must have known her parents went through hell. Vonnie and Len Murphy lost their child, her brother, murdered by someone who thought his life was worth nothing.

Her tears mingled with the rain on her cheeks and she was glad. She didn't want Tobias to see her crying. She put her arm around his narrow shoulders and pulled him to her. He was bundled up in his bright green raincoat and the yellow ear defenders he'd insisted on wearing because of the noise from the other shoppers. With his hood pulled up he looked like Andy Pandy.

'Time to go home, little man,' she said. She blew out a breath. 'Home. Not sure it feels like home, at least, not the one I was hoping for.' She watched the rain fall from the sky in rods for a few minutes more, not caring how wet they got, realising she was simply delaying the moment of their return to the mill.

The relentless rain began to slow. She rang the water out of her hair and pulled her hood over her head, stretching it across the left side of her face. Taking Tobias's hand, she gently pulled him from the bench and walked back in the direction of The Toy Box. The crowds had thinned out because of the rain making the narrow pavement easier to navigate. She pushed open the shop door and couldn't help noticing Mary's furrowed brow as they stood in front of the counter.

'Sarah,' she said, her voice flat. 'Didn't expect to see you in here again today.'

'No, I know, I'd forget my head if it wasn't screwed on. There was something I forgot to ask you.'

Mary's frown deepened and she lowered her gaze to the stock sheet on the counter. 'Oh?'

'I meant to ask if Luke could come over to the mill. We need a couple of bolts put on the old garden door in the basement. It's just for added security, really. He seems to be the person around here to ask.'

Mary's expression changed and Sarah detected a faint sigh of relief. 'Oh, he'll appreciate it. He's been a bit short of work these last few weeks. When would you like him to come?'

Sarah shrugged. 'Whenever he's free…A.S.A.P. really.'

'First thing Monday?'

'Great.'

Early July 2019
30

When Sarah returned from dropping Tobias off at school Luke was sitting on the steps leading up to the porch. He was smoking an e-cigarette, the thick white vapour floating around his head as he exhaled.

'Good to meet you at last, Luke. Something smells nice,' she said with a smile.

He clicked off the cigarette and stood, blowing out a final mouthful of vapour. 'Yeah, it's Gummi Bear. Got it from the States. You can get anything from the States.'

'Gummi Bear? I've heard it all now. For goodness sake don't tell Tobias,' she laughed. 'He loves Gummi Bears,' she said, laughing again, but he didn't join her. Instead, he nodded silently to indicate his acknowledgement of what she'd said, his mouth a frosty straight line.

She ran up the front steps and as he followed her into the hall she went into the kitchen, filling the kettle and putting it on the hob.

'Your mum tells me you're the handyman in the village and that you can turn your hand to anything.'

'Yeah, well, I do me best.' He seemed ill at ease and swiftly changed the subject to divert attention away from himself. 'What was it you wanted me to do?'

'Dan wants a couple of bolts put onto the garden door in the basement. Heavy duty, he said.'

'Right. Can you show me where so I'll know which one will do the best job? It's unlikely I'll have the ones you need. Probably have to go to the hardware store in Southampton to pick them up if it's okay?'

'Yes, of course. Do you need money?'

'Er, yeah. Probably.'

'Have you ever been here before?'

'Here?'

'Inside the mill.'

He shook his head. 'No, never.'

'Okay. I'll take you downstairs and show you what we want. Coffee?'

'Nah, I'd rather get on with it if it's all the same to you.'

Sarah got the key from out of the biscuit tin and unlocked the utility door to the basement, switching on the light. Leading him down the steps she pointed at the old, once beautiful door.

'It's there.'

Luke went over to it and ran his hand lovingly down the wood. 'Looks like the original. Seems a shame to have it hidden down here. Could do with a lick of paint as well.'

'Could you do it? Have you got time?'

'Yeah, but it'll mean the bolts won't go on until tomorrow.'

'We've lived here for nearly six months without bolts on the door. I shouldn't think one more night will hurt.'

'Colour?'

'I really like the old fashioned chalky bluey-green.'

'Mm, probably be Farrow and Ball. Pricey.'

'It's fine. Just let me know how much money you need.'

The following day Luke returned and fixed the bolts to the door. They were huge brass bolts requiring a key to unlock them.

'Are they the ones you wanted?' she asked him. He nodded without commenting.

Suggesting Luke did the work wasn't the only reason Sarah wanted him at the mill. She'd worked out he was the Luke who had lived down the end of their street on the estate, the Duffield's old house, and one of Aaron's friends. She hoped he would have a different take on what happened to him. She was sure he was also the Luke who played with them in Slaughter's Wood, and wondered if spending time at the house where Aaron had been murdered unnerved him. I've got to ask him, she thought. I might not get another chance.

She made some elevenses coffee and took the mugs and some biscuits on a tray down to the basement. He glanced up as she went down the steps and she thought she caught a scowl cross his face.

'You want to watch yourself,' he said. 'Those steps need redoing. Fall down there and you'll know all about it.'

'Have a coffee break, Luke,' she said. 'I'm not a slave driver.'

He downed tools and took a mug off the tray. Sarah sipped her coffee and decided to break the silence as it seemed Luke wasn't keen to.

'So, did you know the little boy who was murdered here?' she asked him. 'You must have been about the same age?'

He took a breath, a beat of a pause. 'Yeah, I knew him.' He shuffled his feet in the detritus on the floor. 'Bout time you cleaned up this basement isn't it?'

'Was he a friend?'

'Yeah.'

'A good friend?' He nodded. Sarah knew she was being brutal but she was past caring about the feelings of such a judgemental community. 'You'd rather not talk about it?'

'Mum said you were asking about it.' He looked directly at her. 'You seem very interested in it.'

'She shrugged, trying to make it look as though she was only asking in passing. 'The mill is my home now. I was…shocked, I suppose when I found out what had happened. I wanted to know more about it.

'People round here don't like talking about it.'

Sarah raised her eyebrows. 'No, so I gathered.'

'To be honest, Sarah I would prefer it if you didn't mention it to Mum again. Or Dad come to that. People round here want to forget about it and if you keep raking it up it's going to cause a lot of bad feeling.'

Sarah felt a twinge of anger in her stomach, a twist of resentment unfurling in her chest and flooding her senses. How dare you, she thought. How dare you tell me I can't remember my brother, someone who was once a friend to you no matter what other people thought of him? You just want to sweep him away like a piece of rubbish. You're the same as all the other gossiping, backstabbing people in this damned place.

'Why would it cause bad feeling? I don't understand. It's part of Newton Denham's history isn't it. Everywhere has a history.'

'Yeah, but it's a history we'd rather forget…'

Sarah took the mug from Luke's hands.

'Perhaps if everyone hadn't been so disapproving of the family…'

Luke frowned. 'What d'you mean?'

'It's all online, Luke. I had to search for it but I read the interviews. Your own mother gave an interview to a national newspaper about the Murphys and she wasn't the only one. There was a thread running through all of them and it was ridicule. The family was despised, run down by the locals even though they'd lost their son, a little boy who didn't deserve to die.'

'Some people reckoned they brought it on themselves.'

She frowned and gave him a hard look. 'Some people? And how did they bring it on themselves?'

'By not looking after their own. It's what we do here. We look after our own and they didn't. If we all did it there wouldn't be a problem. They left their kids to fend for themselves. Aaron Murphy was uncontrollable, wild, and they left a daft girl to look after him so they could go down the pub and get pissed. And not for the first time.'

'Right. And where was the sympathy? Where was the compassion for a mother and father whose little boy had been taken from them?'

'No one was happy about it.'

'So why didn't the people here say as much?'

'Because we needed people to know we're not all like them here. They cost us. My mum and dad nearly lost their business because there weren't enough tourists to keep us going. They got into terrible debt. We lost the council house on the estate they'd bought from the government because we couldn't keep up with the mortgage and we had to move into a one bedroom flat over the shop we rent from a private landlord. I still don't have my own bedroom. I have a pull-out bed in the living room which is why I try and stay at my mate's places if I can. And don't talk about me getting my own place. I'll be a bloody old man before that happens. We suffered because of them.'

Do it now Sarah, she thought. 'And what about the girl?'

'What girl?'

'His sister. The one who allegedly murdered him.'

'Allegedly? What's that supposed to mean? She did kill him?'

'And you know it, how?'

'She was convicted and sent to prison. It means she done it. She wouldn't have been sent away otherwise, would she? She was a weird sort anyway. I can remember her having her head shaved. Running with lice those kids were. My mum wouldn't have them in the house.'

'It wasn't...' she blurted out.

He frowned and pulled a smirky, "What are you on about" face. 'What!'

'I... I mean don't they have stuff for that kind of thing. I didn't know they shaved someone's head because they had lice.'

'They used to. If it was bad. My mum told me. It would have taken a shedload of stuff to get rid of what she had running around on her head from what I heard.'

Sarah turned away, distraught. Head lice wasn't the reason she'd had part of her head shaved. She'd suffered from nervous eczema as a child and her scalp had become infected. Luke had reminded her of a time she wanted to forget, awful for a young girl. The itching had stopped her from sleeping and the pain from the infection and the humiliation of having to go to school with half her head shaved had been almost unbearable. The medication stank to high heaven as well and the other kids had called her names. She'd forgotten it until now. Thanks to Luke she knew what they were really saying about her.

Time to get to the nitty-gritty. Now I want to know what you really think.

'She might be out of detention by now. It was a long time ago. This is her home isn't it? She might want to return here.'

Luke's face darkened and his raised his forefinger to her face. 'Let me tell you something. She'd better not come back here because I can assure you she'd regret it. We're a very tightknit community in Newton Denham. She's a killer. A child killer which is worse. She wouldn't be allowed back here. If people found out she was back the visitors would stop coming and we'd go through it all again. It can't happen.'

'And how would you stop her? Doesn't she have a right to be here? How could you stop someone returning to their home if they really wanted to be back in the village where they were raised?'

'Steps would be taken. We don't need her sort here. She's killed one kid so what's stopping her killing another?' He shook his head. 'Take my advice, Sarah. Forget it. And forget her.'

She swam up to the surface through bubbles of sparkling oxygen fizzing around her face. Underneath her were long tendrils which undulated in the current and touched the soles of her feet making the tiny hairs on her face and neck stand on end. As she broke the surface and opened her eyes she could hear a voice.

'Saha?' Tobias whispered. 'Saha, open.' She screwed up her face as little fingers unsealed her eyelids, pulling them apart and holding them open.

She sat up with a start, wiping saliva from the corner of her mouth with the heel of her hand, squinting into the dark.

'Are you okay?' she asked him softly. 'Do you want to get in with me?' She pulled the duvet over but he frantically tugged at it trying to drag it off the bed. 'What? No, Tobias? What is it?'

'Saha. The other boy. We go. We go now.'

'Go? Go where? Sweetheart, what are you talking about?' Tobias pulled the duvet even harder, trying to drag it from the bed onto the floor. She reached out and grabbed his hand. 'What are you doing?'

Tobias look frightened. His eyes were unblinking, and as she held his hand she felt it tremble. 'The bad man here,' he whispered. 'The boy say, tell Saha. The boy say bad man here.'

'What bad man?'

'Aaron bad man.'

Sarah froze. 'Where?' she whispered. 'Where is he?'

'Down.' Tobias flattened his hands and pushed them towards the floor.

'Downstairs? In the kitchen?' He shook his head. 'The living room?'

He frowned, looking frustrated. 'More, more down.'

'The basement? Is he in the basement?' Tobias nodded.

Sarah threw back the duvet and got out of bed. She put on her dressing gown, took Tobias's hand and went out onto the galleried landing holding a finger to her lips, shaking her head to let him know not to make any noise. Kneeling at the top of the stairs she pulled Tobias close to her. She waited and listened. There was no sound. She rubbed Tobias's back and tried to smile so he wouldn't be frightened but Sarah's heart was beating like the wings of a bird captured in a net. Maybe he got it wrong. She reflected on Aaron. Tobias told her Aaron had warned him, and she accepted without doubt she should heed the warning.

They were like statues at the top of the stairs, a shaft of moonlight from the leaded-light landing window highlighting them in the darkness until Sarah was confident they could move without being seen. If they stayed upstairs and the intruder made it to the landing there was no way out, they would be cornered.

In her mind's eye she saw Vernon Locke creeping around the basement and up the stone steps, his laboured breath exiting his open mouth, his nicotine stained fingers turning the handle on the door, and she shuddered. Taking Tobias's hand and with her forefinger to her lips, she led him down the stairs and tiptoed silently across the hall into the kitchen. As she was about to unlock the breakfast room door she heard the basement door in the utility room being unlocked. Sarah was astonished. The key to the basement door was still in the biscuit tin on top of the cupboard. The utility room door creaked opened and the increasing shadow of a man broke the shaft of moonlight streaming in through the window. She put her arms around Tobias and got onto the floor behind the island, praying Tobias wouldn't say anything. Putting her finger to her lips again she stared at him and he nodded his understanding. Her heart tilted with love for him.

In the darkness she could hear the intruder's footsteps on the wooden floor. He was wearing trainers, the squeak of rubber soles on the polished wood unmistakeable. Desperate to get an idea of where he was she made a sign to Tobias not to move, gradually leaning around the island, expecting to see Vernon standing by the table, but he'd left the kitchen and was standing in the hall, looking up the stairs.

The moonlight shining in through the breakfast room door illuminated him, outlining his huge body against the wood panelling. He was wearing a dark, hooded fleece, jeans and dark trainers. She watched him for a moment, waiting to see which way he would go. She prayed he would go up to the galleried landing, hoped he would assume they'd be in bed. Then she saw it and her throat tightened with fear. In his left hand was a machete. The curved blade sent a shaft of laser light into the kitchen as it caught a beam from the moon, streaming in from the vaulted window in the breakfast room. Now was not a good time to lose her nerve. If he went upstairs she was confident of them getting away, but if he turned into the breakfast room...where was Plan B?

The seconds ticked away. He held the machete firmly in his hand, his large fist clasped tightly around the handle. She could even smell the stench of nicotine tinged with body odour coming off him. Had the strange happenings at the mill been leading up to this moment; the dead fox, the beheaded magpies, the feathers and stick figure? Vernon Locke had to be responsible for the tsunami of misery brought down on her head since she'd lived at the mill.

The Lockes lived closer to them than anyone else. He could easily stalk them, following their every move would take little effort with their house just down the lane from the mill, seconds away in fact. He must have known when Dan was away from the house. All he had to do was wait and watch. He had time too, time to stand and stare at the children playing across the river in Slaughter's Wood. Time to stand on the bridge in the dark and watch her and Tobias. Time to enter the mill and leave a mutilated fox in the basement, its entrails spread across the flagstones, and then clean up afterwards. Time to kill dozens of magpies and behead them.

What kind of person would kill something to make a point, just to scare someone?

What kind of person killed Aaron?

With one swift movement he pushed down his hood. Narrowing her eyes she struggled to focus on the figure in the gloomy hall. The darkness and the pale shafts of moonlight cast transfiguring shadows and distorted her vision. Surely this could not be right?

Standing in the shadows and partially obscured by the darkness of the hall...was Ray Duffield.

Her mouth dropped open and she inhaled a sharp breath. He lowered his head in an almost patronising movement and slowly raised his eyes towards her. He knew she was there, had probably known all along. Her eyes locked with his and he walked towards the island, stopping just short of it.

'It's over, Lacey,' he said. 'I gave you enough chances to get out of here but you're a stubborn little cow, aren't you? If only you'd taken the hint and left Newton Denham. I know who you are and I want you gone, and I don't care what I have to do to achieve it.'

She stood unsteadily, pushing Tobias down behind the island. She prayed Ray didn't know he was there.

'It was you, wasn't it?' she said evenly. 'The fox, the magpies, even the stick figure. What have I ever done to you? I don't get it.'

'And I don't get why you came back here. Anyone with half a brain cell would have stayed away from the people whose lives they ruined.'

She shook her head. She felt wrong-footed, disorientated. It was as if she had been cast back in time as she protested her innocence to someone who had no intention of believing her.

'I...I didn't know...I didn't know it was here. I wasn't right, for a long time. I blanked it out, had to, to survive what happened, to get through being locked away for so long.' He watched her struggle in silence, his lip curling with hate, his face devoid of empathy. 'Don't you understand? I was wrongly accused of killing Aaron. Do you have any idea of what it did to me?'

'I know you were looking for him the night he was murdered, and I know what you said you would do to him. I heard you, everyone heard you.'

'But I was a child. It was just something I said. Kids say things, don't they? I loved Aaron. I would never have hurt him.'

'Well, you're going to have a hell of a job making anyone believe it. Everyone in Newton Denham knows you've been asking questions and they don't like it. It's unsettled everyone, made them remember it all. We've worked hard to put it behind us, to move on, and along comes Lacey Murphy and starts raking it up again. Just because you call yourself something else...it doesn't change who you are. You're still Lacey Murphy and you're still a child killer.'

She stared at him. 'I want you to go.'

'No chance.'

'Just go, and we'll forget about it.'

'But *I* won't, and neither will anyone else. You need to be silenced.'

He raised the machete and lunged towards her. Sarah screamed and put her arm up to protect herself. As she staggered backwards Tobias ran out from his hiding place and threw himself at Ray, sinking his teeth into his leg. Ray roared with pain and swung the machete again, aiming it at Tobias. Sarah grabbed Tobias by the arm and ran into the utility room shutting the door behind her, pushing the old bolt home and jamming the kitchen steps under the handle. She looked around her to see if there was something she could use as a weapon but there was nothing. She heard Ray at the door, trying the handle then shoulder barging it. Bending down in front of Tobias she took both his hands and looked into his eyes.

'Tobias, I need you to listen to me.' He stared at her, then nodded. 'If the man comes in here I want you to run. I want you to run as fast as you can upstairs and go into the bathroom. You have to lock the door, do you understand. You lock it by turning the key. Can you do it?'

He looked away. 'Tobias.' She put her finger under his chin and turned his face towards her.

'Lock the door.'

'Yes, you must lock it, sweetheart. Don't forget. Please don't forget.'

His gaze was unwavering. 'Saha?'

She shook her head and gently rubbed his cheek with her thumb. She smiled when all she wanted to do was weep, realising it might be the last time she ever saw him, the last time she would look into his beautiful face.

'I'll be fine. Don't worry, okay. Sarah will be fine, but you need to run faster than you've ever run before.'

'Faster than a frog?'

'Much faster than a frog.'

The legs of the kitchen steps scraped along the floor as they were pushed further and further into the utility room as Ray barged the door again and again. The rusted bolt was holding up, but Sarah knew it was only a matter of time. She hugged Tobias to her, her eyes on the door, waiting for it to give way, ready to push Tobias away from her so he could run. She shivered as a distinct drop in temperature floated around her, an icy draft whispering by her ear making her tremble.

'Lacey.'

Sarah's eyes widened. She felt someone standing behind her and she turned. The door to the basement was wide open. She led Tobias to the door and stood at the top of the steps peering down. 'Who's there?'

'Laceeeey. Laceeeey. Come and play.'

Tobias pulled on her hand. 'Other boy,' he said. 'Saha. Other boy.'

'You heard it? Tobias, did you hear it? It was Aaron, wasn't it?'

He pulled her towards the top step. 'We go down, Saha. Down to Aaron.'

She flicked the light switch, and as they went down the steps Sarah heard the splintering of wood as the utility room door gave way to Ray's shoulder.

'Oh my God. Quick. Tobias. The garden door.'

As she pulled Tobias towards the door the overhead light went out and Ray ran down the steps. He illuminated the torch on his phone. 'Stop right there. It's over, Lacey. You can't keep running. It must be awful to have to run from everywhere. I can end all of that for you, all the worry and guilt for what you did.' She made for the garden door and Ray lifted the machete. 'Touch the door and he's dead. I mean it. I'll kill him first with one swing of this, and I'll make you watch while I do it.'

'Just let him go. Please, Ray. He's done nothing to you.'

Ray's lip curled. 'He'll tell them what he's seen and I can't have that.'

'He won't tell. He has autism and very little speech. He isn't able to tell.'

'I'm surprised anyone would let you near their kid after what you did. Does he know, Lacey, your bloke? Does he know you're a child murderer? Can't do. He wouldn't let you within a mile of the little lad.'

'I've already told you, I didn't kill Aaron.'

'Is that right? So who killed him if it wasn't you?'

She shook her head. 'I…I don't know.'

At first it was no more than a shimmer, a pale gleam of light illuminating that part of the basement where there was no light, where it was musty and black and hung with wreaths of dust-covered cobwebs like bunting around the walls.

The glow grew larger and brighter until Aaron appeared in the centre, his face tinged pale grey, his lips ringed with blue, his eyes black sunken cavities. Around his image was a pulsing ashen beam, noiseless and menacing. Ray turned his head, his mouth falling open as he held the machete to his shoulder, ready to attack.

'What's this?' He turned to Sarah, who was mesmerised. This was a different Aaron, a ghost from her childhood nightmares. 'You stupid bitch,' he yelled. 'This is no time for playing games. What the fuck is going on?' Sarah said nothing, but kept her eyes on Aaron's ghost, gripped by his presence. She watched transfixed as he gently and deliberately pursed his lips and blew a puff of sparkling ether into the room. It expanded like a huge balloon, dappling the walls with luminous flecks of effervescence, which, as it hit the ceiling, swiftly transmuted into a swarm of angry hornets.

Ray opened his mouth to scream as the swarm flew towards him. He swung his arms, dropping the machete as he screamed and hit out at the myriad insects buzzing around his head and flying into his face. Sarah pushed Tobias behind her and crouched behind a packing case as Aaron opened his mouth wide and filled the basement with echoing, tormenting laughter, clearly amused by Ray's anguish.

A figure ran through the garden door and grabbed Ray from behind, pulling his arm over his head as the swarm dissolved into glittering flecks that fell to the floor. Sarah grabbed Tobias's hand and ran up the basement steps, through the utility room and into the breakfast room where she unlocked the doors with shaking hands and stumbled into the garden. She took Tobias onto the slope leading down to the river and watched at a distance as the two men grappled in the basement, each fighting to get the upper hand. It was violent, each of them big men, each prepared to do anything to overwhelm the other. Suddenly a large fist rose into the air and came down with a heavy thud, blood spattering the garden door. The struggle suddenly stopped and Ray Duffield lay unconscious, half in the basement and half out of the garden door.

Vernon Locke staggered forwards holding onto the wall. He leaned against it panting hard, his fist pressed against his chest until he could speak. Sarah took Tobias's hand and walked up the slope towards him. 'My asthma always gets me. I should give up the fags. I'm lucky he went down when he did.'

His face was slate-grey and he winced each time he took a breath. A cut across his eyebrow oozed with blood and he put his fingers up to his forehead to staunch the flow. Squatting on his haunches he rested his head against his arm, then put his hand in his back pocket and retrieved a mobile phone. He waved Sarah towards him and handed it to her.

'Call the police. Tell them what happened,' he said, his words staccato with the effort it took for him to speak. She took the phone, her eyes not leaving him as he struggled to get his breath back. As she spoke to the police Vernon went back into the basement and checked on Ray. Taking Tobias into the house she turned on the lights and wrapped a shivering Tobias in a blanket. After a few minutes Vernon appeared at the breakfast room door. 'He's out for the count,' he said, still breathing heavily. 'Nothing to worry about now.'

'How did you know?' she asked him, still wary of this man she'd been so frightened of, the one she was so certain had made her life a living hell.

'I saw him. I knew it would be soon.'

Her brow knitted and she could hardly believe what he was saying. 'You knew it would be soon? You knew what would be soon?'

'I've watched him, y'see, seen him many times in the woods across the river from your garden. He is a determined man. If he takes against you he doesn't give up. My mother and I know only too well. And others in the village. They're as bad. They follow him like sheep. What he says goes. They're probably frightened to go against him. My mother has a cleaner who lives in the village. She told us the things he was saying about you. She said you were stirring things up again in the village about the child who was murdered here. They all want to forget. Ray Duffield didn't want you here.'

Before Sarah had the chance to ask him more the police arrived. She and Vernon explained what had happened, and when Ray regained consciousness he was arrested. Vernon was also taken to the police station which Sarah couldn't understand.

'Why does Mr Locke need to go with you?' she asked them.

A female officer put a hand on her arm and led her to a chair. 'Ms Anders, you've had an ordeal. We need Mr Locke to come to the station to answer some questions.'

'But if it wasn't for him...'

'We're aware of his actions, Ms Anders. May I suggest you and Tobias get some sleep if you can? We'll come and see you tomorrow. We'll need to talk to you.'

She stared at the officer. 'You know who I am, don't you,' she whispered.

The officer nodded. 'Yes, Ms Anders. We have to know.'

'Why, Ray?'

Ray Duffield sat with his elbows on the grey and cream mottled Formica table in the purposely bleak room. He was self-assured, his shoulders straight, his head erect, confident he'd get away with a light sentence, maybe just a fine or some pathetic community service because of the extenuating circumstances. No one in their right mind would question why he did what he did. It was the act of a concerned member of the community of Newton Denham, his only interest the people who lived and worked there. He should be hailed as a hero, not treated like a criminal, and he couldn't understand why he'd been held in this room for so long. On the table in front of him was a crumpled packet of cigarettes and a white plastic cup, half-filled with water. The chairs were black moulded plastic with metal legs, not designed for comfort, but no doubt chosen for exactly that reason.

Two detectives sat opposite Ray, D.I. Jack Cumberland holding a file of reports and photographs, and a colleague who sat silently observing, a trained officer watching Ray's every facial expression and movement, waiting for him to display the body language of a guilty man. There were no windows in the room. A screen with a computer in front of it dominated the space. In two corners were CCTV cameras, and on the table was a digital system for recording both verbal and video evidence. Ray Duffield was under the microscope, and he knew it.

'Well? Come on, Ray, this is your chance to explain. Why did you attack Sarah Anders?'

Ray sat back in the plastic chair and observed the detectives through half-closed eyes, his attitude bullish and arrogant. He smirked and rubbed his eyes with his fingers. 'Are you telling me you don't have a clue who she is, because I don't believe it?'

The detective threw the file onto the table and crossed his legs, rocking his chair back and forth with his foot. 'The information we have says she's Sarah Anders, and for reasons known only to you, you broke into her home and attacked her and her partner's five-year-old son.'

Ray sat forward and looked straight into D. I. Cumberland's eyes. 'Do I need a solicitor?'

'As I'm sure you're aware it's your prerogative to have a solicitor present, but you were caught in the act, Ray. There's not much for you to defend, is there? We're just curious as to why you would take the trouble and not inconsiderable risk of breaking in to the home of someone you barely know and attack her with a machete, a not inconsiderable weapon. Not much of a welcome for someone recent to the village.'

Ray rubbed his chin as though weighing up his options. 'Well, that's the point isn't it? I do know her and she's not who she says she is.'

'And who do you think she is?'

'It's not about who I think she is, it's about who I know she is, and I know she's not Sarah Anders and I know you know it too. She's Lacey Murphy, the girl who killed her brother in Slaughter's Wood twenty years ago.'

The detective's expression did not change. 'And why do you think she's Lacey Murphy?'

Ray shook his head, frowning. 'Because it's who she is. Why are we playing games? Don't tell me you don't have knowledge of her whereabouts, you and every force in the country. You lot always keep tabs on killers out on licence. She might call herself Sarah Anders now, but it's not who she really is.' Ray paused...for effect as much as anything. He wanted them to know he wasn't a pushover. They could protest her innocence all they wanted but he knew. He knew. 'I've been waiting for her, see. Waiting for her to come back here and cause mayhem like she did before. There's a way about her I've never forgotten. She might be an adult now and have that scar down her face but I recognised her. She's a killer after all. That's something you don't forget.'

'And say she *was* Lacey Murphy, which I'm not confirming one way or the other, but if she were why would you attack her?'

'Because we don't want her sort around here. I gave her enough chances to leave us be, to go and infect somewhere else with her evil but she chose to ignore it, which was a mistake. Clearly the messages I left for her weren't strong enough. I was just trying to put the wind up her.'

'How did you get in?'

'What?'

'The mill. How did you get in?'

Ray sighed. 'I've got a key. To the basement garden door. By the wheel. And one to their utility.'

'And how did you come by them?'

'I used to be the caretaker. There's been so many comings and goings there no one knew who had a key and who didn't. I just didn't give mine back to the agent when that bitch and her bloke moved in.'

'But didn't Luke fix some bolts onto the door recently. It's what Dan Kenyon, Ms Ander's partner told us.'

'I told Luke not to push the bolts across when he'd finished the job. Just to give them the keys and make them think it was locked.'

'So Luke knew what you were going to do.'

'No, course he didn't. I told him what I've told you. I just wanted to scare her off. Get her out of Newton Denham.'

'With a machete?' D.I. Cumberland frowned. 'You had a machete in your hand when you were apprehended. You must have been planning to do something with it?' Ray averted his eyes. 'What was it, Ray? Was she asking too many questions? We've spoken to Dave Crowther. He says Sarah Anders was doing a lot of digging, asking about the history of the mill and what happened when Aaron Murphy was murdered. Did she get too close, Ray, too near to the truth?'

Ray hardened his jaw and the detective fixed his eyes on him.

'She was upsetting Mary. Kept on about it. Wouldn't let it rest. You know what happened here, Jack. You're as much a part of this community as I am. We all know each other. We don't want rubbish like her here. I was just making sure we could all carry on the way we have for the last twenty years. She started turning it all over again, so I let her know she wasn't wanted here. You should be thanking me not bloody questioning me for hours on end. I'm not getting this.'

D.I. Cumberland knew he was about to deliver a coup de main.

'We have Luke in custody.'

Shock dissolved the cockiness on Ray's face. 'Luke? Why have you dragged Luke in? He wasn't at the mill. He didn't even know what I'd planned. He hasn't done anything apart from not bolting a door, and that wasn't a criminal offence when I last looked?'

'You sure he didn't do anything?'

'What d'you mean, am I sure about it? What's he done?'

'I think that's my line, Ray. What did he do?'

Ray eyes searched the room, then he rolled his eyes and stared back at D. I. Cumberland. 'He didn't do anything.'

The detective saw him swallow, a "tell" to indicate a lie if ever there was one. He pushed his chair back from the table, the legs screeching against the vinyl flooring, and stood, picking up the file from the desk and banging the end down on the table top to straighten up the papers inside. The noise jarred the atmosphere and his eyes narrowed. He raised his eyebrows to the other detective who also stood and carefully and silently placed his chair under the table. 'I'm going to give you some time, Ray. I want you to think about what we've discussed. If you want a solicitor I'll arrange for the duty solicitor to come in and have a word with you. She'll be in full receipt of the information we have in our possession. In the meantime, I'm going to speak to Luke.'

'What about?'

'About the murder of Aaron Murphy in Slaughter's Wood on the 15th of December 1999.'

Ray slumped back, his face turning ashen. 'Why are you talking to him? It's nothing to do with him. Why the hell would you think it's got anything to do with him? He was only eight for fuck's sake.'

'A witness has come forward, someone who says they saw what happened.'

Ray stood abruptly, knocking the black plastic chair over. It clattered against the hard, grey vinyl tiles as he thumped the table with his fist in frustration. 'You know what really happened. The bitch at the mill killed him. She did time for it so why you're talking to me about it I don't know. And why Luke? Leave him out of it.'

The detective didn't answer. As he and his colleague left the room a uniformed officer stepped in and put his hand on Ray's shoulder, who closed his eyes and put his head in his hands. Tears trickled between his fingers and his thoughts went to Mary, the wife who had stoically accepted his determination to make the decisions for them, shaping their life together, the woman who had been by his side for thirty years. He had often called her a nagging old harridan under his breath when he was fed up with her, muttered she was lucky to have a man like him in her life seeing as she wasn't exactly a looker. He had shrugged off her scorn when she'd said he couldn't do anything without making a mess of it. It was beginning to look as though she was about to be proved right.

'You've been cautioned, Luke? And you've been made aware this interview is being filmed and recorded.'

Luke Duffield gritted his teeth and took a breath. 'Yep.' He rolled his head around on his neck to relieve the tension in his shoulders, wishing more than anything he could speak to his dad. At least he'd know what he'd said to the police. He couldn't work out why he'd been brought in for questioning over something Ray had done, apart from one thing, and it was impossible for anyone to know about it. Ray had told him it was impossible. No one knew and no one would ever know, he'd assured him of it. He'd told him to put it out of his mind and not to worry. Plain sailing, he'd said, and advised him to get on with his life, even when Luke had wobbled a few months ago. Ray had patted him on the shoulder and guaranteed it was all under control. When Luke said he didn't know what he meant, Ray said better he didn't know. 'To be honest, Jack, I don't know why I'm here.'

'While you *are* here, it's Detective Inspector Cumberland. This is an official enquiry, Luke.'

'Official as in what?'

D.I. Cumberland pushed some photographs across the table. 'Official…as in this.'

Luke lowered his eyes to the photographs and his stomach flipped. He frowned and swallowed the nausea rising in his throat. He pushed the photographs back across the table, glancing up at the two officers. His eyes locked with Detective Cumberland's. 'I don't think you should be showing me them photos. I don't get it. Why are you showing me? It's disgusting.'

'Do you know who's in the photographs? We're pretty sure it's someone you knew.'

'Of course I know. It's Aaron. Aaron Murphy.'

'Friend of yours, wasn't he, from school?'

Luke shifted uncomfortably on his chair. His mind was in turmoil. Was he supposed to deny everything or was he supposed to say what he knew? What had Ray told them? If he got the story wrong he'd never be forgiven. Not by his dad or his mum. 'I want to speak to Dad.'

D.I. Cumberland shook his head. 'No can do. Just tell us what you know, Luke.'

'I don't know anything.'

D.I. Cumberland breathed in heavily through his nose, held the breath and slowly released it. It was an action he'd used to great effect before. For some reason it unnerved suspects and he could sense Luke was wavering. He wasn't enjoying it like he usually did. He'd known Luke Duffield since he was a baby. He pushed the photographs back across the table, forcing him to look at them. Luke paled.

'What would you say if I told you we had a witness and a signed statement to what happened?'

'A witness to what?'

'To Aaron's murder.'

'It depends on what they're saying.'

'They're saying you and Aaron were in Slaughter's Wood on the night of the 15th December 1999. They're saying you were arguing. They heard you shouting at him, and saw you pick up a lump of wood laying outside the den you were playing close to and whack him over the head with it, knocking him unconscious.'

'Well, it's bollocks. They're lying.'

'Why would they lie?'

'You tell me. Maybe *they* did it and they're trying to shift the blame onto me.'

'You were in Slaughter's Wood weren't you? You were seen, with Aaron.'

'I might have been. Jesus, I was only eight. How the hell am I supposed to remember that far back.'

'You were a big lad for eight if I remember rightly. Capable of swinging a lump of wood and knocking out a six year old.'

'Well, I might have been capable. Doesn't mean I did it.'

'You didn't do it though, did you? You didn't kill Aaron Murphy.'

A shadow of relief crossed Luke's face. 'I just told you I didn't.'

'No, you just battered his head in, then your dad came along and finished him off. That's right, isn't it? It's how it was?'

'I...I. Am I not supposed to have a solicitor or something?'

'Do you want a solicitor? Do you think you need one? Just say the word. We can get a duty solicitor in here in minutes.'

'I'm not sure. If I have a solicitor does it mean I'm admitting something? I don't think I've done anything wrong. We were just playing. He was a little shit, always getting me into trouble even though I was older than him. I dunno, I didn't care at the time and all the other kids liked him.'

'Why?'

'Because he didn't care what he did. He'd do anything for a laugh and he always had cigs on him.'

'So, what were you arguing about?'

'I can't remember.'

'But you did hit him didn't you?' D.I. Cumberland waited. He was close, very close to getting the conviction to exonerate Lacey Murphy. He'd been a young P.C. when Aaron Murphy had been murdered and he remembered seeing Lacey in the interview room, had remonstrated with her father when he'd refused to see her and forbidden her mother to have anything to do with her either.

Lacey Murphy wasn't a big child, scrawny with huge eyes circled with shadows. She looked as though she would have benefited from a decent meal and he'd wondered how she could have found the strength to bash the kid's head in, but the evidence of her fingerprints on a log found in the den along with Ray Duffield's sighting of her going towards Slaughter's Wood had damned her. Some of their other neighbours had heard her calling him, and they'd all said she sounded as if she was gunning for him. He softened his voice. 'Come on, Luke. You were a kid yourself. It was hardly your fault.'

'He wound me up. I hit him a couple of times with the log and I thought he'd get up and start messing about but he didn't. He just lay on the ground. There was blood coming out his head, and…some other stuff.'

'How many times did you say you hit him?'

Luke met D.I. Cumberland's eyes. He knew the detective was aware of exactly how many times he'd hit him. 'Four or five…maybe.'

'Right. Not just a couple of times, as you said. What did you do after?'

'I ran back to the house and got me dad. I didn't know what else to do.'

'And what did your dad do?'

Cumberland saw Luke swallow and he knew he had him. 'He said Aaron was nearly gone and it was only right to put him out of his misery.'

'What did he do?'

'He picked up the wood and hit him…until he was sure.'

'Sure of what?'

'Sure he wasn't breathing.'

Cumberland momentarily closed his eyes. These were people from his own community, people he'd grown up with and thought he knew. Ray Duffield was a familiar figure in the community, popular with some, vehemently disliked by others because of his cocky demeanour. Arrogant some would say, so overconfident he thought he was untouchable. Cumberland knew people avoided him. He also knew Mary did as she was told and he wondered how many times she'd been threatened or worse, and how much she knew about Aaron's murder. His throat dried up so he reached for the plastic cup in front of him and took a swig of water.

'Right.' He moistened his lips. 'But why? What was the reason for taking his life?'

'So he couldn't say anything, tell anyone what I'd done. Dad knew I hadn't meant to hurt him and he knew what Aaron was like. He said I had a good future in front of me and he didn't see why it should be ruined by the little shit. He said Aaron was scum and no one would miss him.'

'What happened to the wood you and he used? Was it the same log?' Luke nodded. 'So what happened to it?'

'Dad burnt it at home. In the grate. He broke it up so it was small enough.'

'What about the fingerprints on the log found near Aaron's body?'

Luke's eyes suddenly welled with tears. 'She had likely touched all of them. The three of us built the den together a couple of days before and she'd made the bit at the front. It was like a secret clubhouse. Dad pulled one of the branches out of the den.'

'And the blood? How did it get on the branch?'

'Dad…smeared blood and the stuff coming out of Aaron's head on it.' He wiped his nose on the back of his hand.

'Your dad's fingerprints. How were they not at the scene?'

Luke held up his hands. 'He was wearing gloves. He burnt them too.'

D.I. Cumberland rubbed his eyes with his fingers. 'Jesus.' He was suddenly exhausted as though a great weariness had overtaken him. It didn't matter how long he was in the force he'd never get used to what seemingly ordinary people were prepared to do to get what they wanted or to cover their tracks. He'd never taken to Ray Duffield but he'd never had him down as capable of doing something so horrific.

'And he told you to keep quiet about it?' Luke nodded. 'And do you think it was the right thing to do?' Luke didn't answer. 'You're an adult now, Luke. Do you think the decision your dad made when he finished Aaron Murphy off was the right one?'

Luke stared down at his hands. He knew he was about to condemn his father, but he'd already convicted him by telling the police what had happened and he didn't think it could get much worse. 'I was only eight. I thought my dad was the best person in the world and could do no wrong. He was the boss. He said he did it for me.'

'And now?'

'Now I wished he'd helped Aaron. We might have been able to do something for him.'

'Even if it meant you were in trouble?'

'He might still be alive and I wouldn't have had to walk around with him in my head for the last twenty years. I've lived in my own prison. When I was a kid I just wanted to forget about it, do what Dad said, but as I got older I realised it'll never be possible to forget, not for me. The lies have gone on long enough, and if me and Dad have to be punished so be it. I'll never forget Aaron Murphy. He might be dead and buried but he'll never be gone to me. He's always there, in my head, just as he was, the little git with the filthy face who didn't care what he did. I liked him. He was trouble right enough. But he was alright was Aaron Murphy.'

Sarah sat in the corner of the sofa with her legs tucked up underneath her. D.I. Cumberland and a female officer had just left and Dan was in the kitchen making tea.

She was numb. The hollow feeling inside her was making her feel sick and there was only one person on her mind. Aaron, the little boy who was at the centre of everything.

She wanted to sleep, to close her eyes against the spotlight and not wake up for days so she could put it to rest and not have to think about Luke and Ray Duffield. If she thought too much about Luke she would have to decide whether he deserved sympathy, and she wasn't ready to think about it. He was only eight years old when he attacked Aaron. Did a child of eight really know what he was doing? Did he mean to hurt Aaron or was it just a game? From what D.I. Cumberland said it sounded as if it hadn't been in his mind to hurt Aaron, but how would she ever know for certain? Ray Duffield had used the excuse of protecting his son to kill Aaron. But was the reason he gave all it was? He'd hated the Murphys and never liked Aaron, and had tried to stop Luke from being friends with him. Did he use the circumstances he found in Slaughter's Wood to get rid of the boy he thought was a millstone around his son's neck?

And there was the witness. Vernon Locke. The man she'd been so certain had caused her pain and anguish, who she was sure had threatened her and made her question the certainty of her own mind. He'd been standing on the slope of the Locke property and had watched Luke and Aaron as they'd messed about by the river and witnessed Luke hitting Aaron; actually counted the amount of times he'd struck him.

When Luke had left Aaron to go back to the estate to fetch Ray he'd left his garden, run down the lane and entered the mill via the gate behind the summerhouse. Vernon had always been an overweight man and disabled by asthma, and by the time he'd got to the mill Ray and Luke were in the woods. They walked across the bridge onto the mill garden and he'd hidden behind the summer house and watched helplessly as Ray finished Aaron off. He'd been too late to save him. D.I. Cumberland told them Vernon had wept in the interview room, telling them he hadn't come forward before because he knew what the villagers thought of him and was sure he'd get the blame for Aaron's death.

He told the police he usually went out walking late at night so as not to meet with anyone along the lane. He'd been bullied in the past because he was different; a pack of youths had stoned him a few years before and it had frightened him so he didn't go out in daylight. On one of his walks he'd spotted Ray Duffield stalking the mill, hiding in the woods, so he made a point of watching out for him. Vernon had recognised Sarah as Lacey Murphy the day she and Tobias visited his mother and he had kept a protective eye on them because he was sure Ray Duffield would do anything to get rid of her.

Sarah shook her head. Poor man. Poor, poor man. I did it too, she thought with bitterness and guilt. I judged him, and I know better than most how destructive it can be. All he was doing was trying to protect us.

Tears ran down her cheeks and she pulled her knees up in front of her, resting her forehead on them. Justice for Aaron meant Ray Duffield would be punished for his crime, even Luke if it's what was decided. If he hadn't hit Aaron in the first place none of it would have happened, he should be punished, but it didn't really matter to her now. None of it mattered. She'd paid a heavy price for Aaron's murder and he was still dead. Nothing would bring him back.

At the trial their neighbours had spoken out against her, saying she was a strange child, often alone and surly when spoken to. They said they thought she led Aaron astray, encouraged him to steal from the local shops. After all, what six year old stole packets of cigarettes without being instructed? Six year old boys stole sweets not cigarettes. And now she knew they had condemned her because the people of Newton Denham abhorred her parents and couldn't wait to get rid of them from the community. They'd heard the screaming and shouting coming from their house when her Mum and Dad were arguing; the swearing, the accusations, and her mum crying when her husband had hit her, and in truth they wanted to see the back of the Murphys and they didn't much care how they achieved it.

But the most damning evidence of all had come from Ray Duffield. He told the police he'd seen Lacey in the street on the night Aaron had been killed. He had run away from the house and she was looking for him. She was angry, he said, because she knew she would get into trouble with her parents for allowing Aaron to leave the house. He'd told her not to go into the woods because it was dangerous and he'd heard her calling Aaron's name, screaming expletives at him on the edge of the wood, saying what she would do to him when she found him.

She took the offered mug of tea from a saddened Dan who had remained silent, giving her the space to speak if and when she wanted. She warmed her hands around the mug. It was a beautiful summers' day, the garden bathed in sunlight, warm and inviting, but Sarah was chilled to her bones as she envisaged Aaron's funeral, the one they wouldn't allow her to attend. How could it ever be forgotten, the awful day when they'd buried her brother? It was the day she had cried from the moment of waking until she'd fallen asleep, exhausted with sorrow at her loss. No one had comforted her, no one had been by her side. She'd sat alone in her room and grieved for him, wondering why she was being punished for something she didn't do.

'Do you think they went to his funeral?'

Dan sat by her and put his arm around her shoulders, unable to imagine what she was going through. He kissed her hair and shook his head. 'Who knows? Who knows what people will do when they're backed into a corner? Whatever they did they were playing the part of a family grieving for another family. Don't think about them, Sarah. They're not worth it. The police will deal with them and they'll get what they deserve.'

'But why didn't they care, Dan. He was only six. How could human beings not care?'

'Because they were saving their own skin. Ray Duffield's as evil as they come, a psychopath who'll do anything to get his own way. He doesn't care about anyone. He used what happened as an excuse to vent his anger against Aaron.' A tear rolled down his cheek. 'I'm so sorry, Sarah.' He took her hand and pulled her to him, stroking the hair back from her face, her cheeks sodden with tears. 'Have you ever thought of going back to your old home? Do you want to go back? Would it help you…I don't know…get closure? I know it's what everyone says, but it might help. I'll come with you.'

'I don't know, Dan. I know the estate is only the other side of Slaughter's Wood but it's almost like I never lived there. All I'll see is Aaron and how it used to be when we were together. When we were a family. I don't know.'

She imagined the Duffields standing by Aaron's grave looking sad when deep down they were congratulating themselves for getting away with murder. Her thoughts went to Mary, a mother herself who must surely have had some empathy and at the very least a little compassion for a mother who had lost both her children, one to death, the other to incarceration. Was it possible they went to the church, the holiest of places, and said prayers with other mourners, sang hymns praising goodness and truth when all the time they were encouraging their eight year old son to lie, swearing him to a secret he would be coerced to keep for the rest of his life? It was beyond wickedness.

Late July 2019
34

The journey back to Newton Denham was stifling. The train's air conditioning had given up and everyone in the carriage was quietly melting in the heat. Bottles of water were in abundance on the tables as were magazines being used as fans, but nothing gave any real comfort.

Sarah stared out of the window as the train sped through the countryside, relieved she had at least had the good fortune to get a seat. More often than not she'd had to stand much of the way, but Marcus had shut the gallery a little earlier after calling her in to see one of their most important clients. As usual Sarah hadn't failed to deliver and Marcus had said their arrangement had worked so well he was happy to make it permanent if it suited her. He'd given her the weekend to think about it. All she wanted was for things to go back to the way they were, although she'd had to acknowledge it was unlikely anything would ever be the same again.

The only real constants in her life over the past six or seven months had been Marcus, Eve, and the gallery. Sarah understood her place there, knew who she was in the environment and what she was capable of. They were her people, separate from her home life. The gallery was where her identity as Sarah Anders come in to its own. She was proud Marcus and Eve were her friends and colleagues, and of the position she held. Not going back would mean a complete shift in the way she saw herself. Would she be a stepmother who worked, or a career woman with a stepchild? She sighed and rubbed her hand across her forehead, her palm wet with perspiration. The journey between Newton Denham and London would be something which beyond doubt she wouldn't miss. It was definitely a suggestion worth consideration.

The train pulled into the station and Sarah waited for it to come to a halt before leaving her seat. The other passengers rushed to the doors, flinging them open against the side of the carriage with a clang, eager to get out of the dusty, airless atmosphere and into the fresher air. Sarah held back. She couldn't face the contest to be out first onto the platform or the race up the steps to the turnstiles.

She walked across St. Denys station car park to her car. Inside she switched on the radio and hummed along with the songs as she drove, thinking about Dan, hoping he'd remembered to pick up Tobias from school on time. As flavour of the month at his company he'd managed to swing a day off meaning Sarah could go to the gallery. She was glad she'd been able to get away from the mill, even if it was just for a day.

The rumour mill in Newton Denham had gone into overdrive. The arrests of Ray and Luke Duffield and the potential arrest of Mary had given the gossips enough fodder to keep them going for months and Sarah didn't want to be part of it. Up until now her name had been kept out of it. The gossips were far more interested in what Luke and Ray had done twenty years before, and not really concerned about Ray breaking into the mill and threatening to kill her. As Sarah Anders she wasn't important to them. If it came out she was Lacey Murphy she was aware it would be an entirely different matter.

As she turned onto the mill's gravel drive she noticed a car parked down the lane, just behind the summer house. It was a car she didn't recognise, an old, rather beaten-up Mercedes. She locked the car and ran up the steps to the porch, letting herself into the hall.

'I'm home,' she called as she closed the front door.

Dan came out of the living room, nervously rubbing his hands together. 'We've got visitors.'

'Oh. Who?' Sarah followed him into the living room. Sitting on one of the sofas was Yelena and Andrei. Tobias was sitting on Yelena's lap, and when she saw Yelena's arms around him and Tobias looking contented her breath caught up in her throat. 'What's going on?'

'Yelena and Andrei have come to talk about Tobias.'

Sarah felt her jaw harden. Are they seriously expecting us to let them take him from us, she thought. 'What about him?'

'They want to discuss access.'

She turned on her heel and went into the hall. 'I need a shower.'

Dan followed her. 'Can't it wait?'

'No. Sorry.'

She ran up the stairs with anger burning in her chest. She opened the airing cupboard on the landing, looking for towels, and banged the doors shut again, hoping they could hear her. In the bedroom she opened drawers and slammed them shut. She wanted everyone to know how she was feeling. In the detention centre one of the psychiatrists said she was passive aggressive, needing to expel all the anger inside her but not aiming it correctly. Well, she was bloody angry and she knew exactly who to aim it at.

She turned the shower to hot. It scalded her as the powerful spray of water hit her skin and she breathed in deeply then released the breath through pursed lips and tried to let go of the anger coursing through her. After everything they'd been through, after all the progress they'd made with Tobias, were Yelena and Andrei honestly expecting them to give him up to them as if nothing had happened, as if Yelena had never dumped him off and walked away without a backward glance? Is this why they were here? She knew what she had to do.

She dressed in a sleeveless orange and cream patterned shift dress which showed off her tanned arms and legs, and slipped on a pair of nude kitten heels. If there was to be a fight she needed to be confident and this was the tried and tested way to make her appear more self-assured than she was actually feeling. She went downstairs and joined the others in the living room, apologising for keeping them waiting.

'The train was packed today, and very hot. I hope you understand.' They both nodded, and just for a moment, and completely beyond her understanding, she felt sorry for them. She took a deep breath. 'Now, what's all this about.'

Yelena glanced at Andrei. Neither seemed eager to speak. 'We wanted to talk with you about Tobias,' Andrei began. 'Yelena accepts she made a mistake when she brought him here.'

Sarah stared at them. She glanced across at Dan waiting for him to say something. 'It's taken Yelena more than six months to decide she made a mistake,' Sarah said. 'Why did you change your mind, Yelena?'

'Dan told me if I wanted to be in Tobias's life there would need to be agreement about access.'

Sarah widened her eyes at Dan as if to say, 'Oh, really? When did that happen?'

'Yelena was under the impression the best thing for Tobias would be if we were together as a family,' said Dan, 'but I told her it was impossible and it would never happen. And, Sarah, I want you to know, I've apologised to Andrei, for...for what happened. I feel totally responsible and Andrei has accepted my apology. He loves Tobias and wants the best for him.'

Sarah was tempted to laugh. She was pretty sure Yelena never once thought about what was best for Tobias, but rather only what was best for her. 'And what are you expecting to happen now?' She directed her question to Yelena because she felt sure this was where she would get the most candid answer regardless of how unpalatable it was.

'I would like to see my son,' Yelena answered, softly, her face taking on a benign expression. 'Maybe one day to live with me...and Andrei.'

'I'm sorry, Yelena,' Dan interjected. 'Tobias will never live with you, and if I have to go to court to get custody of him to prevent it, I will.'

Yelena's face hardened. She pushed Tobias off her lap and leaned towards Sarah and Dan. 'So answer me, who will look after him? Which one of you? You, or your career wife?' Andrei put his hand on her arm and frowned at her with a straight mouth, shaking his head as if to say, 'You're losing points.'

'I'll take care of Tobias,' said Sarah. 'Full time.' Dan stared at her as she continued. 'I've organised it with the gallery. I'll work from home, but Tobias's needs will come first. Every time.' Dan smiled at her, his eyes full of admiration. 'But at the same time I understand you want to see Tobias, Yelena. He is your son, and I'm sure we can come to some arrangement to suit everyone, especially Tobias. We don't want to part you from your child and he needs to see his mother. I just don't understand why you did what you did. If you had gone about things differently perhaps the bad feeling between us could have been, if not avoided, at least managed better. You don't have to fight us. We all want what's best for Tobias. And as for you expecting Dan to leave me and make a home with you, frankly it was ridiculous.'

Tears rolled down Yelena's cheeks which she brushed away with the sleeve of her shirt. 'Andrei clearly loves you, Yelena,' Sarah said more gently and with greater understanding than she had expected to feel. 'Why would you want to leave him? You wouldn't have brought him with you today if there was nothing between you. You left your home country with him. You came to the UK together as a couple. You and Andrei must mean a lot to each other.'

To her surprise Sarah felt a strange kind of affinity with Yelena. She realised it was possible they had more in common than either she or Yelena would have expected. Her life had clearly been hard. She'd probably received some bad treatment from people who should have known better, and Sarah knew how it felt to be a puppet with someone controlling the strings who didn't have her best interests at heart. The hardness left Yelena's face and she suddenly looked very young.

'Please. Try to understand. I had nothing. Andrei had nothing. We were so poor. We came here to make a life. We thought life here would be easy but it is not. We had no one here, no family, just each other. Andrei did the best he could, but...we had to pay rent, and sometimes I only got money for dancing for men in a club. Sometimes they wouldn't pay and there was nothing I could do. The clubs didn't pay the girls. We had to make our own money. We struggled. Andrei got a job in a nightclub. Security. The owner said I could be a hostess but sometimes I would have to go abroad, for business meetings. To make men comfortable and happy.'

'So, you didn't get paid for anything else?'

'No. Nothing more. This is the truth. I have never done that.'

'Yet you slept with Dan.' Sarah heard Andrei inhale, and he glanced away, his eyes filled with sadness at Yelena's betrayal. She looked at Dan who lowered his eyes.

Yelena nodded. 'I made a mistake. I was hired as a hostess. I got drinks, food. I had to look pretty. When the meeting was over...' She grabbed Andrei's hand and rested her head on his shoulder. 'Things happened that should not have happened. It was my fault too.' Andrei put his hand on her arm. 'I am so sorry.'

Late July 2019
35

She'd gone down to the basement again. Dan was at work and Tobias at school. The place where she'd felt so much fear, where she had experienced so much horror brought her a strange kind of comfort when she was on her own. She knew there were rats hiding in the gaps in the bricks behind the packing crates, their sharp little claws scuttling and scratching on the flagstones. Cobwebs like lace curtains hanging above her were studded with dead flies and spiders waiting for more prey, but she was sure if she didn't bother them they wouldn't bother her. Sitting on the crumbling stone steps, three up, twenty-two down, she stared into the distance, watching the dust motes as they played and danced in the narrow shards of daylight piercing the darkness.

She closed her eyes and took a deep breath, slowly releasing it, allowing the muscles in her body to relax. In her mind's eye she searched for the child inside herself and found a girl. She was small and skinny, her face pale with dark circles under her eyes. Her hair was a short bob clipped to the side and tied with thin blue ribbon in a bow. Sitting on a bed moulded into the wall of a small room devoid of warmth, she hung her head and clasped her hands in front of her as tears rolled down her cheeks. Every cell in her body was infused with sorrow and all she could think about was Aaron. She swallowed hard and raised her head to stare at the ceiling, thinking about her mum and dad and the friends she'd had to leave behind. Her parents had deserted her and the other children in the institution avoided her. She'd heard them whispering to each other. 'Murderer,' they'd said.

'I didn't do it,' she said under her breath to the four walls. 'I didn't do it.'

Sarah took another deep breath and imagined herself opening the door to the room. She sat down on the bed next to Lacey and took her hand. The little girl regarded her with haunted eyes, tears shining on her cheeks. Sarah smiled warmly and put an arm around her shoulders, hugging her close. She felt the child relax with relief. At last, someone had hugged her. Someone cared.

'I'm here now, Lacey,' she said. 'You're going to be alright, sweetheart. I'm here now.' In Sarah's mind's eye they sat together like this for a long moment until she gently pushed the little girl from her. 'Shall we speak to Aaron, Lacey? Shall we tell him we're here?'

The little girl whose tears still glittered on her cheeks nodded, smiling, and the vision faded from Sarah's imagination.

She stared into the darkness at the back of the basement.

'Aaron, it's me,' she whispered. 'It's Lacey.' In the haziness of pale light and sparkling flecks he appeared. Every movement he made was in slow motion, as though he was frozen in time.

She wanted to reach out and touch him, to hug him to her, to warm his little body with hers and to kiss better the wound on his head caused by the violence that took him from her. She smiled and gently raised her hand to greet him.

'Is it okay for me to talk to you again, Aaron?' He grinned and balanced on one leg his arms outstretched. 'Thank you for taking care of Tobias. You took care of me too. Did you know what the bad man would do?' He slowly nodded his head. There was deep sadness in his eyes and Sarah sobbed, her grief almost choking her. 'Aaron, I'm so sorry, so very sorry. I should have watched you better. I was the eldest and I let you down. I didn't take care of you like I should have. I hope you can forgive me. I pray you can forgive me because I don't think I'll ever forgive myself.'

He turned his face away and her heart sank, but when he turned back he had his fingers in the corners of his mouth, pulling it into a wide grin. He stuck his tongue out at her and waggled it. She laughed through her tears. This was the Aaron she remembered, the one she loved and missed.

'Can you forgive me, Aaron?' she whispered. He pulled his fingers out of his mouth and stared at her. She waited with breath held, inwardly praying he would let her know he didn't blame her. She put her face in her hands, hardly daring to look, scared that when she glanced up he'd be gone. She wiped her cheeks with the back of her hand. Suddenly, his face broke into a smile and to her relief, he nodded. 'Thank you,' she breathed. 'Thank you, Aaron. You'll always be my best friend. The bad boy and the bad man are gone now. They'll never hurt you again. And they won't hurt me and they won't hurt Tobias. You've been such a good boy and I'll always love you. I'll never forget you.'

Sarah knew this would be the last time she would see him, but it was the right thing. He needed to go to the other place, a place of quiet and stillness.

'It's time for you to go to sleep now, sweetheart. It's time for you to rest. When my time comes I'll come and find you, and we'll be together again like we used to be.'

He put his head gently over to one side as if considering what she'd said, then grinned cheekily. He slowly raised his hand to his lips and blew her a kiss. Tiny specks of shimmering gold floated towards her and she put out her hand to catch them, then blew on her palm to return his kiss.

'I love you, Aaron,' she said softly, tears coursing down her cheeks. 'I'll always love you. Go to sleep now, darling. Close your eyes and drift away. Go and rest, sweetheart.'

She watched as he gradually faded into the darkness, his image becoming more and more transparent until he'd dissolved into nothing and was no longer there.

'Goodbye, Aaron,' she whispered. 'Goodbye, little brother.'

Saint Nicholas' Church
Newton Denham
Early August 2019
36

They sat on an old wooden bench bleached almost white after decades of blistering summer sun. Years of returning seasons had washed all the colour out of the grain giving it a gnarled, almost fantasy appearance. She held his hand and he stared up at her, his face full of expectation, as though waiting for her signal to leave the bench and wander through the gravestones.

The graveyard was more like a meadow than a final resting place, punctuated randomly by memorials, some covered in moss and lichen with no evidence of anyone caring for them, some recent additions; stark white with black engraving, or black marble etched with gold.

Around them grew ox eye daisies and wild thyme, the bright yellow of Birds Foot Trefoil glowing in the afternoon sun. Anxiety swept through her when she thought about Aaron's gravestone. Would it be like those in the centre of the graveyard, old and crumbling, yielding to the seasons over the last twenty years, or had someone lovingly cared for it as time had turned Aaron's passing into a distant memory? It should have been me, she thought, a surge of guilt reinforcing her anxiety. I should have tended his grave and made sure he wasn't forgotten.

The graveyard was overgrown, but even though it was a place of sadness she acknowledged it was also beautiful. As the sun got lower in the sky and threw long shadows across the ground, it seemed almost appropriate Aaron shouldn't be somewhere neat and clipped and formal. He had been a free spirit, an imp, an earthbound angel with a mucky face and grime under his fingernails.

'Aaron here,' Tobias whispered as if reading her thoughts.

Sarah glanced down and met his eyes. 'Yes, he's here. Somewhere. We just have to find him.'

'Find Aaron?'

She swallowed down her tears, aware he probably didn't know what she meant and perhaps expected to see Aaron as he once was, a little boy, like him.

'We'll look very carefully and find where Aaron is sleeping, and when we find him you can put your lovely flowers there to let him know we remember him and care about him.'

Tobias's eyes didn't leave her face. 'In heaven.' he said softly.

Her eyes widened and the threatened tears pooled at her eyelashes and overflowed down her cheeks. How could she explain the concept of heaven to a five-year-old and show him a gravestone, a cold, hard, unemotional thing. She didn't want Tobias to be frightened, to be scared because Aaron had been laid in the ground. She knew she must find an explanation to satisfy him, to leave him with a sense of comfort rather than fear. She squeezed his hand.

'Shall we look for Aaron?'

He nodded. 'I know.'

'Do you?' He pointed to the far corner of the graveyard. 'Why do you think he's there, sweetheart?'

Tobias stared across the graveyard for a long moment. 'Aaron's my friend. He's there.'

In the far corner was a huge yew tree, its trunk host to a variegated ivy, which crawled like a creature with many tentacles up towards the boughs, sweeping out along the branches, winding around the yew's limbs and clinging with its tendrils over every limb. Tobias slid off the bench and pulled Sarah towards the tree. She followed without question, meandering through the gravestones, her summer dress brushing against the grasses and meadow flowers. She wondered if Aaron's grave was indeed, there.

When they reached the tree Tobias stopped and pointed to a small mottled stone almost hidden by the grasses. At its foot was a posy of meadow flowers tied into a bunch with string.

'There,' he said. 'Aaron there.'

Sarah knelt and brushed the obscuring grass away from the stone. The engraving was partially concealed by brown and green moss, but as she rubbed it with her thumb the inscription could be seen.

Aaron Murphy
Beloved son
Taken too soon.
16th April 1993 – 15th December 1999
Our little sunbeam shining forever

She felt her breath catch in her throat as she read the words over and over again.

'Beloved son,' she said under her breath. She sat in front of the stone and Tobias sat next to her.

'Do you see what the words say, Tobias?' she asked him gently. 'They say he was a beloved son, but he was also a beloved brother. My little brother. And I loved him very much.'

'Like me?' Tobias asked.

'Yes,' she nodded. 'Like I love you.'

Sarah began to clear away the grass growing around the stone.

'Next time we come I'll bring some plants and you can help me make the stone look pretty. Would you like that?' He held up the sunflowers he had brought with him. She nodded. 'Yes, it's the right time. They'll look lovely, won't they?'

Tobias knelt and gently placed the sunflowers reverently in front of the stone. 'Be a good boy, Aaron,' he said. 'Go sleep when Saha says.' Sarah smiled. She wanted the graveyard to be a place of peace for them, somewhere they could come and talk to Aaron.

A movement at the corner of her vision caught her eye and she glanced up. It was Vernon Locke, standing silently by the church gate. Sarah smiled and raised her hand in an uncertain wave. Vernon nodded and raised his hand. After a few moments he shyly lowered his head and walked away with his hands in his pockets, his shoulders bent. She glanced at the bunch of wild flowers on Aaron's grave realising Vernon had placed them there, and stared sadly after him thinking how badly she had judged him, and that if she ever found a way to make it up to him she would.

She and Tobias sat quietly in the grass, enjoying the warmth and the peace surrounding them. When Tobias spotted Dan walking slowly around the perimeter of the graveyard, he ran up to him and put his arms around his legs.

'Hello, mate,' Dan said, bending down to his haunches. He glanced at Sarah and she saw his eyes soften. 'Is this his place?' he asked gently. Sarah nodded. Sitting next to her amongst the grasses he put his arm around her shoulders. 'Are you okay, Sarah?'

'I've found him now. I can take care of him and do all the things I should have done before. I can celebrate him and remember him like he was, so full of life, the rascal with the naughty laugh, a funny little ragamuffin.'

'I want to help, Sarah. Perhaps we could get another stone, one to celebrate Aaron's life properly.' He buried his face in her hair. 'Will you let me be part of it? With you and Tobias? Aaron's part of our family, isn't he?'

She turned her face to him. 'Do you want to be?'

'More than anything,' he whispered.

'Everything we've been through...perhaps it was meant to be. None of it seems worth breaking up a family after what happened to Aaron. I don't want to lose you and Tobias. And now I feel like Aaron is with me again. It's like another chance, an opportunity for us to build something.' He nodded and kissed her and the love he had for her reached his eyes and made them sparkle. She stood, and holding out her hand to Tobias, linked her other arm through Dan's.

'Let's go home,' she said. 'I want to go home.'

They wandered through the graveyard with Tobias between them, lifting him up and swinging him high into the air as they went, his laughter ringing out around the stones. As Sarah and Dan stepped through the gate and onto the church path Tobias turned back. He beamed with delight, his eyes twinkling with amusement, and lifted his hand in a wave.

The other boy was there, jumping from stone to stone, his dirty face pulled into a cheeky grin. He waved at Tobias, then ran with his arms outstretched through the tall, softly swaying grasses and colourful meadow flowers, his fingers rippling them like the gentle gust of a summer breeze.

THE END

Acknowledgements

Thanks and love to my wonderful, beautiful family, the ones who make my life worthwhile. Thanks too, to my supporters, my writing buddies who have been there from day one. I know I can call on you at any time for advice and I appreciate the care and time you invest. Many thanks.

In THE OTHER BOY, Tobias has autism. I wanted to write about a character who has this particular challenge because it has touched my own family; both my young grandsons are on the autistic spectrum, as am I. Autism is one of those issues which is extremely difficult to pin down; my grandsons and I have various challenges to overcome, but when we achieve something we know it is a time for celebration. We may not be the most gregarious of people but when we're together as a family we know how to party; to dance, to sing and to provide friendship and support for each other.

If you or anyone you know is on the autistic spectrum or feels they might be, contact…

UK The National Autistic Society – autism.org.uk

or

USA Autism Society – autism-society.org

If you are reading The Other Boy elsewhere, your own country will have its own society. These agencies are where you will find advice on how to begin the journey to a diagnosis, and how to manage strategies to lead a healthy, productive, and happy life.

Best wishes
Andrea Hicks

If you loved THE OTHER BOY you'll love…
THE DESTRUCTION OF BEES

…the new psychological suspense set to be the publishing hit of 2020

You can pre-order THE DESTRUCTION OF BEES on Amazon
Go to www.andreahicks-writer.com for a FREE excerpt.

Nina Gourriel is on the run. After collapsing from the effects of a contaminated heroin fix she is taken to hospital where she quickly recovers, but instead of being discharged she's held in a secret government facility known as Plan Bee and monitored. She is not allowed to leave the sealed facility known as Plan B, and no one provides an explanation…until she meets Cain, one of the scientists working on Plan Bee who tells her why she's being held and the dangers she will encounter if, or when, she's released. She's wanted, and she knows the only way to save herself is to run!

Printed in Great Britain
by Amazon

41235047R00151